CINDY

— 2011 —
Happy Mother's Day

COYOTE SMART

A NOVEL

ISBN: 145384774X
ISBN-13: 9781453847749

AUTHOR'S NOTE

Dear Readers,

I hope you have enjoyed my first two novels, **Keeping Faith** and **Promises Kept**, and are anxious to read book three where you'll find out what Faith has been doing in the last several years, plus a whole lot more as other major characters develop along the pages.

Like my other books, this is a work of fiction, and although it too deals with a delicate and a controversial topic like **Keeping Faith**, it is meant to be a literary adaption of life at the border, not a manifesto about a political or social issue.

Clearly, illegal immigration is a multi-faceted and very complex matter to say the least, and, unfortunately, it has become a subject that divides folks across the nation. There are, however, far too many pieces in the immigration puzzle for me to try to solve it, even if I were smart enough, which I'm not. So, in this novel I don't attempt to offer solutions to the problem except to emphatically indicate a need to secure the border and punish the human smugglers, known as coyotes in the States and polleros in Mexico.

Instead, I do try through words to portray a picture of lives touched by the complicated border dilemma. To do this I have created characters who reflect the best of the best, along with those who are truly flawed, all engaged in an intricate plot of survival. This is a story that starts out about life and death along the U.S./Mexican border, but it is not confined to a 2,000 mile stretch of unforgiving land and broken dreams. Instead, it takes you on a long and winding journey where the weak and strong collide, good and bad meet, reason outlasts power, and love is stronger than the forces of evil.

I hope you enjoy the twists and turns of the plot and get lost in the settings. In the end, I think you'll agree that our destinies are usually determined by the road we choose to take just like they did for the characters you came to love or loathe in this work of fiction.

⌘　⌘　⌘

ACKNOWLEDGEMENTS

As always there are many who helped me bring my thoughts to fruition in this novel. Sometimes it was only a "you go, girl," that gave me motivation to spend another long day at my computer or a quick email from a friend with a compliment about my first two books.

Others gave graciously of their time, reading my draft hours on end, giving suggestions and editing recommendations. I would be remiss if I didn't say a huge, bigger than huge thank you to Carlene, who listened patiently as I read passages and then after hearing something over and over, still read and gave me help, forever encouraging me, never allowing me to slack off. Judy, as always, you support me by telling me to live my dream and fill in by helping with mundane chores that I tend to let slide when the juices are flowing on a lengthy chapter. You're also really good with those "twists" to the story ideas. It must have something to do with so many years in education.

To Gayle, Iris, and Spanish Teacher Extraordinaire Señora McDaniel, thanks for copy reading and finding all the little mistakes that in my haste I often missed. Another who provided much needed assistance was Ignacio Estoraga, whose knowledge of the Border Patrol and the land they guard was tremendously helpful in my understanding of the inner workings of all the agencies, organizations, and individuals who make their living, both good and bad, along the United States/Mexican border. Thank you, Ignacio, for sharing your time with me, answering my questions, and helping me sort through this complicated process. And Jan, you were great about answering my silly inquiries about life on the farm. I never knew that much went on!

Another very important person in the success of my endeavor is Chris, my publicity agent, who also keeps me on track, and sees to it that the website, blogs, and all forms of online marketing are running smoothly and efficiently. Someday, when I grow up, I hope I am just half as smart as you are.

Most of all, thanks to you, my reader friends, who buy my books and comment on my website, who support me and motivate me to continue on this writing voyage.

⌘ ⌘ ⌘

PRAISE FOR CINDY BRADFORD'S BOOKS

Cindy Bradford has managed in **KEEPING FAITH** to write a heavy subjected book in a way that we feel sadness, happiness and shock at all the right spots. I like that she was able to pull back just when you thought your emotions were going to burst. For a first novel, Bradford scored one out of the park. Once you pick up the book, you'll want to cancel all your plans just to be able to finish it. ~ Josie Kramer—*The Book Journal*

In **PROMISES KEPT** the descriptions of the various travel locations are well-written and well-researched and add nice touches to the romantic story. ~ Robin Cain—*Scottsdale Book Examiner*

PROMISES KEPT is a fairy tale for adult women. For any doubters who think romance is dead, this book will reclaim their beliefs in dreams fulfilled. Overall, this is a great book to turn to when you need your faith in love to be restored. ~ Nicole Langan, official reviewer, *Midwest Book Review*, NewYorkJournalofBooksExaminer.com.

In **PROMISES KEPT** Cindy Bradford uses dialogue so well that you can hear the conversations taking place. Every word carries the story along, drawing you into the midst of the events. ~ Joyce Anthony, Independent Reviewer.

PROMISES KEPT presents a memorable heroine, living a challenging life. Faith has triumphs and heartaches, and I rooted for her throughout the novel. She caught my interest sufficiently that she won't just fade from my memory. She has stepped off the pages and into my mind; I would love to know what happens to her next. ~ Diane Ascroft, Reviewer, dianneascroft.wordpress.com.

⌘ ⌘ ⌘

It has been written in mythical lore that:
"A feather fell from the sky.
The eagle saw it. The deer heard it.
The bear smelled it.
The coyote did all three."

prologue

The dying season begins each spring along the 2,000 mile stretch of the United States and Mexico border, but the term is not used in reference to the parched land or the animal carcasses that waste in the dry gulches and deep gullies littered with cans, bottles, clothing and syringes.

Instead it applies to human beings: poor, desperate people in search of a dream. In many cases, the dream turns into a deadly nightmare. They come by foot, across treacherous mountains and desert wastelands, mostly Mexicans but others from as far away as El Salvador and Honduras. Along the way, the weak die from dehydration, starvation, hypothermia or drown in the swift currents of the river contaminated with pesticide runoff and raw sewage.

Often, they wait for days, without food or water, in the "lay up" for the smugglers or coyotes, as they are called, to pick them up. More times than not, before they hear the long awaited honk from the smuggler's truck, it is too late. The Border Patrol guards, who know that they hide in brushy areas or deep culverts, have found them and sent them back to the other side. But they will try again...and again, until they make it or die. Many times, it is the latter. Those who live are often taken to dingy, dirty, crowded "safe houses" to wait again. The name is a misnomer because these shabby hotel rooms, tiny trailers or what is left of a falling down house are anything but protected refuges. Sometimes the smuggler never comes, only the dreaded Border Patrol. The lucky ones get further only to be crammed into hot, airless trailers or overcrowded trucks and driven to often isolated, dangerous locations and left to their fate. The worst part is that many have saved for years to pay their coyotes for their trip to nowhere.

⌘　⌘　⌘

part one

chapter one

Everything about Maxwell Collin Ridgeway III was oversized. At six feet, four inches and three hundred pounds, his barrel chest protruded as predominately as his ego. But Maxwell hadn't always been so large nor did he, in the beginning, have a big name.

Born two months premature to Consuela de la Peña, a slight Mexican woman who had migrated illegally with her husband from south of the border in Puebla to West Texas, he was christened Enrique de la Peña Jr., but called Kiki for short, a name he hated.

María, the midwife who delivered the tiny boy, had placed him in a dresser drawer, stuffed with crumpled newspaper and a ragged, torn blanket, doubting that he would live and warning his frail mother not to bond. To complicate matters, the new mother had difficulty making enough milk and what little she did, the baby had trouble nursing.

María had delivered countless babies for immigrants, but never a blond, with light blue eyes. Trying to hide her surprise, she dared not mention the distinctive characteristics of the newborn, noticing how Consuela shifted her gaze whenever their eyes met. María had hurried for it was getting late in the day, and she had not wanted to be in the house when Enrique Sr. came into to see the baby for the first time. Maybe he already knew. Maybe Consuela had told him, but from the look in the new mother's eyes, she doubted it. She didn't want to take any chances of seeing his reaction; one she knew would be of utter sorrow and disappointment.

When she closed the door, leaving Consuela alone with only her thoughts and the sickly baby, the bitterly cold winds of January blew through the rafters of the dilapidated shotgun shack. Consuela hated the wind, but on that day she was glad that over time it had blown the dust between the cracks in the walls, turning it to mud when the rains came. At least that kept out some of the cold. The old black iron wood burning stove located in the corner of the one room that served as the kitchen and living area gave off little heat because wood was scarce in these parts, and Enrique had not had time lately to find and cut scrub mesquite.

Consuela felt a sudden chill, but it wasn't only because of the frosty air. She was scared, scared for herself and for her husband. Why had she not told Enrique when it happened? Why had she waited? Because she had hoped; she had prayed that this would not be the outcome. Over and over she had asked God to let the baby be Enrique's. And she couldn't even remember how many times she knelt, touching her rosary beads and appealing to the Virgin Mary for favor. Even in the last month, when it was difficult to lower herself to a kneeling position, she did, and repeated: *Por favor, María, Madre de Jesús*, let the baby be Enrique's. But it was not to be. She drew her son to her breast and wept, thinking about her life with Enrique. What would he do now? She had felt so safe and happy when they first arrived here.

⌘   ⌘   ⌘

As she wiped away her tears, her mind took her back to the time she thought they were so lucky, so fortunate to have made it here from Mexico, finding work in the cotton fields of West Texas, proud that they could send money home, a little to her parents, and more to Enrique's brothers and sisters who needed it the most.

They had come on their own, walking for miles in the cover of darkness until it seemed their legs would no longer carry them. When finally the sun came up they would rest for a while until the temperature rose to an unbearable degree and they could take no more mosquitoes biting through their clothes. The trees were a trade off as protection from the sun, but they brought the bugs, black swarms of them. After a few hours of fitful sleep, Enrique would finally tell her they would move on, in spite of the dangers of being spotted. She wondered if he had slept at all because he was always on the lookout, even jumpy at times. It was too miserable to stay still, and they were running out of water.

They had shared the last tortilla the night before when they were able to jump on a freight train that took them west through flat lands dotted with mesquite trees and blowing tumbleweeds. With every stop there was renewed fear of being caught, nerves frayed with the thought of being sent back after they had travelled so far. When the train reached its last stop before it turned around, they hitchhiked. At first the teenaged driver had seemed nice enough until he demanded Enrique empty his pockets. Fortunately, he didn't realize that most of their savings, not quite two hundred dollars was rolled into Enrique's backpack. Again, they walked, always off the roads, far away from passing cars.

They counted the cows to pass the time. Twice Enrique stopped to cut a prickly pear cactus, careful to select the thin young tender pads and even more cautious to cut the barbs and burn off the spines. Then they chewed on the nopal until the moisture came. He told Consuela how his mother used to boil them with an old Mexican copper coin to thin the sap. She had smiled with memories of her own, though it made her sad to think about how far away her family was, not knowing when she would ever see them again.

When a large expanse of green and white fields came into view, they saw Mexican men and a few women bent over picking the soft, fluffy cotton fibers. Others hoed weeds that had somehow found cracks in the dry, reddish-brown soil. Enrique hesitated, and then walked over to a man who looked like he might be head of the crew. It was a chance and he took it. If he had only known, he would have kept walking, but then all he knew was that he had found work and a roof over their heads, and food, though meager, for their growling stomachs. Yes, they had felt blessed because this was before so many smugglers had dominated the routes, before the unscrupulous and despicable coyotes. But even without them there were dangers; Consuela had learned that all too soon.

⌘　⌘　⌘

When Enrique saw the baby, he grew pale and turned away, trying to hide his tears. But once he regained his composure, he looked directly at Consuela, who was cold with fear and simply asked, "*Por qúe?*"

She began sobbing uncontrollably. "*Tenía miedo,*" explaining to him that she was afraid, and it was not the way he thought. She had not been with anyone willingly. He was the only man she had ever loved, would ever love.

And then he knew. He believed her, his Consuela, his Connie as he called her when they chased each other down the dusty streets in the little barrio where they grew up. They had fallen in love when they were only children. They had made this pilgrimage to what they thought would be a better life together. There had never been any other for either of them.

Thinking back it now made sense. He recalled an evening in early summer. He had been working long hours, taking advantage of the sun setting late when he came in from the fields to find her crying, a painful, haunting mourning. He had been frightened when he heard her and went to her immediately asking what was wrong, searching her eyes for a sign. But she would only say that she was sick—a woman sickness, so he asked no more, but he worried. He noticed her lip had been bleeding, and he pressed her to tell him what had happened. She responded that she had felt faint, then fallen and hit a chair.

Several months later when she told him she was pregnant and she was sick every day, he worried that she might have something more wrong with her that was making her weak and unable to keep any food down. He had never seen his mother so sick when she was pregnant with any of his little brothers and sisters. He woke up nights afraid he would lose her and held her close. In the fields each day, he could not get her off his mind. Life would be nothing without his Connie. Now he understood that it wasn't a disease at all, but a terrible, reprehensible act imposed by a horrible human being without a conscience, without a soul.

He turned to look at the baby again, who was now cradled in Consuela's arms. He knew without further explanation that this baby belonged to his boss. What he didn't know was just how vicious and savage the land owner had acted or what force Maxwell Collin Ridgeway II had used on Consuela, how he had repeatedly raped her, and then hit her when she whimpered. He knew she would never tell him just how bad it had been. He wasn't sure he even wanted to know.

Without saying a word, he grabbed his hat and gun and was out the door. In the distance he heard Consuela calling to him to return, begging him not to do something he would regret. "I need you; this baby needs you. Please don't say anything, don't do something crazy. It will only make it worse," she screamed in Spanish. In her heart, although she wanted the man who did this to her dead, she was praying that Enrique would not kill him.

⌘　⌘　⌘

For over an hour Enrique walked down the long winding path leading to the big ranch house. The estate would be a more fitting term. He walked with the purpose of a man possessed with an anger that could explode any minute, and then he finally stopped and leaned his tired body against a railed fence that he had helped build, and cried like a baby. He was alone in a country where he did not belong, with the knowledge that he now had a son who did not belong to him. His chest heaved from the sobs and then there were no more tears.

He stood, taller it seemed, and took off walking in a different direction, veering into a clump of mesquite trees where he sat down, his back to a stump. Coming to grips with his destiny, he had to make a plan. He knew they could not stay here, but it was not the time of year to leave. Neither Consuela nor the baby could survive a journey on foot in this weather. He would wait until spring, but he would stay no longer than that. He would find other work in a safe place for his family. And he would love this baby. That was his plan.

⌘　⌘　⌘

chapter two

Against all odds and the worst winter since 1951, Kiki not only survived, he thrived with his mother hovering over his every need. Enrique was relieved that the baby seemed able to travel. On the day before spring was official he told Consuela they were leaving at dawn the next morning. The shock on her face must have startled him because he paused for a few minutes before explaining that he had made this plan back in January. If he stayed he knew he would kill Ridgeway should he ever come close to Consuela again.

Taking only what they could carry and the clothes on their backs they set out again on a journey together. Only this time, there was a baby, a little boy. Although neither mentioned it, both knew they could take him away, but the color of his skin and eyes might someday draw him back.

The journey along the back roads was no safer than it had been a year ago, and they feared the Border Patrol or anyone who might turn them in to the authorities, but this wasn't a choice for a better life; it had to be done. Silently they walked while their feet hurt and their stomachs groaned in hunger. When the sun was high, Enrique stopped and took off his backpack. It felt good to straighten his back once the weight was lifted. But it was not as bad as working the fields with the short handled shovel that he was forced to use. No matter, he felt so much older than his nineteen years as he looked at Consuela, who managed a smile when she saw him gaze at her. She placed the baby on a blanket and unrolled the tortillas that she had made the night before. Tearing open the deer jerky that Enrique had dried earlier in the month, she handed it to him. He knelt down and gently kissed her cheek. She took a bite of a tortilla and a sip of water, afraid that they might run out before they found a place to refill.

Enrique admonished her for being frugal; reminding her she needed her strength for the many miles ahead. She wanted to ask him where they were going, where this was leading, but she stopped herself. Enrique always knew best. She would trust him.

Just as she was finishing her meager lunch, Kiki began to cry. She drew him to her breast and was so thankful that she had finally begun to make enough milk to satisfy her growing son. She nursed and alternately patted him on the back, and then changed his wet diaper, carefully saving the dirty one in a plastic bag, hoping she had clean ones to last until she could wash these somewhere along the way. It had been so much easier traveling without a baby, but she would not trade him for any easier experience in the world.

When the baby began to doze, satisfied by his mother's milk, Enrique bent over and took him, fitting the child into the pouch he had made for Consuela's back. It was time to start out again. Time was precious and they had miles to go before sunset. Before, they had traveled primarily at night because there was less danger of being spotted, but with the baby it was too precarious. In the darkness, Consuela might fall; a wild animal might attack. They would have to take their chances and be cautious.

⌘ ⌘ ⌘

For three days they walked until Enrique saw a small ranch house with a barn twice the size of the house and a couple of pickup trucks parked alongside a cotton trailer with two gentlemen leaning against one of the trucks. He knew he was about twenty miles north of Abilene and hoped he was in the right place at the right time. Three older men from his village had been in this area several years ago as braceros, and they talked about a farmer who had been kind to them. Could he be so lucky to find the right place? They had described the place and the long gravel road that led to the home place.

He saw the ironwork with the name MOSS. *Por favor mi Jesús*, he whispered to himself, hoping this was the place and that there was work. Signaling Consuela to hide behind the tall cedar windbreaks, he ventured forward. If this didn't work out, he didn't want anyone to know he wasn't alone. He wasn't taking any chances.

⌘ ⌘ ⌘

He need not have worried. The gentleman farmer was, indeed, kind and fortunately in need of help. With the braceros gone, a crop to sow and a garden to plant, Enrique was quick to explain that he could do most any work required, and that his wife could help with cleaning if there was a need for that in the ranch house. The farmer smiled, seeming to understand most of the Spanish, mixed with a couple of words of English that Enrique stammered. He held up four fingers and said "Ninos," as if to indicate his wife could definitely use help since there were four kids to clean up after and cook for.

Within an hour, he had Enrique, Consuela, and the baby settled into a two room house with a wooden outhouse located about twenty feet away. He brought two clean blankets, an old iron skillet and a soup pot and pointed to a well a couple of hundred feet from the house.

"My wife sent these," he said, handing Consuela a plate of warm biscuits, six slices of ham and a jar of homemade blackberry preserves. He doubted she understood a word he said, but the smile on her face showed she understood a language that needed no translation.

Taking Enrique outside, he pointed to the barn, held up six fingers and said, "Mañana." And then he was gone, leaving the young couple to their first warm meal in four days.

⌘   ⌘   ⌘

chapter three

The work was grueling and the hours long, but Enrique had never felt happier or safer. He got paid every Saturday morning, and after that his boss took him into town to buy groceries and supplies. He was able to put food on the table and clothes on his family's backs, and that made him feel proud. Never shying from work, he was up before dawn, doing his own chores before meeting his boss shortly after the sun rose against the stark backdrop of West Texas.

The first year was difficult because Enrique had to learn exactly what his boss expected, but he was a patient man and a good teacher; showing Enrique how to run the tandem, grub up the useless mesquite trees that only got in the way of the tractors and precisely how he wanted the fences built. Before long, Enrique was welding trailer parts. Although Mr. M., as he was known, was indeed selfless he was particular about his land and extremely tidy. Any stray weeds in the wheat or cotton fields brought a frown to his ruddy face and a look that Enrique didn't want to see. It was important to please this man who had given him a chance and trusted him. If this meant hoeing into the darkness to keep the fields clean, then Enrique persevered.

The first spring slipped into the second, and the second faded into the third, as the years rolled softly into one another. Before long Kiki was a tall, skinny four year old whose best friend was the oldest Moss boy, Jan, who though a year older, stood a good three inches shorter. Both had eyes the color of the sky in summer, but the physical resemblances stopped there. Jan's hair mocked the same shade as the cotton his dad raised in the fields and his shirtless chest glowed white, save the chestnut mud that clung to it in the summer heat. Kiki's hair had finally taken on the chocolate sparkle of his mother's, though not nearly so rich and dark and his skin had only a faint hint of a perpetual tan. Enrique was grateful for what little ounce of Hispanic heritage that could be noted in the boy, though there was no other visible characteristic to reveal any chance of his being the father.

The boys were inseparable and played together almost every waking minute, except when Jan went to the farmhouse for a hot lunch, and Kiki trudged back to the little structure he called home for a cold tortilla and a cup of warm beans. He wasn't allowed to play in the farmhouse or go past a certain point that led to the main house. Although it was not marked by any special designation, it was understood, and strangely enough, even the two mischievous and often less than obedient boys, never pressed the issue. Neither Kiki nor Jan understood why this was a rule. They never questioned it out loud; instead they just shrugged it off and chased rats out of the prickly pears or rode bareback through the turn rows, Jan on the old brown horse and Kiki on the white clumsy one. Both animals were too old to be otherwise useful except to two young boys, one whose life extended past the farm and one whose life stopped at the road.

"I hate to think about starting first grade. I know I won't like school. You can't play or anything, I hear. And you have to do arithmetic and read. Yuck," Jan said to Kiki one lazy summer afternoon in July as the two boys splashed in the tank that Mr. M. had dredged to hold water for his cattle. In West Texas that almost always meant a place for boys to swim and jump off a makeshift diving board made from a two by six, welded to a metal frame. Absent any spring in the board, the boys were content with jumping as high as possible and then landing with a splashing thud on the brownish red water that they shared with any thirsty cow that might decide to drink.

Jan had turned six in February, and in his mind, escaping private kindergarten had been a blessing. With no public kindergarten in town, his mother had hoped they could send him to the only private one when he turned five, but when she had approached Mr. M. with the idea he just shook his head no. The reason was money or lack of it, and there was no real cause in his mind to discuss it. Of course, Jan and Kiki were thrilled. But now the inevitable loomed closer, and both boys dreaded it.

"Did you hear what I said, Kiki? School! There is no getting out of it. And on top of that my mom wants to take me shopping for school clothes. My sister is all excited, but I can't think of anything worse." When Kiki still didn't respond, Jan yelled, "Are you even listening to me, stupid?"

"Yeah," Kiki managed to say in a low tone. "I don't want to think about it. What will I do? I ain't got no other friends to play with."

"We can still play when I get home every day."

"It's not the same. It'll probably be dark when you get off the bus. That's what I want to do the most. I want to ride the school bus."

"That's no big deal," Jan said, now trying to act big and all-knowing. "You can the next year. I asked my dad and he said they let Mexicans ride it too. If you even are a Mexican. I never saw a blue-eyed one. Anyway, you might have to sit at the back, but I don't care. I'll sit with you."

"Promise?" Kiki asked, not seeming convinced. The remainder of the afternoon he was quiet and withdrawn.

"Hey, if you are going to act like a big baby, I'm going home," Jan announced as he pulled himself up on the bank, which was covered in overgrown weeds. "Ouch, I got a sticker."

"Now, who's the baby?" Kiki mocked, as Jan sat pulling a clump of cockleburs from his big toe.

"I'm going home," he said with a pouty mouth.

"I'm not ready."

"Too bad, so sad. I'm leaving your butt," Jan said as he tromped up the slight incline to his house, forgetting that his dad's rule was to never leave anyone in the tank alone.

⌘ ⌘ ⌘

An unusually dark cloud had formed just as the sun went down causing the sky to go prematurely very black when Enrique knocked rapidly on the backdoor to the main farmhouse. This was something he never did unless there was a serious problem so when Mrs. M. saw him through the tiny window she was immediately alarmed. Could something have happened to her husband? His heart! "Oh please Lord, don't let it be his heart," she murmured out loud. It was late, but he was often late, chasing a stray cow or mending a fence that he had missed earlier in the day, but now Enrique was knocking. Her face went pale as she opened the door.

"What is it Enrique?" She asked with a panicked tone.

"It's Kiki. We can't find him. Is Jan here?"

"Why yes, he is," relief coming to her voice. "Come in."

"No ma'am I can't. Consuela is waiting for me. We are so worried. I just thought if Jan is home he might know where Kiki is."

Just as she turned to yell for him, he appeared, all color drained from his face, saying nothing.

"Have you seen Kiki?" Enrique and Mrs. M. pressed at the same time.

He lowered his head, and then stammered, "N...N...Not in a couple of hours."

"Where was he then?" Enrique cut in, obviously worried and anxious.

"We were just down at the field."

"Jan, tell Enrique where Kiki was the last time you saw him, and tell him this very minute," his mother scolded.

Realizing the seriousness of the situation, he looked up and meekly said, "In the tank."

Upon hearing that, Enrique took off running. It had started to rain, sprinkled with tiny pellets of hail that grew larger by the seconds. The hail stung his arms, but he barely noticed, his only thoughts on the muddy water and a little boy who he wished belonged to him.

Turning swiftly to her son she admonished, "You go to your room, right now. Just wait until you daddy gets home. I'm going to Consuela. You better pray that baby is okay." She grabbed her umbrella, which the wind caught the minute she stepped outside. She headed for the small house where she could see Consuela pacing just outside, oblivious to the weather that was growing increasingly worse.

Suddenly, the headlights of her husband's truck appeared out of the darkness. She had forgotten that just minutes ago she was so worried that the news was about him. The vehicle turned the direction she was running and stopped just short of the front door where Consuela was now standing, looking small and afraid. Mr. M. got out quickly, his clothes were dripping wet and he was holding Kiki in his arms. "Are you looking for this little fella?" He asked, handing Kiki over to his trembling mother.

Her eyes showed only appreciation. "Enrique's gone looking for him. Where was he? Before she heard his answer, she released her son's hand and brushed his hair from his eyes, pulling him close to her waist. "Are you okay, Mijo? Your father and I have been so worried."

"Jan said he don't think he's my dad, says he can't be because I have blue eyes. He said he has never seen a Mexican with blue eyes."

Consuela looked away, embarrassed that her husband's boss and wife had heard her son's accusations, and even more concerned that their son had been the one to notice. What would they think of her? Did they know? Had Kiki run away because of this? She had no answers at the moment.

Mr. M. turned to see Enrique coming toward him, drenched and covered in mud, but looking relieved as he saw everyone crowded around Kiki who was apparently unharmed. Mr. M. put his hand on his wife's shoulder, and silently nudged her to go home. He walked over to his helper and slapped him gently on the back. "Get some rest. Tomorrow's going to be a long day. Can't tell yet what this hail has done to the crop."

⌘　⌘　⌘

Kiki didn't see his friend for a week, a long and boring week. He knew this was going to be the way he felt when Jan went to school. But right now he was mad because they were losing a whole week of summer. What he didn't know was how lucky he was that it was only a week that Jan was grounded. At first Mrs. M. had said that he couldn't play outside for two weeks, but after seven days of a sullen, pouty six year old fighting with his older bossy sister and a baby underfoot, she gave in to save her own sanity.

The morning of his freedom, he ran to Kiki's house yelling. "Hurry, my dad's taking us to see the new baby calves." Kiki was out the door in a flash, and within minutes they were in the back of the pickup, bouncing along the rough terrain, screaming to the top of their lungs for no reason except they were on an adventure. When they arrived at the pasture, they jumped out before the pickup had come to a stop.

They were followed by Mr. M. who took his time getting out of his truck. Adjusting his hat, he drawled, "You boys are going to hurt yourselves doing that one of these days." But before he had finished his sentence, Jan, oblivious to his calm warning, was chasing after a lone calf that managed to stay several feet ahead of the lanky kid. Accepting defeat and out of breath, Jan pleaded. "Daddy, can we rope one, please?"

The farmer's face broke into a slight grin as he reached over into the pickup and tossed a lasso to his son and one to Kiki. "You can try, but it doesn't look like you can get close enough."

"I want to ride one." Kiki said as he looked at the lasso. "If I catch him, can I ride him?"

Mr. M. smiled again as he walked over and cajoled the young animal with a handful of hay as Jan tossed the rope only to wrap it around his own foot and then fell smack on the ground. "I don't believe they are ready to be roped today, son. We'll try it again.

Here, help me feed their mommas and then we'll go for a ride into town. I need some supplies at the hardware store."

"Can Kiki go?"

"I don't see why not."

Jan looked at his friend who in all these years had never been into town with him before. Kiki looked back in disbelief.

⌘ ⌘ ⌘

Chapter four

Enrique and Consuela began to adapt to the pattern of their lives and into the expectations of the seasons, of the continuous cycle of life. Wheat was sowed in late fall as soon as the cotton was stripped and sent to the gin. As it began to turn yellow in the waning days of April, Enrique knew that the harvest looked good for late May.

When grain sorghum was in the ground of a small section of the land, all attention was given to sowing cotton in June and in some cases early July, depending on the rain, which seemed to control most of everything on the farm. Mr. M. had told him about the long, hard drought of the 1950s. He had thought he might lose everything, but finally after five brutal hot and dry seasons, the skies had opened up and rain had been consistent, if not almost plentiful in recent years. The crops had responded, and he was able to pay off the bank, but it had been a difficult time, and he had worried from season to season, from year to year. His bad heart may have been a result of the stress or it might have been from the malaria he contracted in World War II, Enrique didn't know. His boss didn't really talk about it much, but he had explained to Enrique about the nitro-glycerin pills he carried in his shirt pocket and on occasion, Enrique saw him grimace and reach quickly, popping one into his mouth. The strain was often noticeable, and it caused Enrique to wonder if his boss would live to see his newest son grow to be a man.

Enrique was always glad to see a rain shower after the cotton crop was in because it meant that his boss, who needed a reprieve from the stress of the farm, would load up his wife and children and head for the mountains of New Mexico for a week of cool air and family fun. There wasn't much time for that most months on a working farm, and Mr. M. insisted on being the one to feed the cattle and drive the combines.

Enrique smiled when he saw the cows running toward his boss's pickup truck each morning. He wondered if that was why Mr. M. wanted this task for himself. Maybe it was the bond between animal and man or maybe it was the land that he just liked to be close to. Whatever, Enrique admired his boss's work ethic, but most of all he just liked him because he was kind and gentle, with a tender side that men from these parts often didn't show.

October, November, and December were the busiest time of year because of ginning season. Since his boss ran the gin as well as harvested his own crop, Enrique carried most of the responsibility for stripping the cotton, getting it onto the trailers and to the gin. This year would be special for him because Mr. M. said he could let Kiki and Jan ride on top of the soft cotton all the way from the farm to the gin, almost six miles. Depending on the weather and his place in line with the other farmers who were waiting to unload, it could take several days before the cotton was off the trailers, days that were wasted if he didn't find other chores on the farm. But there were always tasks, big and small, and Enrique never waited to be told.

⌘　⌘　⌘

chapter five

The news of Consuela's pregnancy brought a new spring to Enrique's step. She had waited until she missed her third period before she told him, fearful that something might happen. Although it had taken years for Consuela to conceive, and she and Enrique had worried they might never have a child together, this pregnancy felt different, with none of the morning sickness or spotting that had occurred with Kiki. She actually felt good, and her skin glowed with a radiance that she couldn't explain.

Perhaps it was her happiness, knowing that this baby beyond any shadow of doubt belonged to her beloved Enrique. This baby would be theirs, a connection and a bond that only they could make. This baby would bring them years of happiness and a shared joy that Kiki refused to allow. Although it had never been mentioned again after the night Kiki had run away or hidden, whatever the case, it was obvious that even at his young age he knew there was something different about his skin and eyes, and that he looked nothing like Enrique. Often Consuela would watch the two together; Kiki stiffened when his father reached to ruffle his hair or touch his shoulder. There was a chasm between the two, and it wasn't because Enrique didn't try. She saw the hurt in his eyes when Kiki pulled away or didn't answer a question directed to him. She ached for him when her husband brought home a toy on Saturday morning after a trip to town, a gift he had scrimped and saved to buy, and Kiki would barely notice, much less respond to favorably. Maybe this baby would bring a positive change to the boy; she could only hope.

Yolanda de la Peña or Yoli as her parents called her was the most beautiful baby girl Enrique had ever seen. Her skin was the color of roasted almonds and her hair the silkiest, black curls that ever graced a perfectly formed little face. But her eyes were what thrilled him most. They sparkled and shone a deep mahogany and followed his every move. This was his Yoli; she had her daddy's eyes.

At first, Consuela was worried because the baby never cried. She smiled even in her sleep. The mother wasn't used to a baby like that. Kiki had been so fussy and fitful with difficulty sleeping, but Yoli lay in her crib that Enrique had built out of scrap lumber and cooed for hours before dropping off to a sound, sweet sleep. As time wore on, Yoli would cry occasionally when she was wet or hungry, but she was simply a happy baby.

Consuela had made her a quilt from the scrap fabric Mrs. M. had brought over all through the pregnancy. And as a surprise, Enrique had brought home yellow yarn and a crochet needle he had bought at the hardware store. Although the directions were in English and Consuela was still struggling with the language, she was able to read a few words and study the picture diagrams that led her swiftly through the process. She loved the handwork, and within two weeks had made a throw for Yoli's crib.

Enrique was so pleased when he saw her creations, but even more excited about her determination to learn English. Each day he would tell her new words he had learned, and together each night they read scriptures first from their Spanish Bible and then from the English, carefully comparing each word. He would place Yoli in his lap while Consuela read to him, and then when the baby had drifted off to sleep, he would take his turn reading and translating. When his eyes became heavy and he began to nod off, Consuela would kiss him gently on the cheek, and persuade him to get his rest for another long day in the fields.

Kiki refused to pay Yoli any attention, and was sullen when anyone else did. What Consuela had once tried to pass off as his shyness, she now had to face was a much deeper issue. Even when he and Enrique had not been close, the two of them had been. He related to his mother or at least it seemed that way, but now he was pulling away from her as well. And no matter how hard she tried, she couldn't reach into the deep inner workings of his five year old troubled personality. She hoped when school started, and it was just Kiki and Yoli that he might decide that having a little sister might not be so bad, but September came, and Kiki withdrew more.

During the mornings, he played outside in the dirt with his little cars, building intricate tunnels that were not easy to carve out of the dry, parched West Texas dirt. In the afternoons, he lay in the shade of a mesquite tree and taught himself to read. He loved books. When Consuela had first noticed him trying to make out words in her Bible, she knew she had to figure out a way to find him some children's books. Finally she had Enrique ask Mr. M. if there was a chance he could get a library card. Mr. M. had laughed and said he really didn't know because none of his kids liked to read and would think a library card was punishment, but the next day he appeared with one in Enrique's name.

⌘   ⌘   ⌘

The first week of school, Jan cried everyday at the bus stop. "I don't want to go," he wailed as his mother stood along his side trying to convince him that it wouldn't be so bad once he got to know some of the other kids. His sister, one year older who now considered herself a seasoned student, pleaded with him to dry his eyes. She loved school, especially recess, and couldn't understand why he was being so obstinate. When the bus arrived, she forgot her little brother was even there and immediately jumped on, anxious to find a seat by one of her many equally chatty little friends. Jan begrudgingly dragged himself up the steps, and plopped down in the first vacant seat he could find, mumbling under his breath.

Every day after he got off the bus, he dropped his books off and ran to find Kiki who at first seemed anxious to hear his stories, but as the weeks wore on Kiki became less interested. Some days he appeared glad to see his best friend and on others he told Jan he just wanted to be left alone. More and more the two boys argued and then the day came when out of nowhere, Kiki punched Jan in the face and yelled, "I hate you." Before Jan got to the back door, the skin under his eye was turning blue, but when his mother asked what happened, he told her the fight was entirely his fault.

As the years wore on, Jan adjusted to the idea of school, although he would have quit in a second had that been an option, but Kiki grew more and more agitated once he was in school. What he thought would be a way to get away from the farm was far from a sanctuary. Although he liked the lessons and excelled in every class, he didn't fit in. He fought with the white boys and refused to have anything to do with the few blacks and Hispanics. He ignored the girls completely.

On the occasional weekends when the boys still crawled around in the hay stacked high in the barn or jumped around giggling and chasing the headless chicken that was on its way to being supper at the Moss table, Kiki seemed almost happy. One night when the boys had been catching fireflies and were lying on the cool grass looking at the stars, Jan asked, "What do you want to be when you grow up?" Without hesitation, Kiki said, "Important, somebody famous who people look up to. Somebody big! What about you?"

"Oh, I don't know. Maybe a bootlegger like my grandpa. He makes moonshine, but my momma said never to tell anyone. She's not happy about it. Says the people at the First Baptist Church would think she was bad if they knew, but I know a lot of people who think he's pretty smart. I know he makes a bunch of money because I've seen folks put folding money in the boot he leaves by his back door. It seems like they just drop by and leave money. Yep, that's what I want to be. Then you get to drink as much of it as you like. He's pretty funny after he's had some of the moonshine, except one time I saw him get really mad and slap my grandma. Hey, look at that shooting star. Quick, make a wish!"

"I already did," Kiki mumbled.

"What was it?"

"If you tell, it won't come true, and I'm not taking any chances."

The next Saturday it rained and the boys rode washtubs down the bar ditches and dug for oil in the soft soil that was rare during most of the year. But even in play Kiki had developed a cruel way of laughing when Jan fell out of the tub and hurt his leg and again when he smashed his finger on the bar he was using to dig. It was totally different when he was hurt. The time he was trying to learn to walk on the wooden stilts that belonged to Jan, and fell off bruising his knee, he picked up the one closest to him and beat it against the ground until all that was left were pieces of splintered boards. Then with all his strength he threw the other one straight at Jan's head. When his friend ducked, Kiki pounced on him and pounded him in the stomach.

He was always restless, never satisfied with the activity at hand. Neither was he afraid of causing trouble. One day when they were about ten and eleven, he convinced Jan to help him steal pomegranates and peaches off the neighbor's trees, and when they got caught, Jan confessed, but Kiki denied he was even with his friend. Most of the time when the boys got into trouble it was minor, but then one incident led to another, and each time it became more serious as Kiki grew older.

First, Kiki stole a hunting knife at the hardware store, and Jan once again took the blame, which meant he had to go to the store and pay back the six dollars that the knife was worth and offer to work two Saturdays as community service. His dad never asked to see the knife, knowing that Jan could not produce it, and was proud of him for taking the punishment although he worried about Kiki and what other pranks he might have in mind. Jan hated giving up his Saturdays while Kiki played, acting like he was innocent of any wrong doings and smirked when Jan mentioned he had "worked to save his friend's butt."

Although Jan would never admit it to Kiki, the penitence wasn't all bad because he loved wandering through the old hardware store that held about anything a farmer or anyone in his family could ever want. He had heard his dad and some of the other farmers laugh and say the store had everything one needed from the womb to the tomb because the owner sold baby diapers and caskets alongside every kind of kitchen utensil one could ever need and every farm implement imaginable. When the second Saturday's work ended, he stepped outside expecting his mother to be waiting and instead saw his dad standing by his pickup talking to a rancher friend who had just left the store with a bale of fence wire and a posthole digger.

As Jan approached the truck, the two men were finishing a conversation about how wheat prices were falling again. "Guess I'd better get this boy some food. He's a good worker if you can afford to feed him." With that he snubbed out his cigarette, pulled himself into the truck, started the engine and drove to the Super Dog Drive Inn where he bought each of them a hotdog and cherry lemonade. Jan couldn't remember being happier.

Several months after the knife stealing incident, two yellow kittens that Jan's sister had brought home from school on the bus disappeared. A week later, Enrique found them in a trough, dead, covered in kerosene. That mystery was never solved, because no one really wanted it solved. When Jan found out he asked Kiki if he knew about it, but Kiki just shrugged his shoulders and looked straight through him.

Enrique and Consuela worried. They were not blind to their son's antics or his attitude. But nothing seemed to work in reaching him. Consuela tried. Enrique tried, but Kiki grew further and further away, and his temper tantrums increased. When he slapped six year old Yoli for no apparent reason, Consuela had enough. She took a switch off the closest peach tree and swatted him on his arm until she saw blood. Then she stopped and cried. Kiki just glared at her, steeling himself against tears.

Though the boys continued to hang out together, Jan made other friends at school, and began to see Kiki less and less. The summer after Jan turned fourteen, he decided he needed extra money and so during cotton season, Mr. M. told him he would pay each boy fifty cents for every tow sack they filled, but after less time than it took to fill one sack, Kiki threw his down, and stomped away. "I will never pick cotton. I hate it here. I don't have to do this. I ain't no Mexican."

With a puzzled look on his face Jan stared at his friend, picked up his sack and trudged after him. "What's the deal, Kiki? I thought we wanted to make a little money."

"I don't need your daddy's money. My daddy has lots of money, lots more than yours!" Kiki said, with defiance and anger in his voice.

"What are you talking about? Your daddy works for mine."

"He's not my daddy, and you know that. I've heard talk at night when they think I am asleep. My daddy is rich and important. Now leave me alone. Just leave me alone." he said, turning to brush away a tear that he didn't want Jan to see.

That night, the whole Moss household was awakened to a crashing noise and a flame that lit up the night sky. By the time, Mr. M. got outside, the barn was just a burning heap of lumber. The hay was gone as were all the tools, and the old wagon that had belonged to Jan's grandfather. Enrique had arrived first and tried to salvage anything he could, but the wind and the hot dry air cooperated only with the fire. It wasn't until the sunlight hit the embers that the full scale of the damage came into sight. Nothing was left.

⌘ ⌘ ⌘

Chapter Six

That morning Kiki was gone as well. His mother found his room stripped of the few books he had checked out at the library and his favorite jacket. Scrawled on a single sheet of paper left on his pillow, were the words, "I hate you. Don't dare look for me."

What Enrique and Consuela didn't realize was that Kiki had a keen ear. On the night when he had first run away briefly, and returned telling his mother he knew Enrique couldn't be his father, they had a long, and whispered conversation about Enrique's former boss, and his forceful and intimidating personality. Kiki had learned spotty details as he eavesdropped over the years, but that night he finally heard a name—Maxwell Ridgeway. It was said in complete contempt as was the off-hand mention of Lubbock and the big ranch house located not too far away.

Since that time, Kiki had conjured up a plan. He sold his stolen knife and the watch he had gotten as a Christmas present to an older kid at school for ten dollars. He knew exactly when the train came by on the way to Wichita Falls and then on to Lubbock every morning and when another returned each evening on its way to Abilene because he and Jan had walked the half mile through the neighbor's pasture more times than he could remember. They had watched the hobos and put pennies on the track for the train to run over. He carried one of the many smashed coppers as they were called by the local boys in his front pocket as a reminder that this was his way out of town. He needed to go north, and he promised himself he would.

Hopping a freight train was considerably more difficult than Kiki had thought, and if his legs had been shorter, it would have been almost impossible. Although he had just turned thirteen in January, and stood close to six feet tall, he was still a clumsy, awkward kid who knew nothing about the real dangers of "catching out" a train. As he waited and the train approached, he grew more and more nervous. Grain car after grain car passed; he could tell by their cylinder shape, until there were only three remaining cars—boxcars.

Wiping his sweaty hands on his jeans, he ran, jumped and caught a bar next to the metal ladder attached to one of two boxcars, but his feet missed the rail, and for a minute he was simply holding onto a speeding train with one hand. With every ounce of strength he had, he was somehow able to pull himself up and grab the ladder. As he stood shaking, one leg on the plank separating the two train cars and one on the ladder, it hit him that in the struggle he had dropped the books he had so carefully packed in an old tow sack.

Looking down, he realized he was lucky not to have fallen onto the tracks. Cautiously, he put his other foot on the ladder, and took a deep breath before stretching first his right leg and then his left to the front ledge of the boxcar, and hoisted himself around and through the open door. Relieved, still shaking from the ordeal, he dropped to a sitting position in the side not filled with shingles and lumber, and put his head in his hands. Not only had he underestimated the difficulty of hopping a moving freight train, he had overestimated his abilities. More than anything he regretted the loss of his books.

Just three miles down the road he heard the loud, lonesome whistle and felt the train slowing down. They were at the grain elevator, which he had visited on several occasions with Enrique. The train now came to a full stop. Had he checked out the train schedule more precisely he would have known that during grain harvest, the train stopped at both elevators, and he could have probably boarded the train at either. Now that he was on, he felt lucky that this was the second elevator because each stop would make him more vulnerable for being seen and taken off. Now, not only was he upset about his miscalculation, he didn't know what to expect. Worry overwhelmed him because the car wasn't full and he was fearful that more dry storage might be added to his car. A sick feeling came over him.

He couldn't remember how the grain was loaded. Raising his head just enough to see out, he felt the train move as the empty cars were replaced with those filled just to the top of the open rails with wheat. By now he was sweating, so he removed his jacket, and hunkered down. He had come too far to be caught and kicked off the train. He waited, and then just as quickly as the loading started, it was over. He began to think his nervousness was a lifesaver since that put him close to the back of the train, but the downside to his placement was that the smells from all the first cars drifted back, which was proving to be anything but appealing as the day began to heat up.

As the whistle blew again, and the low pitched rhythmic rumble of the locomotive began, Kiki relaxed for the first time. Combined with a sense of relief and the whine of the wheels against the old steel tracks, he nodded off, lulled into a gentle sleep. When he woke, he was surprised that he had slept through the track noise and the hissing of the train that reminded him of the way a tornado had sounded as it came close to touching down near the farm last spring.

With the wind blowing hard against his face, he looked around at the scenery that didn't seem to have changed much since he had boarded the train. He had studied pictures of all parts of Texas, and longed to see the pine trees in the eastern part, the Gulf of Mexico to the south, the mountain ranges of the far west, but right now he was content to see anything since he had never been more than a five mile radius from his house.

After what seemed like a long time, the train began a slow descent into what he hoped was Wichita Falls. Now he wished he hadn't sold his watch, but he needed the money more than he needed to know the time; however, he would give back part of the amount to know how long the journey had been so far. He figured it had been at least three hours since he boarded, but he couldn't be sure.

Although he had heard stories about the train stopping for a few minutes to load cargo, and then proceeding to Lubbock, he wasn't absolutely sure if it even went that direction—and even if it did what he was going to do at the end of the tracks. But one way or the other, he would get to Lubbock and he would find Maxwell Ridgeway. Right now all he could do was hide and wait, something his parents had done once before his birth and once with him in tow. They, however, were much better prepared and it showed as his parched throat began to remind him that he should have at least brought water. But if he had, he would have probably lost it on the ascent between the cars. He shuttered again as he thought of his close call.

The stop was quicker than he had imagined, but this time he was joined by a stranger who appeared surprised to see him. Kiki was taken back as well, but tried to act nonchalant until the old hobo mumbled a muffled hello. He returned the greeting and slowly inched back, closer into the corner.

Noticing his nervousness, his rail companion smiled through a toothless grin and said, "Boy, I ain't gonna do you no harm. I'm just trying to make my way down the rails, just like you. Here you look hungry. I'll share my grub." He pulled two apples out of his dirty knapsack and tossed one toward Kiki who was caught off guard and fumbled it in mid-air. Embarrassed about dropping the apple and that the man had perceived his tentativeness, he frowned.

"You are hungry, ain't you?" He asked as he took a rusty pocket-knife from his pocket and began cutting into the fruit. "When I was younger, I had pretty good teeth like you boy, but now I can't bite into this hard stuff. Need to take care of yourself. Don't want to wind up like me."

"Thanks for the apple; I am hungry." Kiki said, biting down.

"Yeah, I thought so. Noticed you are traveling light. Sure look young. Your first ride?"

"Uh-huh." He looked away, avoiding eye contact with the stranger.

"Well, everyone has to have a first," he said, appearing anxious to talk. "I remember I wasn't much older than you. I told my momma bye and hopped on a freighter near Pecos. Me and a bunch of canta-loupes on that train. I wasn't any more prepared than you. I got hungry and crawled over and stole me two. Busted them right there in the car and ate them with my hands. Best cantaloupes I believe I ever ate."

Kiki wiped his mouth with his sleeve. He was beginning to warm up to the old man and curious to know more, "Have you been doing this ever since?"

"Not all the time. Tried to settle down once. Met me a nice woman in Ft. Worth, but she didn't like the fact that I didn't bring home much money working down at the stockyards. Besides I missed the rails."

"But how do you get enough money to live on?"

"Don't need much. I work a little now and then, but am getting too old to do much. He took off his dirty baseball cap lined with salty sweat and ran his fingers through what few long scraggly hairs he had left on either side of a bald spot. "Mainly, good folks give me food along the way. Never gone hungry, and never been sick a day in my life, despite all the germs you hear about on these ol' cars. Guess I'm just a hearty soul. My only regret is that I can't see too good anymore, which bothers me. I like to read my Bible, but I'm having trouble with these old eyes. Course I say my prayers every night. Just me and God out here together most nights." He paused briefly and looked out at the drab land that seemed to go on forever, "Where you headed?"

"I hope Lubbock. Do you know if this train goes there?"

"Yep, sure does—everyday. What's in Lubbock that has caught your fancy?"

Kiki hesitated, but figured there wasn't any problem in telling now. "Going to find my dad."

The hobo scratched his whiskered chin, and with his beady, diluted brown eyes looked straight at the young traveler. "I never knew my old man either. For awhile it bothered me, but then it didn't seem so important. Guess he never thought so either." This time he looked away, appearing to be absorbed in thought. For the longest time he said nothing, and the silence was broken only by the rhythm of the train rolling along the tracks.

Finally he asked, "Have you ever met him?"

"No, I've never even seen pictures, but I know he's rich, and I'm tired of being poor."

"There're worse things, boy, worse things by far. Just remember that. Think I'll catch a nap." He pulled the cap down over his eyes and leaned his head against the rumpled knapsack that he nestled against a stack of shingles.

⌘ ⌘ ⌘

The sun was setting as the train pulled into the yard in Lubbock. Both Kiki and the hobo had slept until a few miles out, and now the old man began stretching his legs, slowly turning and reaching for the rumpled bag that held all his worldly goods. "Gotta move these old legs for awhile or I won't be able to walk. Remember when I was young, it never bothered me, but now I have arthritis or rheumatism, something that sure makes me stiff. Least I have my legs. Seen more than one young man lose a leg trying to jump a train."

Kiki started to tell him about nearly falling, but stopped short.

"Well young man. It's late. What you going to do for the night?"

"I'm not sure. I thought we would get here earlier," realizing that once again he had miscalculated and that he didn't have a plan. Slowly and cautiously, the riders climbed out of the car and lowered themselves down the ladder. Kiki's legs felt limp, and he shook first one and then the other. The old man straightened his shoulders and reached to rub the lower part of his back and then his neck.

"There's a park not too far from here. I'll walk and show you. Do you have any money?"

"Ten dollars," Kiki said reluctantly, suddenly afraid the man might try to take it.

The hobo must have sensed his hesitation because he smiled knowingly. "Well, get yourself a bite to eat at the little café across the street from the park. It's going to be a long night for you, I'm afraid, since you haven't ever done this before. You'll have a lot of time to think about what you are doing. You might even change your mind."

They walked slowly along an asphalt road until they came to a clearing and fork in the road. "Just head that way," he said pointing. "You can't miss it. Now, you take care, boy. Good luck." And then he disappeared; for a minute Kiki wondered if he had been a dream. Trudging down the road, he felt incredibly alone, but determined. He couldn't let himself get discouraged. Tomorrow he would find his father, and everything would change.

⌘　⌘　⌘

Enrique, Mr. M. and six other men from town were finishing a long day of clean up among the rubble of the burned out barn. After culling the metal from the plow sweeps and wagon wheels, the men had raked up bolts and screws and anything else salvageable, and then used a tractor to push the ashes and other debris into piles. What few boards that hadn't completely burned, they stacked, and striking a match, turned them into the same useless ruins as everything else. When all the tasks were completed, Enrique turned to Mr. M. and did what he had dreaded all day. "Boss, I don't know what to say. We'll leave if you want us to, but I would like to try to stay and work out paying for a new barn."

Mr. M. took off his hat and rubbed his forehead with his sleeve. He looked at Enrique and felt only compassion. "Some things you can rebuild and some things you can't. A barn is one of those things that luckily we can replace pretty easily. "Let's just be glad no one was hurt."

Looking down, Enrique was engulfed in sadness. He kicked a mixture of soot and dirt with his worn boot, and pondered his next words. "You and I both know Kiki did this. Neither of us knows why. I'm sorry. You have been so good to us, and Jan has been like a brother to him. I don't understand Kiki, and I never will. He left this morning without telling us. I don't know where he went or if he's coming back. He's only a kid, but he thinks he's a man. He thinks he knows more than his ol' dad. Well, more than me, anyway." He looked down again. "You must know Kiki is not mine."

"I guess anyone who gave it much thought might have figured that out, but it's not my place to judge any man or his family."

"I never felt the need to explain before, but if you have a minute, boss, I'd like to now."

"It's not something that I need to know or you have to talk about."

"I know, but I think I want to. I know you're tired, but will you just give me a few more minutes of your time?"

"Then in that case, let's sit down and have a beer." And for the first time in nearly thirteen years, the two sat side by side on the porch and talked.

The next morning Enrique rose earlier than usual and walked the route he thought Kiki might have taken to catch the train. Once he crossed the neighbor's property he didn't have to walk far. His instincts were right on target and when he saw the tow sack, he picked it up and looked inside to find the books, knowing that Kiki wouldn't be coming back. Slowly, he tossed the sack over his shoulder and walked back to break the news to Consuela. She would be expecting it, but he was doubtful it would make her feel any better.

⌘　⌘　⌘

chapter seven

Kiki had seen the lights lining the Big Top immediately after coming out of the coffee shop, and he couldn't resist. When he was little the circus had come to town, but his mother said they didn't have the money. Jan and his sister had gone and said it was a circus and fair all rolled into one. Both had won stuffed animals, ridden the Ferris wheel, and seen the elephants.

Now he had the chance to see the elephants and ride the rides. Unable to resist, he tried throwing wooden circles over the top of Coke bottles to no avail, telling himself he didn't want a silly stuffed animal anyway. After spending three dollars and eating two bags of cotton candy, he started back to the park, but out of the corner of his eye he had seen a small booth with a fortune teller. She was dressed in a long flowing black skirt and a dingy multi-colored blouse, her head wrapped in a gauzy black scarf. When he approached her, she looked up with a hard, tired look in her eyes and smiled faintly. Seeing the cost scrawled on a handmade sign,

Kiki plopped out four quarters and waited for her to speak. "I guess that means you want your fortune told?"

Kiki nodded and followed her through a set of worn blue satin curtains, and sat down across from her at a small table that was covered with a deck of tarot cards. It took him a minute for his eyes to adjust to the small room lit with only three flickering candles. She picked up the deck of cards, shuffling them carefully, all the while watching his face. When she noticed he was growing impatient, she stopped, told him to cut the deck with his left hand, and then very slowly she placed five cards in the shape of a horseshoe on the table. Picking up the first card she said, "You are quite lucky for I have dealt the King of Pentacles. You are a very smart boy."

He smirked. "Tell me something I don't already know."

Rubbing the cards, she held the card up again, and continued. "And obviously lucky—this is one of the best cards to draw because the King card not only represents knowledge and acquired experience, but the pentacles mean wealth and prosperity. You may be the giver or the receiver."

"It has to mean I will be the receiver because I sure don't have any money. My father is very rich, he boasted. "What else?"

"Patience, young man. It takes a little while to see into one's future. Oh dear, this is the most powerful and dangerous card in the deck, but it is difficult to read, and often misunderstood. I must study it and be very careful. This is the Devil card."

"Why, what does it mean?"

Slowly, the old woman studied the card, laying it down and clasping her hands together. I must draw strongly on my sixth sense, which helps me to better divine what lies ahead."

Nervous now, Kiki fidgeted, "Well, you're the fortune teller; you're supposed to know the future. I'm paying you to read these cards."

"This card is about the god of pleasure and abandon, of wild behavior and unbridled desire and ambitions. The figure represents erotic power, aggression and money. I can interpret it no further than that."

She picked up the third card and studied it carefully. "Ahh, this is much better. This is the Temperance card, and it shows promise. Even happiness and success. The angel is holding two cups, one with silver spilling into the second one holding gold."

Smiling, Kiki pressed her to hurry. "What about the next one?"

Ever so cautiously, she peered at the card, and put it face down, a sudden frown on her weary and worn wrinkled face. Picking up the card, she turned it over and laid it flat. "Look at the card and tell me what you think," as she ran her finger over the man lying face down on the card with ten long swords stuck in his back.

"Hey, I don't know. You tell me," he snapped, with agitation in his voice.

"The Ten of Swords foretells misfortune. Notice the sky is black. I predict that things will not go smoothly in your dealings with others. But there is hope, because the outcome of what this card foretells can be controlled with mental activity, with good choices."

Pointing to the part of the card reflecting a calm sea, she continued. "The sunrise is appearing in the distance beyond the mountains. Because of its place in the horseshoe, this card tells me about your near future, how near I do not know, and there is a small chance that this is the very close past. You have let go of something so now you can expect a turn for the better. I wish I could say for sure, but for some reason I am having great difficulty with the cards tonight."

Kiki was wishing he had never stepped into this lion's den, but he was too curious to stop now. He sat quietly waiting for the next card, hoping that if he sat still, it would be a good one.

"This card symbolizes the far future," she said, taking it in her hand.

"Well?" He grumbled impatiently, unable to control his eagerness.

"Are you sure you want to know?" But before he could answer, she asked to see his hand, which she took and turned to trace his palm. Looking again at the card she began. "There are seventy-eight cards in my deck, and this card is zero, also called the Fool card. Let me explain what I see." as she pointed to the card.

"The young man in this picture is standing at the edge of a cliff, staring at the sky. He has just emerged from the darkness of a cave shown here in the background, and he carries a knapsack of his talents. On the knapsack you can tell that it has an eagle on it, a sign to me that he aims high. The black rose troubles me because it brings to mind that this young man may have malice in his heart, and the tattered sleeves on his shirt portray an irreverent disregard for others. The feather in his cap shows pretense and arrogance. The dog at his feet symbolizes his animal instinct. On the other side of the cave are snowcapped mountains which tell me that this young man is willing to climb whatever heights he must, but the clouds indicate a storm is brewing."

"So, what exactly does that mean?"

"That is all I can tell you, the rest is up to you."

"Hey, you're supposed to tell me the future. You took my money, and then you just leave me hanging."

"The Fool card is, perhaps, the hardest to read. It can go many directions; after all it is the wild card. You told me you were smart. Figure out the symbolism."

He frowned and stood up, disgust in his body language.

"For fifty cents more, I'll read your palm," she offered.

He dug in his pocket for two more quarters, and put them begrudgingly into her wrinkled outstretched hand as she stood up and took his hand once more. "When I looked at your palm earlier, I wasn't going to tell you, but you seem so bent on knowing what lies ahead. I don't see a long life line. You should be cautious; remember the last card shows a young man standing on a cliff." She paused as he waited for more.

This time her patience ran out. "I'm done. I spent more time with you than I should, but your cards were very complex. Now, good luck."

As Kiki left the small enclosure, he noticed that the crowd had grown and the lights twinkled in all directions. But his excitement had faded and his shoulders drooped as he trudged back to the park bench he had spotted earlier.

The glow of the rising sun woke him from a restless, broken sleep. Although the park was well lighted, he had heard noises that frightened him throughout the night. But it was what the fortune teller had told him that made him first lie awake for what seemed like hours and then sleep fitfully, waking often in a sweat. As he leaned up from the metal bench with wooden slats, he stretched his sore muscles and looked around the empty park, remembering his encounter the night before, wishing that the visit to the fortune teller was only a dream.

Realizing he was starving, he stood and began the short walk across the street to the little café where he had eaten a burger the night before. The same young woman who had waited on him then was now working the morning shift. Although she had been too busy the night before to start a conversation, she recognized him and greeted him warmly when he sat down at the long, stainless steel counter, pocked with dents. He ordered orange juice and studied the lengthy breakfast menu.

"What'll it be young man?" she asked.

He thought a minute longer, and then ordered scrambled eggs and bacon.

"Branching out this morning, aren't you darling?" She drawled.

Managing a half-hearted smile, he said, "Just sounded good, but could I have extra toast?"

She turned and yelled, "Order," although the cook was only a few feet away behind an opening above an inside counter, covered with utensils, jars, and little individual boxes of cereal. Once she had completed the order, she turned back to him and asked, "You're not from around here are you?"

At first he didn't meet her eyes, but then he looked up and said, "No, but I might be moving."

"Really, what brings you here?"

"Work, I want to find work."

"Why darling, you're still wet behind the ears. You ought to be in school," she admonished.

He straightened his back, took a long swallow of his juice and said, "I've been to school."

"Yeah, and what?"

"Order up!" The cook yelled in the same manner she had earlier.

Kiki was glad to see the food because he was hungry, but most of all he wanted a diversion from her questioning.

"Hot plate, darling. Now you enjoy. I'll let you enjoy your breakfast. No more twenty questions." She smiled a pleasant smile, and Kiki thought she was almost attractive, save her oversized nose that looked like it might have been broken at some time.

He forced a weak returned smile, buttered his toast, and ate the triangle of bread in one bite. The diner was beginning to fill up when an older man who seemed to know everyone in the room walked in saying greetings and shaking hands with various men who had gathered for coffee. He walked over to the round swivel seat next to Kiki. "Mind if I sit here?"

Kiki looked up from his eggs. With his mouth full, he nodded his head to give approval, and then finally said, "Go ahead," but the gentleman in the big Stetson had already sat down.

The waitress smiled broadly and asked, "How are you this morning, Mitch? You're looking good as ever. Where have you been?"

Taking off his Texas-sized hat and placing it carefully on his knee, he answered, "Oh, I had to run up to Kansas for a few days to pick up some cattle. Does that mean you missed me?" He winked and thanked her for the coffee.

"You know we do. Say, this young man is looking for a job. You got anything?"

He turned to Kiki who was wishing he was finished with his breakfast and out the door. "That so, how old are you, boy?"

"Looks young, don't he?" The waitress chimed in without any provocation before Kiki could answer.

"Well?" The rancher pressed.

Kiki gulped and weakly lied, "Fifteen."

"Oh, that's too bad; I generally only hire guys who are sixteen."

"I'll bet Maxwell don't care how old they are as long as they can do dirty work," the waitress said, laughing.

Kiki's ears perked up. "Maxwell Ridgeway? You know him?"

"Honey, everyone within two hundred miles of here, maybe further, knows Maxwell Ridgeway and the Triple R Ranch."

"Well, I'm supposed to see him. How far is the Triple R?"

"About five miles from here is where it starts, but who knows where it ends. Goes on for miles," she said with admiration in her voice.

"So do you have an appointment?

"No, he just said, to come whenever I could."

"Is that right? Doesn't sound like the Maxwell I know, but who knows, he seems to be mellowing slightly with age. And I do mean slightly." Both he and the waitress laughed.

"You got transportation? If not, I'm going out that way after breakfast. Maxwell owes me a little favor. What do you say you ride with me and I'll drop you off?"

"Okay. I mean thanks."

"Just let me have my usual, and we'll be on our way," he said to the waitress, and then turned back to Kiki. "By the way, what's your name?"

"Uh, Ricky," he stammered. Why hadn't he thought ahead and prepared for such a question?

"Was that a hard question?"

Kiki smiled, "Oh I just didn't know if you wanted my formal name or what I go by."

"I see, well what you go by is fine with me, Ricky." He finished his breakfast and wiped his mouth with the extra white paper napkin the waitress had placed at his plate. "Here, I'll pay for this young man's breakfast. He can pay me back some day when he gets a job." With that he twisted his athletic frame off the stool and reached to lay a twenty dollar bill on the counter. "Keep the change since you missed me." He smiled and winked.

"Thanks Mitch. You're a good guy."

"Yeah, yeah, that's what they say. Let's go, Ricky, don't want to keep ol' Maxwell waiting."

⌘   ⌘   ⌘

Kiki held back, waiting to see which pickup belonged to Mitch. There was not a car in the parking lot—only pickup trucks of various sizes and shapes. Mitch signaled for Kiki to get in. The sun bounced off the chrome of the extended cab pickup. A shiny aluminum tool chest in the bed of the truck glistened with dew on the sunny, but chilly morning. Opening the door, Kiki saw the prettiest hand carved deer rifle he had ever seen.

Noticing Kiki admiring the gun, Mitch offered, "Pretty gun, huh? I actually won that in a contest Maxwell hosted out at his place years ago. I've never seen another one like it."

Kiki wanted to ask what kind of contest, but he wouldn't allow himself.

"Yep, I've known Maxwell for almost as long as I am old. We played together as kids. He was the bully. I was the good guy." He said with a laugh. "Naw, he can be okay. That is if you do exactly what he says. So if he hires you, just be sure to jump at every command."

Kiki didn't like what he was hearing. Although he had heard the disparaging remarks coming from Enrique and his mother, he had still pictured Ridgeway as a benevolent and rich rancher and nothing more, so he remained silent.

"So you never met Maxwell?" Mitch asked, looking incredulous.

"No, just heard he was hiring," Kiki said with some timidity.

"Maxwell is always hiring...and firing. People come and go out there like flies at a picnic.

Look at me a minute. I swear, if I didn't know better I'd say you look like him. But guess that's not possible." He smiled as he drove along the bumpy road. "Although anything is possible with Maxwell. He's had his share of women. I'd say there isn't a woman safe for a thousand miles." He laughed deeply as he brought the truck to a stop. "Well, there it is—the Triple R Ranch, the biggest ranch until you get to Amarillo."

Kiki looked at the gate in awe. Flanked on either side by huge river rock cemented together, the black metal sign was wider than Kiki's house. Cameras stuck out from both ends. The electric gate opened only after Mitch answered the voice at the end of a metal box. "Maxwell may be a little paranoid, but I guess with his money, he can afford to be." The gravel sprayed underneath the truck as Mitch revved the engine. "I do this because it makes Maxwell mad. Just wait, he'll be standing outside when I get to the house."

And when they pulled to a stop, Mitch was right. Standing just outside the massive dark Spanish Colonial parota wood double front doors, that would have dwarfed anyone else, was perhaps, the biggest man Kiki had ever seen.

"Damn you, Mitch Parker. How many times have I told you not to kick up my gravel?"

Mitch opened the truck door, and slid out, his long legs hitting the driveway within seconds. "Calm down, Maxwell; it's just a few pebbles here and there. You can replace them anytime. I brought a guy with me who needs work."

"Well, then why didn't you hire him?" Maxwell growled without even looking Kiki's way.

"Said he only wanted to work for you. Hurt my feelings, but heck, we all know everyone wants to work for you, right Maxwell?"

Maxwell turned to look at Kiki. "Wait in the truck. We'll be awhile, but that's okay, it won't kill you to cool your heels. If you are going to work for me, you'll get used to waiting on me." He slapped Mitch on the back, "Come on in. What's on your mind?"

⌘   ⌘   ⌘

An hour and a half later, Mitch came out to his truck where Kiki had fallen off to sleep.

"He wants to see you now. Don't keep him waiting!"

Kiki jumped out of the cab, brushing his hair with his hand. He wished he weren't so crumpled and had on clean clothes. He climbed the steps and knocked gingerly on the huge door, and waited for what seemed like a very long time.

Finally, the doors swung open and he saw the powerfully large man for the second time.

"Now, what is this I hear about your wanting work?"

Kiki caught his breath and mustered his courage. "No, that is not exactly what I wanted."

Glaring at Kiki, Maxwell said, "What do you mean that is not exactly what you had in mind. Don't waste my time, boy, or you won't get work anywhere in these parts."

Kiki started to speak, but the words wouldn't come. Maxwell's voiced boomed as he yelled, "Talk boy, or get on your way."

"Did you need me boss, I heard you from the kitchen," came a timid voice from a small Mexican lady who stood a few feet from the opened door.

"No, I was talking to this mute. He seems to have forgotten what he came for."

Finally, Kiki found his voice and his courage and quickly said. "I came here to live. You are my father, and I came here to live."

Maxwell's eyes danced with rage. "I'm your what?"

"My father."

"Well, you may be right about that. I've had my pick of women over the years, but tell me why you think I would believe you?" Maxwell and Kiki were still standing on the expansive porch. "Here, sit down in one of these rocking chairs, and tell me your little story."

Kiki waited until Maxwell had taken his immense frame and wedged it into the one rocker that was obviously his. "Sit down, you're making me nervous, all fidgeting around, sweating and jumpy," he ordered in a loud voice.

Kiki complied, but not in the rocker next to Maxwell.

"If a man can't sit by you and look you in the eye, then he's not much good for anything. Now, get up and sit in this chair." He ordered, pointing to the one next to him.

Kiki rose and then sat down again in the rocker closest to Maxwell. "Okay, I'm waiting!" Maxwell's voice boomed as his face turned crimson.

Kiki began, explaining what he had heard his mother and Enrique say.

Maxwell's mouth turned into a sarcastic smirk when he said. "You know, I'm thinking I remember her now. I went down to the house to see if there was anything they needed, you know blankets, food, any supplies, and while I was there she seduced me, right there in the little room where they lived and ate their meals. I'm telling you, she came on to me, which is not really anything new, but I really didn't expect it of her. You know, she was so quiet and kind of shy. But right there she plain begged me to take her to bed, so I couldn't let her down. No, that wouldn't have been neighborly. She was a real tiger, fighting me and begging me for rough sex."

"Is that why she had that scar above her lip?"

"Probably so, believe it got wild there for a few minutes cause she wanted me so bad. Obviously she had never been with anyone of my caliber. Well, tell me, how IS your mother?"

Kiki looked down. He wanted to like this man, but he hated what he was saying about his mother. He didn't believe any of what this man was saying, but he didn't want to give him any indication of those feelings. "She's fine. She and Enrique have a girl now. She looks just like them both. I look like you."

Maxwell ignored the last part of his answer. "That's good. I never saw her again. Her husband took off with her shortly after that. That's right, I remember now his name was Enrique. Ran out on me during planting season. Boy, was I pissed! Felt sorry for her though. That wimpy husband of hers would never be able to satisfy her again after me." he chortled in a loud, menacing tone.

"So, now we have established that you might, just might be my boy. But remember, she was in Enrique's bed too, so there is certainly a chance that you are his, you know. But let's say you have my blood running through you, what is it you want?"

"I want your name, and I want to live here," he said nervously and in a high, almost squeaky voice. He hated it when his voice did that to him, but it was changing, and occasionally he sounded more like a girl than a boy.

Maxwell stood up, all three hundred plus pounds of him, and started pacing. He bellowed, "Let me get this straight. You want me to claim you, a half Mexican, as my own." He laughed to the top of his lungs and continued until Kiki couldn't stand it any longer.

He stood and took his place next to Maxwell, trying to make himself taller. "It didn't seem to bother you that she was Mexican when you were with her. Look at me. I have blue eyes just like you."

"Sit down and shut up. Don't ever get in my face again. I told you I was just doing her a favor. She needed me, and I just accommodated her. Do you hear that?"

Kiki stiffened but didn't answer.

Stomping over, Maxwell leaned in close and slapped the boy hard on the right side of his face. "I said answer me."

"I...I...I forgot the question."

Maxwell appeared to have forgotten it as well, but continued. "I said she was nothing but a Mexican tramp, and I just gave her what she wanted. Guess she wanted a half white kid too from the looks of things." His voice trailed off, and for a minute Kiki thought he was softening. He reached up to touch his stinging face. If Enrique had ever done that he would have hit him back, but he simply sat and held his face and looked at the man who was his father, once again pacing the porch.

For what seemed like a long time there was total silence, save for a sound of birds foraging in the nearby sunflower patch. "Let's go inside," Maxwell commanded.

Just inside the mammoth room, Kiki's eyes grew wide. A distressed chocolate brown leather sectional sofa with reclaimed wooden end tables on either side sat directly in front of a gargantuan rock fireplace that touched the twenty foot ceiling. A large sturdy coffee table with an iron base revealed hand carved edges. To one side was a poker table and six chairs and to the other was a huge leather recliner which appeared to be reserved for Maxwell. Next to it was a smaller wing back chair in a rich warm hue that complimented the other furniture. The two chairs were separated by a small glass top tree trunk table that held a slate lamp and an ashtray in the shape of Texas.

A chewed on, half smoked cigar teetered on the side of the ashtray. Western art adorned every wall and hand painted Mexican pottery was visible throughout the enormous room. A hand woven wool rug in geometric shapes of reds, oranges and browns covered half of the Brazilian wood planked floor. "Rosa, bring this boy a glass of lemonade and me bourbon, straight up. And don't go telling me it isn't even lunch. I don't need your advice, you hear?"

Within seconds, the helper appeared with the lemonade and then went over to behind the fifteen foot mahogany bar, inlaid with copper and turquoise. She carefully placed two cubes of ice in a highball glass and filled it with Johnny Walker Black. "Here you are,

Sir," as she stood patiently waiting for Maxwell, who seemed preoccupied or distracted, to reach for his drink from the silver tray. She turned to Kiki and offered him the lemonade.

"Thank you," he said quickly and politely.

Realizing he hadn't asked the boy his name, he said, "Introduce yourself to Rosa."

"I'm Kiki," hating the sound of it.

"No wonder you want to change your name. That's a sissy name." He turned and called to Rosa. "He thinks he's big enough for my name." he laughed, his voice ricocheting off the dark walls. "What do you think about that?"

She smiled gently and gave no answer.

"He's going to be here a few days, so make a bed for him. Give him the Ponderosa Room. He might think he's Billy the Kid or somebody for a day or two!" Again, his voice boomed as he laughed heartedly, obviously pleased to hear himself.

Kiki stood in disbelief, afraid to move, fearful he might change his mind. Although he hadn't made a commitment, it was a step in the door, and Kiki knew he had made progress.

"Where's your gear, boy?"

"I don't have any. I had to leave my books behind," he lied. "That's all I miss, really."

"Well, there's a whole library in that room over there. Any book you could want, you'll find. Help yourself, but leave it when you go. I don't like folks taking things with them that I don't give away."

Kiki's heart sank, maybe he wasn't going to get to stay, but he nodded in agreement.

"When you finish your lemonade, Rosa will show you your quarters. Just be glad you're not having to bunk with the other guys. And if anyone asks, tell them you're my nephew. You got that?"

"Yes," he stopped short of saying sir. He had never used the word, and he didn't want to start now.

Maxwell noticed, and turned back to face Kiki. "You got any manners?"

"Yes, sir."

⌘   ⌘   ⌘

Kiki sat on the Ponderosa Pine canopy bed with cowhide headboard and panels, and looked around the room. The floor to ceiling window overlooked miles and miles of prairie, dotted with mesquite trees, Longhorn cattle and oil wells, pumping rhythmically along the expanse of land. He wanted to see what the three-drawer nightstand held, but refrained from looking. Instead, he rubbed the turquoise inlay with his fingers, and noticing his dirty fingernails and grimy hands, realized he hadn't had a bath in two days. Peering into the adjoining bathroom with a claw foot tub and large, inviting beige towels he asked himself what good it would do since he would have to put the same soiled clothes back on.

As if reading his mind, Maxwell hollered from downstairs. "Hurry up. Gus is on his way up to take you to town to buy some clothes and get a haircut. You can't hang around here smelling like a hog. I have enough of them out in the pen."

⌘   ⌘   ⌘

part two

chapter eight

The few days that Maxwell had said Kiki would be staying turned into a week, and then a month passed, and another and another. Neither Kiki nor Maxwell mentioned the extended stay until summer was almost over.

But that was not to say Maxwell had not thought about it...a lot. In all the years he had lived in the big house on thousands of acres, a child had never shared his life. Many years ago when he was married to Sarah, he had wanted a son, someone to carry his legacy and the Ridgeway name, but she had left him after just two years because he was unfaithful, not once, but many times. After she left, he never married again, but there were always women, coming and going, because Maxwell grew tired of them quickly. To him, they weren't companions or anyone to love, but merely possessions or trophies that he bragged about. He treated his cattle better than most of the women in his life.

He had long ago put aside any thoughts of a son, but often he had thought about what it would be like to have a child who shared his bloodline, a son who would mirror his thoughts and mimic his actions. And now fate was tempting him.

One hot and dusty afternoon in mid-August when Maxwell was sitting on the veranda reading a hunting magazine, Kiki approached him to say he wanted to go to school, and he didn't want to start classes being known as Kiki. Maxwell ignored the conversation, and took a puff off his cigar.

After a long pause, Kiki insisted, "I really like school, and I'm smart. You'll see. I'll prove that to you."

"Oh, I believe you. Guess you're a chip off the old block. I always say, the acorn doesn't fall too far from the tree. School's not the problem—the name is."

Although that wasn't exactly what he wanted to hear, Kiki was stunned, but tried not to show his surprise because this was the first time that Maxwell had, even remotely since the first day, acknowledged being his father. He sat patiently hoping Maxwell would continue, and after a long pause, he did. "What grade are you in?"

"I was in the seventh when I left to come here, but since I didn't finish I guess I still am."

"And you're how old?"

"I'll turn fourteen in January."

"Then if you are as smart as you say, you should be at least in the ninth grade. No boy of mine is going to repeat a grade—maybe skip a grade is more like it. Yep, that's where you'll be—ninth grade," Maxwell said emphatically.

"But I don't have a report card or anything to show."

"Precisely, I guess we need to visit my friend Harry at the law office."

"What can he do?"

"Well, to start with he can give you that damn new name you are so set on having. You can go by Max until you leave here for college. After that I don't care what you do. Right now the spread of land isn't big enough for two Maxwell's, and besides it's too damn confusing. Why can't you be satisfied just being Bill or Tex or anything simple?"

"Because your name is big and important...like you. That's what I want to be—big and important."

Maxwell beamed an obviously proud smile. "Well, you've come to the right place for big and important. Anyway, as I was saying we'll talk to Harry to see what he needs to do to fix you up for school. Now, go fetch me a bourbon; all this talk is making me thirsty. And get you one. Guess this calls for a celebration. If you're going to have my name, you're going to have to learn how to drink. I'm going to make you as mean and tough as a junkyard dog and a hell of a lot smarter."

Unable to hide his excitement, Kiki stumbled over the rocker and fell face down in front of Maxwell. Embarrassed, he jumped up and without saying a word, ran into the house.

⌘ ⌘ ⌘

Three weeks later Kiki started ninth grade as Maxwell Collin Ridgeway III with a new red GMC pickup, compliments of Maxwell II. The driver's license, birth certificate, and school records were a product of the Law Offices of Henry F. Herrera, Jr., better known as Harry the Fairy to a certain segment of the county. But to Maxwell he was a long time friend who he had known since first grade. When Harry had come out of the closet, it was Maxwell who had supported him when others took their legal issues elsewhere. Friends were astounded that Maxwell, the rough and tumble rancher, would still stick up for Harry once everyone in the area knew his sexual preferences. When one asked him about it he replied simply, "If a guy can be gay and survive in West Texas, he's a tougher son of a bitch than me. Besides, Harry's the damn best lawyer in the state even if he is crooked as a country road. I don't give a rat's ass who he kisses or for that matter does anything else with as long as he covers my ass when I need him."

And Harry had done just that for more than thirty years. When Maxwell needed papers for an illegal alien, one way or the other Harry managed. When Maxwell needed a DWI expunged, it was taken care of in less time than it took Harry to find a new lover. If a pay-off to a local official was the only way to get a job done, money was transferred without any questions asked. But it was the big stuff like sexual assault that Harry handled flawlessly, and Maxwell needed his expertise because it had happened more than once. Only once had any such accusation gone all the way to court. Harry had managed to ruin the woman's reputation as a whore and a gold-digger, but it had taken several months and thousands of dollars. The results were all that mattered to Maxwell. Winning was the most important thing, not to mention escaping jail time.

Of course, Harry didn't work for free, and Maxwell reminded him often that he had seldom paid someone that much money without so much as a single kiss. Harry would smile and tell his longtime friend that he wasn't his type. But let no one be fooled, Harry might have been gay, but he was certainly no pansy, nor was he a loser at the courthouse. Maxwell Ridgeway II picked no losers!

⌘   ⌘   ⌘

chapter nine

If Max was worried about being the new kid at school, it never showed. Transitioning into ninth grade went smoothly. The boys thought he was cool because he had a new truck and money in his pocket; the girls saw him as the next Paul Newman. When Maxwell asked Max how it was going he always answered the same, "Smooth."

"Yeah, well so are these castrations I'm overseeing every day, but these guys have a lot more to lose," Maxwell growled.

"Maybe literally, but this fitting in is pretty important to me."

"Fitting in is not the point. You need to be the leader. I want you to run for president of the student body, and find some sport to excel in. It's too late for football this year, but you can play baseball...that's it—baseball."

"I've never really been all that great at baseball."

"I know the coach at Texas Tech. I'll call him tonight. Have him send someone over to help you every afternoon. You'll be the best kid on the diamond by the start of the season."

"But what if I don't want to play baseball?"

"You will, and you will be damn good. Lots of things I don't want to do that I do. You think I wanted to take in a teenage boy out of nowhere? Hell no, but I did because it was important to you. Now, this is important to me. I make the decisions here, and you will do as I say. Got it?"

"Got it," Max said, although not completely happy about it.

⌘   ⌘   ⌘

Max learned quickly that if he wanted to live in a big house, drive a new truck, and have money in his pocket, there was a price to pay, but even at his age, he had figured out that in life there are tradeoffs. In the end, this would all be his.

So, he did what Maxwell told him, and in return, Maxwell bailed him out of all his scrapes, which were many. Usually, it was Max's attitude that caused most of his problems, but there were actions as well. Each time, he came out on top, and learned by example that if a person had enough money, power and reputation, the sky was the limit.

He took full advantage, and as the years went by learned by watching Maxwell step on those who were defenseless and crush those who crossed him. And he became the leader that his father had said he would, but not necessarily in a good way. It was Max who encouraged his school buddies, and he had many, to outrun the cops, to steal street signs and mow down mailboxes. He pushed anybody around who disagreed with him, bullying the boys in the high school band, and convincing the girls he was the perfect male to take away their virginity. On several occasions, Maxwell received calls from Max's teachers who explained that his smart mouth and less than desirable actions and language were disrupting their classes. Finally, he was suspended, and Maxwell had to go to school to get him reinstated, but underneath his bluster when he yelled at Max, he was secretly pleased that his son was showing signs of supremacy and dominance.

Max also learned about the ranch, which interested him less than Maxwell would have preferred, so he insisted that Max participate in every aspect of its workings, except the books—accounting was off limits. No one, not even an accountant saw the books, which only served to heighten Max's curiosity. But there was one other part of the business he didn't quite understand. There appeared to be a constant flow of workers coming and going, with relatively few of them there for more than a few days, except for those who had been Maxwell's longtime ranch hands. The bunkhouse was often a flurry of activity, almost a changing station. When he asked Maxwell, the only explanation was "these people find out how hard the work is, and they move on."

But it was more, and Max persisted until Maxwell finally said. "It's called smuggling, stupid. I guess I am pretty damn good at it since my own son can't even figure it out, and I've been doing it right here in front of your nose for years."

"But why? You have more money than you can ever spend!"

Maxwell laughed his usual boisterous, booming laugh and replied, "Oh, the money is, indeed, good, but it's much more than that. I'm the Godfather! I'm King of the coyotes, the general in charge—El Patrón, they call me. My lieutenants, hell, the whole organization answers to me. I own the border, and I decide who comes in and who doesn't. And if somebody screws with me, then they pay with their blood! This ain't no charity. Hell, these people are totally expendable. Nobody knows who they are or exactly where they come from. If they make it this far, fine. If not, who gives a shit? They lie in the desert until some vulture eats them or their brains fry in the heat."

"But why are they coming here? Why not just drop them off at the border, and let them get somewhere best they can?"

"I still do that for the most part, but now I've taken it a step further because I am such a good guy. For a little bit of extra money, I let a few get this far and find them jobs. I don't know of another coyote anywhere that does that—never hurts to work hand in hand sometimes with the drug cartels. Guess you can call it sharing the routes. You scratch my back and I'll scratch yours. The farther the drugs get, the more money and the more power. See your old man is just so damn nice, don't you think?" The room almost shook from the roar of his laugh.

"Has anybody ever questioned you, anybody get suspicious?"

Maxwell stood and started pacing. "Questioned me?" He asked incredulously, his voice louder than before. "I don't have Harry working for me for nothing. He keeps an ear to the ground, and he has money to use in exchange for dirt, or anything else for that matter. This is the first time I've seen you interested in anything on the ranch except the oil wells. What's the deal with this sudden beam of light around your eyes? Think you're big enough and smart enough for this, do you, huh?"

Max smiled a cunning, crafty grin. "It's good to be King! Count me in."

"Whoa, first, you have to go to college, get that piece of sheepskin to hang on the wall. That's all it is, but it's my requirement. Then, we'll talk."

⌘   ⌘   ⌘

As was Maxwell's wish, Max attended Texas Tech, where he partied the nights away, and slept away the days, rarely going to classes. But when time came for grades, one call from his father to the dean and that was taken care of swiftly.

In the last semester of the four years, there was one scare that Max didn't know how to get out of so he quickly ran to Harry for help.

"You know I can't do anything for you without your dad's knowledge."

"All I am asking is for a doctor who will give her an abortion. That's all Harry. You know someone? I know you do, even if we have to go to Mexico. You're the best."

"Don't go giving me the sweet talking, ass licking crap, Max. I get enough of that from your old man, but he pays me well, and you don't."

"I can get the money. I just need a name and address."

"So is this what the girl wants?"

"I don't know. I haven't told her yet!" Max exclaimed, exasperated.

"What do you mean you haven't told her? Don't you think she will make that decision?"

"It's not her decision to make. I'll make it, and she is not going to have my baby. End of story."

"And all these years I thought your dad was the most controlling asshole in the world, but I do believe you have one upped him."

Max smiled, "Well, thanks for the compliment, Harry. Now, the name of the doctor?"

Harry was not finished. "What if she tells you she wants this baby; I can't see that there is much you can do at this point, at least not legally."

"This is not about legal shit. If I have to drug her to get her to a doctor, and wait there while he cuts it out, I will."

Looking stunned, Harry continued. "But if we can draw up papers that relinquish you from child support or any claim to the baby, what do you care?"

"I know what it is like to be born into that circumstance, and I will not have it. If you don't help me I will find someone who will. Thanks for nothing, Harry!" The slamming door vibrated the room as Harry picked up the phone to call Maxwell.

⌘   ⌘   ⌘

When Max arrived back at his apartment, Maxwell was waiting, but not patiently. As the door opened, he rose and walked over to Max, his eyes menacing. "What in the hell have you gone and done now, you stupid little shit?"

"Well, obviously your little prick of a lawyer has already told you, so why the question?"

"Don't you dare get smart with me or I'll have your legs cut off. Then you'd have to look up to me. Seems you are forgetting these days who's boss." In the last year Max had surpassed Maxwell's height by an inch, and it was not something that the elder Ridgeway was taking well.

"All I wanted was a doctor's name where she could get an abortion. What's the big deal?"

"The big deal is that she's pregnant and you're the stupid bastard who didn't have any better sense than to get her that way. Haven't you ever heard of a condom?"

Max's eyes froze in contempt. "In other words, do as I say, not as I do?" Before the last syllable came from his mouth, Maxwell hit him hard in the stomach, knocking him off his feet. Then when Max started to get up, Maxwell took his foot to his chest and pushed him back against the floor, penning him to the ground. "You're not getting up until you have apologized to me."

"That's not going to happen in this lifetime."

"Well, I can stand here as long as I need to." He eased one foot off and placed the other on Max's stomach. "Who is this girl anyway? Where's she from?"

When Max didn't answer, he applied more pressure. "Better still, how old is she?"

"Let me up and we can talk."

"Say it or you stay on the ground."

"Okay, old man, I'm sorry, but it sure seems a lot like the same circumstances."

Maxwell released the force and Max struggled to stand. His gut hurt, and his head was spinning. "She's sixteen."

Maxwell's face went pale. "You stupid, dumbass, son of a bitch."

⌘　⌘　⌘

As with every tight space he had ever been in, Max knew in the long run Maxwell would save his butt. In the end, the girl, under extreme pressure from her parents, and twenty thousand dollars riding on the outcome, agreed to the abortion. Always the business man, Maxwell required papers from the doctor and all manner of agreements signed by the girl and her parents in front of Harry. But Max was cleared, and his life went on whether another's did or not.

With graduation behind him, Max took a trip, but not to Europe or Asia or any other place where most young graduates would choose. Instead he went first to the flat parched Texas border and then to the mountainous desert land that separates the state of Arizona from the country of Mexico. Walking along the dusty trails dodging mice, snakes and stinging nettles, he saw firsthand how the coyotes worked, and in his mind justified the process. He couldn't wait to start.

⌘　⌘　⌘

Chapter Ten

Within days of returning to the ranch, Maxwell sent Max back to Arizona on his first assignment. "When you've been in charge as long as I have, you can sit on your ass, but right now you have to learn the trade. To do that you have to be there—to smell the land and the people, feel the heat, literally and figuratively, and get the rush. Ah, the rush. There's only one thing that feels better," he winked at his young protégé. "Report in often. Be safe, but most of all act smart. And remember the real coyote in the wild is cunning and fast. The key is he walks with only his toes touching the ground."

Max thought for a minute before responding. "Were you ever really in the trenches? I mean like I am going to be?"

"No, I was too old when I got into this business, and it's changed a lot in the last few years. It's a lot more dangerous now for everyone—the coyote, the Border Patrol and the one being smuggled. You'll learn from the ground up, but trust me I won't leave you in that position for long if you do well. In other words, bring a group with you quickly, and you might get promoted."

"What's the most important thing?"

"Never flinch. Keep your ears to the ground and your eyes open. Above all, be smart!"

Max sat thinking about that comment, and then rose to leave when Maxwell stood and walked over, extending his hand with a crushing handshake. "I'll see you soon. And Max, take care."

Max realized that was about as sentimental as Maxwell could ever get. He had noticed though as he sat listening that for the first time, his dad was looking older. Tiny lines and bigger creases were beginning to show in his face, and absent was the old customary swagger in his step that was so familiar since the very first day they had met. Although they had never discussed his age, Max figured he had to be approaching his mid-sixties. Despite his lack of love for the old man, he had come to appreciate his strength and resilience, not to mention his guts.

⌘　⌘　⌘

He flew to Tucson, and rented a Jeep to Naco, on the border where he met Maxwell's first lieutenant Sergio, who gave him the details of his first assignment. Taking orders was not something Max took well, and he was testy and argumentative with Sergio, who detected his attitude immediately.

"Hey, you should know this is not as easy as it looks. The Border Patrol guys are like ants right now and the heat is sweltering, if you haven't noticed. I have arranged for you to pick up your first group tomorrow night. I'll walk you over to the lay-up where they will be waiting. If anything happens and you're late, they'll wait, but the longer they wait, the better chance they will be caught."

"So, we have their money, right? What do we care?"

"We have half of their money, and we care because right now we have a pretty good reputation with the illegals. As your father says it's exponential because if people we take across are happy, they tell their families who tell their friends."

"Hey, they need us a lot more than we need them. Who's going to get them across if we don't?" Arrogance filled every word he spoke as he kicked a creosote bush with his heavy boot.

"Technically, you're right, but they'll come with or without us. And although we are the biggest organization, we're not the only one. There are still a lot of mom and pop businesses out there," Sergio added.

"Yeah, and the good thing is it's a win-win. We never lose the product. The Border Patrol guys always put the illegals back into the system sooner or later. Most of the time they don't even process them—just see that they are sent back to Mexico, and surprise, here they are again. Suckers keep trying. Can't lose in a deal like that. Better than smuggling drugs where they might take the drugs if they catch you, which means that trip is a wipeout, but not with these guys. They never stop trying."

"Unless they don't pay up quickly."

"If they don't pay the second half, I say we kill them," Max said coldly.

"They're worth more to us alive once they are here. We can make them work and pay it out. Of course, we can always put pressure on their families in Mexico."

"Those guys are expendable," he said in a cocky tone, mimicking the elder Ridgeway.

Sergio frowned, "That they are—in some cases. Look, your dad told me to teach you everything you need to know. I don't want to talk to you anymore than you do me, but I have my orders, so let's make it easy for both of us. Here's the plan. As the sun begins to slip below the western mountains, José will go across and meet up with the first group, and then the stragglers, if there are any. Pay attention because you will take his place tomorrow night. Be here in the truck by midnight. Okay?"

"Yeah, where can a guy get a drink around here?"

"There's a tiny bar in town, but I don't suggest you be seen. That's not the way we work."

"Yeah, well that's the way I work. I'm thirsty. I work better when I'm not," Max said, walking toward the Jeep.

"Be here by midnight. I don't want your dad on my ass because of some ungrateful bastard like you."

"I'll pretend you didn't say that because within six months I will be in charge of this operation. Where will you be?"

Sergio turned and shook his head. He had met bullies but this guy was the worst of the worst. He didn't wish him any harm, but he didn't like him; that was a fact.

⌘   ⌘   ⌘

Shortly before midnight on what had turned out to be a cloudy, moonless night, a lone Border Patrol agent using night vision saw six heads almost two hundred feet away, but in the time it took to adjust his eyes, he lost them. Stopping, he stood motionless, listening. He thought he heard a branch break, and then nothing. Hating to put his goggles back on because they sometimes caused him to become disoriented, he waited. The silence was deafening. In the pitch darkness, he didn't see the dead limb, but he heard it snap the minute his foot came down on it. It distracted him, and he almost fell.

Damn, he thought but dared not open his mouth. Suddenly, he heard movement, and turning saw the figures of at least twenty people of various heights. Pulling out two flashlights simultaneously, he kept one in his left hand at waist level while he raised the one in the right hand to his shoulder, and then flipped them on at the same second. "Stop! U.S. Border Patrol," he yelled in Spanish, trying not to let fear or any hint of emotion creep into his order. But as always when there were so many of them and he was alone, there was a moment of trepidation.

Fortunately, they immediately stopped and hit the ground, lowering themselves into sitting positions. That told him they were not new to this. Rookies would have run or panicked. These guys knew the drill, and had obviously been on this route and caught before. And tonight would not be their last attempt; they would be back until they were successful.

"Take off your shoes," he commanded in Spanish. He couldn't remember if this was against protocol or not, but right now it didn't matter; he couldn't take any chance of them running. They knew better than anyone what lay on the desert floor and that it was useless to try to run without protection for their feet; they were compliant, but they held their shoes close to their chests, and the officer sensed their hope that he wouldn't take them.

What disturbed him even more was he had lost his sense of direction and wasn't sure how far he had moved away from his original position where the truck was parked. All he could do was walk until he found it. In Spanish he yelled, "Put your hands on the shoulders of the person in front of you and walk."

Noticing a man who looked to be about twenty holding a hand of the only woman in the group edge toward the back, he walked over and crammed one of the flashlights under his chin. "Some may get away, but not you. I'll see to it you're going with me even if you are the only one. So move it, and move it fast."

He knew that more than likely, the coyote was with them, but they would never give him up so it was useless to try to determine who it was. Somewhere there was a second coyote waiting to take this group away from the border, but it wouldn't be tonight.

⌘   ⌘   ⌘

This was not what Max had expected; he had waited like Sergio instructed, but it turned out to be a total waste of time. On the second night he was less than enthusiastic about sitting around waiting, so he started drinking at the bar around nine and by midnight was drunk. "What the hell," he said to no one as he approached his Jeep in the parking lot. *Those damn Mexicans have waited this long, they can wait until tomorrow*, and he drove to the trailer Sergio had rented for him just outside of town.

When he awoke, his head hurt and his throat was dry. He made himself a half a dozen scrambled eggs and four pieces of toast. By the time he showered and dressed it was after eleven o'clock, and the temperature was climbing fast. But still he took his time, and it was nearly one o'clock when he reached the lay-up and honked. People flew out of the brushy area like ants out of a mound. Two young women carried babies, but most were men of all ages and sizes. Each looked tired and listless.

As Max watched, they kept coming, and he wondered how they were going to fit in the back of the Ryder truck. One thing for sure, he wasn't coming back, so one way or the other, they were going to fit. When the last person had climbed in, Maxwell jammed the metal door shut, and slammed the bar into place. He was not looking forward to the drive to Phoenix, and because he had not done his homework; he had failed to get directions. For four hours he drove more or less in circles until finally out of frustration he stopped at a convenience store for directions. When he learned he had more than two hundred miles to go, he called a cab, and left the truck in the parking lot of the store.

After it sat for two more hours, a cashier became suspicious and called the Border Patrol who arrived to find ninety people stuffed in the back of the truck, most with no water and all in terrible physical shape from dehydration and stifling temperatures of more than one hundred and twenty degrees. When they tried to trace the truck back to the person who rented it, there was no paperwork and no one was talking. Transferring all the migrants into enough vans took more than five hours, and then they were taken to the border and unloaded as agents ensured they crossed into Mexico, a temporary holding place until the following day, when they would try again.

⌘　⌘　⌘

Maxwell was furious when he heard that Max had left the truck and basically walked away.

Screaming into the phone he cursed and swore and berated Max for more than fifteen minutes before he paused, let out a long breath, and started ranting again.

Finally Max got in a sentence. "I didn't go to college for four years to drive some fucking rental truck all over this God-forsaken shit hole of the world."

"You didn't exactly go to college for four years. You farted around and played for six years while I covered your ass and saw to it that you got a sheepskin. Now you listen to me, and you listen real close. I told you that you are going to learn this from the ground up, and that is exactly what I meant. You are going to get dirty, sweaty and thirsty until you know every cactus, every drag road, and every cattle guard and safe house there. You are going to be able to tell me the color of every Border Patrolman's eyes. And when you have driven across enough times to get at least five guys in a car with a secret compartment and again that many with forged papers that you have secured yourself, then you can come home. But not until then!"

Stopping to catch his breath again, he shouted, "And by the way, why were you so late picking this group up? I swear, if I have to come down there myself, I will. And that won't be pretty. Do you understand me?" He was yelling so loud that Max held the phone out for more than a foot.

"Calm down old man. You're going to have a heart attack."

"You wish!"

⌘ ⌘ ⌘

chapter eleven

And so it was for two years that Max learned the business. He found an official at the U.S. Consulate Office in Nogales who on four different occasions sold him three different pre-approved visas with fake numbers for three thousand dollars. These would easily go for five thousand a piece so he would hold on to them until the right people came along, people who were willing to pay the big bucks for a ten year visa that allowed them to come and go as they wished.

"Good work, Max," Maxwell praised after he heard his son explain. "Now, find as many polleros in Mexico as you can. Put the squeeze to them. Tell them they owe us fifteen thousand a month for us to leave them alone. I'm sick and tired of them taking part of our business. They can work for us, but not against us. Tell them that if they don't see it our way, we'll turn their polleros into chicken shit."

"Max laughed. He loved it when his dad talked like that. His Spanish wasn't as good as his son's, and Maxwell had visions of all the Mexican smugglers turning into chicken shit. "Gotcha, old man."

But Maxwell knew exactly what he meant, and he meant business. The small time mom and pop Mexican polleros, as they called themselves, didn't have a chance competing with Maxwell's organization. "Quit calling me that. I don't like to be reminded. Call me tomorrow," he commanded. "Do you understand?" But Max had hung up before the end of the question.

⌘   ⌘   ⌘

Tomorrow came and went, and Max didn't call, nor did he report in to Sergio, who was now his dad's deputy and gave all the orders. He had sent Max across the border to bring back three fairly high profile guys in a car. They were part of the Mexican Mafia, and Max had sold them two of the forged visas, but the third guy didn't have enough money so he was to be hidden in the new vehicle with the six thousand dollar magnetic-electro compartment that not even x-rays could detect. The trouble with dealing with the Mexican Mafia was that they were just as criminally motivated as Max and considerably more careful. About ten miles from the U.S. border, they had him stop the car. The guy in the front ordered Max out while his friend proceeded to get in the front seat and drive off, but not before taking out a shotgun and peppering Max in the stomach with buckshot from fifty feet away.

Lying in the middle of a dusty road in the middle of nowhere, he figured he was going to die, until a woman in a bright blue Mustang convertible pulled up and saw him bleeding. In a smoky voice, she asked him in Spanish what happened. He answered sarcastically in English that his girlfriend had gotten mad at him for something he had said, shot him and left him for dead. The young woman returned the conversation in English, and told him she was on her way to Mazatlan to her condo for a month.

"You're going the wrong way," he remarked halfheartedly.

"No cowboy, you're going the wrong way. You might lie out here 'til the vultures get you. You want to go with me, we'll stop at the next hospital, and get you fixed up, or I leave you here and get on my merry way. What do you think?"

He liked the sound of her sultry, sexy voice. "Guess, I don't have a choice, do I?" He said with a smile, dragging himself closer to her car so he could pull himself up.

"Hold on cowboy; I'll help you," she said, stepping out of the car to reveal long tanned legs. Quickly, Max noticed that her mini skirt left little to the imagination, especially from his vantage point, and he was suddenly glad he had made the decision to go with her. As she bent over to help him, her cleavage was even more noticeable, and he thought for a minute her breasts might fall out of the tight crop top. Disappointed that they hadn't, he leaned in close to her pretending he needed her assistance and brushed against her. Obviously liking his attention, she squatted down, and brushed his hair back from his eyes. "Are you going to be okay to travel?"

"I am now," he said, unable to take his eyes off of her, as he took her hand in his and tried lifting himself up by holding onto her and the running board. Falling back, he pulled her down on top of him, and let out a yelp. "If I didn't hurt so bad, that would feel so good."

Rolling off of him onto the dusty road, she laughed. "I don't even know your name, cowboy, but I think you might be real fun when we get you all well. Now, let's try that again."

The next time, he was successful, and he eased around and opened the door to the passenger seat of the car, falling into the seat. She got in beside him, and leaned over the console and pulled his shirt up to see where the bleeding was coming from. "Oh, you've got some nasty little pieces of BBs in you, yet, we're in luck; I think you'll live. It may be a long fifteen hours for you, but I think you'll be better off waiting to see my doctor in Mazatlan. We'll stop for the night when you get tired; how does that sound? I know just the perfect little hotel with private casitas about five hours down the road. I'll be ready for a swim around dark thirty. Wish you could join me."

"Yeah, me too, My name's Maxwell," wanting to impress; "but my friends call me Max, what's yours?"

"I'm Isabella. My mother's Mexican and my father's Italian so it was a name they could easily agree on. She reached over and touched him on the leg. "Poor baby, I'll bet I have just the medicine you need." Smiling, she put on her extra large tortoise shell framed sunglasses and revved the engine. "Here we go!" The wind caught her long black hair and she looked beautiful to Max. All he could think about was she would be perfect for his convalescing. His belly didn't hurt as much as it had earlier.

⌘ ⌘ ⌘

After spending several unnecessary nights in hotels along the way, they arrived in Mazatlan where Max reported in. Fabricating most of the story, he told his father how the three thugs had taken him as far as Topolobambo, robbed him, shot him and stolen his car. He had been in the hospital ever since, but someone from a local church had heard about his situation, and the family had taken him in. It would be several weeks before he could travel, but they promised when he was able to fly they would take him to the airport in Mazatlan. Not exactly the truth, but he figured it would buy him some time with his latest toy.

He turned to put the phone on the hook, and then leaned over in the bed and began stroking Isabella's long black hair. Within minutes he was on top of her again, and for the third time in three hours he thrust himself into her waiting body. There was nothing loving, nothing caring or even remotely gentle about the way he took her, and when he was finished, he rolled over and out of bed. "I'm taking a shower, and going to the bar."

Pulling the covers on top of her, she looked up, and asked. "Will you wait until I can shower and dress?"

"You know where to find me," he said as he stepped behind the shower curtain and turned on the water.

Isabella had never had a shortage of men, and had shared her bed with many more than she could count, but never had she met anyone like Maxwell Ridgeway III. In some odd way, she was drawn to him, yet there was a small part of him that frightened her a little. Maybe it was the way he stared at her; at first she thought he was attracted to the point he couldn't keep his eyes off of her, but then it seemed he looked right through her with an almost menacing glare. And in bed he used every ounce of his brute strength to show her that he, and only he was in command.

"Oh, come back. Let's just be together a little longer. I'll rub your back and make you happy. Don't be grumpy," she teased. He pulled back the curtain and stepped out of the shower dripping water onto the floor. He had an insatiable sexual appetite, and she was tempting him beyond control. Without even reaching for the towel, he fell onto the bed and drew her near.

She looked at his strong arms and long torso. He was, indeed, a handsome man, and charismatic in a bold and strange way. She sat up and began massaging his damp back, kneading it like soft dough being readied for bread. "You have a wonderful body, but then you know that, right?" She moved her long sensual fingers down to his thigh, and reaching touched him between his legs, feeling him come to life again. "I thought I could maybe interest you again," she said, almost as a challenge. He turned, pushed her against the mattress and straddled her.

"Do you ever get enough or am I just the best you've ever had?" When she didn't answer as quickly as he thought she should, he climbed on top and began forcing his mouth hard on hers, taking her breath away for a second. "If you don't want to talk, we'll do something else," as he once again thrust himself roughly into her. She whimpered slightly, which only made him more forceful. As she whispered to him that he was hurting her, he replied that she asked for it and proceeded to pin her closer to the bed. "I'll make you wish you didn't want me so bad," he said as he dug his teeth into first one breast and then the other. Then he released her, and laughed.

"I don't understand you, Max. Why did you do that?"

"Don't call me Max. To you I am Maxwell. Only my good friends call me Max."

"That's what you said your name was, and by the way what do you think I am?"

Thinking for a minute, he smiled and said, "Guess!"

She rose to get out of the bed, and he pulled her back hard. She yelled, "What do you think you are doing? If you remember, this is my bed, and my condo. I saved your ass on a dusty dirty highway, and this is what I get. Get out!" She screamed and jerked from him as he lay on the bed naked, laughing.

"Hey, now don't get so upset. Can't you take a little teasing," he said, insincerity dripping from every word. She looked back at him and noticed he had an erection."

"What are you going to do with that now, big boy?"

Jumping up he grabbed and caught the tail of her robe. "I'll show you." He pulled her back onto the bed. As she began to fight, he slapped her, again and again.

"Don't ever touch me again! Do you hear me! Get out, and I never want to see you again!" She hurled the words across the room, just as he took hold of her hair. As she started to scream, he held her down and hit her hard in the stomach.

"Don't you talk to me like that, you fucking bitch. Nobody, talks to me like that. Do you hear me?"

Now frightened, Isabella knew she should be quiet, but this man had really made her mad. "You lousy, ungrateful bastard. Get your clothes and get out of my condo before I call the police."

With that, his anger exploded and he picked her up and slammed her against the wall. As she slid to the floor, he wasn't sure if she was dead, so he picked her up again, and twisted her neck until he heard it snap. "Why'd you make me do that?" He mumbled under his breath, returned to the shower where he turned the water to its hottest. As the water beat down on his back he felt the tension release in his body. Then he stepped out slowly with a certain degree of accomplishment, dressed, packed his suitcase and caught a taxi to the airport.

⌘　⌘　⌘

chapter twelve

Max returned to Texas at the same time a hurricane was brewing in the Gulf of Mexico, and there was relatively little difference in their bluster and urge for power. In Brownsville, people were boarding up windows and filling sand bags, when all he wanted to do was to get off the plane and find the nearest bar, which he did in a matter of minutes. Inside it was dark and dank, and filled with shrimpers who had managed to bring their boats to safe harbor before the brunt of the winds began to blow.

Max wondered if it was always so gloomy or just because the plywood covered the windows. Neon signs against the dimness gave the tiny place a gloomy feel, but he loved the Tejano music playing on the jukebox, reminding him of one of the señoritas he had met on another trip to Mexico. He couldn't remember her name, but he could remember her—tall and sleek, and full of sexual tricks.

She had gone back to the hotel with him late into the night, but when he awoke, she was gone and so was his wallet. In spite of that setback and misfortune, he considered it worth the thousand dollars she had stolen; he just wished she had hung around for a morning special. He smiled momentarily, remembering.

Suddenly, he was melancholy—maybe a woman would make him feel better—yes, a woman and a bottle of whisky. He looked around the bar, now that his eyes were accustomed to its darkness, and saw only men. The door swung open, a little Mexican man came in with rain dripping off the brim of his short brimmed hat. "It's beginning to blow hard. The man on the television says it's gonna be a CAT 3 hurricane—supposed to hit in a couple of hours. Damn! I don't know how many more of these I can take. Gimme a Tecate and lime," he demanded, as he sat down on the stool next to Max, his white shrimper boots muddy and slick with wear. "You don't look like you're from around here. Gonna ride this out?"

"Do I have a choice?"

"Doubt if you can get out if you stay much longer. Where you coming from?"

"I just flew in from Mexico. They said it was the last flight or I would be on one right now to Lubbock," he mumbled aloofly.

"Miguel, how long you staying open?" The little man asked the bartender.

"Til the electricity goes, I guess. Sure as hell won't be able to see in here. Generator rusted out so when the lights go, we go. Might finally get a night off."

"Yeah, then what you gonna do? Man says this is gonna last three days. Streets are already filling up with water. Saw a stalled out car on Boca Chica just before I came in. Heard Matamoros is already flooding. I hear we're sending police over to help. Poor folks in the low lying areas. Last hurricane, more than a hundred went missing. Found a few bodies, but not all of them," rambling he turned to Max. "Ever been in a hurricane?"

"No, and from listening to you, I don't think I want to. Where're the women around here? Wouldn't be so bad if I had a few women to keep me company when the lights go out."

"Good luck; tonight's not such a good one to be out on the prowl. Just gonna get worse before it gets better. I'll have another beer—two limes this time and a salt shaker. To hell with the blood pressure. I may blow away anyway." He and the bartender chatted about the most recent drug cartel happenings and a shoot out in a colonia in Valle Hermosa. "Guess this might slow them down for a couple of days. Heard a guy was kidnapped right by Los Tomates Bridge just yesterday."

Max's ears perked up, and for the first time since the man came in his mood turned hospitable. "Who do they think kidnapped him?"

"Obviously, one of the cartel guys. Lately, they have been kidnapping store owners and giving them a choice—your life or your business. Last guy chose the wrong one, and they hung him right in front of his family."

"What about the smugglers? What's the latest with those sons of bitches?" Max asked tauntingly.

"Same ol' shit. Those sorry bastards just keep making money at everyone else's expense."

"That so? I've heard, but never talked to anyone who really knows."

"Yep, a friend of mine told me all about the way they treat people. It's terrible. He had a cousin who came through using a coyote. They left him in load-house purgatory for ten days. All he had to eat was a pot of beans and dried out tortillas, but that even ran out after a while. Had he known he was going to be there so long he might have rationed himself. Finally, they came for them, but one of the women died in childbirth while they were there. They left the baby behind."

Just as Max started to talk, the lights flickered and the power went out. The room became still and silent as conversation came to a halt. Wind racked at the windows while Miguel began lighting candles. "Last call."

"I want to buy a bottle of VO."

"Sorry, but that's against the law," the bartender said without inflection in his voice.

"Would a hundred dollar bill make it more lawful?" Max said with a smirk, aware of the bartender's attitude toward either strangers or him personally.

"That it would. Be right back." In a minute he returned from the back with a bottle wrapped hurriedly in a brown paper sack. He took the money as discreetly as he could and slipped it into the back pocket of his Levi's. "Hey, about women, you might could find one on Fourteenth Street, although I don't know about tonight, with this weather and everything. If you do, be careful, some of them are infe…" Maxwell wasn't sure if he said infested or infected, but it didn't matter. No woman was worth a case of the claps. He had had them once, and thought he was going to die every time he peed. He remembered it felt like he was pissing razor blades.

Come to think of it, there might be one woman worth it, and he wished she was here, or better yet he wished he was there in Trinidad, lying in her bed. Her agility and feminine prowess amazed him, but it was her rich chocolate skin, her supple, yet perky breasts, polished in shimmering softness that aroused him.

She was the only woman he had ever been with who had outlasted him. After they had screwed more times than he could count, he fell asleep and when he woke up she was still on top of him, her chin propped up on her hand, smiling right straight at him. She was ready to go at it again, and he was limp as a rag. She had told him he made funny noises as he slept, and he had countered that she made them when she screwed, a fact she took as a challenge rather than a put down. Normally, Max was a bigot, but he never let that get in the way of his choice of women. He had decided in his early twenties that white women were the most inhibited anyway.

"Can you get me a cab?" He asked, wishing he had rented a car at the airport. Now it was too late, too late for much of anything on a night when the winds were blowing with gusts up to eighty-five miles an hour, with predictions that the weather was going to get much worse before it got better. At this point even if he could rent a car he doubted if the roads were open as far as Corpus Christi.

"Shit," he said loudly, waiting for the taxi driver who was either very slow or caught in the storm.

"We're closing up, man," yelled the bartender.

"Well, what the fuck am I supposed to do, wait outside in the damn hurricane?"

"Not my problem."

With that, Max sat down the bottle he had been holding and grabbed the bartender by the throat. "Don't think just because you are some cocky kid who runs this bar, you can talk to me like that. Do you understand?" When he didn't get an answer, Max tightened his grip. There was no one else in the bar, and only a few candles were still lit, but he could see the fear in the young man's eyes. Finally, loosening his hold, he said, "Now, what do you say we just sit down and wait until my driver picks me up? And while we wait, I'll have another drink."

Hastily, the man complied just as the cabby arrived. Max slammed back the drink in a single gulp and brought the glass down so hard on the bar that it shattered. Picking up his bottle he said sarcastically, "Guess you have a mess to clean up, but who cares? This piece of shit may blow away so I'd wait until tomorrow before

I went to any trouble," he snorted, laughing when he banged the door closed.

The driver explained that many of the roads were impassable. "You're in luck. I was about to quit for the night, but my mother called and wanted to stay at my house for the night. I need to pick her up. Her house tends to flood, and every since my father died, she gets really scared when there's a storm."

"What's that have to do with me?" Max asked gruffly, caring nothing about the driver's story or his mother.

"I was close by, and needed the money. I make most of my money off trips to and from the airport. Today hasn't been so good because most of the flights got cancelled."

"Take me to the Sheraton," he commanded. "And shut up. I've got a headache already from your bullshit."

At the hotel, Max poured himself a straight whisky and turned on the television, which flickered off every few minutes as the power lines swayed. He needed a shower, but since he didn't have a change of clothes, he doubted that it mattered. Instead he stripped to his underwear and propped himself up in bed. In the middle of the program, and after his third drink, the electricity went off, taking the air conditioning and lights with it.

When Max woke at ten in the morning, he was sweaty and hung over. The darkness and heat told him the electricity hadn't come back on. Dressing, he looked out the window. The wind had lessened, but the rains were torrential. He tried calling to see if any of his men were still in the area, but apparently the towers were down. He was stuck, and not in control of Mother Nature, a fact that made him so uncontrollably angry that he banged his hand on the wall until the plaster cracked.

The hotel restaurant was dim but open, yet only serving coffee with the help of a generator. Two other guests sat at a table grumbling, and Max listened as one explained to the other that the hurricane had made landfall between Brownsville and South Padre Island about two in the morning, pounding the area for more than four hours. Then after the eye went over, the winds came from the other direction, causing even more damage. Power was out all over the valley, with no predictions when it might return. The biggest concern now was flooding, which Brownsville was prone to do.

The more he listened, the madder Max got. Turning to one of the men talking, he asked why he was in town. "Checking on some work at a maquiladora—we make circuit breakers. I'm down from Kansas. We have our share of tornadoes, but I've never been caught in one of these. Can't get into Matamoros today; that's for certain. Doesn't look like anybody's going to be doing much work today except the electric company—they have their work cut out."

"I'll pay you a thousand to get me to the first airport that's flying."

Trying to hide his amazement, he answered, "That would probably be San Antonio," the man said, figuring the time and money. "You've got yourself a deal if the roads are open. We can try."

"I'll be ready in five minutes. Don't keep me waiting."

⌘ ⌘ ⌘

Chapter thirteen

When Max returned home, he was more arrogant and indestructible than ever, and not the least troubled when he learned six migrants had drowned in a lay-up near the border waiting for one of his men to pick them up after the storm. He boasted he was in a bar wasting away as those people did the same thing without so much as a drink.

As time elapsed, he grew more powerful with his dad relinquishing more and more of the daily responsibilities. When Maxwell had his first stroke, Max hired nurses to take care of him around the clock while he took off to the border on a regular basis, giving the excuse that he must check on operations. Usually, if his deputy or lieutenants needed him, they could reach him in one of the local Mexican bars or in a hotel with what he called his harem of señoritas. Even the toughest of his men were disgusted with his behavior and cocky attitude, but nowhere else, in any type of job could they make the kind of money they were making, so they gutted it in, and outwardly showed Max the upmost respect.

And as long as Maxwell was alive, they knew that daddy could reign in the wayward son if things got too out of hand, but when Maxwell suffered his second and third strokes, it was evident that Max would soon be El Patrón. When he demoted Sergio and made José his deputy, the deal was sealed, and there appeared to be no stopping him. When Sergio went to the ranch house to complain, Max warned him not to say anything to Maxwell, but the long time deputy didn't take heed. He went straight to his old boss's bedside and cried like a baby, asking Maxwell to intervene, but the elder Ridgeway was too feeble to do anything but mumble. As Sergio was leaving the house, he stepped off the porch and turned to Max. "You'll live to regret this."

"Well, you won't and he shot him straight between the eyes. He walked over and dragged the body to his pickup and lifted it into the metal tool chest. The next day he drove the truck and its contents to a far end of one pasture where the workers often burned stumps. Sliding the stiff corpse out of the chest, it hit the ground with a thud. Laughing, he lifted it into an empty fifty gallon oil barrel and stood it up, then took a chain saw and cut the body in half at the torso. This time the top half of the body made a dull sound hitting the bottom of the metal drum.

Next, he poured a full can of gasoline into the barrel, and from ten feet tossed a match. Immediately, fire spewed forth. After watching the flames for over an hour, Max went and sat in his truck, pulling out a Cuban cigar and a flask of whisky. Occasionally he gathered a few stray mesquite branches and threw them on the fire to ensure that it continued to burn; then he would return to his truck for another drink and look at pictures of naked women in his porn magazines.

When the sun began to set, he summoned his strength after a long nap in the cab of the truck and went to check on what was left in the barrel. "Damn, how long does it take to burn you up, you stupid son of a bitch? I haven't got all week."

Twenty-four hours later, he buried the ashes in a hole he had dug himself, and marveled at his ingenuity. No one ever asked about Sergio, and if his name came up in conversation, the look in Max's eyes told every man within range that it was a subject best not broached.

José stepped in as if there had been no change in his level of command, but it was obvious that he was Max's man, and that he was a loyal, humble servant. He was a small, wiry guy with thinning hair, and beady black eyes. The left eye was slightly askew, which made it difficult to always know what direction he was looking. When he was tired, it crossed more haphazardly than at other times, and Maxwell would prey upon this weakness by demanding that José look him in the eye, an almost impossible task. His English was flawless, but his Spanish was also such that he could blend in at the border with his knowledge of Tex-Mex or sharpen and smooth it out when he visited the interior of Mexico.

Maxwell thought he was the perfect man for the job, and he paid him well to be his eyes and ears. Never once in their years together had they disagreed, because José was no man's dummy. He knew just what to do to make his boss happy and what to say if he needed a boost. Right now, he needed a boost. "What's the matter, boss? You seem unhappy?" He doubted it was because Maxwell had died a few weeks before. Max didn't even have a memorial service. He just had the old man, as he still called him, cremated and dumped his ashes on the ranch on the way home. José knew that Max could be callous, but he thought this showed total disrespect to a man who had given him everything and who under his tutelage, taught him all he knew about the business.

"I'm bored, José, bored out of my fucking mind. I've been at this almost twenty years now, and it's the same old thing day after day. I'm making more money than I can count. Now that the old man has finally gone to hell and left me everything, I couldn't spend everything if I tried. I need to get away, travel, see the world and maybe find me the most beautiful, sexy woman in the world who will light up my life."

"Well, you can give me a raise, and that would help you get rid of a little of your money. My wife has been really badgering me lately for a new car. The one she has runs okay, but she's acting weird on me—wanting fancy clothes and stuff."

Surprisingly, Max looked up and said, "That's a good idea. Glad you thought of that. How's an extra five hundred a week?"

José was astonished. His boss wasn't known for his generosity. He smiled and asked, "Are you serious?"

"Yep, and take her down to the Chevrolet house, and let her pick out a car. Here, give her this hundred and tell her to buy some fancy negligee. You seem to be a little antsy these days. Maybe some dirty sex would liven you up. She's a looker. You better satisfy her or somebody else will. I wouldn't mind having a piece of her myself." He laughed loudly and slapped his leg.

José hated it when he talked that way about his wife, but it was his own fault. After all, he had brought her up. Still the thought of taking her home a new car and bringing in more money cheered him up.

"That makes up my mind. I need a woman around here. I don't like an empty bed these nights or days for that matter. And these local whores just don't do the trick." He laughed at his own use of words. "Well, they do the trick; that's about all. They just don't have their heart into it. You see, José, I need a woman who is good in bed and loves me. That's been the missing part."

José had seen his boss this way on a number of occasions, and when he did he could usually talk him through it, especially if he gave him a challenge. "Well, before you go running off to find one, we have a couple of problems. First the ranchers in Arizona are eating our lunch. They damn near killed Omar last week. They are shooting at people. I know firsthand that the people we bring in leave a lot of garbage, and the drug people are causing other issues on their land, but that ain't our problem. They are. We need more men."

"First you ask for a raise, and now you tell me you need more men!" His mood had suddenly changed, and José almost wished he hadn't brought up the subject.

"How many?"

"Maybe three or four. We need to maybe open up a couple of new routes, and bring in some guys from further down, more from El Salvador and other places so they have to pay twice."

Max smiled, "Now you are using your brain. I'll give you three, but I want a report in a month about who they are and just what difference they are making. You got that?"

"Yes, boss. But there is one more thing. There's a woman who is working against us every day. It's like it is her mission to cause us problems. She's started her own network. Her people are filling up our routes, and they are getting through without even paying the drug cartel to let them through. It's like they are in cahoots. She's got people on our side waiting, helping them. Some of them owe us money."

"If they owe us money, find her, tell her to pay up or she knows what will happen."

"But she's all the way in Puebla. My men have seen her there. That's a long way, boss."

"Hell, you brought it up. I said pay her a visit. If she is helping, she knows the consequences. Find her. I have some other business in Brownsville so I'll meet you there in my office in three days for a report. Don't keep me waiting. Understand?"

"Yes, boss."

⌘   ⌘   ⌘

Only two days later, Max had been in town an hour before José showed up looking grim, but pleased.

"We found her, boss. Actually, she was almost to Matamoros when we caught up to her. This one wasn't as easy for me. She seemed really pretty nice. She smiled at me when we talked, and she seemed to understand, but she wouldn't budge. She said she was going to continue doing what she was doing until everyone she knew who dreamed of getting across did so safely. She claimed she knew who you are and wasn't surprised when I told her what would happen if she didn't stop meddling in our business. She just kept smiling, and then I pulled the trigger. She didn't even try to stop me. She didn't even try to run."

"Good work, that's done."

"Oh, here boss, thought you might like this little souvenir. I mean it's not an ear or anything. It didn't seem right doing that to a woman so I brought you this so you would know we completed our assignment."

He tossed a shiny object to Max who leaned forward but reached out too late, causing the tiny ring to hit the floor with a hollow sound. Obviously agitated, Max started to yell, but stopped short. There was something eerily familiar about the ring. No, it couldn't be, but in all his life he had never seen another ring like this one with the Virgin Mary's image. It had belonged to his mother's mother, and she had given it to Consuela when she left Mexico the first time. It was to be a symbol to keep them safe on their journey.

His mother had explained the virgin would watch over them, and she had. They had made it safely to their destination and beyond. She told him when he was a small boy that this ring was like a good luck charm to her.

"Where is she?"

"Who?"

"The woman," Max shouted. His face was red, his eyes wide. José had seen his boss go into fits of rage on hundreds of occasions, but this time it was different. For the first time in all the years he had been his deputy, José had never seen this look in his boss's eyes. It almost looked like a hint of fear or vulnerability, if that was possible. Whatever this was, José didn't like what he saw.

"Bring her here!" his voice exploded loudly. He was standing now, towering over his subordinate, staring at the ring he still clasped in his enormous hand.

"Hell, boss, the wolves are probably eating her by now."

Max's face went pale if only for a second, but José saw it and stepped back, suddenly wishing he had not brought the ring. He wasn't sure why he had. Generally, he checked for money or a watch, anything of value and put it in his own pocket. But usually he didn't kill women, yet that is what his boss had said do, and he always obeyed orders.

"I said bring her to me. Don't you dare argue! Do you hear me?"

José stuttered, which was something he was prone to when nervous. Maxwell knew this trait well, but this time he didn't make fun of his deputy as he had so many times before. "B…B…But boss, it is at le…least twenty miles on the other side of M…M… Matamoros. I'm not even sure I can find the body. I wasn't paying all that much attention. I mean. Sh…she was just some woman who had crossed us. You know how risky it is to bring a dead body over the border! W…What if I get stopped at the bridge with a body?" He said, trying to convince himself as much as his boss that this was a bad idea.

"Life is risky! Felípe has the special vehicle. You can put her in the compartment. Call him. He can't be far away because he is bringing four migrants later today. Now, find her, bring her here or you'll be next!" He yelled and then turned away, and lowering his voice slightly said. "And it better be today. You best not get detained. I'll hunt you down, and you won't have a chance."

José knew he had never heard anything so true.

⌘   ⌘   ⌘

He looked down at the woman's face. It had been more than twenty years since he had seen her and he searched her face for familiarity; suddenly, he was taken that she looked so at peace, but his mother would be that way, he surmised. She was a simple sweet person, but damn her, she shouldn't have stepped in his way. She had no right to fight against him.

"Bring a priest. We're giving her a decent funeral and then you can take her back to Matamoros for burial."

"Why, why her? She's just an old Mexican woman. What makes her so special, so different from the rest that you have left for the vultures and buzzards?"

"Just do as I say. And hurry up." But his voice was flat; the command had lost its passion.

The deputy pressed. "Who was she, boss?'

Max hesitated and then looked at his deputy squarely. "Someone I once knew."

⌘   ⌘   ⌘

The priest came with José without asking questions, and said a blessing and a prayer. It was short, and Max looked on, showing no emotion. When the priest had finished, his facial expression was dull and as lifeless as the body he had stared at minutes ago. "Now, get her out of here. There's a little cemetery about five miles into Matamoros—right after the Colonia Ventanas, turn right. If no one's there, just find a spot. And José, find some flowers. I don't care what kind. Just put some on the grave," he said, walking out of the room.

When José went to get the car, it was no longer there. *Damn.* Felípe had picked it up already, not knowing he would need it further. When he tried calling him he got no answer, which meant he was probably on his mission to bring the men across. Now, he would have to figure out a way to disguise the body in his truck, knowing if he got stopped at the bridge the guards would more than likely check the tool chest and maybe the entire truck. The key was in getting a green light and drive right through, but he couldn't count on that. The chance of getting a guard too lazy to check was the next best scenario.

First he had to find a box, and he did at the back of a used clothing store on Elizabeth Street. Back at the office, he placed the body, which now was beginning to emit the pungent smell of death and decay, in it. Retching, he knew he had no more time to waste, as he taped the box with layers of duct tape. Lifting it into his truck, he threw in a few empty paper boxes from the office for disguise, and headed for the Gateway International Bridge. It was crowded, which made him hopeful, as he counted the cars in front of his truck that got a green light and a free pass.

When he pulled up to the electronic monitor, the light turned a sickening red, and he felt his stomach churn. He told himself he could not stutter, and paused for a minute to regain his composure before driving to the waiting guard. The stern faced Mexican official nodded and looked inside the truck as José sat silent, and then the guard moved around to the back of the truck and reached over to move a couple of the smaller boxes, before he noticed the duct tape on the large one.

In Spanish, he began quizzing José about its contents and took a knife from his belt to cut the tape. Taking a chance, José reached in his pocket and pulled out a fifty dollar bill that he carefully and discretely folded to show the amount without being obvious, as he quickly explained he was in a hurry to pick up his ailing mother. The guard looked down at the money and moving his hand toward the car door to grasp the bill, mumbled, "Pásele!"

The deputy gave an audible sigh of relief as he rolled up his window. "Holy shit. That was a close call," he muttered under his breath. He easily found the colonia and wondered where it got its name because he saw no windows, only openings where they should have been in dilapidated wooden structures and occasional cardboard houses.

When he came to the cemetery there were a number of people putting flowers on graves. He had forgotten it was Sunday, often a busy day in Mexico for family to visit loved ones' graves. Trying not to look too obvious, he found an area away from most of the visitors, off to the side of a row of unkempt graves, and taking a shovel from behind the back seat of the truck, began digging a hole in the hard, cracked ground. After almost an hour of steady digging and alternately wiping his sweaty brow, he shoveled the last heap of dirt. Standing back, he studied it for a minute before realizing in his hurry to find the cemetery he had forgotten to pick up flowers. *Damn!*

He was hot, and drained from the incident at the bridge and the digging, and just wanted to be finished. His first thoughts were to walk away, get into his truck, and drive away. *Who would ever know the difference?* But it was the last thing Max had told him to do, and he had never failed an order. Looking around, he noticed the grave-yard was eerily quiet; everyone was gone, save a mangy dog that he saw weaving his way between two tombstones before he stopped to hike his leg on the last one. José shook his head in disgust, walked over to a well-maintained grave, reached down and removed the bouquet that had been so lovingly placed less than an hour before, and tossed the mixture of flowers on the fresh grave he had covered. For a sliver of a second, he wondered what kind of person he had become.

⌘ ⌘ ⌘

About a month and a half later, Max was on the veranda at the ranch house, where he was spending a lot of time lately, still bored and out of sorts when José came by to check in. Without climbing the steps, he yelled up, "Hey boss, all is well. Just got in from El Paso. Those crossings went really smooth for some reason, although Juarez is getting meaner by the minute. Nobody from El Paso is going in unless they have to, but there are sure a number coming out. The BP is stretched pretty thin, so we should pounce on this opportunity. Hell, my men got in fifty-five yesterday and seventy-two for the two days before."

Max was adding up the money in his head. At an average of twelve hundred dollars per head, that was more than one hundred and twenty-five thousand dollars for part of the week, and that didn't include his lieutenants working along the most southern Texas border and in Arizona where he hoped they were bringing in even more than that. He had to admit, however, for the Chihua-hua region this was a very good draw. Arizona was still paying the biggest dividends, and the fee there was generally fifteen hundred per head. Overhead was relatively low although it was costing him more and more to keep good right hand men, men who know how to keep their mouths shut and their ears open. "You're making me a very rich man, Go bring the Patrón. Let's celebrate."

Dutifully, José climbed the steps and went in the upstairs bar, and brought out a fifth of Tequila and two shot glasses. "Pour me a double, José. Hey that sounds like a good country western song. Maybe I should try my luck at that next. Seems like I've got the world by the tail."

He slugged back the tequila. "Ahh, good stuff. Another one, and salt and lime. You know I don't like my tequila without those!" He said, pounding on the table. Knowing it would take a few more shots to get his boss where he was pleasant to converse with, José quickly went back into the house, cut the limes exactly like his boss preferred, grabbed a salt shaker, and took them out to the table on the long wooden upstairs wraparound porch. He poured his boss another double and himself a single. In the same fashion, Maxwell downed it. "I think I could do this all night, and I just might."

The sun was just beginning to melt into the landscape, and it looked as though it was going to be another sticky hot night. "Fuck this heat. Turn on the fans; maybe that will help. I want to sit out here and take in all that is mine." In the eight years his dad had been in a nursing home, and subsequently died, he had taken over the ranch and all the operations, causing his self-confidence and arrogance to grow to proportions unmatched by heads of state or Arabian sheiks. He now insisted that he be called Maxwell or Mr. Ridgeway. Max was only for those very close, and those folks were very few, and subject to change at any minute. Not only that, but because of his unparalleled success, he had become not only greedy, but careless, and that bothered his deputy. This was a risky business on the best day, and a slip up could not only cost a guy his life, it could compromise the entire operation. Maxwell continued to drink, and as he always did, he preceded to tell his stories, embellishing them as he went. Most of them José had heard more times than he could count.

After they had finished off the first bottle, Maxwell ordered his deputy to bring another. "And while you are in there, bring us a joint. If we're going to celebrate, we're going to do it right."

His deputy complied, and by now was beginning to get a bit tipsy himself, but it was important to endear himself to the boss, so he never turned down the opportunity, even if it meant not getting home to his wife for another day. She never knew for certain anyway where his work might take him or when it would bring him home, so another day away would not surprise her.

What he didn't know was she had long ago begun an affair with a local banker who appreciated her smooth, sleek body and uninhibited sexual drive, just not enough to leave his wife. They were rarely able to get together more than a couple of times a week, and sometimes it was for less than two hours at crazy times during the night or day, but when José was away, she took full advantage of the stolen moments at the Motel 6 on the seedy, sad side of town. The desk clerk knew them well, and always gave them a knowing look when the banker discreetly placed a ten dollar bill in his hand, winking and saying, "We're not to be disturbed." Ten dollars and their secret was safe.

Every now and then her lover's wife went to see her mother in Amarillo, giving them the whole weekend to themselves. She wondered where this quiet, almost shy man learned all his sexual techniques that kept her begging for more after an entire night of what she liked to refer to as lovemaking. He knew how to do things to a woman that José either didn't know or didn't like to do, which made it difficult when they were together to keep from sharing those with him.

She wished on these weekends that she spent with her lover that he would take her to a fancy hotel or at least out to dinner. When she pressed the issue, he complained that it would take away time they could share in bed, the obvious reason for his interest. So the pizza delivery boy knew them almost as well as the desk clerk.

Though she had always been home when her husband arrived, she wasn't sure how she had been so lucky. When he came in the door, she realized she had missed him. He always looked tired and worried, so different from the young guy she had married, and at those times she somehow wished she hadn't started the sordid affair.

But it was what she needed; besides she never turned him away when he undressed her wildly and pounced on top of her like a depraved animal. Yet always the sex was the same, quick and uneventful, and he then turned over and went to sleep. When he left her feeling that way, she almost wished he would sleep around to get some new ideas. It was during those times that she convinced herself that both men needed her and wanted her in different ways, and if she could satisfy them, there was no harm done.

⌘ ⌘ ⌘

José looked in the drawer for the joints and a box of matches, and grabbed the second bottle of Tequila—this time a tall, sleek Don Ramón, his favorite. He was a simple man, but proud to have such a lucrative, high paying job, which his wife thought involved taking cattle to market in Kansas and other states.

Because his family had been dirt poor, and most had never been out of the dusty little town in Mexico where his parents, and then he and his siblings had grown up, he saved almost every penny he earned, always fearful that somehow it might disappear. He knew his wife didn't understand, and she wanted pretty things, but he just couldn't let himself spend money frivolously. He tried to keep her on an expense account, and shamed her when she bought skirt steaks for fajitas when chicken was cheaper.

He took a long swig of the tequila, and it felt good going down. He hadn't realized he was so weary, and it was nice to relax. When he joined his boss again, they both had drunk just enough to loosen their tongues. José had watched his boss drink many times, and he knew he could hold enough liquor to fill a ten gallon hat, but he was also aware when he was vulnerable. Finally, when it seemed like the right time, he said, "You know, boss, that lady we had the burial for?"

"Yeah, what about her?"

Maybe he hadn't had enough to drink yet, José worried, but treaded forward, "Well, I was just wondering how a pretty lady like that got into this business, especially from the Mexico side. I mean nobody in their right mind does that, plus this is man's work."

Maxwell didn't say anything for several minutes, and José was nervous that he might throw him off the porch. Then, he took a long draw off the joint, and leaned back in his rocker. "Well, Joe, as he always called him when he was drinking, some folks just don't know who to screw with and who not to. With a lesser man, a lady might have won a battle, but of course not the war. However, she was dealing with Maxwell Collin Ridgeway III, and she forgot or she unfortunately didn't know how dangerous that could be. That was indeed, negligence on her part, and this is not the business to be negligent in, as you well know."

José was wishing that his boss would pay more attention to his own actions in this regard because lately he had gotten cocky and taken chances he should not have risked. "So how did you know her?"

"Did I say I did?" He took another long toke of the marijuana cigarette. "Now this is damn good weed. Of course, those boys know I'll kill 'em if they bring me some kind of cheap bullshit weed mixed with plain tobacco. Believe I'll have another. Fetch, boy," and he laughed loudly like he was especially cool at the moment, and that his employee was once again in his lowly and appropriate place. Obediently, José rose and went for the joints, this time bringing out four.

It irritated him when Maxwell talked to him in that condescending manner and he thought if he feels like shit in the morning from an over abundance of weed and alcohol, then he deserves it. He reached into the cabinet and got out the unopened bottle of Rey Sol Añejo. He knew from buying it and other bottles for Maxwell that this one cost upwards of four hundred dollars. But who was counting money at this time; this was premium stuff, and he had wanted to taste it for a long time. Hell, he figured the Sun King bottle itself, crafted with a design by some Mexican artist, was worth more than the cheap stuff he and his buddies drank.

Returning to the veranda, he put the joints on a special handmade and artfully designed pottery ashtray that Maxwell's dad had probably spent five hundred dollars on years ago. He handed him a fresh shot glass filled with the exceptional tequila and commenced to talking.

"Yeah, boss, you said you had known the lady a long time ago. I saw the look on your face when you saw the ring." He knew he was probably pushing it, but he was getting drunk and he didn't care. He took a slow taste of the Rey Sol, and savored the taste of caramel and spice. It tasted faintly like his mother's flan that he remembered as a kid. He was still waiting for a reply when Maxwell blurted out. "Okay, you want to know, then I will tell you. You stupid son of a bitch killed my mother!"

He turned pale and suddenly felt nauseous. "Why didn't you tell me?"

"It wasn't exactly going to help any. She was dead. She should have known that she wasn't dealing with her little Kiki anymore. By God, she should have known who she was dealing with; I rule the border. It was her own fault. She should have known..." His voice trailed off.

José had never heard Maxwell refer to himself as Kiki, and although he had surmised from her appearance that the woman was Mexican, he never knew Maxwell had a Mexican mother. He knew never to mention it when Maxwell was sober. No, these were words for drunken times. Nothing more would ever be spoken.

Maxwell was caught in a mood between nostalgic and hostility when he told José to bring him the bottle.

"Are you sure you should do that, boss?"

"Did I ask for your opinion? When I do, you'll know."

With that, José retrieved the bottle and took his chances with his choice.

"Glad you picked the good stuff. We deserve it, don't you think?"

Relieved and glad he didn't have to worry that Maxwell would later discover his extravagance, he let out a sigh. Of course, there was a chance he wouldn't remember, but more than likely he wouldn't mention it.

"Did I ever tell you about the woman I killed in Mazatlan?"

"No boss, I don't think you've ever mentioned her," he answered with astonishment obvious in his voice. Maxwell had told him lots of stories, but not two so incriminatory.

"It was a long time ago. She was a beauty, but damn her she wouldn't listen. She pissed me off, and I broke her neck, but before

I did for a week we had the best sex I have ever had in my life. She was a sex manic. We hardly finished until she wanted more.

"Shit. I wanted to go to the beach, and she just wanted to screw twenty-four/seven. She was remarkable at it so I can't say I minded. But hell, a guy has to come up for air every now and again. Besides there were more fish in the sea; I didn't go all the way to the Mexican Riviera to just fuck one woman. One thing's for sure, there's an old blue Mustang convertible somewhere in Mexico that witnessed some kinky stuff on a long ride down the coast. And I had a belly full of BBs in me, but that didn't slow me down. Kind of wish I hadn't done it now. Might not be such a bad deal to snuggle up to that bitch right now."

José looked at his boss. He had never known anyone so insensitive, coldhearted, and cruel. He thought about both of these women and knew that neither had deserved their fate, but he had played a role in one, and he hated himself for it. Up until then he had justified that letting people die on their own accord because they couldn't make it out of an unforgiving desert or leaving them to die in a closed truck or at a rundown safe house was somehow different from looking them in the eye and shooting them. Now, he had done both, which put him in the same disgusting category as his boss.

It was just part of his job, not something that he planned or even wanted to do, he repeated to himself. To Maxwell it was a rush, a devious, calculated act of control. There was a difference, wasn't there? His mind was playing tricks on him. Maybe it was the combination of alcohol and drugs. For a minute he felt sick, and he excused himself to throw up.

⌘   ⌘   ⌘

As expected, the conversation about Maxwell's mother was never mentioned again nor was any of the drunk talk. Within a few months, Maxwell had extended his operation to more OTMs, which meant many of the illegals now were not Mexican, but coming from Guatemala, El Salvador and even parts of South America. Occasionally, there were even some whose route had taken them through Mexico but their origins were anybody's guess.

Once, the word got out, they came from as far as Somalia. Maxwell had studied the routes well, and sent José and several lieutenants all over Mexico and the border. First they had to get them into Mexico for a fee, and then another fee was charged coming into the States. More times than not, those ended up being more than ten thousand dollars per person, and could go as high as twenty thousand.

The lieutenants were happy to be selected for these assignments because how would Maxwell know if they just forgot to turn in the money for one individual every now and then. That would mean more money than they made in months of dangerous work, but this was an even more hazardous game, because if Maxwell did find out, they would never live to spend the money. And Maxwell had his plants; no one trusted anyone else; however, they all knew his loyal deputy would never steal from the boss.

As the operation broadened, Maxwell's interest continued to wane, except for the money. He was spending more and more time flying to faraway places, enjoying luxury hotels and the women they provided. He especially liked Asia where he could find beautiful resorts, exotic women, and every sexual perversion possible, which lately he had found quite intriguing. Because of his size and money, the women saw him as fascinating and equated him to a position of the gods. This was too much for him to resist.

But on the home front, trouble was brewing, and his distractions were causing him to check in less and less, all the while mutiny was close. His men were becoming territorial, and fighting among each other, compromising operations, and getting lax in their efforts. José tried calling his boss, but Maxwell was lounging in some fancy hotel in Bangkok pretending he was emperor. Phone calls could wait.

When Maxwell did decide to answer his phone, three of his main men were in jail, and more than twenty of their underlings were under arrest. The entire organization was beginning to resemble a town after a 6.1 earthquake. A total of thirty-nine of his people had been arrested over a three day period following a series of raids involving shuttle vans and trucks. For the last ten years, this had been one of the most lucrative aspects of the organization where immigrants were provided with phony bus tickets and fake border-crossing cards to avoid raising suspicions at checkpoints throughout Texas and Arizona. Authorities estimated that in the two year period that they had been working the case, Maxwell's organization had smuggled in more than a hundred and fifty thousand people using this method alone.

Then two of the Border Patrol agents that Maxwell's syndicate had working for them were busted, within a period of a week. "El Gordo" as he was referred to was the first. The heavy set agent was actually an illegal himself. Maxwell had arranged a doctored birth certificate for him, although Harry had seemed to see the handwriting on the wall and refused to help, an action Maxwell didn't take kindly to. Within a year of the fake papers, Manny Cervantes was hired by the Border Patrol. For three hundred dollars a head he allowed enough illegals to pass through without question, making far more from this lucrative business than his salary.

It didn't take him long to convince a fellow agent to help, who he knew had, on a couple of occasions worked with women smugglers in exchange for sexual favors. He knew Buzz, his buddy, who sported a cropped haircut that had earned him the nickname, didn't really perceive this as hurting his country. Actually, in the beginning, this ex-marine and now agent supervisor saw himself as the ultimate gatekeeper when he arrived at the border, determined to make a difference in the problem of illegal immigration.

A middle-class former army brat whose dad had been a career officer had shared the same dream when serving in the military. He had joined the Marines right out of high school, earned several medals in Desert Storm, but became disillusioned afterwards and returned to use the GI bill to get a college degree in criminal justice. He even had an American flag tattooed on his forearm.

To most people, he would seem the last person to go astray, but the money Maxwell's organization offered was too much for him to turn down. So when the call came for him to drive to various points of entry to see if they were manned and then relay the information back to the smugglers, he didn't resist. Before long, he was waving carloads on as an arranged covert operation with the smugglers. It took almost two years, but informants finally brought both he and El Gordo down.

If this were not enough trouble for Maxwell, the worst was yet to come, when one of his drivers fell asleep driving through Waxahachie in route to Dallas and killed sixteen immigrants who were huddled in the back of a closed-in truck. Police suspected that many had already died from suffocation before the wreck. Those who lived began to tell horrific stories of captivity in squalid drop houses.

One described having been left there for weeks, with very little food or water, waiting for money from his uncle to pay the coyote. Another of the captured men began talking about how he had tried to get to the United States more than ten times, and had been caught and sent back each time. Each attempt brought him new information and he learned who he thought he could trust to transport him to Dallas and then on to Chicago where his nephew was living. He knew he was dealing with a criminal element, but this group had a reputation for success, even if they were sometimes cruel and deceitful. Every detail in his account and that of others further confirmed to the federal agents they had their man identified.

Over and over the captured migrants had given similar descriptions of whom they considered the main coyote. Although this had proven to be of little help to the authorities in the beginning, consistent stories along with three years of intelligence that began when federal agents infiltrated Maxwell's organization all the way into Mexico and back was pointing to one man—José Escalante who hopefully would lead them to El Patrón—Maxwell Collin Ridgeway III.

The agent Immigration and Customs Enforcement (ICE) used to infiltrate was perfect for the job. Jesús (Chuy) Guerra was born to Mexican parents with green cards, and had always been proud of being an American citizen, yet remained connected emotionally in many ways to his parents' homeland. He had won several commendations for outstanding work and his commitment to the agency.

Although he had a soft spot for poor Mexicans and their plight, he never wavered in his responsibilities and openly said there was a right way and a wrong way to gain U.S. citizenship. When the opportunity came for the assignment to try to bust the largest smuggling ring in the country, he volunteered and was quickly accepted. From Arizona he found his way to Tlacuitapa, Mexico in the central western state of Jalisco, which seemed to be a favorite holding place for those in that region to be picked up.

For two weeks he stayed in a seedy hotel and drank at cheap run-down bars to learn as much as he could about how most migrants were getting to the U.S. After listening to numerous conversations he heard stories that made him cringe and more determined than ever to find out as much as possible about El Patrón and his oper-ation. Finally, after a couple more days he made contact with a vaqueton who agreed to help him for a hundred and fifty dollar fee to get to nearby Lagos de Morenos where he could board the bus for a thirty hour ride to the Arizona border. There the lead coyote would charge another fifteen hundred dollars for the border pas-sage. By now he was anxious to leave Lagos and continue the trip and the conversations with fellow passengers.

He hadn't counted on waiting another ten days until the vaquetones had enough other people to fill a bus. Still he waited, and he listened. The stories of sex favors, deaths along the way and long stays at load-houses were not new to him, but that didn't keep him from being sickened by them. He knew he had help at the end of his journey; most of these people didn't.

The bus ride from Lagos to Agua Prieta, Sonora was excruci-atingly long with babies crying, women singing, and men snoring. Bathroom stops were infrequent, and when they came, it was at filthy roadside hovels. At the end when they reached A.P., as it was known to the locals, Chuy and most of the men bought water, diet pills to stay awake, and what few snacks they could carry. The tiny store was a hub of activity where old toothless men sat out front on wooden benches swatting flies and swapping stories, kids in diapers begged alongside their mothers and a few older children tugged on the pants of any passing visitor hoping to sell a tiny box of Chiclets.

After buying only necessities to get them through the next several days, the men stopped at Café Viva Mexico for a cold beer and waited until night fall to begin the much anticipated border crossing, and the much dreaded walk in the desert. The trip across the desert that night was not to happen. The chequadores had failed to monitor the checkpoints, and the entire group was spotted when one man stepped on a buried motion detector. They were quickly gathered up and returned by the Border Patrol agents to the south side of the border.

"Adiós, buena suerte," one agent yelled, smiling and telling the group good-bye and good luck. Chuy knew he was being sincere. The agents wished these people no harm; guarding the border was simply their job, although it was getting increasingly more challenging and dangerous on both sides. Seeing the white crosses hanging along the fence, a few marked by bright plastic flowers, sent a tingle of fear up his spine. Recently, he had also lost a colleague in Nogales to a bullet from the drug cartel. His co-worker had left behind a wife and two young children. For a moment he felt vulnerable. Undercover brought many risks, and being alone further added to the dangers.

The next day, the smugglers told the group they were taking another route; this time westward through Nogales and on to Sasabe where there was less patrol, but more treacherous terrain. Crammed in a hot open truck the group nevertheless arrived in good spirits and high hopes for safe passage to the U.S. As night fell, they huddled together. Chuy heard a few prayers as he too bowed his head for a quick blessing, which seemed appropriate in this lonely outpost, an area ruled by coyotes, drug lords and rogue Mexican militia and known as 'Drug Alley.'

Slowly and steadily, twenty men made their way "de alambre," literally through the wire into part of the Buenos Aires National

Wildlife Refuge. Trudging through the mountainous terrain and canyons, stomping the grasslands and shrubs and tromping through the few riparian corridors, the men continued for miles of desert, in four days of sweltering heat. Nineteen made it to Three Points, some forty-five miles from the border where they were picked up by their coyote and then driven to a safe house in Tucson.

Again and again, Chuy was deployed to various parts of Mexico, and each time he returned with more information as he paid his coyotes and talked with fellow migrants. On each phone card he collected from a smuggler, he wrote detailed notes and dated them. Every story revealed new information that was getting ICE closer and closer to their man.

When Maxwell returned from a month of orgies and massages, he was met at the Dallas-Ft. Worth International Airport by federal agents. José was in custody. The house of cards had crumbled, and it looked like the Ten of Swords had maybe been right on target. But it was the Joker card that was the most telling.

⌘ ⌘ ⌘

part three

chapter fourteen

José knew he had to find the best immigration lawyer or the best lawyer period in order to have any chance of not getting the death penalty. By living miserly all of his life and holding the spending reigns on his wife, he had acquired a nice savings; one he thought would serve him well in retirement. That was not going to be the case. Right now, he needed it to save his ass, and he had learned quickly that the person to do it was Faith England out of the Law Firm of Jackson, Henry, Jackson in Dallas.

Her reputation was impeccable, and winning in court was her strong suit. Though she looked too young and beautiful to him to have built such a strong résumé, he didn't question her expertise. He still found himself staring at her brilliant blue eyes, perfectly set over high cheekbones that further enhanced her extremely attractive face. Her dark, wispy, tousled black hair, with natural highlights of auburn was cut in a medium length slightly above her shoulders, and the suit she wore was tailor-made and obviously expensive.

He found quickly that convincing her to represent him was not going to be easy as she looked over his case and began their conversation.

"I take an oath to stand by my clients, but you, Mr. Escalante, are lower than dirt; I'm not sure I can look at myself in the mirror in the morning and represent you."

"Please call me José." He was putting forth his best face, but it wasn't working.

"Look, I'm not here to chat. The Feds have everything they could possibly need to throw you so deep behind bars that they will only find you with a map on the day they come to give you the lethal injection."

José grew pale. He knew that her assertion was true, but he had held out a glimmer of hope. "I was just thinking you might help. I'll do whatever it takes not to die. Anything."

"So, when did you get so queasy about the death thing? You certainly haven't been immune to killing a few folks over the years."

"I was just following orders. I didn't like doing it. It wasn't like it was anything difficult—sort of like Chalupa." his voice growing louder in frustration.

"Chulupa?"

"You know, Mexican bingo. You get a picture and you cover it. That's the way smuggling is. You see a face and in your mind you cover it. Once the game is over, you move on. Like in bingo. Sometime you win; sometime you don't."

"Well, tell that to a jury. I'm sure they will be impressed," Faith drawled sarcastically. "You say you will do anything, huh?"

"Yes, you just tell me."

"I've read everything I can so far and talked to the federal prosecutors. The stack of charges against you is so tall it would smother you if it tipped over. All the intelligence focused on you. You were the frontrunner all these years. You are a dead man walking. Your only prayer is to cop a plea and testify against Maxwell. That might get you thirty years, and you can be out when you're seventy-five. With clean living, you might live another ten years to look back and reflect on a life gone wrong. Of course, you're going to have plenty of reflection time."

José was shaking, and visibly upset. "I...I can't do that," he stammered. "He was good to me."

"Well, adios, because he certainly can't help you now. Actually, he may get far less time than you if somebody doesn't start singing." She turned to leave.

"Wait, please. I need a minute to think. What would I have to do?"

"Look, I can't promise you anything, but if you waive your rights, and agree to cooperate with full and honest disclosure about every ugly thing you know of that Maxwell Ridgeway III has ever done, and the prosecution agrees, then we can ask them for a motion to reduce your sentence. Basically, we make a deal."

"I guess I don't have much of a choice."

"I'm not telling you that you have to follow my advice. I'm just saying that your chances of coming out of this with anything but a life sentence or the death penalty are nil and next to none, from my perspective. You have to decide. I will not pressure you to cop a plea, but neither will I try to defend your innocence for the reprehensible acts you have done. Many attorneys will, and believe me there are plenty out there. So, if you want to go a different route, take it."

"But what if I tell you I'm not guilty? A man is supposed to be innocent until proven otherwise."

Faith replied glibly, "Maybe, you should be your own lawyer; you know so much about the law." She stopped and looked at him squarely. "Look, as a lawyer, I have to believe in a person's innocence and his right to a fair and just trial, but you're paying me for my counsel. Think about it, and I'll call or come by tomorrow."

"No, don't go. If you have time, I'll tell you everything I can. But I hope you have a strong stomach, because what I am going to tell you is hard to swallow and even harder to digest."

"I'm strong so give it to me."

José talked for five hours straight, stopping only long enough to drink two Cokes and go to the bathroom more times than Faith could count.

"I guess I'm a little nervous," he said, showing embarrassment when he returned again from the men's room. "What I am going to tell you next, is the worst. The guy killed his own mother!"

Trying not to act shocked, Faith put her hand over her mouth and cupped it, lost in thought. She picked her pen up again and began jotting notes. "Tell me every detail."

José began explaining how it had all transpired, and how he didn't know who the person was until Maxwell had told him that fateful night.

"Did he act upset?"

"At first, maybe a little, and then he said, if she was guilty of working against him, then she deserved it."

"Would it have mattered ahead of time, if he had known? Would he have looked the other way?" She asked, incensed by the brutality of it all.

Thinking for a minute with his head hung low, he looked up straight at Faith. "No, Max would have never cut anybody slack. He would never want anyone to think he was weak. He hated that. The man wouldn't even have white chickens on his ranch because they obviously have white feathers, and he said they symbolize cowardice. He ordered some expensive, special colored chickens for that very reason. Max was very superstitious. He believed in karma and all sorts of mystical stuff, and how symbols mean all different things. I thought it was creepy sometimes."

"So I am assuming no one really knows what happened to this woman. I mean her family. Would there be any way for them to know?"

"Not really, I mean I guess they knew she was dealing in this kind of activity so if she didn't return home, they can only surmise."

"How long ago was this? When did it happen?"

"Let me think. Probably seven months, approximately."

"You said she was buried. Did she have a marker, a tombstone? Could you find the grave?"

Trying to remember, he rubbed his head and squinted his eyes. "I think I could go to the little cemetery in Matamoros, but there was no marker. Seems like maybe I put a rock or something, but I don't remember. Why? What does that matter?"

"I'm just trying to decide how's the best way to find her name, plus I suppose I will have to track down the next of kin and see what they know. First, I'll have to do some searching in the records, which may not be easy if she wasn't documented. Did Maxwell ever say what his name was before he had it changed?"

"No, all I ever knew was Kiki, and I know he hated it. He also hated his mother's husband and his sister."

"Why, what did they ever do to deserve that?

"I don't know. He just said he did. Believe me; Maxwell didn't want to be any part Mexican. He couldn't do anything about who his mother was, but he certainly wasn't going to claim any other Mexicans, including his sister."

"So, does the step-dad or whatever he is to Maxwell still live in Texas or did he go back to Mexico when she did? And what about the sister? Do you know where they live or lived?"

"All I know is that they were at one time somewhere near Abilene, but that's all."

"I'll find out. If necessary, in the end, I'll work with Maxwell's lawyer to get a name. That's the least he can do so I can let somebody know she's never coming back. Okay, anything else you want to tell me today? I need to try to work with the federal prosecutors, but I think they will find all this information very interesting. Keep thinking. I'll return tomorrow."

He nodded, looking tired, weary from re-living what seemed now like a million years.

"And José, for what it's worth, what you did was shameful and loathsome; there is no doubt, but I don't think you started out a bad person. You have some redeeming qualities; unfortunately loyalty was one of those. Now, Maxwell Ridgeway III—that's a different story. I think he is the lowest form of animal there is on this earth."

⌘   ⌘   ⌘

Finding Enrique de la Peña was the easy part; telling him the terrible news was not. When Faith arrived at the small house that her paperwork led her to, it was drizzling a slow, lonesome, rain. She had meant to arrive earlier, but had gotten a late start because her son, Jack, had an ear infection, and she didn't want to leave him with the babysitter without his seeing the doctor first.

Faith had almost postponed the trip, but the doctor had assured her that the little fellow was on the mend, and with a couple of drops in his ear twice a day, he would be good as new. She hated leaving him, but visiting with Enrique had weighed heavy on her mind for two weeks, and she had arranged her schedule so that she could see him, and talk in person. She hoped he already knew the bad news, but doubted that he did.

She knocked lightly on the door, but no one answered. It was almost three o'clock. She returned to her car to wait, not knowing if he was even still living at this house, but it was obvious that someone did. The weather report said it had been raining for two days, making the farm roads muddy, not to mention the fields, but there was still a chance he was in the barn or somewhere else on the farm. If he didn't show soon, she would go back to town and ask questions.

While she was pulling a book from her briefcase, she heard the tires of a pickup truck slosh against the puddles in the caliche driveway, and turned to see a man of Hispanic origin, who looked to be in his early sixties, emerge from it and walk over to Faith's car. She started to get out, and he reached and pulled the door open gently. "Can I help you?" He asked looking confused as to why a young woman would be parked in front of his house. Before she could answer, he questioned her further, "Are you okay? Are you lost?"

She stood and assured him she was fine. Noticing the rain beginning to come down harder, she asked if they could go to the porch. Smiling, he signaled for her to go ahead of him, and sat the small sack of groceries he was carrying by the door.

"Enrique de la Peña?" He nodded affirmatively.

Faith extended her hand, and introduced herself as an immigration attorney from Dallas. Quickly he shook her hand and stammered, "I have my papers, Mrs. England. I can get them and show you. I've had them for years now. Mr. M. helped me before he died. He gave me two hundred acres, and I have fixed all this up. I'm legal here. Honest I am." He was talking so fast that Faith wasn't able to stop him. "Wait here; I'll get them."

Smiling faintly, she said, "I'm not here for that. I'm here about your wife."

"My wife has papers too. Mr. M helped us get everything done right. I swear, but she's not here right now. She's in Mexico taking care of her sick mother. I expect her back any day. She's been gone much too long. I miss her."

"Enrique, may I call you that? And you call me Faith, okay? He nodded again, looking more confused.

"Enrique, I have some very bad news. Your wife has been killed." She watched the color drain from his face.

"Killed, but how could that happen? Are you sure?"

"Could we go inside? Maybe you would like to sit down, and we can talk more," she offered with warm sincerity.

As soon as Faith entered the home, she noticed how the room reflected a simple, cozy taste in furnishings and a strong faith in God. A picture of Jesus and the Virgin Mary hung on one wall and three crosses on another. A worn, but clean couch sat to one side with matching rockers in front of a small rock fireplace. A tiny dining table with three chairs filled a corner of the room.

Looking around she noticed a picture of the family on the mantle, and a Bible on the table beside the rockers. She thought about the tiny ring that José had described. She took a seat while Enrique paced and then finally sat on the edge of a chair. "I need to call my daughter in Abilene. She has to come and hear this too, but first please just tell me what you know."

Faith slowly began the story that she had been told. When she had almost finished she stopped. "I know you don't think it can get any worse than it already is, but I must tell you that the person who gave the orders to kill your wife is her son."

"Kiki? After a long pause, he asked again, in dismay, his brow knitted. "Kiki had her killed?"

"Yes, I'm afraid so, but he goes by Maxwell Collin Ridgeway III now."

His face clouded over. "We heard many years ago that he had found his father and changed his name, but that was the last of the information we found out. It disturbed Connie so much when she heard anything about him, that I finally stopped asking around, and if I did hear something, I didn't tell her. She was so heartbroken about him. So, you mean, he's a smuggler?"

"Of the biggest kind. He is in charge of the largest syndicate in North America or at least he was. He's in jail now, awaiting trial. The man who I am representing made a deal with the prosecution. He's telling us everything in exchange for a lighter sentence. I personally hate plea deals, but in this case it's worth it to put Ridgeway away."

"I just can't believe this. I wish Consuela had just told me she was helping her people, but I'm sure she thought I would try to discourage her, and I would have tried. That's true. None of this really sounds like Connie except that she was such a sweet, caring person, and if she found out people were being treated harshly, she would have wanted to help."

He continued, "I know her mother was sick. She didn't lie to me about that. At first, she wrote me long letters, and then there was an earthquake in the area, and there was some damage. She went to a neighboring village that wasn't hit so hard and called me. She hitched a ride with a friend she told me, and it took all day to get there and back. That's just the way she was—didn't want to worry me. That's the only call though. She didn't like to spend the money to call. Connie was a saver. After that one call, she wrote me about the damage and told me she was helping some with the cleanup. It took a long time for that letter to arrive because service for everything in the area was bad.

"In her last letter, she said her mother's health was declining further, and she didn't feel right about leaving. It's true I haven't heard from her in quite awhile, but it doesn't feel like six or so months. I wish I had saved those sweet letters. Oh, how I wish I could just see her one last time. She was my life. I don't know how I will go on. Will you stay until my daughter comes? She might have questions I can't answer. I'll call now."

"I'll stay as long as you need me. Oh, and one thing I failed to mention. When Maxwell found out, he did get a priest and provided a burial, which is more than he has done for anyone else. She is buried in Matamoros for some reason. Who knows why? After the trial is over, we can work on getting the body moved from Mexico to here if you wish. There will be some technicalities we have to work out, but I'll help you."

"I know you didn't have to come here. You have been very kind. One more thing. I would like to be present at the trial. Would that be okay?"

"Certainly, unless you think it would be too hard on you."

"Losing Connie is the hardest thing for me. From this point on, nothing bad will ever compare."

As he dialed the number, Faith noticed his shaking hands, worn and rough by years of hard labor. Tears streaked his cheeks as he relayed the dreadful news to his only daughter and cautioned her about driving carefully in the inclement weather. "She'll be here within the hour. I feel so badly for her. Her husband is in the hill country near San Antonio. He's taken a new job as a foreman of a dude ranch. They needed a change after Trina died."

"Trina?"

"Oh, I apologize. I'm afraid I am rambling. Trina was Yoli and Cody's little girl. She was diagnosed with leukemia when she was two, and lived until she was five. They thought she would be okay, and she was for awhile. It went into remission, but when it returned it did so with vengeance. Of course, it broke all our hearts, but I think Cody took it the hardest. He came from a family of boys, and having a little girl was special for him.

"His father is a farmer and rancher, and he wanted to do the same. Since he's the youngest of six, there was just not enough land on the family farm to scratch out a living, and all the acres around here are leased out. He got a teaching certificate and taught history and coached—he loves kids. A few months ago this opportunity came up through a college buddy of his, and it is perfect for them. I know Yoli, and now she will be torn, leaving me here, so I have to be strong. They deserve a new start. Too many memories around here. Even more now."

Faith patted his hand and listened as he continued. "You should have heard her voice when I told her about her mother. Like me, she is in disbelief. I know she's been worried about Connie being gone so long, but with lines of communications down after the earthquake, and then the aftershocks, we just figured they were still having problems…She has been so anxious to tell her mother she is pregnant again…" his voice trailed off, and he went over and started a fire in the fireplace although it was only early autumn.

"The room feels cold, don't you think, not waiting for an answer. "Connie was always cold, and would have me build her a fire, especially on rainy nights." He stood looking at the flame, and for a few minutes the only sound in the room was the fire beginning to crackle. It only took a few minutes for Faith to feel more warmth pervade the small room, and she wished she had dressed in layers.

"If you don't mind me being in your kitchen, I could make you some coffee," she offered.

"Oh, forgive me. I should have done that for you. Connie would scold me if she knew." He stopped and frowned. "Do you see what I mean? She is everything to me. We've rarely been out of each other's sight except for me to go to work. I even came home for lunch every day. We were just kids when we married. Love isn't a strong enough word... I'll make us coffee."

"Not for me. I just thought it might sound good to you."

"I appreciate your wanting to help, but nothing sounds good to me. Don't think it ever will." His sentence ended as the door flew open and his daughter fell into his arms.

"Daddy, Daddy, tell me this can't be true," she wailed.

"I wish I could, Yoli, but Mrs. England here told me everything, and she'll have to repeat it for you. I'm sorry I just couldn't wait. I had to know."

Faith stood, and reached out to hug the young woman. "I'm Faith, and I am so very sorry to bring this awful news. Come sit down, and let me tell you what I know." For another hour, Faith talked and tried to answer the daughter's questions, although for many she had no answers. Except for an occasional outburst of tears, Yoli managed to sit calmly until she learned that her brother had ordered the death. She immediately jumped up and ran to put her arms around her father, her emotions unrestrained. "What did she ever do to deserve this, except love him?" She buried her head in his embrace, and cried until she was trembling.

"Unless you need me, I'll go now so you can have time together. I will be in touch with you about the trial, and other matters, but I need your telephone numbers." She smiled faintly at Enrique, and continued. "As much as I would rather talk in person than call, I'm afraid that's easier than driving back out to West Texas." He returned her smile with a wan one of his own, and wrote down the phone numbers.

Walking her out the door, he shook her hand and thanked her for what he called an errand of mercy. "You know, we might have never known if you hadn't come."

"It is the least I could do. And although I know it doesn't help your suffering, I know what it means to lose someone you love beyond reason."

For a minute there was a long pause, and she continued. "My husband, Tyler, died four years ago, and I miss him every day." Almost as a habit she twisted her wedding ring that she still wore, and then patted Enrique's shoulder. "You better get inside. The weather is really nasty now," as a sudden chill crept up her back. "You take care of Yoli. She needs you now more than ever."

Evening was falling as steady as the rain as Faith pulled out of the driveway, her mind slow dancing with memories of Tyler as she compared the way she had felt losing him with what she knew Enrique must be feeling. It was going to be a long drive home, but the twang of the country western music on the radio and the gentle swishing of the windshield wipers brought a welcome relief from the earlier events of the day.

Drumming her fingers on the steering wheel to the rhythm of a steel guitar whining through the car's speakers, she watched the dark landscape speed by, and wished more than anything that Tyler was waiting for her at home. Healing took longer than she had ever imagined and suddenly she felt an overwhelming loneliness. *Would it ever end?*

⌘ ⌘ ⌘

chapter fifteen

Faith looked up from the long narrow bench in the hallway of the federal building and courthouse where she was sitting, jotting down notes, just as a man clad in brown alligator boots, russet western slacks and a matching sport coat approached her. "Mrs. England? Hello, I apologize for intruding, but I wanted to introduce myself. I'm Clayton Derrick. My friends call me Clay." He smiled broadly, and the minute a visitor opened the door to the courthouse, the morning sun light bounced off his blondish, brown hair. He was tall, extremely tanned, rakish and rugged, in a pleasant way. Faith couldn't help but notice a piercing intensity in his deep-set hazel eyes, but when he smiled, they showed sensitivity and warmth. She wasn't sure, but she thought she saw the beginnings of a light moustache.

She stood and extended her hand, which he shook and placed his left hand over on it as to convey his warmth. "You have quite a reputation. I just wanted to meet you, and say thanks for, in an indirect way, helping put the squeeze on Maxwell. I'm here..."

Faith cut into his sentence and smiled softly. "I know why you're here. I'm so sorry about your dad. Please call me Faith."

"Yes, he was a good man, and didn't deserve to die like that. I guess we will never know if it was an accident or just cold-blooded murder. People say it makes it easier if people die doing what they love, but I'm not sure that's true. People just shouldn't get killed checking the fences on their ranch. He was completely defenseless because he was one of the few ranchers who wouldn't wear a gun. Said he didn't want to put himself in the position where he might have to use it. Maybe if he had had one on that day, it would have been different. But who knows?"

He stopped and then started talking again. "The way things are today, he might be on his way to prison for shooting someone. It's crazy; we're not only losing the battle, but also our rights, which further complicates everything. Although, I'm getting better about losing him—it's been two years now; I will never be better about the way it happened. That's the part I can't accept."

"I read about it in the papers, and then when you came into the courtroom, someone pointed you out as his son. Not that the trial can ever bring closure, but are you pleased so far?"

He smiled again. "I will be most pleased when it's over, and I can go home."

"I don't really have to be here this morning; if you can miss a little of the proceedings, why don't we go get a cup of coffee?" Faith asked.

"I'd like that."

"I know just the place right around the corner. Of course, it is always packed with attorneys so you'll have to try to ignore that. More lies told in that building than we could ever count."

She smiled and reached for her briefcase. He made a move to get it, and stopped short, reminding himself that from the stories he had read, she was a very independent, strong woman. Though she appeared in charge and was obviously intelligent, feminine and beautiful were the key words that were coming to his mind. Thinking back, resilient was another word he had heard used more than once to describe her. "You lead, I'll follow. I haven't been able to find a good cup of coffee yet. Hotel coffee has to be the worst. Those single packets in the room, terrible."

"This coffee is especially good. Heck, you think they would serve bad coffee to a bunch of lawyers? We'd sue!" They both laughed and found a table in the corner. As soon as she was seated, he said, "What would you like, and I'll get it."

"I invited you, so it's my treat."

"You can get it next time. Hurry, those folks are going to get in front of me." He smiled a boyish grin.

"I'll have coffee black with a cheese Danish."

He returned carrying a tray with two coffees and four Danish. "Hello Ma'am, I'm Clayton, and I will be your server this morning," he said laughing, as he placed the food and coffees on the table and returned the tray to the neat stack at the end of the counter.

Laughing, she asked, "Who's joining us?"

"I'm starving. I should have had breakfast at the hotel, but frankly I was a little tired of the same buffet, so this sounds good." He paused and opened a creamer for his coffee, and began to stir it slowly. "You asked me how I think the trial is going, what do you think?"

"Since he's not my client, I can comment. Thank goodness he isn't mine. I would never, never defend anyone as despicable as him. Anyway, to answer your question, I think he will get the max." She stopped and laughed. "Hadn't thought of it that way before. Maybe we should carry placards that read, 'The max for Max.' Has a nice ring to it doesn't it?"

"Indeed, it does."

"So, I know your father was a rancher, but what do you do?"

"Of course, I grew up on the ranch, and I really liked it as a young kid. More than anything, my dad wanted me to take over the operations when he retired, but he wanted me to get my education first. That was very important to him. I was torn; I mean, I loved the wide open spaces and the cattle. My dad gave me my first herd when I graduated high school. He knew I was leaving for college, and his foreman would have to take care of them, but I think it was something he hoped would bring me back. I know he realized ranching was not my passion like it was to him. He never pushed me, but the cattle herd was one of his little undercover ways of piquing my interest."

"What is your passion?"

Looking serious, he thought for a few minutes. "I guess I have two passions, and it is difficult to say which is the most significant, but I'll try. Writing is certainly one."

She broke in, surprised. "You're a writer?"

He smiled, grateful for her interest. "I try."

"Fiction or non-fiction?"

"Fiction, although after the trial, I may try writing a non-fiction about my dad and the border."

"This is exciting. Don't tell me you write those Harlequin romances," she teased.

Blushing, he answered, "I wish, but I'm afraid my life isn't exciting enough for that. I wouldn't know enough to fill a page. I write western novels. I like to think of myself as someone between Larry McMurtry and Louis L'Amour."

"I really enjoy McMurtry. Loved 'The Last Picture Show.' McMurtry was my husband's favorite author."

"I heard your husband died several years ago. I'm sorry."

"Yeah, me too. He was a great guy. I think if he hadn't been a lawyer, he would have liked to have been a rancher. Just didn't have that opportunity like you do. He loved going to his parents' farm in West Texas. We were going to retire there someday." Her voice trailed off wistfully. After a few minutes of awkward silence, she continued. "Now, my little boy Jack thinks he's a real cowboy. Can't get him out of his hat and boots."

"I was like that too when I was a kid. I shot everybody who came in the house with my little pistols. My mother wanted to shoot me."

"I want to hear more about your writing, but I'm anxious to hear about the other passion."

After taking a sip of coffee, he said, "Wine."

"Wine? Making it, drinking it, what?"

"All of the above, plus growing the grapes."

"Really? Oh my gosh, you'll have to meet my father. He is big time into wine. Has a small vineyard in Tuscany."

Clay's eyes lit up. "Are you serious? Is he Italian?"

Faith laughed, "Hardly. He's Irish, very Irish. It's a long story. I'll have to tell you that over a glass of wine. Right now I want to hear more about you and your wine."

"Well, I went to the University of California-Davis, thinking I would get a degree in English, but I knew in the back of my mind, I really wanted to study wine. I think at the time, I didn't have the heart to tell my dad, because then he would know I probably wouldn't ever come back to ranching. And it would be hard to grow good grapes in that soil, although I must admit some are doing it not far from the ranch, and there are several wineries in the area. Anyway, I changed my major after the first semester to enology and viticulture."

"After I finished my bachelor's degree, I stayed on for my masters. I'd like to go back some day and get my Ph.D., but at that time,

I needed to start making some money. So I moved to Napa, and got my first job, and as they say, the rest is history. Well, sort of. Obviously, since Dad died, I have been side tracked."

"What do you mean?"

"I felt like I should go back and run the ranch. Mom was in very poor health, so I quit my job as a wine maker, and went back to the ranch. Within eight months of Dad's murder, Mom died, literally and figuratively of a broken heart. She didn't want to live after his death, so she starved herself. I did everything I knew how, but I just wasn't him. She lost down to fifty pounds, and didn't even know me at the end. Her heart simply quit beating. I will always believe people can die from a broken heart."

"So you're there now, back in Arizona?"

"Yes, for now. My dream is to go back to the Napa or Sonoma area and buy a vineyard someday, but at the present, I'm just trying to keep the ranch going."

"So what about the novels?"

"Well, I guess the good thing about the ranch is that I have nights to write. Not much else to do there. I think that is what always bothered me thinking about living there as an adult. To me, it is a lonesome place, and especially now. As a kid, I guess I never noticed because there was so much to do. I had horses. Even did a few rodeos, and of course I was in 4-H. Sold my first project—a lamb, and I think I cried for a week."

"Rodeos? What was your sport, your event?"

He grinned. "I wouldn't call it my sport. I was a miserable failure for the most part, but as all young cowboys must, I tried bull riding. Never lasted more than two or three seconds. Broke my leg and my nose, and hung up my hat. But I had to try."

Faith laughed trying to picture him on a bull. "You've had an interesting life."

Smiling, he said. "Yes, for a thirty-four year old, I feel like an old man."

"Well, you look like a kid. I figured you were about twenty-eight. You look younger."

"Thanks, tell me that when I'm sixty."

Smiling she said, "I guess we better get back to the courthouse. I don't want you to miss any more than you already have."

"I think I have about had enough. The whole deal makes me sick. Needless to say, I don't like the way the illegals are trashing my ranch; this whole immigration issue had to be addressed, but the worst part is how some of these people are treated. Between the drug cartels and the smugglers, it's a perfect storm—one big endless mess. Neither group gives a damn about the sanctity of a human life. Along with them, the OTMs are the next biggest threat. People are dying every day, and everybody turns a blind eye."

"Let's just hope this puts an end to the largest smuggling organization in the country," Faith said.

"Yeah, but there will be others. Until we solve the problem, the Mexicans for sure will continue to come. We might have fewer other than Mexicans, but who knows. They've found an easy way to get in, and I'm not sure we can ever put our finger in the dam."

He paused, "We need strong laws, and more officers at the border. Most of all Mexico needs to figure out a way to help its own, but I don't see that happening in the near future. As long as these people can come to the U.S. and send money back, or even more so, as long as they can bring over the drugs and put cash in their pockets for the short term, the problem will still exist. But maybe, just maybe, the next smuggling leader won't be so cruel and heartless. I can honestly say I have never heard of a man as terribly vile and depraved as Maxwell Ridgeway III. He has to be the lowest form of humanity."

"I couldn't agree more. Thanks for the coffee and Danish, but most of all thanks for sharing part of your interesting life with me."

Smiling, he said, "Thanks for letting me stand on my soapbox for awhile."

"You deserve to do that, besides sometimes just talking about it helps. I know about that. Well here we are. I think I'll just go back to the office for awhile. I have to take Jack to T-ball at three-thirty, so I really need to get some work done."

"How old is your son"

"He just turned five in January so I say five going on twenty. He's quite a little man, as his dad called him. Are you going to be here tomorrow?"

"I'm going to be here until the fat lady sings. Oops, I shouldn't have said that. The Judge is a bit rotund. Sure don't want her to think I'm talking about her. Enjoyed visiting with you."

"My pleasure. See ya soon," Faith called back to him as she turned to leave.

⌘　⌘　⌘

Faith couldn't remember laughing so much in a very long time. She would have to tell Patrick that she had met a wine connoisseur.

Back at the office, she returned phone calls and read a couple of briefs before taking off at two to run errands and pick up Jack whose day care/school was not far from home. She had lived in the house Tyler had bought and refurbished before they married until the year after he died. The memories were smothering and exhaustive, and when she thought she could stand it no longer she found a newly built two-story red brick house in a gated community in the suburbs. Although it made for a longer commute, and she missed some aspects of living close in to the city, the school district was better, and she wanted Jack to have the best educational opportunities when it came time for him to start kindergarten and then first grade.

She and Mr. Jackson had agreed after Jack was born that she could pretty much call her own hours so that she had plenty of time to be mommy, but still have a lucrative practice. She tried to work at home two days of each week so she could have some time to devote to her son, and go to the office on the three days he went to a private pre-kindergarten and day care. It was a relief to her that he loved his teacher because she felt he needed the socialization of the other children his age.

Mr. Jackson and his wife had been life savers to her by pitching in to babysit or help in any way they could if she had a business commitment out of town. She tried not to infringe on their generosity too much, but on occasion, there was no other way. Patrick and Sue were helpful too, but they were out of the country more than they were in, and if she was going to be gone for more than three days, Grandma Alice came up to stay with him.

He had so many grandparents, it had to be confusing to a little boy, but he loved them all, and they spoiled him unmercifully. He had named each of them with Faith's help and they melted whenever he called their names. Patrick was Pops, Sue was SuSu, Alice was Grammy, her Ben was PapaDoc and Tyler's parents were Gramps and Nana.

He never lacked for love, but that didn't take the place of a father, and Faith worked hard to keep those memories alive. Although Jack had been born just days after his dad had died, she talked about him daily to Jack. She wanted him to know who his father was, and what a great dad he would have been.

Today was an actual game day for Jack, and Faith never missed a game. She and the other mothers laughed at the antics of their children, and shared their frustrations and obligations dealing with other parts of their lives. All but one of the other mothers were married, and most griped about their husbands, and how they wished they would help out more around the house. The other single mother, who had been divorced for a couple of years, complained relentlessly about the lateness of her child support checks. Faith had even helped her pro bono with some of her legal problems concerning their breakup and his lack of support, although domestic issues were no longer her main focus. She had learned early on in her practice, that dealing with divorce and custody issues were downers—depressingly so, and thus she had changed to immigration law, although she did still take a few regular cases here and there.

It was particularly hot, and as soon as the game was over, she encouraged Jack to go home for chicken nuggets there rather than stop at McDonald's. He agreed only because his favorite show Sponge Bob was on television at five-thirty. It was a re-run for some reason everyday at that time, but no matter how many times he might have seen a segment, he was glued to the TV.

Faith fed the Collie and the cat, changed clothes, and plopped down in her chair to watch the news as soon as Sponge Bob ended. "Time for your bath, Little Man. She had gotten in the habit now of calling him that after Tyler had referred to him as his little man. It seemed fitting to honor Tyler in that way.

"Ah, Mom, can't I play a little longer?"

"Oh, okay, but I want to watch the news. Why don't you and Judge go out back? She needs to run a little. After that we'll have supper, and then a BATH!"

"Come on Judge, hurry." The dog wagged her tail, and stretched, not exactly excited about leaving her pillow, but always happy to oblige Jack in any way she could. She stood up slowly and took off after him. Faith worried about what both of them were going to do when something happened to Judge. She was eight years old, and beginning to slow down. Faith could tell it was harder for her to get up some days, and she slept a lot more than she used to.

Faith tried not to think about it, but when she was being honest with herself she knew that Judge was getting on in age. Dusty was almost as old, but being a cat had the chance of living much longer. Besides Faith reminded the furry feline that she had a very easy life. But when Judge was gone, another piece of Tyler would be gone as well. Judge was his before she was theirs.

After the news was over, she changed the television channel to her favorite game show, and prepared herself a salad and Jack's favorite meal— nuggets, plus Mac and cheese. She knew she should make him eat less junk food and more nutritious meals, and she tried, but tonight this was easy, and she was feeling a little down. It had been five years since Tyler had died, and although she was doing much better, there were still days when it was harder. For some reason, today was one of those.

After his bath, Faith lay in bed with Jack, and read him a bedtime story, a usual activity for them. She normally read until he fell asleep although she never let him nod off until he had said his prayers. They were basically the same every night. "God bless Mommy, Judge, and Dusty. And especially Daddy. Thank you." She kissed him on the cheek, turned out the light, and went to her room to read.

⌘　⌘　⌘

The next day at court was more of the same; actually Faith thought it was downright boring and monotonous. This trial was dragging on, and there was no real reason that it should. In Faith's mind Judge Hopkins was letting it go way too long, allowing too many witnesses who reiterated the same information. Besides her client, José, had pled out, right off the bat, spilling his guts and incriminating Maxwell on hundreds of counts. The prosecution had everything they needed to convict him. He could easily get life, but she desperately wanted him to get the death penalty. Maybe the Judge did too. She couldn't quite figure it out.

Clay was sitting in his usual seat, and when he saw Faith come in, he smiled and nodded hello. For some reason he looked different today, and she realized he had gotten a haircut. She really liked it better long, but either way she thought he looked ruggedly handsome. She smiled when she saw him loosen his tie, knowing he was tiring of the proceedings also. As the lawyers droned on and on, she found her mind wandering. She really didn't even have to be here. Her work with her client had all been taken care of before the trial started. He didn't even have to testify against Maxwell, but he wanted to.

Faith thought it a waste of their time, but she knew he had a score to settle, and this was the only way he could. She and the prosecution had agreed that he could testify, if nothing else to get it off his chest. Tomorrow, if the schedule held, he would be paraded in front of Maxwell, and allowed to say a very few words. Actually it was part of the plea deal.

At first the defense had fought against it, but finally agreed her client could answer a few questions. The jury already knew the role he played and how the plea worked so no one could really see much harm. After all, he was probably going to spend the rest of his life in prison unless he lived a long time; it was the least she could do for him, except assure him he wasn't facing the death penalty.

She reminded herself often that José wasn't a saint by any stretch, but because he was loyal and Maxwell's most faithful servant, carrying out his every wish and command, he had found himself in a most tenuous predicament, facing the death penalty until Faith had agreed to represent him and in essence help the prosecution win against Maxwell. If she could be instrumental in bringing down Ridgeway, her role would be worth sitting in court when she would have rather been most anywhere else.

But that didn't keep her mind from wandering or her hands from doodling short notes to herself. In a limited way, it was sort of amusing; because this was one time she could actually sit in court and not really have to worry about listening to every word or focusing on the jury. But she did find herself spending time watching each juror, but more for the fun of it than for judicial awareness.

The jury was a hodgepodge of twelve individuals, more eclectic than Faith could remember, starting with the software engineer all the way to the stay at home dad of six, who Faith thought looked the most harried and tired every morning. She didn't know his whole story, but she sympathized with any parent who had six kids. She barely got Jack ready without succumbing to a mild breakdown some mornings.

Most of the twelve looked as disinterested as she was, but she hoped she covered her lapses better. Of course, the high school math teacher took notes every day, though nobody really knew what they contained, or at least she didn't. For all she knew, he could be writing love notes to one of his students. She hoped not or he might have his own front row seat in court some day.

The fashion designer was by far the most interesting to Faith since she sashayed in every morning in a colorfully wild outfit perhaps better served in a New York night club. She nonetheless caught everyone's eye and made a few moments more tantalizing as she swooped down into her seat, her long black hair pulled up so tightly on her head that it shone like a newly oiled engine.

Of course, anyone might have stood out sitting next to the seventy-five year old grandmother who brought her knitting the first day. Faith could never understand how she made it through security and the metal detectors, but she did, and she knitted and pearled right along, until the judge told her to put it away and not bring it back the next day. She looked downright hurt as the Dillard's sales woman sitting next to her patted her on the arm when she was admonished. Later that morning as they were taking a short recess, Faith noticed the sales clerk again consoling the older lady as they were led to their jury room.

The guy on the end of the second row of jurors Faith called "the sleeper," not because she thought he might have an unexpected opinion that would change the force of the trial, but because he slept off and on through the proceedings, his head bouncing uncontrollably until he woke himself up or the architect next to him nudged him. Twice the judge had warned him to pay attention. Later Faith found out the burly guy with tattoos blazing down his arms under the tight short sleeve t-shirt he donned so proudly was a bouncer at a local nightclub, which explained why he needed his zzz's. He also needed a dress code to Faith's way of thinking.

In contrast, the stern Mormon bishop who was the foreman appeared to hang on every word being said by the lawyers and witnesses, taking his position very seriously, never showing a hint of emotion that might give away his thoughts.

Occasionally, Faith found herself wondering what really went through each lawyer's mind during voir dire. These folks represented the community and were supposed to be the spokes that made the wheel of justice go round and round. She laughed out loud one of the first days of the trial as she was leaving to go back to the office, wondering if anyone else thought the curious twelve sitting there together brought a chuckle. The whole legal process she thought was pretty remarkable, how regular citizens who normally see things from their own perspectives and backgrounds could all come together after days of testimony and see things as they should. In spite of her intermittent amusement with their appearances or idiosyncrasies she had confidence in these folks to figure it all out.

Some of the other people in the room caught her attention as well, especially a couple of not so handsome men who always sat at the back of the courtroom. Both were Hispanic, extremely tanned and dark, and she wondered if they worked for Maxwell. She wished she could see their eyes, but both wore dark sunglasses throughout the testimony. The taller one had a mean scar from under his eye to the collar of his shirt that looked like the result of a bar fight gone really bad. The other guy, who was much smaller, hung close to his friend and appeared to be extremely uncomfortable in a legal setting. She meant to make a note to ask José if he recognized them when he was in the courtroom, but got preoccupied with the droning of the defense attorney and forgot.

She always wondered about people who hung around a courthouse, and there were always some who did. She had been at other trials where the same person came day after day, and when she inquired, the individual would shrug and say it was a hobby or something to do to pass the time. She thought that strange until at one trial she noticed an elderly woman who was neat and clean, except her clothes were the same each day. It was apparent that her hair needed some attention and the handbag she held closely to her side was old and tattered. She was the first to arrive every day, and never mingled or talked with anyone else, leading Faith to believe she didn't belong to any family represented by either side.

For several days, Faith simply smiled and nodded, busy preparing for the proceedings, until her curiosity got the best of her.

She stopped the woman early one morning as others were taking their time dragging in; weary from sitting in the same wooden benches, with looks on their faces that said they would prefer to be anywhere else in the world. She had seen these looks so many times on the faces of family members who came to support those who probably didn't deserve it, but they came out of a sense of duty, many taking time off from jobs they needed just to make ends meet.

To her surprise the lady appeared happy that someone had spoken to her and they struck up an almost friendly conversation, but the woman offered no explanation as to her presence, and Faith decided to respect her privacy. The next three days she wasn't there, and the trial ended.

Oddly, Faith couldn't get her off her mind, and mentioned it to the bailiff who shook his head and proceeded to explain. "She started coming here a couple of years ago when she moved into the shelter downtown. At one time it appears she had a nice little house in Oak Cliff where her husband owned a small body shop, not exactly a shade tree type, but not much bigger. They scraped out a living because she did alterations and took in ironing. On weekends their only son helped his dad at the shop. One Saturday night they were working late because the husband had promised to get a car back to a guy around the corner who had managed to knock the front fender off his wife's new Chevrolet Malibu.

"They had exactly a hundred and thirty-one dollars in the cash register when two thugs walked in and robbed them, and then for no reason at all shot both of them in cold blood. After that, Mrs. G. as we called her, I've actually forgotten her name, stayed at the house for a short while, but then moved into the shelter.

"They never caught the guys; only reason she even knew what they sort of looked like or how many there were was a neighbor who lived by the shop saw them running after he heard the gun-shots. So for two years she has been coming here almost every day just hoping that maybe they've been caught and their trial is up. No one ever had the heart to tell her she was wasting her time, especially here at this court, but she makes the rounds. Time's no longer on her side. She told me last week that she's been diagnosed with congestive heart failure. Sweet woman. Sad life."

Faith nodded, "We see a lot of that, don't we. But we keep coming back trying to help the ones who deserve it. Thanks for telling me."

When she returned to the office she had confided to her boss that she almost felt sorry for Maxwell's defense team. It wasn't that they were inept or ill-prepared, they were tops in their field; it was like they were coaching a team of midgets who were playing the Harlem Globetrotters. This trial was a slam dunk because the prosecutors had everything going their way.

Of course, the key was her client, and most people at the trial knew it, though she never brought the slightest attention to it. His testimony was powerful, and she had pulled it all out of him in such a way that no one but an insider would have been able to relate the gruesome details that evolved from being in the throes of Maxwell Ridgeway III.

⌘　⌘　⌘

For some bizarre reason that Faith could not comprehend, Maxwell had asked for the chance to meet her early in the pre-trial stages, and since that time had requested she visit him on more than a few occasions, although he was keenly aware she was representing his deputy. At first she refused to see him at all, emphasizing that it was a conflict of interest, and she had stressed to him and his attorney that she didn't think this was a good idea. Upon Maxwell's continual and unending insistence, his attorney threw up his arms and went to Faith. "Just talk to the bastard. Besides he doesn't listen to me. Just don't talk about the case, and it's no big deal."

"Then what is there to talk about? I'm not exactly a friend or confidant. My client has told me how he disrespects women, how they are just dirt under his fingernails. What does he want from me? I'm certainly not going to share anything about my client with him, and if he tries, I'll not go back."

"Probably just to ogle. I understand he's quite a ladies' man no matter what your client says. I think it would be good for him to be in a cell with a woman like you."

She flashed him a collegial but go to hell look. "What's that supposed to mean?"

He laughed and smiled. "For once in his life he can't have his way with a woman. You should hear how he brags about his prowess and how all the women want him. It's sickeningly funny. He is so perverse. But hell, he's my client so I'll defend him til the day is long."

"I must admit I am a little intrigued by the way his brain works or in some incidents seemingly failed to work. Listening to him would be a lesson in psychology that might help me in future cases," Faith revealed.

"Hell, I don't care, and it can't hurt. I'll draw up a statement that he can sign that it is his request so he can't come back on appeal and try to use it against us. Maybe after he gets some of his pontificating out of his system, he'll calm down and plead guilty."

"Remember we are not going to talk law. I can't believe I am agreeing to his request, and I don't exactly know why, but I'll see how it goes." she said, not sure if she wanted to give up her time to listen to a man she knew in her mind was guilty as sin though she was pledged to the concept of innocent until proven guilty, at least in public.

After two sessions, she began to think Maxwell truly believed he was going to beat this rap like he had every time before when he had been caught doing something wrong from the time he was a kid until now. She had read somewhere that the coyote, the animal, was known for its trickery, and it had even been noted that he often tricked himself. She didn't know how much of that was truth and what part was merely legend, but it was beginning to fit Maxwell, the human coyote.

He talked, or in many cases rambled on and on as long as the guards allowed, which was generally longer than it should be because Faith was a lawyer, and they liked her. He told her all about growing up and how he had come to be a smuggler, how he hated his dad, but admired his brilliance and utter disregard for failure.

"He was a very smart man, and very important one, although he could be cantankerous in his old age," he repeatedly told Faith. Sometimes she wondered if he really hated him, or just had long ago convinced himself he did. Most of all she realized from talking to him that power was an aphrodisiac to both men. And both could obviously reason themselves into believing that everything they did was right.

One aspect of his dad she knew Maxwell could absolutely not deal with was the fact that he had been told he had Alzheimer's shortly before he died. He repeated to Faith that his dad would have rather died ten thousand deaths than lose his mind. "He was a proud man, you know, and that's not how a person needs to get." Faith wondered if it were pity he was showing or fear that it might be an inherited part of his DNA, genes that he so very much wanted to run through him at one time in his life.

"Maybe it is a curse, you know for treating people the way he did," Faith finally said.

Maxwell grew red in the face, his intense eyes glaring, and he began pacing, saying the same thing over and over, "He never did anything to anyone they didn't deserve. He could be hard, but he wasn't bad."

"Sort of like you huh, Maxwell? You don't see yourself as evil either, do you?" She asked with an ephemeral, cynical smile.

"Not in the least. I'm good to my people. I pay them well. Give them time off when they need it. I'm probably too good. Sometimes they take advantage of me."

Faith laughed loudly, "Yeah, right, Maxwell. You are so sordid, you don't even know it."

He was agitated and yelled, "Get out of here if you are going to talk to me like that."

She rose to leave, "Hey, you are the one who asked for me. I'll be glad to leave. You're beginning to wear on me. I'm losing patience," she said almost casually as she walked over to the door, but before she could reach for the button to let the guards know she was ready, he jumped up. "No, please don't Faith. I didn't mean it. It's just that sometimes I get a little antsy in here. These bars are wearing on me."

"We'll, if you think they are now, wait a few years or better yet, maybe you'll be one of the lucky ones who runs out of appeals early on and gets the lethal quickly."

The guard was now standing just outside the cell. "Are you ready, Mrs. England?"

"Give us a minute," Maxwell said, gruffly, seeming to disregard what she had just said.

Faith nodded to the guard indicating she was okay. Maxwell turned to her and with a tone of disgust asked, "You really hate me, don't you? You and José really want me to die in here don't you?"

"I don't hate you Maxwell and I can't speak for my client. I hate what you've done, and who you are," she said icily.

"I've never done anything to you." He winked and gave her a reassuring, yet suggestive smile.

"You better have something in your eye right now," she said glaring at him. "No, you certainly haven't affected my life one way or another, but you have hurt countless others."

"I can explain everything," he said without one hint of remorse.

"No, Maxwell, this is one time I don't believe you can. One thing I know for sure is that you have a lot of issues or should I say hang ups."

"Yes," and then from out of nowhere he said, "And the biggest is you, Faith. I love you. I can't help it. I've never felt this way in my life, and I can't even explain it to myself, let alone anyone else. I've watched you day after day. I want to hold you in my arms just one time."

"Stop it!" She was shocked and taken back. She had never given him any reason to believe she had anything but contempt for him. "That will never happen, and if you ever say that again, I will never return. You don't know what love is! Anyone who kills his own mother is incapable of love."

"I've told you over and over I didn't know the person he was talking about was my mother."

"It doesn't matter. It's all the same. She could have been anyone's mother. That person was a human being and you snuffed out that life like it was a burning ember of a camp fire that you had no use for after it cooked your big fat steak. You did it in a blink of an eye. Just another calculated order to your man, José, who thought you ruled the world. I guess you did...the underworld. That's what you do, Maxwell, if you don't need it, you get rid of it. Just like that, no matter who you hurt."

"I would never hurt you."

"You are so right, because you'll never get the chance."

He reached over, undeterred and quickly brushed Faith's face with his hand. As hastily as he did, she pulled back.

"Don't ever do that again. Don't touch me or I will have the guard in here faster than you can imagine. As a matter of fact, I'm out of here," and she called for the guard.

Maxwell was accustomed to being the one who gave the orders, but he backed up and threw up his hands. He knew he was beaten and he hated that feeling. It had been years since he had let himself show any signs of weakness. Suddenly, he was a boy again. God, how he didn't want his brain to take him back to those days. He never wanted to be that little, that unimportant, a half Mexican, half Anglo poor kid. He had come too far. He straightened his back, turned and looked at Faith as she was leaving. For a split second, he opened his mouth to respond to her comment.

Her eyes flashed a 'don't you dare' look, and he allowed a half smirk to come to his face before he slumped down onto his chair. He knew she had gotten the last word. No woman had ever done that to him. If he ever got out of here, he would make her pay… dearly; loving her even had its limits.

⌘ ⌘ ⌘

Later that night she couldn't get the incident out of her mind. How could he say that to her, but more than that what made him even think that. She had never known anyone as narcissistic. She had read about serial killers and even done case studies on some; he had many of the same characteristics, but reading about and knowing one was totally different. She felt a chill go up her spine, and decided then and there not to return to his cell; furthermore, not to talk to him again. He unnerved her, and now she knew why.

He was like a caged animal that was used to roaming his kingdom, who not only stalked his prey; he killed and ate them or spit them out to decay in the wild. He was the most despicable human being she had ever encountered.

Faith had interviewed countless criminals, but she had never seen a look on a person's face to compare with his when he knew he had been beaten, when he knew he had been outsmarted. That is what brought the look, she decided. Maxwell thought he was so damn coyote smart, and when he realized he wasn't, his mouth sprayed venom; his eyes darted with wicked intensity. She wondered how many women had fallen prey to his smooth talk the few minutes before they ruffled him and anger spewed out of every cell in his body. More than that, she speculated about how many people he had killed or had someone else kill. One thing she knew for certain was that he had no conscience, no soul. And from what she had heard, neither had his father.

In a twist of irony, Faith's mother-in-law knew of the Ridgeway family and was familiar with many of the stories surrounding them. Before the trial started, Faith had called to tell Joy that she might be interested in following the case because it involved a well-known West Texas rancher's son. Faith was sure it would eventually be on all the West Texas news channels and she wanted her mother-in-law to know she was going to represent a guy who was testifying against him. Being from Midland and having grown up not far from Lubbock, Joy had heard stories about the older Ridgeway for years. There had been talk about his arrogance and his money for as long as she could remember. She related that many years ago there had been rumors that he had raped a woman from Raton, but nothing ever came of it.

As the trial developed, and more stories were emerging, she would call to tell Faith the latest gossip since the event had obviously become the talk of beauty parlors, as they still referred to them, and coffee shops. She told Faith that his lawyer had put him in a nursing home away from Lubbock because he knew the old man was proud, and would never want anyone to see him less than strong and vital. Then he moved him to another place because the facility there wasn't able to meet his needs, and then suddenly he died, and there was not so much as an obituary, no service— nothing. Folks claimed Maxwell III acted as if there had never been a Maxwell II. The day he died just unfolded into another, and one of the richest, and most notorious men in West Texas was gone without a place in the family plot, without a prayer muttered, without a tear shed.

Likewise, each week, Faith called to give her a report, and of course, to talk about Jack, and his latest achievements. Faith still went to see her in-laws on a regular basis, and they visited in Dallas often. She knew they still missed their son tremendously so she wanted them to spend as much time with Jack as they could. Furthermore, Jack was particularly close to his granddaddy Tom or Gramps as he generally called him. Watching them, she wondered if it was because Tom and Tyler had so many of the same characteristics and that Jack knew that in some unexplainable way.

⌘ ⌘ ⌘

chapter sixteen

Three days later the trial ended abruptly; it was almost as though everyone but Maxwell had heard enough. He had seemed to revel in the proceedings, enjoying the attention and notoriety, oblivious to the potential outcome. Faith wondered if he had convinced himself that he was invincible. He had been for a long time. Closing arguments on the prosecution's side were especially short, with the federal prosecutor summarizing the evidence and asking the jury to return a verdict of guilty. The defense took longer, enumerating all the positive attributes of his client, and stressing that he had a stellar record with no prior convictions.

Without any pomp or ceremony, the jury found Maxwell Collin Ridgeway III, guilty on more counts than anybody at the Federal Courthouse could recall, including harboring illegal aliens, conspiracy to transport undocumented immigrants, extortion, bribery, weapons trafficking, narcotics trafficking, and murder. As he was being escorted out of the room, he recognized a familiar face from long ago, and hesitated as the man stepped up in front of him. The guards quickly intervened.

"Please this will only take a minute. I just want to say hello to an old friend." As the older of the two guards pushed Maxwell to move on, he suddenly stopped and pulled back when he heard sarcasm slip into the man's voice.

"Well, Kiki, oh, excuse me, should I say Maxwell? I remember now that neither of us liked our names—thought they weren't big enough or mean enough for us. I kept mine and it's served me pretty well. How's yours working out for you?" His old friend Jan laughed.

Maxwell frowned, and finally muttered. "Why did you come?"

"Well, I thought I needed to be here—not for you, obviously. You never really needed anyone or so you acted. Hey, I really appreciated you burning down the barn. My bike was in there. Never got another."

Maxwell looked away. "You survived."

"That I did, and more. I guess we both got what we wished for—you got famous or should I say infamous, and I... well I make a little whisky from time to time."

The first smile of the day came to Maxwell's face. "Maybe after my appeal we can drink a glass or two."

"Don't think so; I'm sure I have other plans. Besides as my dad would have said, you have a long road to plow, and it isn't looking too good." He paused and looked long into Maxwell's eyes. "Well, Kiki, I never got to say good-bye the last time so guess this is my chance." He turned, reached for his wife's hand, and winked, "Adios, Amigo!"

⌘　⌘　⌘

A week later, based upon a recommendation of the jury, the judge sentenced Maxwell to death by lethal injection. As he was leaving, Enrique asked the guards if he could say a word before Maxwell was ushered out. Faith stepped up to explain his connection, and the guards nodded approval, keeping a strong hand on Maxwell's arm, although he was shackled with his hands to his back.

Enrique looked up at Maxwell to meet his eyes. "All those years I wished you were my son. Now, I am so glad you aren't, and I wish you weren't Consuela's. You are a bastard at the lowest form—a bad seed planted thoughtlessly in the most beautiful of gardens."

Enrique's deep set brown eyes began to water, and he steeled himself to continue. "Your mother did everything for you. She was never the same after you left. I watched her day after day as the sun was setting and the darkness beginning to cloud over our little borrowed house. She would sit on the bed and look out the one little window in our bedroom hoping she would see you coming down the road, wishing you would return and share just a little of the love she had for you. Every night of her life she said a prayer and lit a candle for you. And then in the morning, she would look again, but you never came."

Maxwell looked at him with pure contempt and turned to walk away. With all the strength he could summons, Enrique grabbed Maxwell's left arm, while the guard held tightly to the right, and continued, standing taller than Faith could ever remember him looking.

"You are not walking away from me this time. You are going to listen and you are going to understand. No new papers, no new name will ever make you anything but a sorry, soul-less bastard. May your sweet mother rest in peace, and may you and your so called real father burn in hell. You are worse than him, and I thought that not possible." For an instant his mind took him back to years before when he had first learned that the baby did not belong to him, but rather to the rich and mighty landowner. He remembered how helpless he had felt, how utterly useless, and how low his emotions had taken him. And then he took control of his thoughts again, remembering the good times he and Consuela had shared together and the look on her smiling, but drained face right after the midwife delivered Yoli, sweet little Yoli, who had his eyes and her mother's mouth.

He looked over at Yoli, who had grown into a beautiful, young woman, full of humility and grace. Already she had experienced the terrible loss of a daughter and the joy of a young son. Now she and Cody looked forward to another child on the way, only this one would never know his grandmother's touch or fall asleep in her lap as she read a bedtime story.

Seeing Yoli, Enrique knew that he and Consuela had done things right, in spite of being poor. If a shortage of wealth was their only failure, then so be it; they had been rich in other ways. His daughter's presence gave him the strength he needed to continue. When he had said everything that had been pent up inside of him for years, he smiled and finished with, "Now you can walk away, Mr. Big Maxwell Collin Ridgeway III," the words no longer paining him to say. "Go ahead, walk on. That's what you have always done best." With that done, Enrique lowered his head in his customary way, looking tired and older, but for the first time in a long time, content.

Faith looked first to Yolanda who was now at her father's side, looking at him proudly, and then to Enrique. "It's been a long day. I'll drive you both to the hotel."

"I'd like you to take me to the bus station. I'm ready to go home. Yoli will be driving back to San Antonio tomorrow. She's got her responsibilities there, and she's already been away too long. She'll be okay tonight without me." Yolanda looked at her father and understood. He wasn't a complicated man. She knew this had been hard for him, but he had done what he needed to do.

He had done it for her mother, and now he was ready to get back to where they had once had a life together, the only place he was comfortable. With the money and land Mr. M. had left him and what he had saved, he had added on to their modest little house and made her a garden, which he had tended to carefully and lovingly in the months she had been gone. That and the land he now farmed for himself, were calling him gently to return. His daughter knew he needed the land as much as it needed him, so she didn't try to persuade him differently.

But Faith didn't know him as well and she persisted, "But Enrique that will take all night."

"Yes, what else do I have to do? Nights are the hardest time for me. Maybe the crying babies and snoring men will put me to sleep. If you'll just let me get my bag from the hotel, I can catch the nine-forty."

Faith looked over at Yoli for support, but his daughter just smiled and nodded, indicating that her father had made up his mind, and even two women were not going to change it.

Faith acquiesced. "Well, we have time for a sandwich and cup of coffee. Will you both join me?"

Enrique smiled. "I'd like that, but let's not talk about today." And then he faltered and as if he couldn't stop himself he added, "I never want to see him again. I remember the first time I ever saw that boy. He was too pink, not dark like me and his mother, and his eyes..." His voice trailed off. "I knew immediately, but I loved him because Connie loved him. I'm positive that she loved him til her dying moment, even though she knew he was rotten to the core.

She was just that way. Now, that's the end of that. That is the end of him."

He reached down and picked up his three year old grandson, Matt. "This is the best little boy in the world," as he gently squeezed the boy's right cheek. "I'll miss you, buddy, but granddaddy will come visit soon." A smile came to the youngster's face, and he leaned his head on his grandfather's shoulder.

Faith couldn't remember ever feeling so sorry for another human being, and she had seen some sad cases, had heard some gut-wrenching, heartbreaking stories, but the look on Enrique's worn face was a story all its own.

"Tell me what it was like growing up in Mexico," she asked quickly to change the tone that had grown so incredibly sad.

"It wasn't so bad. We were poor, but so was everyone else. I had three sisters and four brothers. Seems like there was always a new baby, another mouth to feed on a very small budget. But we loved each other, and the older kids took care of the younger ones, not that there was a lot of difference in ages.

"I was the oldest so most of the responsibility fell on me to help out. Early on I worked at the El Mercado, running errands. Then after a few years of that I worked alongside my dad making and hauling concrete blocks. What I like to remember most is that we all loved music. Me and three of my brothers carved out our own guitars, and they sounded pretty good. The two oldest girls got tambourines for Christmas one year so we formed ourselves a little band, and on Saturday nights we would go to the square and perform, if you could call it that." He stopped and smiled, obviously re-living those times for a few moments.

"Some people would throw change into a sombrero my sister had placed front and center. I'll never forget, one night there was a group of teenagers from somewhere in the States doing mission work, helping build a little hospital. They were having a great time at the square, and they started putting money into the hat. I mean real money, dollar bills. My little sister dropped her tambourine and started dancing and they just kept adding money. Anyway, when the night was over, we had almost twenty-five dollars, more money than we had made all the Saturday nights together. The next day, my mother took the little ones to town and bought them shoes and candy. You should have seen their faces, all smiles, chocolate and peppermint coated."

He stopped and looked over at Yoli. "I remember you liked candy too, didn't you?"

"I still do," she said returning his smile, noticing that her son had drifted off to sleep in Enrique's arms.

As he related the story so eloquently, Faith was reminded of all he had overcome, and as always when he talked she was amazed at his English. For a person with very little if any education in Mexico, and knowing only a few words of English when he arrived, he had managed to teach himself not only the language, but much more.

"So how did you decide to leave, to come to Texas?"

"When Mama died in childbirth, Papa started drinking. Everything changed. The kids were always hungry and dirty. My aunts tried to help, but they had kids of their own. I knew I had to get some money, and there was no way there to ever get ahead. That's when I asked Consuela to marry me, and shortly afterwards we left for the border. As soon as I could I started wiring money home.

"One by one, the boys left and the girls married." His voice trailed off. "My daddy died in a brawl in a tacky little bar on the outskirts of town. He was drunk, and smarted off to some guy about his date, and the guy broke a beer bottle on the back of his neck. He bled to death, or at least that's what the cousins said."

Continuing he added, "Something bad was bound to happen, but death certainly doesn't come early just to those who do wrong. We all know that, don't we?" He looked at both women, and then turned and gently patted Yoli on her very protruding tummy. "God gives and he takes away...Now let's get those sandwiches, and don't let me miss my bus," he said. Slowly they all walked to Faith's car, with Matt still sleeping soundly, his head on his grandfather's shoulder.

⌘　⌘　⌘

chapter seventeen

The message light was blinking on the phone answering machine when Faith walked into the house, but she passed right by, instead heading straight to the sun porch where Grammy and Jack were playing. When he saw her, his whole face lighted up and a grin was quickly pasted on his mouth. "Mommy, Mommy, Guess what? Grammy took me to the movies and to get ice cream. And she bought me three toys!"

Faith looked over at Alice and smiled, not surprised at anything she did for Jack. "And what did you see?"

"*Thomas and Friends.* It was so good."

"And can you come give Mommy a kiss hello or have you used them all up on Grammy?"

He jumped up from his pile of stuffed animals, Lego's and plastic cowboys and Indians that were strewn across the floor and flew into his mother's arms.

"I missed you today," Faith said, as she nestled him against her.

"I missed you too, Mommy, but me and Grammy had fun."

"I'm glad. Are y'all hungry? I'm sorry I'm so late."

"He wasn't really hungry after popcorn and candy, and then ice cream," Alice admitted, sheepishly. "But I made him eat a half of a peanut butter and jelly sandwich just so we resembled some kind of schedule, and he wouldn't wake up hungry. I ate the other half, and drank a glass of Pinot Grigio. Isn't that classy?" She laughed. "Have you eaten?"

Faith allowed Jack to wiggle out of her arms. "Yes, let me get a glass of wine, and I'll tell you all about my day. You want a refill?"

"Sure, I thought you'd never ask. Oh, and by the way. Some guy named Clay called and left a message. I didn't answer."

"And you didn't listen either, huh?" Faith teased.

She went to the kitchen, and poured herself a glass of wine and refilled Alice's, and then pushed the button to listen to her message. *"Hello Faith, this is Clay. I looked for you after the proceedings today. Don't know how you got away so fast. One minute you were there and the next you were gone. Anyway, I just wanted to thank you for your work on the case, and the important role you played in seeing that justice prevailed. I'm flying out early in the morning for Phoenix. If you are ever out that way, I'd love to see you. Bye"*

In her haste to talk to Enrique she had forgotten to say anything to Clay before she left the courthouse, and now she felt bad. For reasons she couldn't explain, she also felt strangely let down, and didn't know why.

Looking at her watch it was almost nine o'clock and she wondered if it was too late to call him at his hotel. She decided it was since he had an early flight. Besides Alice was anxious to talk, and she had been patient all week while Faith was either gone or busy. Patience was not Alice's strong suit, but she was much better now since she had Jack to entertain. Faith handed her a glass. "I'll be right back. Just let me get into something more comfy."

⌘　⌘　⌘

When Enrique arrived in Abilene, it was close to dawn, and he rubbed his sleepy eyes as he headed for his truck that he had left at the station parking lot. The windshield was so dusty he was afraid he couldn't see, causing him to take out his handkerchief and wiped it as best he could. In some ways he dreaded going home, but in other ways the little house comforted him, even though the sound of silence reverberated off the walls. Driving the lonely highway, he saw only an occasional eighteen wheeler, going much faster than the allotted speed, and wished he was in such a hurry.

As he approached the flat dusty area filled with scrub shin oak, he saw the first pale colors of the emerging sun, and marveled how fast the shades changed into vibrant oranges and reds. Although he was always up before sunrise, he rarely gave the beauty of it much thought as he rushed to do chores and get to the fields.

Looking over at the landscape, he remembered driving through this area when Kiki was young and he had mentioned that it was known as the shinnery. Always inquisitive, the boy had asked why it was called this, and Enrique had explained that the dense scrubby oak that only grew shin-high, was like a parasite, taking over the land, and sucking what little nutrients there were from the soil, giving nothing back of any value. He couldn't help but think about the symbolism of his answer and the similarities this dusty bush had with the boy who grew up to be a smuggler.

Today the sun was different; it was hard to ignore it or the memories of years before. He was glad it was morning, and that he wouldn't have to go into a dark house. As he pulled into the driveway, he noticed in the last remaining vestiges of darkness that he had left the light in the kitchen on, and scolded himself for his carelessness. But then he saw a small figure inside the house, and all he could think of was a burglar. Normally he would have his gun; he never went anywhere without it, but he had taken it out of the truck since it was going to be parked indefinitely at the bus station. If his truck were stolen he would be upset, but losing his prized gun would have brought him much sadness, since it had been a Christmas gift from Yoli and Cody. Carefully, he got out of his truck, and as his boot hit the first step of the porch, the door swung open, and a voice cried out, "Enrique, my darling Enrique, where have you been? I've been so worried."

His heart pounded. *Was he seeing an apparition?* It couldn't be. He looked straight ahead. "Connie? Is that you?" He asked, his voice shaking and his legs almost giving way.

"Enrique, what's wrong? You look like you have just seen a ghost. You are as white as a sheet. Let me help you." She rushed out the door and down the steps.

He reached for her and drew her close, sobbing uncontrollably. He then held her at arm's length and looked at her face, and then down her whole body. She was much thinner, and her long hair was showing the first hint of graying, but she was very much alive. "Consuela, I thought you were dead."

"Dead? Why on earth would you think that? I was so worried about you. I arrived at the station two days ago and called and called. Finally, when it was getting late, I took a taxi, which cost me twenty-five dollars. I couldn't believe it. When I got home and you weren't here, I panicked because no one I asked knew where you were. I didn't even know where to start looking. I called Yoli and couldn't reach her or Cody. Are you going to just stand there looking at me or come in the house?"

"Connie, Faith told me you were dead."

"Enrique, who in the world is Faith?"

Realizing he wasn't making any sense, he hugged her again, and motioned for her to sit down. As he related the details surrounding the circumstances of what he thought had been her death, she sat looking at him with stunned emotion.

When he explained about the ring, she started weeping softly. "Oh, poor Blanca. She was so committed to helping the people of the village. She had heard so many awful stories, so many tales of heartbreak and meanness; no one could talk her out of what she called her mission. We all knew how dangerous it was for her, but she was passionate about it so when I knew there was no changing her mind, I gave her my ring with hopes it would lead her on a safe journey like it had done for me."

Enrique reached over and kissed his wife again. "I don't want you ever out of my sight. I have missed you so much, and I thought I was going to have to live the rest of my life without you. I never told Yoli, but I really didn't want to live."

"Oh, Enrique, look what would have happened if you had taken your life. Oh, we are so blessed to have each other." She reached and touched his head, running her hands through his dark hair that was now streaked with specks of gray. "When is the last time you had a haircut? And look at your mustache. I have never seen it so untrimmed."

He smiled sheepishly. "I know; I haven't really paid much attention to those things lately. I'll do better."

"I'll get the scissors for later, but first I must try calling Yoli again."

"Yes, I think she has some news for you," he said with a wink. Maybe she is still at the hotel."

"What news?"

"She'll have to tell you."

"Oh, Enrique, please, please, I can't stand anymore suspense or drama on this day."

He teased, and kissed her again, this time, a long passionate, loving kiss. "Oh Consuela, I love you so much. I missed you, and wanted so badly to hear from you."

"But I mailed you a letter each week. That is why I was so surprised when you weren't home. The last letter said when I would arrive."

"I haven't heard from you in months. Did you get my letters?"

"Yes, and I answered each of them. I don't understand, but now I know why you were so worried. Now, would you get Yoli on the phone while I start breakfast? You are hungry, right?

"Yes, for the first time in a long time."

After they had talked to Yoli and lingered over a long breakfast, Enrique told Consuela the hardest part of the story—the part that included Maxwell. It pained him to relay the details, but he knew she had to know, and the sooner the better. When he had finished, she sat stone faced, and no tears came, only a sad, and protracted frown that gave away her hurt.

"I can't cry anymore for him. I loved him since before he was born, but I truly believe I can say he has killed those feelings. I know that is terrible for a mother to say, but if I said I loved him, I would be saying in part that I condone what he did. Oh, Enrique. How can he be such a monster? Part of me lives inside him. How could this happen? Part of this is my fault."

He drew her near, and held her for a long time, rocking her gently. "You are not to blame for any of this. You were his mother, but you were also a victim. He was born not from love but from hate and wretchedness. If God has a purpose, I wish he would show us, because I have tried to figure it out, but I can find no answers."

"I can't question God, but I can honestly say, I prayed for answers long before I knew this, and lit more candles than the Pope, but all the light is gone. I'm glad I wasn't here for the trial. I don't know if I could have faced him. I wouldn't want to see any of me in him."

When she finished, she stood up and walked over to the mantle where the last photograph she had taken of him as a twelve year old sat in a small wooden frame. Studying it, she reached for it and drew it to her breast. *"I don't know you, Kiki. I guess I never did."* And then without further thought, she took the picture and dropped it aimlessly in the kitchen trash. "I'm sorry, but Kiki is already dead; Maxwell took his place, and Maxwell is not my son." Then, the tears begin to fall as the glass broke into tiny pieces.

⌘ ⌘ ⌘

chapter eighteen

Faith was totally caught off guard and astonished at the news that the call from Enrique revealed. Of course, it didn't change anything in terms of Maxwell, but it gave Enrique and Consuela back their lives together, and Yoli back her mother, and Matt, his grandmother. Finally, there was some good news to share. Although she realized Clay was probably on his flight to Phoenix, she decided to call with the news, and apologize for not saying good-bye. She was surprised when he answered.

"Hi Clay, I figured I would have to leave you a message. What time does your flight leave?"

"I postponed it a day. There are a few things I still need to do here," which wasn't exactly the truth, but he couldn't bring himself to tell her he stayed hoping to see her. "What a nice surprise to hear from you. I'm glad you called."

"Well, first, you are not going to believe this," and she continued, telling him the entire story about Consuela. "Is that not wonderful?" But before he could answer, she explained why she wasn't around to say good-bye. "I'm really sorry, Clay."

"Well then, why not make it up to me by having dinner tonight?"

She hadn't expected he was still in town, and certainly wasn't anticipating a dinner invitation. "Gosh, Clay, I don't know. I haven't been on a date in five years. I'm not sure that's such a good idea."

"Then let's not call it that. Why can't we say that two friends are going to enjoy a Texas- sized steak, and adult conversation," he said persuasively. There was a long pause on the other end, and he added. "I promise not to keep you out late if you are worried about Jack."

Softening to the proposal, Faith said, "Actually, my mom is here for a few more days. Let me check her plans. Can I call you back?"

"Sure, or what about me calling you in an hour or so?"

"That's great," she said, hanging up the phone. Her heart began to pound, and her stomach grew suddenly queasy. *What am I doing? I can't do this!* She was still in her robe, and realized Jack and Alice must be sleeping in, noticing it was after nine. What a switch that was. Alice was usually the first one up, and Jack was not far behind. Walking into the kitchen to get her first cup of coffee, she heard the television in the den, and peered around. Jack was curled in Grammy's lap, eating a pop tart and watching cartoons. Normally she would have scolded him for eating in the den, but what could she say? "Good morning, you two."

"Hi Mommy, we've been really quiet, huh?"

She looked over at Alice who beamed, knowing they were breaking house rules. "We thought we would let you sleep in. Had we known you would catch us eating on the couch, we would have brought more food with us, right Jack?" The little boy had moved to the floor and was petting Judge with one hand and eating with the other.

"You are spoiling him, and when you're out of here, I'll have to pick up the pieces."

"So?" Alice was in one of her customary, witty, bantering moods, which Faith loved. This was quintessential Alice who loved life and everything spicy and a little rebellious about it. But there was a serious side as well, and that was the other characteristic that Faith admired; together these two traits had been instrumental in developing Faith into the strong and optimistic young woman she had become. Alice was her rock, and it was very difficult to get mad at her, and impossible to stay that way.

"I've actually been on the phone. Let's go into the kitchen where we can talk without the TV blaring and little ears listening." Alice sat at the table in the bright and airy breakfast nook as Faith poured them each another cup of coffee, and grabbed two muffins from the refrigerator to heat. "Want a muffin?"

"I was thinking more of an omelet, bacon, and French toast!" Alice teased. "I ate a bagel when I made Jack's breakfast."

"You mean when you handed him the box and let him grab a pop tart." Faith laughed.

""Hey, just because you have the most magnificent kitchen in the Dallas area doesn't mean I want to use it." The kitchen was indeed exceptional with tall cherry cabinets, granite swirled in earthy tones, and stainless steel appliances. Venetian Murano glass pendant lights along with dark wood floors gave the rooms a classic tone. She was especially proud of the lights because they were a gift from her Italian friends Stefano and Carmella whom her father had met many years prior. Her second favorite feature was the wide island in the center.

"Glad I'm not supposed to go to the office today. I'm not sure I could concentrate. First, I have a story…and she began to tell about Consuela."

"That's about the most interesting, good thing I have heard about lately. I feel like I know them, him at least because of everything you have told me. I'll bet that is the best homecoming in history," Alice noted "I'll be anxious to meet her. Okay, now here is story number two, actually it's a dilemma. Remember the guy I told you about from Arizona whose dad was the rancher killed a couple of years ago? He asked me to go to dinner tonight!" She paused, waiting for a reaction.

"So, what's the dilemma? A guy asks you to dinner."

"Mom, I haven't so much as looked at a man since Tyler died. The thought of a date scares me to death. Besides I would feel incredibly guilty."

"Faith dear, first of all, he isn't asking you to sleep with him or marry him, unless there is something you aren't telling me. Second, I think it would do you good to go. I know you think you would be disloyal to Tyler by going. Hon, you are going to have to get past that. You are young and vibrant with a life ahead of you. Tyler wanted you to move forward. You know that. No one could ever have loved anyone more than you did him…and he returned that love, but we both know that with Jack that will live on, but that's all, Hon. You have to let go."

"Mom, I've been thinking lately of using some of his frozen sperm. I want another child—his child."

Alice's face didn't hide her surprise, and her frown revealed even more. "Faith, Faith, please listen. You need to think long and hard about that. That's a big step, and I'm not sure that would be the smartest thing I have seen you do."

"I know, but sometimes I get so sad, missing him, wanting more of him."

"Well, you can have children 'til the sperm run out, but that won't bring him back. Now, listen to me. Jack and I already have plans for tonight," she lied.

"Yeah, like what?"

Thinking fast, Alice explained. "We're going to play miniature golf and to eat pizza til we pop."

"And what if I wanted to go with y'all?"

"You're not invited, so unless you want to stay home alone, I'd suggest you go out with the rancher's son. Does he have a name?"

"Clay." As the word was coming out her mouth, her cell phone rang, and she looked at the caller ID. "Speak of the devil," as she answered, "Hello."

When she hung up, Alice smiled broadly. "Order the most expensive thing on the menu. If he asks you out again, then you'll know he's not a cheapskate. Let's go get manicures and pedicures, and then lunch. I'll call Sue, and run Jack by for a couple of hours."

"What about work? I really should finish some projects I brought home to work on."

"What about it? You've been working twelve hour days for weeks. You need to relax."

"You are not a good influence, you know?"

"Oh, I don't know. We've managed to do pretty well together, don't you think?"

Faith stood up and reached to hug her mom. "Magnificent. I'll watch Jack while you shower, and I'll see if we can both get in at the spa. If not, I guess we can go to the little salon at the mall."

⌘   ⌘   ⌘

Faith was uncharacteristically nervous when Clay rang the doorbell. In court battles with some of the most vicious and tough lawyers, she felt totally confident, but going out to dinner with Clay terrified her, and she couldn't understand exactly why. She was so glad that Alice and Jack had left early because she wasn't ready for Jack to see a man taking her anywhere. If she wasn't ready she could only imagine how he might feel. Perhaps, she thought that might be part of her nervousness. As she opened the front door, Clay smiled, a slight furrow in his brow, and said hello, and as if a cloud had cleared, she immediately felt at ease.

"Would you like to come in?"

"Well, if you're ready, we can go. I found a really unique little wine bar that I thought we could go by for a drink before we go to Del Frisco's. What do you think?"

"I think that's great."

"You're not going to believe this place—especially in Dallas, maybe in California or New York, but Texas. I can't believe it."

"Hey, what do you mean by that?" She looked at him quizzically.

"You'll see, and I bet you agree."

⌘   ⌘   ⌘

The wine bar was close to downtown and located in a strip shopping center between a Chinese take-out and cleaners that promised one day service. Clay joked that all that was missing was a doughnut shop since he figured both establishments were probably owned by the same family who hadn't had the chance to buy the storefront space that housed *The Wine Geek*.

When the couple walked into the bar, Faith was stunned at the eclectic décor of the first room, filled with simple stainless steel racks holding bottles and bottles of wine, opposite wooden boxes holding others. A long haired, flat-nosed black and white cat was curled inside one of the boxes. There were no tables, only a single stainless bar with more racks overhead, and three overstuffed, worn black leather chairs and several pedestal ashtrays. Faith was beginning to wonder what Clay could possibly see positive about the place until they ventured into the second room with another long bar, this one with wine menus projected onto it. She looked at him in amazement. "Is this a virtual bar or what?"

He smiled. "See, I told you. I could have guessed a lot of cities that might have one of these, but not Dallas, not yet, but I'm pleasantly surprised. What about you?"

"I can't believe this. What I really can't believe is that my dad doesn't know about it!"

He took her hand and led her to a bar height table in the corner where they sat opposite each other. "I came here the other night after I read about it in a magazine at the hotel. Watch this; you can scroll through more than a hundred selections." He touched the screen, and hit a button with the words, light and crisp. "What will it be? Red or white, Italy, France, USA—you name it!"

"Let's see. I think I'll have a Pinot Grigio from Italy." He screwed his face in a mock frown. "Italy, where is your loyalty? Just kidding. I always feel a bit guilty drinking wine from places other than California, but I must admit I like wine from all over. You want to select on your computer or you want me to choose?"

"Let me play around with it a few minutes. This is fun," as she scrolled down the menu. At this rate, it will be time to go before I pick one. Go ahead. Surprise me with something white."

He selected a dry, straight forward Pinot Grigio for her and a toasty, yet soft and creamy Chardonnay for himself.

"Does a robot bring it or do they still have servers?"

"Right now, they have servers, but the owner told me they are planning to expand with self-serve Enomatic machines placed strategically around the room so that people can stroll around and taste different wines while interacting with others."

The server placed the glasses in front of each of them, and Clay proposed a toast. "To the best and most beautiful immigration lawyer in the United States. Is that okay to say?"

Faith smiled. "I'm not complaining. I am just so happy that it turned out the way it did. How's your wine?"

Clay swirled it again and took another sip. "Just enough oak to make it interesting, shaded with a hazelnut note," he said grinning. Do I sound like a wine geek?"

"You sound like my father. Did you end up getting a California one?"

Meekly he confessed. "Yes, from the Russian River area. Just couldn't pass it up. So what do you think about this place?"

"I like it. I don't think I would like it in large doses because I favor quiet, quaint places with rich wood and soft lighting, but this is great for a change, plus it's interesting to see technology come to wine—I think, but I'm not sure."

"The owner told me there is some real resistance to it, especially by the sommeliers he knows. There is some fear they'll become obsolete, and it does seem cold and mechanical, rather than warm and romantic in some ways."

"I was a little taken back when I first came in. That first room doesn't exactly match the second."

"No, and it seems backwards. The first is now the smoking room, which makes no sense. That should either be in the back or outside, but originally it was the only room, and they have expanded. Plans are to change that room eventually. It seems to belong to Casey the cat."

"You sure learned a lot on one trip here."

"I have to admit. This is my third visit. I was so bored at the hotel, I couldn't stand it. Everyone is friendly here so I just came back the second time and now with you." He looked straight at her, and continued. "I know it was hard on you to join me, but I am really glad you did."

Faith blushed slightly. "I'm glad you stayed over another day, and this is a nice diversion for me. So what will you do when you get back to the ranch?"

"Feed horses and cattle, mend fences, bale hay, clean barns, stalls, and corrals, and maybe even write a little in between those fun activities."

Faith frowned, "Doesn't sound like much enjoyment."

"Well, at least we don't still have goats, sheep and chickens like we used to. Since dad died, I've sold all of them. Oh, Shane, my ranch hand, keeps a few chickens, but I don't have to deal with them. I've also sold a lot of the horses. Just no need for them anymore. Dad simply loved horses so he had too many."

"Good thing you aren't afraid of hard work."

"The work I don't mind. It's the isolation that drives me crazy. When I ride my horse and feel the wind against my face, there's no feeling quite like it, but after awhile, day after day, it gets lonely. So to be around people, I write. That way I can create them myself and tell them what to say," he said with a broad grin.

"Describe one of your characters so I know what to expect."

"Well, there's Jake the bounty hunter, whose best friend is his horse Choco and his only possessions besides the clothes on his back are his rifle and .44 Colt that he won in a gun fight. Of course, he has his pick of women and he drinks way too much whisky. A western novel is a little like a country western song. You have to have certain components. If you don't have a saloon, a livery stable, a jailhouse, and damsels in distress, you don't have a book," he chuckled.

"Well, I must meet Jake. Who knows when I may need to be rescued?"

"That reminds me. Tell me, what was it like talking to Maxwell in jail?"

Laughing, she thought for a minute. "I guess it is appropriate that we are in a wine bar, because I suppose one could say he is layered in complexity, flinty, and very acidic. Certainly not fruity!"

He laughed and then suddenly became more serious. "You know, I watched the guy. Actually I became fixated by him because he never showed one ounce, not even a hint of emotion throughout the trial. I mean, wouldn't you think he would frown or smile or even smirk once in awhile? I'm not sure he blinked."

"I can honestly say, I have never met or talked with anyone as complicated and convoluted, so evil and vile. Yet somehow he has convinced himself that what he has done is perfectly normal and okay," Faith said.

"The only time I saw any response at all was when some guy who was apparently his friend as a kid talked to him after the trial. I think it caught him totally off guard, and he doesn't appear to be the kind of person who takes well to the unexpected."

"No, I would love to be a fly on the wall when he sees his permanent cell at Supermax. He won't exactly be super Max anymore. It's fitting."

"I'll drink to that," he tilted his glass momentarily towards her and then emptied the last remaining drops into his mouth. "Are you hungry?"

"I'm always hungry," she said jovially.

"Good, let's go get a Texas-sized steak. It might be my last one from the Lone Star state for awhile."

His comment was unanticipated, and for a moment, she found herself thinking about how much she was enjoying his presence, how his steady hands guiding her out of the bar provided her with a sense of wellbeing. Their time at the restaurant was equally enjoyable, and when it was time to leave, Faith almost wished the night wouldn't end. When they drove up to her house, he parked and killed the engine, and hesitated before he opened the door. "Could we just talk a few minutes more?"

A long silence stretched out, and Faith finally said. "I really need to go in. My mom leaves tomorrow, and I really need to spend a little time with her. I hope you understand. I had a wonderful night."

"Yes, me too. So if I ever get back to Dallas can we do this again?"

"I'd like that." She said softly as he reached for the latch of the car door.

"Wait, I'll walk you to the door."

"Really, I'm fine."

"I know, but I insist."

⌘　⌘　⌘

chapter nineteen

Maxwell was no more prepared for prison life than he was for the verdict. Actually, he was in complete denial about it all; it could not happen to him. He was too big, too strong, and too smart. But it did happen, and reality set in as he took his first shower that lasted only minutes before shutting off, compliments of the automatic prison timer. His seven by twelve foot concrete cell and furniture made from poured concrete that included a desk, stool, and bed allowed for an eerie quiet and hollow, void feeling. Save for a four inch by four foot window designed to prevent him from knowing his specific location, there was nothing to see, and this tiny slit only allowed a miniscule view of the sky and roof.

ADX Florence, the only Supermax federal prison in the United States, is reserved for less than five hundred prisoners who are deemed the most dangerous and most in need of control. Sitting at the foothills of the Rockies, one hundred miles south of Denver, it comprises thirty-seven acres near the heart of Colorado, close to the San Isabel National Forest with snow capped mountains and spring flowers. It is a seemingly wasted space for a prison where inmates spend their time in solitary confinement for twenty three hours of the day. And in the hour allotted outside for exercise, fettered by leg braces and handcuffs; once again only concrete is visible.

This control unit maintains a multitude of cameras, motion detectors, laser beams, pressure pads, and attack dogs that guard the area between the prison walls and the razor wire. Fourteen hundred remote-controlled steel doors round out the security. Meals are hand delivered and television station choices in black and white only are remotely controlled by a special programming system.

Known as The Alcatraz of the Rockies, it has a way of killing the psyche, which is not by accident. For a man like Maxwell Collin Ridgeway III, isolation and the lack of communications with the outside world were the most difficult. The absence of human touch ran a close second. For when the door slammed shut, he was a forgotten man, with only a limited number of books to read and his twisted mind to contemplate his actions. A polished steel mirror, bolted to the wall, showed the reflection of a prior existence but very little evidence of a future, as he peered straight ahead. He had always been able to work his way out of a hole, and this would be no different he told himself. The appeal would have a positive outcome. He would be free, and when he was, he would show Faith England that she would love him, if it was the last thing he did.

⌘　⌘　⌘

Maxwell's federal criminal appellate attorney, C. Steven Morris, saw dollar signs for his time as he filed the notice of appeal, but he knew that getting a reversal down the road for murder related to the smuggling of aliens under **8.USC. 1324** was a long shot.

Less than six percent of federal cases result in reversals, and he knew quickly this one would probably fall into the losing category also. Certainly, if Maxwell had a chance, it would require Morris' best work ever and a great deal of creativity with the law. As he poured through the transcripts it was apparent to him early on that providing the court with an objective rendition of the facts of the case, followed by a persuasive argument that specific legal errors had occurred, was going to be difficult. In fact, he had never dealt with a case that appeared so flawlessly presented and technicalities so well adhered to. Since Maxwell was far from indigent, had hired the best team of lawyers money could buy, and had no recourse for racial bias, the task ahead of him was formidable not to mention dealing with Maxwell, which had already proved to be thorny.

Federal appeals are frustratingly slow, taking months or even years, a fact that Morris explained to Maxwell the first day he had met with him, but as usual, his client would hear nothing of it, showing uncontrollable bouts of rage when the process was delineated. "Get me out of here before I go crazy. I can't sleep or eat."

Morris began seeing degeneration in Maxwell within the first six months of his stay, with noticeable panic attacks and even hallucinations. His jumpsuit began to sag and his face showed signs of worry and anxiety. The more the lawyer tried to reason with him, the more unreasonable he became, until Morris quit visiting, and instead plodded forward with research and writing.

He had practiced criminal appellate law for almost thirty years, but in all that time, he had never met a person so totally self-absorbed, but even love for one's self can only take a man so far, and eventually the mind follows the body into decline. Morris wondered if his client was losing it completely. He was beginning to think Maxwell Ridgeway III had already gone to hell, and from talking to those affiliated with his trial and his life, the consensus was they hoped this was the case. Only time would tell, and best he could determine that was all either of them had in this process— months and months of waiting.

⌘ ⌘ ⌘

In the beginning José didn't fare much better than Maxwell except that he wasn't in a maximum security complex. Although his crimes were heinous and he was serving a thirty year sentence for murder related to smuggling, the judge determined from countless mental examinations and discussions with Faith, his attorney, that he wasn't a severe threat to himself or others so he was placed in a federal correctional complex that allowed for more privileges than might have been earlier expected. Once he was no longer under the influence of Maxwell, he had actually reverted back to his passive, almost shy self, and had cooperated completely with everything the court asked.

But that didn't mean he had adapted to prison or fully accepted his plight for the next very long phase of his life. Within the first three months, his wife had filed for divorce and managed to take most of what was left of their savings, and a fellow inmate had attacked him, claiming José was trying to horn in on his relationship with a cellmate because he kept looking at him suggestively.

Stuttering, he tried to explain that he was not looking at the other guy at all, which was easy to understand since it was extremely difficult to tell what direction he was looking. Unfortunately, that didn't stop the fellow prisoner from beating the crap out of him.

After a brief stay in the medical facility, he was moved to another area of the prison, but he was marked by the homosexuals as an interested party, an unfortunate mistake that would cause problems for him off and on. "So much for trying to fly under the radar," he had told Faith on one of her infrequent visits. Although Faith didn't condone any of his prior actions, she had tried to muster some empathy for her client, but simply couldn't get past the horrific things he had done to his own people—people just like him who had dreams for a better life. As Alice would also remind her, he had made his bed, and now he must lie in it. Nonetheless, as his lawyer, she tried to visit him on occasion, and noticed that after awhile, his luck began to change, and he started to make the best of his situation.

As she listened to him she found his stories almost humorous in a warped sort of way, and generally laughed to herself as she drove the long drive home. His latest adventure, if it could be described that way, involved a woman whom he had been corresponding with through letters for two months. She had proposed to him, and he was considering marriage. Faith had known of this happening on several occasions, and could never quite understand the purpose or what could possibly run through a woman's mind that would remotely encourage this option. But it certainly appeared from the letters he shared with Faith that Tami, as José referred to her, was interested in making a commitment to a man who would be penniless, in his mid-seventies, if he lived that long, before he was free to consummate whatever this feeling might be.

Times like this made her wish she could talk to Tyler. He would understand these crazy stories that they never told students about in law school.

⌘   ⌘   ⌘

chapter twenty

On the long drive from the airport to the ranch, Clay thought of little else but Faith, although he felt it was a waste of emotions. But try as he may, he couldn't get her off his mind. When he arrived at the ranch, he felt incredibly lonely as he walked, looking around the grounds. Although his foreman, Shane, did a good job of keeping the place in good condition, it lacked the touch of those who truly loved it, and that showed in both the land and the house. Since his parents' deaths, he had done very little except return.

His heart simply wasn't in it. He realized the ranch needed more than paint and other refurbishing, it needed someone to nurture it, find the beauty in the crumbling cliffs of red and yellow earth that gave way to the rugged mountains. It needed to belong to someone and that person to belong to it, like it had to those before him. That was never going to happen with him for he longed to be anywhere else.

There were things about the west and the ranch that he liked, but he preferred writing about it rather than living it. In his novels he could make the mountains as high and rugged as he wanted, the streams as crystal clear as bottled water, and the sunrises and sunsets always perfect. The cowboys he depicted were rugged heroes and hardworking giants who slept next to crackling campfires on long trail drives through rolling hills and sweet sagebrush. They sat tall in the saddle and though quick to fight, always came out the winner. Having lived on a working ranch, he knew it wasn't so dramatic or romantic. To him, it was more work than pleasure, more headache and sore muscles than glamour.

As he opened the door, the room was well lit, and the blades of the old ceiling fans swirled in rhythm with the music on the radio. Shane had tried to set a positive scene, and Clay made a mental note to thank him, but it still wasn't enough.

He flipped on the television to a local channel, and almost immediately saw a story about his neighbor's watchdog being poisoned and his water tanks drained. Film footage showed food wrappers, dirty diapers, water bottles and toilet paper scattered over the ditches and culverts. Plastic bags clung to the purple-hinged prickly pear that his mother had loved. Nothing had changed while he was in Dallas at the trial, except his heart.

Frustrated, he clicked the TV off, and the computer on, and typed in the email address Faith had given him the night before. *Hi, just wanted you to know I made the trip safely. Doesn't look as though I have missed much here. Had a great time last night. Hope we can do it again. Regards, Clay.*

As he pushed the send button, he wondered if it had been the right thing to do. Sending a message to a woman who was still in love with her husband who had been dead more than five years was crazy. She had never given him any reason to think that she wouldn't still feel that way twenty years from now. But it was only an email, what could possibly be wrong with that?

Within minutes he heard a ding, and looked at the screen. *Hi yourself! Good to hear you are safe. Hope you found everything okay on the ranch. I had a wonderful time last night, and I think you know that wasn't my original intent, if I am going to be completely honest. Perhaps, I need to embrace the dating situation—just not sure. When is your next trip? I know you are too restless to stay put on the ranch. Later, Faith.*

Clay was filled with exhilaration, but quickly reminded himself not to get carried away by one brief email. He reread the email and decided that maybe, just maybe there was a slight crack in the armor. Suddenly, without further cautiousness, he found himself trying to figure out a way to see her again. He had not even unpacked, and already he was planning, trying to devise a meeting place.

The next morning as he rode his black stallion along the narrow path that bordered a long fence, separating his ranch from the neighboring one, he continued to think about Faith and miss her. He also missed the California wine country, when suddenly it made sense that the two went together. Maybe she would meet him for a long weekend in Napa Valley.

He knew he was probably pushing his luck, but he would make it easy and comfortable for her by getting two rooms at his favorite little bed and breakfast in Calistoga and then having dinner at the French Laundry in Yountville. His mind was racing with all the things he could show her and places they could see. If only she would agree. The day, although extremely busy, crawled as he weighed the possibilities and mustered his courage to call.

After Shane and a couple of the extra workers did their usual morning feedings of the cattle and horses, Clay helped Shane medicate several of the horses. The vet lived twenty miles away, and as a teenager his dad had taught him how to give intra-muscle injections and other routine medications that might be necessary. That was back when there were more than a hundred horses on the ranch and they bred Appaloosas and Arabians. He could remember getting up at five in the morning, helping his dad feed before school. He liked reining and cutting and joined the rodeo club in junior high. Even the smell of fresh mown hay in the morning didn't bother him then, but in high school he had grown restless on the ranch, knowing there was more to him than a solitary life in southern Arizona.

He was a dichotomy in many ways—captain of the football team, yet editor of the literary magazine. Though tough as nails building fences, he was brought to tears watching his first horse put down. His interests were far broader than any of the other kids at school, and it didn't go unnoticed by his teachers or peers. Voted **Most Likely to Succeed** by his friends, they were in awe of his creativity, lofty goals and dreams of seeing places they only knew on a map. Many, who had no plans of ever moving more than fifty miles away from where they were born or doing anything else but ranch, had written in his yearbook that his success was inevitable. Several added a big question mark as to where his dreams might take him, but they knew it would be somewhere besides the dusty fields of southern Arizona. To those who knew him well, his future looked bright because he shone his light in a wide circle, and it was obvious that Clay Derrick didn't fit into their same mold.

As he and Shane rode, the foreman brought him up-to-date on everything that had happened while he was away at the trial, although the two had stayed in communications almost daily.

"What's next, boss? Are you staying for awhile?" Shane asked, glad that Clay was back. He had missed him, and looked up to him like he was a big brother. Clay liked him as well, and appreciated his work ethic and willingness to accept most of the responsibilities of the ranch. He knew that Shane loved the outdoors and would never be content working inside, although he too in recent months had become disillusioned with the way the illegals were trashing the land.

"I don't really know Shane. I did a stupid thing in Dallas."

Looking stunned, Shane asked, "You? What?" Knowing his boss was steady and solid; he couldn't imagine him doing anything stupid.

Clay laughed, "It's not what you might think. I let myself fall for a lady, and I really don't think she feels the same about me or ever will."

"And who is this lady?"

"A lawyer."

"Oh, boss, that's the worst kind. Independent, smart, strong-willed. How'd you let that happen? You know there are hundreds of women around here who would line up to have a relationship with you. And they would be downright submissive."

Grinning, Clay looked at his youthful ranch foreman. "Sometimes things just happen, and a man has to take what comes his way. Be careful, Shane. Shit happens and so does love; sometimes you even step right into both. Boots don't even help with the latter."

Finally, after he and Shane finished a five hour struggle to round up stray cattle that had wandered away after a fence was cut, he showered and dressed in old jeans and a faded orange T-shirt, poured himself a glass of Pinot Noir, and sat down on the front porch with his cell phone. As he practiced what he would say, he laughed out loud at his nervousness.

Dialing her number and feeling the sweat on his palm reminded him of how he felt as a teenage boy asking a girl to the prom. Thinking back, he remembered the first girl had turned him down, claiming she already had a date, but later he found out she was waiting for his best friend to call. The second call was more successful, and the night turned out to be okay until he fell off a step leaving the ballroom. Clinging to his hand, his date landed next to him, crushing her corsage into a hundred petals. The reminiscing or the wine eased his tension, and by the time he heard Faith's voice, he was prepared. "Am I calling at a bad time?"

"Hi Clay. No, I just finished making Jack a sandwich, and decided I'm not ready for dinner. He's sitting in front of the television chomping down on his favorite—ham and cheese with a side of Mac and cheese. I'm telling you that kid is going to turn into a cheese stick. I promised myself when he was old enough to walk that I wouldn't let him eat in front of the TV, but that's easier said than done. Besides, we have our sweet moments together at bed time. Gosh, that was a long explanation, wasn't it?" She said, laughing.

He laughed too, but quickly said. "It's good to hear you sound so upbeat. But come to think of it, I don't think I've ever heard you otherwise."

"Oh, I have my moments, but it's not my nature to be down. Can't do a darn thing about it. So how was your day?"

Clay explained about the cattle and the frustration with the way the ranches were being trampled and overrun by drug runners and illegals. "They cut the fence to make access easier, and then cattle get out. You know they're not the smartest animals in the world, so they sometimes try to eat the trash, and get sick or die. I'm talking about the cows, not the people." He chuckled again.

"The people are obviously smarter, but that's not why I called. Please listen before you say no, okay?"

"Gosh, you have my curiosity piqued."

"I was thinking maybe you could meet me in San Francisco some weekend soon and then drive to Napa for two or three nights." He paused, but when she didn't reply he continued. "I know a lot of folks in the area, and could get us a couple of rooms at a nice

B&B, and maybe even get a reservation at the French Laundry. Is there any chance you would join me."

"This is a surprise Clay. I don't know. Maybe I shouldn't. I mean..."

"Faith, I'm not asking you to rush into anything. I know this isn't easy, but I know we could have fun. I don't expect anything more."

After a lengthy, drawn out awkward pause, she said, "Would you let me think about it overnight?"

"Certainly. I can call you about this same time tomorrow night if that's okay?"

"Sure, but wait Clay, tell me what you're doing tomorrow?" She hoped she wasn't obvious in prolonging the conversation, but she really wanted to talk.

"Probably, more of the same, but I need to go buy supplies and groceries. I thawed out a steak and frozen vegetables for tonight, but otherwise things look pretty slim for the rest of the week. So what's your tomorrow look like?"

"Just work. I have a luncheon appointment with a client, and I need to catch up on everything I've let slide the last couple of weeks. Seems like I don't get as much done when I'm working at home, but I wanted to spend time with Jack—besides he's more important than anything else. I can't believe he will be in kindergarten next year. He's so excited because tomorrow is kindergarten round-up.

"They have it in the spring so the little kids can see the school and know what to expect when school starts. My next door neighbor is the principal at the elementary school where Jack will attend, and he thinks she's wonderful so he's not the least bit worried about school. Anyway, I'll take him to that at two-thirty."

"That's a good idea for the school to do that, because it can be scary at first. I remember being excited about going to school so I could play with other kids. The ranch is pretty far out, and I didn't have brothers or sisters. All I could think about was playing; and then my teacher said we had to do math. Was I ever disappointed?"

"Yes, he needs to be around other kids too. That's also why I wanted him to go to day care some too. I know I smother him, and I really try not to, so at least on those days he can be independent."

"So, do I ever get to meet him?"

"Sure, I'm certain he would be very impressed with your boots."

Clay laughed. "Then I guess I need to send a picture of my Shetland ponies."

"Oh, my gosh, he'll wet his pants! Speaking of the Little Man, I guess I had better get him ready for bed. Convincing him that a bath is a necessary ritual is not easy. Don't forget to call."

"Don't worry. And please give Napa consideration."

"I will. Good-night."

"Good-night, Faith."

As she hung up the phone, she thought about him so far away in the old ranch house he had described as having good bones, but needing some tender loving care. The hacienda he called it, because it was a spirited mixture of Indian, Spanish and Mexican influences, like many of those in the desert southwest. She could almost visualize him sitting on the porch, surrounded by the courtyard, which he had told her was his favorite place to write. He said the rustic elegance of the thick walls bathed in earthy hues of burnt ochre along with the blue and yellow Talavera tiles and a round, cascading fountain gave him inspiration for his writing, but no comfort for his soul.

As she went to get Jack, she couldn't help but think about Clay's invitation. Deep down she wanted to go, but she didn't want to admit it to herself or anyone else. She liked Clay, and he was fun to be around, but she wasn't ready for a relationship—or was she? The inner conflict tore at her, and when she looked at Jack's sparking blue eyes and chestnut hair, she saw Tyler. "Time for a bath."

"Oh Mom, can't I skip tonight. I didn't play outside much."

"Jack, that is not the point. You need to bathe every day. Besides you have fresh pajamas and sparkling sheets so you have to be just as clean. How about a bubble bath, and I'll sit with you."

His eyes lit up again, and he ran into his room peeling off his shirt and tossing it on the bed.

"Uh, hold on. All your clothes need to go in the clothes hamper. You know the rule. I'll run your water."

He appeared at the door naked and grinning. "Ready."

Faith smiled and then laughed. "Look at you. You're as naked as a jay bird, but a lot cuter."

As he climbed into the tub, she covered him with bubbles and began washing his hair, which he hated. "You didn't say I had to wash my hair."

"It'll only take a minute. Do you want your toys?" She asked as she reached into the container by the tub.

"Sure."

"Are you excited about round-up tomorrow?"

"Yep. I can't wait to see the school!"

"Now remember, you can't call Carly by her first name. You have to say Mrs. O'Conner."

"That's gonna be hard. I've never called her that."

"I know, but all the other kids have to call her that so you do too."

"Why?"

"Because that is the polite thing to do. Kids are supposed to call adults by their last name."

"But I always call her Carly."

Realizing that this was going to be harder to explain than she expected, she changed the subject. "What are you most excited about?"

"The clowns. Carly, I mean Mrs. O'Conner said she has clowns hanging all over the school."

Faith smiled, "She told me after you and all the other kids tour the building, you are going to have snacks in the cafeteria and then get to play outside on the jungle gym and swings for a whole hour. Won't that be fun?"

"I can't wait!"

"I'm going to get your P.J.s. Do you want the space ships or the cowboys?

"Cowboys!" His head went under the water, just as he answered and he came up with bubbles all over his face and head.

"Now, you're going to have to rinse your hair, silly goose. I'll be right back." When she returned she sat and watched him play, but her mind kept taking her to Clay's offer. She didn't want to think about it, but she knew she had to give him an answer tomorrow night. She needed a sign, something to help her make the right decision. She reached over and grabbed a towel. "Okay, time to get out," as she stood to dry him off. "You're getting so big, I won't be able to do this much longer," she said wistfully.

"You need another little boy," Jack said from out of nowhere.

Trying not to show her surprise she turned away for a slight second, and then looked at Jack. "Do you want a little brother or sister?"

"A brother, not a girl."

Faith's startled response now turned to laughter.

"Can we get one?"

"Well, not anytime soon."

The warm bath must have done the trick because Jack said his prayers and fell asleep before Faith turned the first page of his book. She kissed him good-night, and then went to the den to find the novel she had started weeks earlier. After reading the same paragraph four times, she knew it was hopeless. Concentration wasn't there. Staring at the cover of the book, she began to think about Clay's books and wondered what his covers looked like, what the stories were really about, and how he developed his characters. Where did he get his ideas?

Although he had told her they were westerns, and described one lone character, she realized she knew very little about him or the books he wrote. Who was this guy who rode horses, made wine and wrote novels? She was tempted to Goggle him, but thought that seemed unsavory—like she didn't trust him or something. Yet, she really wanted to know more about him; that she had to admit. Maybe she would go by Barnes and Noble tomorrow so she could at least buy and read one of his books. Maybe she would meet him in California.

The phone rang as she was undressing for bed, and she was surprised to hear Patrick's voice at that time of night since he knew that Jack's bedtime was at eight-thirty.

"Is everything okay?" She asked with noticeable alarm in her question.

"Geez, Faith, I wasn't paying attention to the clock. I'm sorry. No, everything is fine. Sue and I were just sitting here talking and decided if it would be okay with you, we'd like to take Jack to Disney World next weekend. When you mentioned kindergarten round-up, we started thinking that it will be harder to just jump up and take him somewhere next year, so we better do some spoiling right away."

Faith laughed, "He is so excited about the round-up. But when he hears about Disney World, he will be hard to control. When do you want to go?"

"We thought we might get flights for Wednesday and return on the following Wednesday. We might go to Epcot and drive over to the beach. Just take our time. Would that be okay?"

"That's wonderful. Uh, dad, while we're on the phone. I wanted to talk to you about something anyway, but I was going to think through it a little more. But with your taking Jack, maybe this is the sign I was looking for."

"What in the world are you talking about, Faith?"

"Do you remember the young rancher/grape grower/wine maker/novelist that I told you I met at the trial?"

"Yes, you said he wanted to meet me. So, what about him?"

"I went to dinner with him Sunday night."

"And?"

"He's invited me to meet him in San Francisco and spend some time in Napa where he used to live."

So, what's there to talk about? You are going, aren't you?"

"I don't know, Dad. I'm so confused. I want to, but I don't. You understand, don't you? I mean, not a day goes by that I don't think of Tyler."

"But honey, Tyler made it clear in his letters that he wanted you to move on with your life. It's been a long time, and you've spent many lonesome days and nights. I think you have been very respectful of his memory, but it's okay to find someone. You are too young to live only on memories. You need to create some new ones. This may not be the right guy, but you'll never know until you learn more about him. Take it slow, but take it."

"I'm so glad you called. Maybe I will go, but yes, I'll take it slow. He knows how I feel, and I really think he understands. He's supposed to call tomorrow night for my answer. I guess if next week's not too soon for him to get rooms and for me to get a flight that would work out. It would be great for Jack to be with y'all. I don't want him to know right now."

"Why don't you let me know what you decide, and we'll plan our trip around what works best for you. Faith, you have always made the right decisions. You will this time. Since it's so late, I'll tell Sue all this news and she can talk to you later. We love you."

"I love y'all too. Thanks for listening. Good-night."

"Good-night."

Peeking in to check on Jack, she walked over and touched his hair, moving it gently away from his forehead like she had done countless time to Tyler. She was still stunned that Jack had mentioned wanting a baby brother. Perhaps, in her efforts to protect Tyler's memory she had been too cautious, too shielding. Maybe she should use some of the cryo-preserved sperm that they had banked before Tyler's radiation or maybe it was time to let life itself decide. She went into her bedroom, turned off the light and slept better than she had in weeks.

⌘ ⌘ ⌘

Clay couldn't sleep, and he tossed and turned until he finally got up and went to his computer to write, but before he picked up where he had left off on chapter six, he pulled up his email and sent a message to Faith. *Hi, It's three in the morning, and sleep eludes me. My daddy, if he were here, would say I don't have a clear conscience. That was one of his favorite sayings because he never had trouble sleeping. Maybe it was because he worked dawn to dusk or maybe he was right about that conscience thing. Whatever the case, I've given up, and I'm sitting at the computer getting ready to work on my novel. I went outside thinking I could get some inspiration, but do you know how still and quiet it is on a ranch in Arizona in the middle of the night? Crazy when it's too quiet. Seems like that would be the best time to think. The stars are bright, but not as big as they are in Texas, or so I'm told. It is a beautiful night, but I don't see the man in the moon like I did when I was a kid. I guess things do change.*

I decided while I was flinging the covers around trying to make myself sleepy that I would write a children's book about a little cowboy named Jack. How does that sound? Of course, eventually, I would need for him to come to the ranch and ride one of the Shetland ponies, and rope a calf and several other things so I could get photographs for the book. But of course, that is a ways down the road. Right now, I just need to convince his mother to meet me in San Francisco. I promise to be a gentleman. I haven't had so much trouble getting a yes for a date since the prom. Am I losing my touch? Thinking about you. Clay.

Once he had written the email, he had felt better and more relaxed. After three hours of nonstop writing, he went to the kitchen to make a pot of coffee, and turned on the radio for the weather forecast. It was a habit, and a useless one he decided because this time of year the weather rarely changed—hot days and cool nights, and rarely a drop of rain or a smidgeon of humidity. The sun was just coming over the mountains and through the small kitchen window where he could see some of his mother's flowers beginning to peek through the dull brown-gray dirt. He reminded himself to water them later in the morning.

This was one of his favorite hours while it was transforming from night to day, still cool from the brisk desert night air, but not so chilly that sitting on the porch was uncomfortable. Taking his coffee mug with him, he went to the courtyard and moved a canvas pillow to the back of his much preferred wooden bench, sat down and propped his feet on a small wooden stool. Needing to stay busy, he plotted his day. He felt silly feeling this way. What was it about Faith England that had made him resort to practically begging her to meet him in one of the most desired places in the United States?

He thought about Sandy, his latest girlfriend, who would have jumped at the chance to go with him to Napa, to go anywhere with him. He had broken it off with her before the trial; she was too clingy he had decided. They had met in Phoenix where she taught high school English and drama, and actually hit it off from the start. Both were avid readers, and liked to go to the local productions where on occasion she starred in a play. She even enjoyed the ranch, and could ride a horse as well as anyone he had known. But the fire wasn't there, and although he enjoyed her friendship and gourmet cooking, she wanted more, which he simply couldn't give her.

He didn't like hurting anyone, and he knew he had broken her heart. She called him every night for awhile, and they went out to dinner the night before he left for Dallas the first time, but it was futile. He could never love her, and she deserved more. At thirty, she was restless to marry, settle down and have children. He had told her he wasn't ready, but now he wondered if he had been dishonest. At the time, he thought that was true. Now, that was what he wanted, just with a different woman. Maybe, his falling for Faith was punishment for not loving Sandy the way she wanted him to.

He had dated many different women both at the university and after, and never had he lost touch with his emotions. Always he was slow to embrace any kind of feelings beyond friendship. Not that he fought loving someone; it simply hadn't happened, and in spite of trying, he came up hollow and knew it wasn't right to string someone along because he enjoyed their company. Needing another cup of coffee, he went back into the kitchen the back way through the old screen door his dad had added a few years after the house was built. Glancing over at the computer, he noticed he had mail, and his heart skipped a beat.

Well, it's the middle of the morning here. I forget your time is two hours dif-
ferent. I slept like a baby. Guess your dad was right. You've made me an offer I
can't refuse. Please call tonight, and we can see what dates, etc. you have in mind.
Don't fall asleep on your horse. A cactus might do some damage to that handsome
face. Later, F.

"Yippee," he hollered, glad no one was around to hear. With
that news, he showered, shaved, dressed and got in his Dodge Ram
pickup. With the windows down, he bounced along the dusty road
feeling like he did as teenage boy who had just won the blue rib-
bon at the fat stock show, only this was better. He wasn't sure if he
would take home the grand prize, but he knew he was closer to it
than he had been yesterday. He had a lot of work to do, but he was
up for the challenge. Faith England didn't know just how persuasive
and persistent he could be when it was important to him. He had
some calls to make and some favors to call in. This needed to be a
magical weekend, even if it meant sleeping alone.

⌘　⌘　⌘

Will Rogers Elementary was teeming with five year olds or
those soon to be when Faith and Jack arrived. Uncharacteristically, they were running a few minutes late, which drove Faith,
an extremely punctual person, crazy to say the least because Jack
couldn't decide which shirt he wanted to wear. She had thrown up
her arms and told him if this was the way it was going to be at five,
what on earth would he be like later, but then she had to smile,
remembering that he got this trait from Tyler. She reminded herself
to ask her mother-in-law how early it had manifested itself in him.

Once they entered the school, Jack could have cared less if he
had on a shirt. Immediately, he saw friends from the neighborhood,
and off they went until Mrs. O'Conner gathered them all up for

the tour. *So much for holding my hand, and staying with me,* Faith thought. She wanted him to be independent, but wasn't sure she was ready for it so quickly. Nevertheless, she and a host of other mothers tagged along as their soon-to-be kindergartners pranced merrily behind the principal as if she were the legendary Pied Piper.

The first stop was the library, and it was difficult to keep the children in line when they saw the giant stuffed monkeys, giraffes, and turtles. The theme, LEARNING IS FUN UNDER THE BIG TOP, was evident everywhere one looked. Library columns had become trees made out of green and brown colored butcher paper. Papier-mâché' monkeys in vibrant shades and tones hung near the trees, and bright colored clowns were suspended from the thin metal strips that held the ceiling tiles in place.

Everywhere the children looked there were colorful displays. On top of each book shelf, children's books with animal titles stood waiting for little hands to touch and marvel at the words and pictures. The reading corner was even more inviting with bean bag chairs in each of the primary colors tossed around on a gigantic rug that looked more like a painting of a zoo than carpet. Wooden pieces of a jumbo zebra puzzle was scattered on one end of the rug, evidence that tiny fingers couldn't resist the temptation.

If this place didn't stimulate an interest in reading, nothing would. The librarian smiled at the children and handed each a bookmark with a picture of a purple monkey scratching his tummy saying "itching to read." For a fraction of a second, there was silence as each child touched and studied the small gift before handing it off for safe keeping to a waiting mother or father.

Classrooms were the next stop on the tour, and all three kindergarten rooms in the kindergarten-first grade wing were equally decorated to draw attention to learning. Stepping into the first room the children saw a huge sign that read: Welcome to

Kindergarten—The Greatest Show on Earth. The teacher, Ms. Evans, a tall blond who looked not a day older than sixteen, welcomed the excited group and explained that the students who were assigned to her class would be known as the lions, and she pointed to the alphabet decorating the lower part of the wall circling the room.

Each letter had a picture of an animal or something related to a circus. Similarly, a row of numbers from one to twenty was posted on one wall at average five year old eye level. "We will learn all this next year, and a whole lot more," as she took the hand of one of the little girls who appeared fidgety. "Can you find the elephant?" Immediately, the child relaxed and pointed to the giant E. "Very Good. Well, you have a lot more to see. So have fun, and see you in August."

They all waved good-bye and headed for the second classroom where a pudgy middle-aged smiling teacher was waiting below a sign that read: Be A Highflyer in Kindergarten. Plastic parachutes hung from the ceiling, and pictures of tigers flanked every wall. "Hello, little tiger friends. Welcome to a magical place where you as tigers will be powerful top cats of kindergarten."

She pointed to a cardboard circus train where each car was filled with beanie-sized animals, and a sleepy tabby cat curled in the corner. "Tab is our resident cat. She lives here, except on weekends when she goes home with me. She's very gentle, and if you are in my class next year, you can pet her when you finish your work, if you can find her. She likes to hide. We will have so much fun while we learn next year. Come back to see me," and with that the kids proceeded to the final classroom that was painted a soothing blue, with an aquarium filled with colorful fish and coral arches.

A slender young woman of Asian descent greeted the children. "The big top has land and sea, and my room is like a colossal ocean because we are the walruses. I lived in a house that faced the Pacific

Ocean when I was your age, and I love everything about water. You will too if you are in my room." A collection of sea shells lay scattered on top of a low shelf. The teacher picked up the largest, a conch, and put it to Jack's ear. "Can you hear the ocean?" With eyes sparkling, he smiled shyly and nodded yes.

It was time for snacks, and the children were ready as they held hands as directed and walked to the cafeteria where cupcakes decorated with clowns, boxes of animal crackers, and bags of popcorn had already been placed on the long metal tables. Watching, Faith couldn't help but think what a job the custodian was going to have after this adventure was over, but surprisingly, each teacher came along with white plastic trash bags as the children were almost finished, showing them how to put all the leftovers and spilled food in the awaiting sacks.

Looking at her watch, Faith was reminded that Clay would call in a couple of hours, and she was glad she had made her decision as she watched Jack looking so poised and grown-up. Whether Clay was right for her or not, she knew that time had come when she should think about a future that perhaps included sharing it with someone else, maybe not marriage or anything serious, but something more than she had known in a long time.

She was jolted back to reality when the principal announced that everyone should make their way to the gym and adjoining covered outdoor play area. Pandemonium almost occurred when the children saw the face painters, jugglers, and clowns. On a makeshift stage, middle school gymnastic students were performing. One of the clowns was blowing up balloons and stretching them into funny looking animal shapes, which the kids grabbed excitedly. Jack ran outside to the Jungle Jim set and proceeded to climb and swing on the bars.

By now, Faith was beginning to tire of standing, and made her way over to several of the mothers who were sitting on a concrete bench watching the activities. Conversations quickly led to other responsibilities and all agreed the children had much more energy than they did. Laughing, one mentioned that maybe all this excitement would lead to an early bedtime. After what seemed like an insurmountable length of time, the principal thanked everyone for coming, and announced that round-up was officially over. Jack came running. "Five more minutes, please."

"Nope, times up. You heard Mrs. O'Conner. She's the boss of the school. Besides I need to stop at the store for some milk and bread."

Ah, Mom. I hate going to the store!"

"Well, you don't hate your Fruit Loops. It will only take a minute."

"That's what you always say," as he took her extended hand.

"You want to ask Casey to go with us?" Casey was Carly O'Conner's oldest, a fiery red head one year older than Jack. Since both of her parents were Irish and red headed, she hardly had a chance to be otherwise. Freckles covered her nose and cheeks, and the fact that she had lost her two front teeth, made her cute, but certainly not pretty. Her vivacious personality, however, lit up a room, especially when she danced and sang, which she did often. "Her mom probably has to stay at school awhile. We'll walk her home after y'all play. How does that sound?"

"Great, I'll get her," and he was off to fetch his friend while Faith asked Carly. Normally, Jack didn't like to play with girls, but Casey was a tomboy who liked the same activities as him, so she was okay, which is how he put it.

It was almost five when they arrived home, and as Faith unpacked the groceries that had grown to include more than milk and bread, just as Jack had predicted, she yelled for Jack and Casey to let Judge in from the backyard. In less time than she could put the bread in the pantry the television was blaring, the door slamming, and the dog's tail wagging. She flashed Judge a smile, and petted her head. "So much for our peace and quiet, huh girl?" The dog cocked her head as if to indicate agreement.

"Let me change clothes, and I'll get your food," she said, knowing that the Collie well understood the drill and would follow her to the bedroom and wait patiently. Within minutes, Faith was wearing madras tennis shoes, faded jeans and a UT sweatshirt, which was now raggedly short sleeved as a result of a combination of dull scissors and Faith's lack of talent for anything related to sewing or cutting.

Taking the dog food sack from the closet in the utility room, she signaled for Judge who obediently followed her outside to the flagstone patio. She was glad she had bought a house in one of the few neighborhoods that had trees. Being from the piney woods, that was important, although in this case she had to settle for oak and one large pecan, which was messier than she liked when the pecans fell. As Judge started eating, Dusty crawled through the cat door, stretched and brushed Faith's leg with her head to let her know she was ready for attention.

Reaching to pick her up, she said, "You little lover. You're not exactly subtle are you?" She sat down, placing the cat on her lap and reached for the steel comb to untangle the long thick coat. "I spend more time on your hair than mine," she said admiring her silky fur. Purring softly, the cat relaxed like a limp rag. "Don't get too used to this today. I'm running behind schedule."

After another few minutes she lifted the cat and started to set her down when at the same time the feline spotted a lone squirrel. Jumping out of Faith's arms she sprang into action, chasing it halfway up one of the oak trees. Faith picked up the dog's leash and stuck her head in the back door, yelling, "I'm taking Judge around the block. Want to go?"

Realizing they couldn't hear for noise of the TV, she ran inside, and announced it again, but Jack, engrossed in the cartoons, raised his hand to wave her away, which pleased her because this wasn't going to be an extended walk, although she never knew who else would be out for a short stroll and stop her to say hello. If she stayed away from the park, her chances of a quick getaway were best. Luckily, the path was empty today. It wasn't that she didn't want to be friendly; she had a lot to do before Clay called.

Shortly after supper of grilled cheese sandwiches, pickles and chips, which Casey had stayed over to share with Jack, the phone rang, and Faith stepped outside to answer, glad that Jack had a friend to keep him company while she talked.

Clay told her about his day, and how he had heard from his agent with good news. The latest edit he had sent to the publisher had gone through with remarkably few needed changes—music to his ears since this was the fifth edit, a task he hated. Then he turned the conversation to her. "I can't say I had nearly so much excitement," as she went on to explain about the uneventful lunch meeting with a client, and the lengthy round-up of overly exuberate five year olds. They laughed and talked easily for more than twenty minutes until Casey's mother called on the other phone.

"Can I call you right back?" She asked Clay, and he was glad because maybe that meant their conversation would be extended. After she and Jack walked Casey home, she explained to her son that she needed a few more minutes on the phone, which he accepted happily because it meant prolonged playtime.

Clay picked up the phone on the first ring. "So, when can you get away to the wine country?"

"What are you talking about?" Faith asked teasingly, before she explained about her dad and mother wanting to take Jack to Disney World the next week.

"That's great. I can make it work. Is Thursday okay? Could you stay until Monday?

"I think I can arrange that."

"Great. I'll call right now, and get airplane tickets."

"I can get mine," she answered quickly.

"I won't hear of it. I invited you so that is my treat."

"So, does that mean if I invite you to Dallas I have to pay?"

He was so excited to hear her say that, he almost forgot to answer, and then laughing, quickly goaded her. "Well, I was hoping Paris or London, but Dallas will work. After I get everything arranged I'll email you if that's okay," not telling her that he had already checked on rooms and taken his chances with possible dates, reserving two rooms at his favorite B&B next to the Napa River.

⌘ ⌘ ⌘

chapter
twenty-one

Clay was waiting at baggage claim when Faith arrived. Seeing him, she realized again why she was attracted to him. His broad smile matched his broad shoulders, and he looked handsome in his khaki slacks and black Polo. This was the first time she had seen him without boots, but he seemed even taller than she remembered. Not sure how to react to her, he waited until she hugged him gently, and then he embraced her with both arms. "You look great."

Dressed in sandals, and a multi-colored peasant skirt with cerulean highlights and a solid cobalt lightweight sweater, her blue eyes glistened; she appeared relaxed when she smiled and thanked him. "I guess you discovered quickly that the plane was late. It is always so reassuring when the captain comes on and tells you they are working on a mechanical problem and it will only be a few minutes. I want them to take as long as they need, which apparently they did. Oh, that's my bag—the blue with the ugly flowers." She pointed to it as it bounced along the conveyer. "I figured no one else in the whole world would buy luggage that dreadful—so far I've been right."

"I like your hair."

"Thanks, as you can see I got it cut. My regular stylist was on vacation, so stupid me, I went to someone new, and she cut it shorter than I wanted, but I tell myself, it's just hair. It'll grow." She had told Tyler the same thing many times during his chemo, but she didn't want to think about that right now.

"Well, I think it looks super."

She reached and ran her fingers through the wispy, slightly wavy style that sprang right back in place. "Wait 'til it hits the humidity in the bay area, and tell me then."

Smiling, he gathered her luggage and took her carry-on, leaving her with just her purse. "This is great. I usually have my bags, Jack's, and all his junk that he insists on taking. I have never understood why it is necessary to take a pillow, stuffed animals and other miscellaneous odds and ends on a two night trip."

He eyed her large suitcase and grinned.

"Stop it," she said, hitting him on the arm. "That look didn't get past me!"

"I'll get the rent car." Noticing it was almost one-thirty he asked, "Are you hungry?"

"A little, but I can wait if you want to go straight to the Napa area or wherever."

"I know a great little dive overlooking the bay that has magnificent appetizers and a la carte small plates that would keep us from getting too hungry before dinner. How does that sound? We would still get to the B&B by four-thirty, get checked in and have time to walk around some."

"Let's do it."

⌘ ⌘ ⌘

A gentle breeze kicked up a light spray from the water, but the tiny restaurant was high enough on a cliff overlooking the pristine waters of the San Francisco Bay to protect the couple from the cool dampness. Clay suggested a crisp white wine, the grilled prawn appetizer, langoustine and cucumber canapés, and a small cheese plate, which he described as being a great pairing and a light selection. Faith shook her head in agreement, but added, "I thought you said we were having a light lunch?"

"The portions are small"

Looking at the view, Faith let out a sigh, "This is spectacular."

"I'm so glad you agreed to come. I have so much planned; you'll probably yell calf rope."

Laughing, she said. "I haven't heard that saying since I left home. Mom used to say that."

The server brought two tiny carafes of wine and glasses. Carefully, he poured a portion of the wine into each glass, leaving the miniature decanters half full on the mauve table cloth.

"I thought you said this place was a dive."

"Well, by San Francisco standards it is." He held up his glass, and toasted, "To a memorable weekend."

Clinking her glass gently against his, she smiled and took a sip of the chilled wine. "Now, this is good."

"Baby, you haven't tasted anything yet."

⌘ ⌘ ⌘

The Calistoga Elm Tree Bed & Breakfast was exactly as he remembered, and his good friends Kathy and Mike greeted them with open arms. While Mike and Clay retrieved the luggage, Kathy began showing Faith around the inn at the foot of the St. Helena Mountains, which included five bedrooms overlooking the Napa River among a grove of elms and assorted other old growth trees.

"I thought you would like this room," Kathy said, as she opened the door to a small, but beautifully appointed corner room with a queen size bed, night stand, a small armoire, and an outsized window overlooking a patio and fish pond. "You can't see the river from here, but from the patio downstairs you have a wonderful view. Folks don't tend to spend much time in their rooms here with so much to do elsewhere."

"This is perfect. I am so glad it doesn't have a television." Faith laughed.

"I've heard that before. People just want to come here to get away, eat delicious food, and drink wonderful wine," Kathy added. "I hear the guys coming up. Clay's room is across the hall. Although his has a view of the wisteria covered brick patio and fountain, I still think you have the best one," she said winking. "He told me not to give him the master suite although it is the only one with a deck overlooking the garden. It also has the spa tub, but he declined."

"I think he was being protective of me, which right now, I especially appreciate," Faith confided.

"He's a terrific guy, but I'm sure you know that. We've known Clay about five years. All his friends were just sick when he moved back to Arizona, but we understood. He was a very popular guy, and could have been married ten times if he had wanted. Several of my friends included."

Faith smiled. "He is quite handsome, and a genuinely sweet guy. That's what I like about him. Reserved, but lots of fun. Speak of the devil, I think he's trying to listen," as she heard a slight knock on the door, and then saw Mike peering around. Clay was holding back with her luggage.

"Can we come in?" Mike asked.

"I think you are. Here let us step out, and you can put the suitcase right over there," pointing to the luggage rack with dark espresso burlap webbing. "It's a bit crowded," Kathy said, squeezing past him.

"Where are you headed first, Clay? Sometime, you must have wine with us on the patio. Will you work that in?" Mike asked.

"I'm counting on it. After we unpack, I thought we might walk to town, and just look around; then have a late dinner."

"We'll catch you tomorrow for a longer visit, but come on down when you're ready. I know how long it takes a woman to unpack. We might have time for a glass or two. So when did you snag the elusive table at The French Laundry?"

"Saturday night!" Clay grinned." Tomorrow morning, if I can convince her to get up that early, I wanted to take her on the hot air balloon ride."

"Yeah, that's pretty early, but it's worth it."

If she agrees, then after brunch, we'll drive around, see the vineyards and stop at several of the wineries. I know she wants to shop some too."

"See you downstairs."

Faith found the two men on the larger of the two patios, sipping on champagne from crystal flutes. "Aren't you two fancy," she teased.

"Well, we were going to be good, and refrain, but look at that view. I couldn't resist," Clay remarked sheepishly."

"Hey, you're on vacation. You should do as you please," Faith encouraged.

"I know, but I need to get you to town."

"There's plenty of time," as she reached for the flute Mike was handing her. Looking out over the lawn and beyond she commented,

"It has been a long time since I have seen such a gorgeous garden. May I go look?"

Kathy rounded the corner of the patio as Faith finished her question. "Am I missing a party?"

"Yes, you are," Mike said. "Clay and I were just having a little innocent drink of the bubbly and now here we are. I'll get you a glass."

"Kathy, are you the gardener? I was just going to look."

"Wait, let me get my drink, and I'll walk with you." Reaching to retrieve the glass, she paused, took a sip and joined Faith. "I wish I could say I was the gardener, but we have help with it. Otherwise, the B&B and everything with it would be too much. Mike is adding a vineyard across the street, so we just keep expanding. When we decided to do this eleven years ago, we were just going to open a small hotel, you know, a few rooms, and nothing more, so we could make enough to get by and enjoy the region. Now, look at us."

"Are you happy though? That's what is important," Faith offered. She already felt comfortable talking with her as the two strolled along.

"Very, Mike is a wonderful man. I was married before, and it was a disaster. I grew up in Oregon and married my childhood sweetheart. I could have stayed there forever. The wine areas are beautiful there as well. As a child we lived in the country, and my dad had a small vineyard, but he worked in town about twenty-five miles away. But after we were married, Rob wanted to move to San Francisco so we did. I worked days, and went to night school to get my teaching certificate, then finally got a job teaching eighth grade science, which I hated. Anyway, turns out, the reason he wanted to live there was he was gay. I guess I really didn't know him after all. Anyway, we lived together a couple of years after he broke the news to me, and then we finally just gave up and separated. A year after that we divorced. Believe it or not, we're still friends."

"So, how did you meet Mike?"

"I came up here one Sunday afternoon with some girlfriends to wine hop, and he was working in one of the wineries. He poured me a fantastic sauvignon blanc, and told me its history, and all about this area, and I was hooked, on the wine and him. He was everything Rob wasn't—a little rugged, and scraggly, an earthy, but sensitive kind of guy. Maybe, it was the beard," she laughed. "Thank goodness, he was single.

"For the next month, I came up here every weekend, and when school ended I quit my job, and moved in with him, without a clue as to what I was going to do to make money. When he told me he had always wanted to own a B&B, we started looking around, and found this place, which we could not come close to affording. In the meantime, another couple bought it, and it quickly fell into disrepair and later foreclosure. By that time, we had married and had managed to save enough to put a down payment on it when the bank agreed to sell it."

"Well, it is beautiful. Just look at it. The location couldn't be better. Oh my gosh, these roses are unbelievable," reaching down to smell the slight fragrance.

"They're called Betty Boop," Kathy said laughing. "They grow really well here on the banks of the river because they get lots of sun. The soil has just the right amount of moisture because it drains well."

The ivory roses with red edges were just a small part of the garden that extended for more than fifty feet across the back of the lawn. Showy red and purple flowers of the tree mallow shrubs flowed gracefully into the clusters of bell-shaped white tinged pink flowers of the abelia, surrounded by yarrow, society garlic, lantanas, salvia, and lavender. Two flowering dogwoods and big, bold statuesque Corsican hellebore with leathery leaves and pale green cups added lush greenery to the backdrop.

"This reminds me some of Italy, although it is perhaps more verdant and rich, at least right here. I love that part of the world, but I'm beginning to think this would be a wonderful, much closer substitute," Faith said, wistfully, remembering her trip to Italy, which resulted in Jack being conceived. "My husband and I went there some years ago. I had been trying to get pregnant for a long time, and it was a magical time there… because it finally happened, but wasn't long afterwards that Tyler got sick again."

Seeing the stunned look on Kathy's face, Faith continued. "He died five years ago, but we had a beautiful little boy together."

"I'm sorry, I didn't know. Clay didn't say anything, but he was so cautious about the two rooms, that I wondered about your relationship."

"I told him I wanted to go slow. He's actually the first person I've dated since Tyler's death. I'm not sure I'm even being fair to Clay"…her voice trailed off.

"Well, if anyone can woo you, he'll be the one. As I told you, he's a special guy. I don't want to see him hurt, but I understand your wanting to be careful."

"Hey, are you two going to talk the rest of the afternoon, or are we going to town?" Clay yelled.

Smiling, the women turned around and sauntered toward the patio. "We could talk all afternoon, you know," Faith teased. "I guess we had better see part of the town. You are welcome to join us," looking first at Kathy and then at Mike.

Mike quickly said, "We've seen it a few times. Do you want to ride bikes? We keep some here for our guests."

Clay looked at Faith for a reaction. "That sounds like fun, but give me five minutes to change into pants," she answered, as the guys went to the shed to retrieve two older model, firecracker red Schwinn bicycles.

"You guys have fun," Mike called as they pedaled off down the road that led to town.

⌘   ⌘   ⌘

An hour later, after seeing some of the local highlights and stopping to shop in a couple of quaint stores, they parked their bikes and went into the Hot Springs Grill where the owner, another friend of Clay's seated them at a corner table by a small gas fireplace. "I forgot that it gets cool at night here in the spring; it may be a bit chilly on the ride back to the B&B," Faith said, already liking the warmth that the fireplace emitted.

"Not if we jump into the hot mineral bath afterwards"

"You mean there's one there at the B&B?"

"Well, sort of. It's actually Mike and Kathy's personal spa, but they offered it. Does that sound like fun?"

"Now, I know why you said to bring my swimsuit. At the time I thought you were crazy, and then I forgot to ask you about it. I'm game. What's this about a balloon ride?"

"It's right after sunrise; they pick us up and provide coffee and muffins so you can see how the balloon is prepared, and then after an hour's flight they serve a champagne brunch. How do you feel about getting up that early?"

"When in Napa, do as the visitors do," she said, cheerfully.

The owner sent over two glasses of Merlot and an order of pecan-roasted lobster bites. "Compliments of the house," the server said. "Enjoy."

"That was nice."

"See why I miss this place so much?" He laughed, "Not the free stuff, the friends."

"I'm feeling it. Kathy told me you were quite popular with the women."

His cheeks flushed as he probed. "And what else did she tell you?"

"That's the gist of it."

After a few minutes of silence, they sipped on their wine, and Clay reached across the table and took Faith's hand. "Someday, I'm moving back here, when I can figure out what to do with the ranch. My neighbor is slightly interested, but he doesn't really want to pay me what it's worth, but that may be the only answer."

"Life's too short to wait to do the things you love..." She stopped, realizing her words sounded hollow. Here she was lecturing him when she almost hadn't allowed herself to meet him in California. She took the last sip of her wine, and placed the glass down slowly, looking at him thoughtfully. His deep set eyes carried a look of serious, yet playful imagination that she guessed helped him see the world in an optimistic and exhilarating way. He was an interesting individual, who seemed generous and open, and she found herself liking him more and more, despite her unwillingness to give in completely.

"Are you ready to order?" Clay asked, as he handed her the menu. "I already know what I want."

"And what's that?"

"The ahi tuna with bacon and chanterelles. But to start, the chef here makes a dynamite pear salad with toasted walnuts, blue cheese and white wine vinaigrette."

"The salad sounds good, but not the tuna. I think I'll have the prosciutto wrapped halibut with artichokes."

"Do you want a Chardonnay or Pinot Grigio with that?"

"Pinot Grigio."

Following dinner, Faith turned down dessert, which was a rarity, with the promise of a glass of Port in the spa. As expected, the night air was chilly on the ride back to their rooms, but the wine and good food had left them both feeling warm. Mike and Kathy were in the mineral bath when they arrived so they quickly changed and joined their friends, who regaled them with stories for the next two hours before Faith announced that if she was going to be able to open her eyes at five in the morning she had to call it a night.

Shivering as the crisp cool night air touched her skin, she reached for a towel, but before she could pick it up, Clay wrapped a warm, fluffy white robe around her shoulders. "Good-night," they called to their friends, as they entered the warm main sitting area and headed up to their rooms. For an awkward moment, Clay stopped at Faith's door, and gently kissed her on the cheek, before he turned to go into his room.

Faith was asleep before her head hit the pillow, and it seemed like only a few minutes had passed when the alarm rang at five. She hurriedly took a shower, fixed her hair, and put on a hint of make-up, determined to be ready at the appointed time. When she heard a delicate knock on the door, she opened it quietly, not to wake the other guests. She took his outstretched hand, and they crept down the stairs.

"Did you sleep well?" Clay whispered.

"Like a rock."

"Yeah, me too."

The van was waiting for them, and took them directly to the launching area, and true to the advertisement, steaming hot coffee and warm muffins were set out as soon as they arrived. Because they were the first balloon in the air, they were able to watch the others ascend and marvel as the bright colors of each balloon rose above the golden glow of the sun, the perfect backdrop for the miles and miles of vineyards that blanketed the landscape below. Within minutes they were floating above the morning mist. "This is breathtaking, Clay. Worth every minute of lost sleep."

He flashed her a huge smile. "I was hoping you would see it that way. Don't you feel a part of the wind?"

"It's wonderful," her wispy curls blew slightly against her face as they glided above the majestic vistas. When they landed an hour later she admitted she wished it had lasted longer.

The champagne brunch was set in an old winery that had since been turned into a restaurant, but it had maintained many of its original features, which led to its old world charm. Because they had stayed back to talk to the pilot, there were no small tables available so they were forced to join a couple from New York who had never been to California wine country, but shared endless stories about wine in the North Fork, praising its superiority. They explained that they owned an antique shop/trendy boutique in an area sandwiched between Peconic Bay and Long Island Sound, just about ninety miles from New York City.

Known for its savory seafood bounty, farms, and wineries, this region offers views more splendid than they had ever seen in California, they noted loudly before Clay or Faith had a chance to ask questions or make a comment. Faith tried to talk about Tuscany, but they continued to interrupt with stories about their area being the best kept wine secret, how everyone knew the Finger Lakes of New York but no one was taking the wines on the Sound as serious as they should. While Faith and Clay listened and she pinched and kicked him under the table, the New Yorkers described the hamlet where they lived with its apple orchards and potato farms.

Faith found them totally obnoxious as they dominated the conversation, and appeared to be quite knowledgeable about every subject that arose. She was glad when they excused themselves to look around the building. Clay smiled at her mischievously. "I know what you are thinking."

"And just how do you know?" She couldn't help but grin as she asked him.

"Your eyes gave you away, not to mention the bruises on my leg"

"I guess I let my guard down. I work on not showing how I feel with my eyes all the time when I'm in the courtroom, because I'm afraid that will happen. Those two were pretty loathsome, don't you think? Plus, he ate with his mouth open."

Clay chuckled. "He had to; he never shut up."

"Well, I'm glad we agree. I am also happy that they have someone else captured besides us. Look they are talking to that couple from Oregon we met earlier. Guess they are telling them their wine in Oregon sucks also. Do you ever drink wine from New York?"

"Not often, but it's okay, especially if you like Riesling, which I don't. I must admit though wine from the Sound must be a pretty good secret because I haven't tasted any from there, only the Finger Lakes."

"If I ever do, it will bring Mr. and Mrs. Know-it-All to mind and ruin it for me," Faith said, not soon to forget her brunch conversation. "So, what's next, tour guide?"

"How does a massage and an herbal wrap sound?"

"Oh, my gosh, that is the most heavenly news I have heard. Are you going to do the same?"

"Not hardly, but I made an appointment for you at ten-thirty just in case. If it's okay, I'll visit with some old friends that I'm afraid I'll miss otherwise and pick you up at the B&B about two.

The spa is only about three blocks away, an easy walk. Afterwards, we can ride around the countryside and maybe go to a couple of my favorite wineries. We have to see St. Helena, Rutherford and Napa. If we have time, I'd like to drive over to Sonoma as well, but that might have to wait until another time."

"Whatever you choose. I'm anxious to do a tasting, and see some of the actual wineries."

"It might be fun to have a late picnic at V. Sattui or we could even bring it back here and sit out on the patio."

"That sounds like the most fun, a picnic; maybe Mike and Kathy would join us."

⌘   ⌘   ⌘

When Clay drove up to the B&B, she met him at the car, smiling radiantly. "I had the most wonderful time. Do you want to hear?"

"Sure, do you want me to drive or give you my undivided attention?"

"You can drive and listen. Oh, before I tell you all about it, first I must admit, I had a thirty minute nap."

"Hmmm. That's why you are so cheerful!" He teased, and reached over and patted her leg. "So tell me."

"Well, first, she did a grape-seed/rosemary exfoliation, with chardonnay oil. Then she used a gentle polish of essential oils, herbs, lemon and papaya. She called the massage eclectic because she combined Swedish, reflexology and deep tissue. After an hour full body massage, I had a rose/geranium wrap that felt sooooooooooooo good, followed by a jasmine/rose bath."

"So which of the two hundred ingredients do I smell?" He joked, but she was killing him. He could visualize her laying on the table naked, her sleek body stretched out, every seductive curve glistening with warm oils. He wanted to hold her and feel every inch of her, but he snapped out of it, careful not to reveal that he was aching inside or that there was a bulge forming in his slacks.

⌘ ⌘ ⌘

Three wineries and several tastings later, they stopped to buy four bottles of local wine, two white and two red, in case Mike and Kathy decided to join them and enough sandwiches, cheese, and fruits for them all. A bright orange sun was slipping slowly behind the mountains as they neared the B&B. "I'm tired, are you?" Faith asked as she looked over at Clay.

"A little, maybe we should turn in early," wishing she would agree to share his bed. How he wanted to take her in his arms, and slide under the cool covers with her nude body against his, but when they had finished the picnic dinner with their friends, and said their good-nights, she didn't join him in his room or invite him into hers. What he didn't know was that a part of her wanted to; her heart was telling her yes, and her mind was saying no.

As she undressed, she thought about how he had looked at her several times on the trip, especially tonight as they lingered over the wine. She wasn't naïve; she saw the wanting in his eyes, and she knew that all she had to do was knock on his door. He would meet her with open arms, and have her clothes off of her in minutes. She could see his thin, muscular body waiting for her, needing her. For a second, she paused and stopped unbuttoning her blouse. It had been so long since a man had undressed her and shared a bed, cradling her body, exciting her and making long, slow, gentle love to her. Would she ever allow anyone else but Tyler to touch and kiss her in places no one else had ever gone? She was so close, but she finished taking off her clothes, pulled on her silky sleep shirt, and turned off the lamp.

⌘   ⌘   ⌘

Saturday morning dawned bright as Faith tried brushing the sleep away along with the thoughts of the night before. Sun had often been a therapeutic balm for her, and that proved to be the case when she pulled the curtains back and glanced down at the fish pond. She was glad she hadn't let herself weaken, although she couldn't get the picture completely out of her mind.

Although it was nearly seven-thirty, she decided to take a luxurious bath with the special salts and oils that were strategically placed in a basket by the claw foot tub. She had always loved this style of bath tub, so she ran it as full as she wanted, and relaxed under the soothing waters, until the phone rang. Dripping, she stepped out and answered Clay's cheerful voice.

"Good morning, did I wake you? I'm downstairs having coffee, but Kathy has some wonderful fruits and breads when you're ready."

"I'm having a bath so if it's okay I may be awhile. Go ahead and enjoy your breakfast."

"No hurry. I'll have coffee, read the paper, and visit with Mike. Just enjoy your time. We don't have to be anywhere at any certain time."

Stepping back into the tub, it had cooled off slightly, and rather than add more hot water, she hurriedly finished. She wasn't used to hovering, and it was a little annoying, knowing she had become extremely independent over the years. Trying not to be bothered by the early call, she talked to herself, and dressed, realizing she was on an emotional rollercoaster that she had to try to control.

Clay was in a perfectly splendid mood, and it showed. It was obvious that this atmosphere worked wonders for his psyche, and smoothed out any stress he carried because of the ranch. When he stood and smiled at her, she scolded herself mentally for ever being the least exasperated with him. "I need coffee, strong coffee."

"Didn't you sleep?"

"I did, but for some reason, I'm running on empty this morning."

"Try one of these." He passed a basket of assorted breads to her. "The homemade honey butter is excellent."

"Does Kathy bake this?"

"She has help in the kitchen, but she does all the baking."

"Mmmm. This is good. And the coffee is too. I'm better already"

"You better eat as much as you want because we can't eat much lunch—have to save room for tonight at The French Laundry."

"What time is our reservation?"

"Seven. I know that is a little earlier than we might normally select, but this experience will take three hours at least."

"Three hours?" She looked at him, her face in disbelief.

"You'll see. This is an event!"

I'd like to get back in time to freshen up, and call Jack. I'm not sure why since the last time I talked to him, he was much more interested in the Magic Kingdom than me. Guess I should just be glad he isn't missing me," she said smiling. "Anyway, I'm so excited about eating there. My dad is so jealous. He's tried to get reservations three different times, and to no avail."

Clay winked, "It's all about connections."

⌘ ⌘ ⌘

Visitors driving by the turn-of-the-century two story stone building housing The French Laundry would likely pay little attention to the nondescript place that started out as nothing more than a saloon in the 1880s. After a town ordinance directed that no alcohol be sold and served within two miles of Yountville, the building became a brothel, and finally in the late 1920s a French steam laundry. In 1994, Chef Thomas Keller bought the building from the local mayor who had rescued it twenty years earlier and turned it into a restaurant.

Because it is known all over the world for its unique nine-course tasting menu, each a series of small, focused dishes, some no bigger than a cupcake, with whimsical names and a gourmet twist, reservations are extremely difficult to score. The menu is primarily French with an American influence, and a trip inside the famous blue door, becomes a memorable food experience, an expensive one. With wine, a bill for two can easily exceed a thousand dollars. Yet, some of the cult wines themselves top that amount, without the fixed price meal that cost two hundred fifty dollars per person.

Clay and Faith arrived early so he could show her the garden, which was offering up spring bounties of snow peas, lettuce and cabbage that would expand to tiny, fairytale eggplants, luscious stone fruits and heirloom tomatoes as the weather warmed.

Once inside, the couple was seated upstairs in one of the two rooms created by a staircase in the middle of the exposed stone walls. Fresh flowers adorned the white tablecloths set with white china. Although every table was taken, the restaurant had a comfortable, private feel because of the arrangement of the tables, and immediately Faith was enamored by its coziness. The waiter brought the wine list and the menu choices for the night.

"I have never seen a wine list with so thick with pages," Faith said as Clay passed it to her. "Or so heavy. She handed it back to him. "You decide, but then I just want to look at it a few minutes."

"What do you think about a sparkling wine to start? The Anderson Valley, Roederer Estates is recommended, and I've had a glass before, and I thought it was excellent."

"That's perfect. I'll have to write all this down so I can antagonize my dad."

He laughed as he ordered a bottle, and handed the menu back to Faith, who was unable to control herself when she saw the price. She whispered in disbelief, "Clay, surely you didn't pay a hundred and forty dollars for a bottle of bubbles."

"Keep looking and you'll think I'm a cheapskate; some are fifteen hundred."

It took thirty minutes for the couple to decide on their order, which Clay explained was one reason he had allowed so much time for the dining process. When Faith tasted the signature "Oysters and Pearls," she said, "This melts in your mouth. Oh, it is so good." For the next two hours, they alternated food with conversation, punctuated by a half bottle of Martinelli Zinfindal from the Russian River area.

"So, what was your favorite?" Clay asked as he ended his dinner with the pane di ricotta alla griglia.

"Well, unless I had the menu to read the ingredients in some of the dishes, I'm not sure I would know, but I think the Dungeness crab boudin. What about you?"

"Definitely the tar tare of Japanese blue fin tuna."

She frowned. "I've really tried to like tuna, but I just don't. My East Texas upbringing shows. I only like it out of the can, dressed up with pickles and mayo, and hard boiled eggs."

Grinning, he said, "Your sophistication shows in other ways." Looking at his watch, it was ten minutes after ten, which meant his prediction about the duration of the meal was right on target. "Are we ready?"

"I think we should walk back to Calistoga. Maybe in a few miles I might feel better."

"Just think, we have a gourmet lunch on the train tomorrow."

"Oh, my gosh, Clay. I'm going to weigh two hundred pounds before I get back to Dallas."

"You would still be beautiful," as he took her hand and led her out into the cool California night. Surrounded by glittering stars, the full moon shone brightly against the darkness. Back at the B&B, they once again went to their separate rooms where alone they fought the temptations and desires that were drawing them to each other, mindful that it was getting more difficult to resist.

⌘   ⌘   ⌘

Sunday lunch in the vista dome of the 1952 Pullman railcar was the perfect way to see more of the countryside in the elevated observation style dining car, refurbished using Honduran mahogany paneling, etched glass, and brass accents. After a four-course meal and more wine, Faith told Clay a nap was in order, which he agreed to whole-heartedly.

When Faith woke at five, she found Clay sitting outside alone, cradling a half-empty glass of red wine. She stood back watching him for a few minutes as he stared straight at the river, seemingly oblivious to a hummingbird darting from flower to feeder not more than five feet away. For a minute she felt like an intruder.

He gazed up at her, clearly in a melancholy mood, and noted that she had changed into tight jeans, which drew attention to her long thin legs and a casual sweater that accented her well proportioned chest. She studied his face and walked over and put her arms over his shoulders, forming a v around his neck. Without thinking she kissed him on the cheek, and then, smiling sat down next to him. "What's on your mind?"

Trying not to show his surprise by her actions, he swallowed hard, and she couldn't help but notice how his slightly protruding Adam's apple made him look sexy. "I love this part of the world. I hate to leave it. I hate to leave you. I guess I'm just a little sad, although I'm the luckiest guy in the world to be right here, right now."

"It's okay to feel that way. We all have our ups and downs, and I know it must be lonely there on the ranch."

"Do you think you will ever visit—maybe even bring Jack?"

She hesitated before answering. "Would that make you feel better?"

"That would make me feel great." His face shone with eagerness. "So how soon can I expect you?"

Faith laughed, "I was afraid that might be the next question. I'm not sure how I am going to handle this with Jack. I mean, how to introduce you two. Kids have all sorts of questions, and it is important to me to be honest with him, although I don't have to be detailed."

"Can't you just tell him we're friends? That wouldn't be anything but true, unless I have missed something that suggests otherwise." He winked, his mood noticeably improved. "Want some wine?"

"Not right now. Seems like that's all I've done is eat and drink for four days."

"Want to change things up. I know a nice little room upstairs," he asked with more nerve than he had shown previously.

Smiling faintly, she answered, "I know this has been incredibly unfair to you, Clay, but as I told you before we came, I need time."

"But Faith, it's been five years since Tyler died. At some point you are going to have to move on," he said, with a hint of impatience in his voice.

"Are you saying you won't wait any longer?"

"No, I'm not saying that at all. I just need to know that you have some feeling for me, that there is a chance." He reached over and took her hand in his, waiting for her response, which seemed to take forever, although it came in less than a minute.

Tears welled in her eyes, and she felt an unexpected pang in her stomach as she searched his gaze for understanding. "I know that in spite of all my efforts to fight it, I'm falling for you, but I'm not sure that is the best for either of us. After all, my life is in Dallas, and yours is in Arizona. I have a five year old that requires my constant attention, and a job that takes up the remainder of my energy. The most we could see each other is maybe once or twice a month, if that."

"People have made it through much more adversity. If you give me a chance I can make it work."

She took a long, deep breath and exhaled slowly, giving her additional time to put her thoughts and words together. "But it takes two, and I just don't know that I can give you all that you deserve. You know how much I loved Tyler; it would not be fair to give you any less. Right now, I'm struggling with my emotional equilibrium. I just have a lot to think about." A tear ran down her cheek as Clay stood up, and took her hand again.

"Let's go for a walk."

For more than three blocks they strolled in silence except for the rustling of a gentle breeze against the foliage along the sidewalk. Finally, Clay broke the quiet. "Look we said we'd take this slowly. Let's just do that—let it, whatever it is we both are feeling, take us rather than we guide it. How would that work?"

She looked at him tenderly. "You don't make it easy, do you?"

"Not when it's something as important as this. I'll give you all the time you have to have, and in the end if it doesn't work out, it won't be because I haven't tried."

The next morning at the airport, Faith agreed to take Jack to the ranch sometime in the next month.

"If I can't win you over fast, I'll work on him," he teased.

"That's not playing fair."

"Nothing's fair in love and war."

Smiling she said, "No, I guess it's not."

Her plane was boarding, as she turned to gather her carry-on and purse, but not before embracing Clay one last time.

⌘ ⌘ ⌘

Jack returned home Thursday night dog tired, but excited to tell his mother every little detail about Disney World. Talking non-stop about Mickey, Donald Duck and the jungle cruise, he barely took a breath before describing his ride on Aladdin's magic carpet. "The camels spit at us," he said eagerly. Patrick and Sue smiled and listened as he related story after story, and showed his multiple souvenirs. Then, visibly sleepy, he climbed up in Faith's lap, and was asleep before she had time to kiss him good night.

"And how was your trip?" Patrick asked, anxious to hear every detail.

"It was good," Faith answered.

"Is that all you're telling? The facts, girl, the facts," he said smiling and waving his hand as if to prod her on. She winked at her mother, and devilishly tantalized him.

"You are much too inquisitive. Actually, I brought you a bottle of wine that you can't get here—it's only sold at the winery. Let me get it" With that Patrick took Jack from her and carried him to his room where the bed was already turned down for him because Faith anticipated he would do just what he did—fall asleep in her arms. She went to the kitchen and retrieved the wine, and returned with an enormous smile.

"Here," she shrugged, showing him a bottle of Cabernet Sauvignon, his favorite. "Don't get too used to it. You can't afford it."

"Was The French Laundry anything like it's purported to be?" Patrick asked enthusiastically.

"Even better," and she went on to explain every element of each course, and to describe the features of the interior and exterior of the restaurant. "Most of all you have to take the hot air balloon ride. The vineyards are magnificent."

"How was Clay?"

"We had a really good time. He wants me to go to his ranch and bring Jack. I don't know if that's such a good idea."

"You'll figure it out," Sue encouraged. "And whatever it is, you know, we'll support you." She stood, "Patrick, it's late. We need to get home, and unpack…and sleep. One week with a five year old is exhausting."

"Tell me about it. I have him every week."

"Yes, but you're younger, and he's less hyper when Mickey Mouse isn't standing in front of him," she said laughing.

Faith hugged them both, as they said good-night to her and walked them halfway to the car. Closing the door, she looked around the room at the new stuffed toys. *How many stuffed animals could one little boy have* she asked herself as she shook her head. She picked them up one by one, and dropped them into the already overflowing basket, and smiled. She was glad Jack was home. It had been much too quiet, and she had missed his sweet expressions. She walked into his room and rearranged the already tangled covers over him. By the sounds he was making, he was apparently dreaming, and she wondered about what. She pushed his suitcase to the corner. Unpacking could wait until morning.

Before turning out the light she checked her email one last time, telling herself that it was okay if Clay hadn't written, but he had, and as usual his note told her she was missed. *Just thinking about you as I ready for bed. Another long day, but I got work done on the house—a little painting and two chapters of my book. I consider that good. Hope Jack had a great time at Disney. Sleep well. Clay*

⌘   ⌘   ⌘

chapter
twenty-two

The call to Faith from Harry Herrera in Lubbock surprised her, but not nearly as much as the news. He had just hung up from Maxwell's appellate lawyer who notified him that Maxwell had hung himself in Supermax, which wasn't an easy task given the tight security. All preliminary findings indicated it was suicide with no foul play, but investigations were still on-going.

Harry was not only the family attorney, but listed as Maxwell's sole contact so it had quickly become his responsibility to formulate a business plan as well as make other arrangements. Fortunately, he had met Faith at the trial, and knew she was familiar with Maxwell's half-sister, who he believed to be the next of kin, pending DNA samples. For some strange reason, Harry explained to Faith, Maxwell II had listed Consuela as the mother when he had Harry draw up Max's new birth certificate and other papers. He had never quite understood that, but was glad now because it would make it easier for the daughter to stake a claim to the inheritance and speed up the process, making the large sum of money he would be receiving for his services that much faster.

There was stunned silence as Faith explained to Harry that Consuela was alive and well.

"As you know, since Maxwell died without a will, this will be a little more complicated, but I think with court records, and my signed affidavit that Maxwell II told me she was, indeed, the mother, we should be able to get this done," Harry explained.

"I'm sure, if necessary, Consuela would agree to give a DNA sample, but of course, she is completely unaware of any of this, so I'll need to talk with her."

"Precisely. That's why I called you. I didn't know anywhere else to start. She stands to gain everything, except my percentage of five percent as executor and my attorney fees, plus all the outstanding bills, but no matter what there's a boatload of money and property. I know both Maxwell's are turning over in their graves at the thought of her getting anything, but that's what happens when they don't listen to me."

"What's your estimate? How much do you think he left?"

"Millions. Probably somewhere close to a couple of hundred million. I know what's in all the accounts here, but who knows where he may have other money stashed. We may never find it all."

Faith gasped at the information, quickly doing the math. "I can't think of a better person to inherit it. Justice may prevail after all!"

"Well, I'll be in touch. Just let Consuela know. I still can't believe she's really alive. Nor can I believe Maxwell is dead. Sorry son of a bitch coward. His old man would have rotted in that prison before he would have taken his own life. Max was never the man his dad was, and his daddy knew it. Used to talk to me about him. Oh well, guess that's life. And in this case death."

"Did you find out how he did it? How he killed himself?" Faith asked.

"With a bed sheet. A lousy bed sheet. Morris said the appeals process wasn't going well, and Maxwell had continued to become more and more irrational and paranoid. He complained that the only sound he heard was the clanging of an occasional metal door. Not that Maxwell was a touchy feely kind of guy, but I can see where the physical depravation would cause him to go berserk. I mean I didn't realize that he had to talk to Morris behind a thick glass wall. Couldn't even shake his hand."

Faith chuckled. "Not going to get any sympathy here, but maybe it's best that it ended this way. Lots of folks find fault with the concept of Supermax—claim it's a form of torture. Who cares? The guy deserved to be tortured, after all he did. But I worry that someday the ACLU or other groups will protest enough that the government will do away with these kinds of prisons. I would have been upset if he had any better treatment."

"Well, Maxwell wasn't a patient man, so I wouldn't have expected him to hang around long though I didn't expect this—not so soon."

"It seems too easy to me. He should have had to suffer longer, but it will be nice for Consuela and Enrique to enjoy his money while they are young enough. All's well that ends well, I guess. Thanks for calling, Harry. Keep me posted."

"Sure."

Faith sat silent for the longest time, taking in the news and thinking. *Maxwell really was a coward after all.*

⌘ ⌘ ⌘

In her excitement she was tempted to call Clay first with the information. She leaned back in her chair and for a second eyed the inbox on her computer, an action she found herself doing more of lately, but the only new mail was a notice of a continuing education course on ethics which was being held the next Saturday when Faith and Jack would be in Arizona on their first trip to see Clay.

She knew it was only right to call Consuela first. After all, she was still Maxwell's mother, a fact that was making her job of relaying the news a little more difficult. Looking at the pictures of Jack that filled frame after frame on her credenza, she tried to put herself in Consuela's position. Stalling a few minutes more, she took a sip of coffee and frowned, not realizing how long it had been sitting cold on her desk. As she scrolled through her list of contacts for the number Enrique had given her, she dialed and chose her words carefully.

Consuela was gracious and reserved in receiving the news, and Faith knew her mind was probably going in a hundred different directions.

"I really don't know what to say, Mrs. England. I am sorry for Kiki, yet nothing I ever said was enough for him, so nothing I can say now would be either. I loved him for so long. Maybe I always will in a way only a mother can, but he broke my heart. And the money—it seems tainted and dirty. Enrique and I will have to talk about it."

"I understand. You'll have plenty of time. It may take several months or longer to settle all the affairs. In the meantime, you talk about it. And Consuela. I'm truly sorry for you and Enrique," she said honestly.

"Thank you for calling," she answered, her voice cracking.

Faith could hear the muffled sobs at the other end, and quietly she ended the conversation with, "I'll call you soon. Bye for now."

⌘　⌘　⌘

chapter
twenty-three

The call to Clay brought her back to a lighthearted mood as they shared their pleasure in Maxwell's demise although both agreed he got off light considering the pain he had caused for so many years. "Suicide was the easy way out." Clay complained.

"Yeah, I think so too, but at least he won't cost the taxpayers any more money for appeals. I just hope Consuela and Enrique will take the money. Her comments made me a little nervous."

"She probably just needs time. Plus, you can help them. They'll listen to you."

"I hope so." Changing the subject, she asked. "So, what are you doing?"

Laughing he said. "Cleaning house for my two guests."

"Jack is so excited. I told him about the Shetland ponies, and of course, that's all he talks about. He wants to know what color they are. Their names, the list goes on and on. He even picked out some clothes he wants to wear, which only happens when he is really excited. Of course, nothing matches, and the cowboy shirt is too small."

"I'm excited, Faith. Anything special you want to do while you're here?"

"I'm excited too. I don't know enough about a ranch to give you input. Whatever you decide will be great with me."

"I just want you to have fun, and for Jack to feel comfortable. Do you think he'll be okay with it?" Clay asked, concern in his voice.

"I've explained that you are a good friend and that you want to show us around. He's good with that. The fact that you are a good male friend really doesn't change anything for him because I have several male friends who I visit with. At his age he takes it at face value."

"I hope so. I really want to make a good impression."

"I know. It's important to me as well. You'll do fine; now stop worrying and get to cleaning. Speaking of work, I guess I better do some myself."

⌘   ⌘   ⌘

Clay had arranged for them to fly into Tucson. At the airport, Faith and Clay were careful not to hug or show any outward signs of emotion in seeing one another in front of Jack, although it was evident in their eyes that they were thrilled to be in each others' presence. Over hamburgers at McDonald's, which Clay insisted on allowing Jack to pick, the couple exchanged small talk until Jack scurried off to explore the play area.

"I'm so glad you're here."

"I'm anxious to see the ranch," Faith answered, still careful not to commit.

Her reaction didn't go unnoticed, and for a moment, Clay hesitated. "I was hoping you might say you were glad to see me."

"Of course, I'm glad Clay," as her eyes followed Jack to be certain he was playing. When she was satisfied, she reached and took Clay's hand. "I'm sorry. I'm a little nervous about all this. I warned you that it might be difficult. Maybe, I'm being too cautious."

"I understand, or at least I'm trying."

On the drive from Tucson to the ranch Jack slept and Faith and Clay talked and alternately viewed the desert landscape, noting the old Spanish missions, the majestic saguaro cacti, and the now defunct small mining towns that still gave the area its western flavor and a glimpse of its history.

Pointing out the giant saguaro, Clay told Faith the story about a man many years ago who had taken refuge next to one of the tall cactus during a storm only to be struck by lightning because the tree is said to hold enough salt to make it a lightning rod. "I don't know how much truth there is to the tale, but it certainly has its place in local lore. Anyway, I don't know many folks around here who would sidle up to a saguaro when it's storming or otherwise."

As they drove up to the ranch, Faith woke Jack whose eyes became wide with amazement, and he wiggled with excitement when he saw the corral with three Shetland ponies.

"Can we ride, Clay, please?" He yelled from the back seat of the truck.

"Sure, but unfortunately it won't be long until sunset. Good news is there will be plenty of time tomorrow. Let's get you settled. I might have a few surprises for you," he said, winking at Faith.

"What kind of surprises?" Jack begged, obviously excited.

"You'll see, but first I'll show you where you'll sleep, and where everything is so you'll know everything you need to know. How's that?" Clay asked, noticing Jack's shoulders slumping slightly. "Tell you what, just let me get your luggage out of the car, and I'll get your gifts. Is that better?"

Jack's eyes lit up, and a huge grin formed on his face. "Yippee. Presents!"

Clay's key slid into the lock on the antique wooden door with hand-forged iron clavos as Jack squirmed and Faith waited patiently. Once inside, Faith recognized some of the rustic colonial furniture that Clay had described in his emails, including the stone fireplace with a rustic, distressed mantel and hand-hewn corbels.

Wooden stools carved from tree trunks sat on either side, but what caught Faith's eye was a wooden trunk with a domed top and detailed lock plate that sat in one corner. Clay noticed her eyeing the old trunk and explained that his dad had found it shortly after his parents were married, and saved it for their first anniversary when he gave it to his mother filled with baby blankets. "I guess that was a hint, but it was five years until I was born. She had lots of difficulty, and they really wanted a house full of kids, but I'm all they got."

"You were probably enough," she said smiling.

Jack busied himself counting the points on a rack of antlers hanging over the fireplace and staring at an oil painting of a cinnamon colored horse that had obviously been painted from a photograph that was tucked into one corner of the frame. "That was my first horse when I was about your size. Her name was Sedona."

"That's a funny name," Jack said innocently.

"Well, there's a beautiful place here in Arizona called Sedona that has tall red rock formations. So she was named that not only for her color, but because my dad bought her not far from there when we went on vacation one fall."

"Where is she now?"

"She died the year I went to college. My dad always thought it was because she missed me."

"My dad died, but it was before I was born. My mom misses him a lot."

Clay looked at Faith, who had stiffened and was noticeably taken back. For a second she felt like she had been hit in the stomach.

"I know Jack; your mom told me."

"He liked horses too."

"Do you, Jack?"

"I luv em. Now can I open my presents?"

Clay smiled. "Sure," as he went into another room and came out holding three big boxes, and handed them to Jack who began tearing them open immediately. Faith, who had been distracted now focused on the packages that revealed a pair of roper boots and chaps, a soft stuffed horse about the size of a Teddy bear, and the biggest little boy's cowboy hat that she had ever seen. The smile on Jack's face was also one of the largest she had witnessed, and she smiled back, glad he was happy in this new setting, and equally happy that he seemingly adored Clay.

"I didn't forget you either," as Clay handed Faith a package wrapped in yellow tissue. "I know your house isn't western, but I thought it might be okay for your office."

Carefully, she pulled the paper off of a hand carved Indian maiden, with an expression that told her story of strength. "It's gorgeous, Clay."

Blushing, he said softly. "She reminded me of you. Would you like to see outside? We can let Jack get a feel for the ride before dark."

The sun set a beautiful pink and orange giving the sky over the mountains a vermillion cast. If Jack had had his way, he would have ridden off into it, but his mom had other ideas as she pulled him off the pony's saddle. "Okay, Little Man, time for supper and a bath. You have another big day tomorrow."

"Oh Mom, just one more ride."

"Jack, it's getting late. Tomorrow is a new day."

"But can I ride tomorrow, Clay?"

"Of course you can, plus I thought you might like to ride with me on my black stallion, Hercules, which I call Lee for short. And your mom can ride the black mare named Madonna, that is if your mom says it's okay," looking at Faith for approval.

She winked at both of them, and said, "Only if you both act nice," allowing the two males to develop a conspirators' bond.

After a dinner of grilled tenderloins, baked potatoes and salad, Faith put Jack to bed while Clay cleaned the kitchen and poured them a glass of Port. "Let's sit on the porch and count the fireflies," Clay said enticingly.

The desert night air was cool. Clay led Faith to the wooden porch swing, and gently wrapped a light blanket around her shoulders before sitting down beside her. He longed to take her in his arms, but instead refrained. For a long time, they sat in silence until Faith broke the quiet. "I know why you get lonesome out here. This would be torture."

"It used to be darker when all you could see were stars and the moon. At least it was peaceful. Now, the mobile surveillance of the Border Patrol lights up the nights sometimes. I hate that because it reminds me of the troubles out here." He took her hand and changed the subject. "I like Jack. He's a sweet little boy. I like the way his eyes sparkle and his mind seems to run on energy powered by a combination of adrenalin and curiosity."

She smiled. "I think he's having a wonderful time. I'm afraid tomorrow may be quite tiring for us. He'll be like a tornado—full tilt."

"That's okay. I just want him to have fun. I'm trying to charm his mother through him," he said, cleverly with a broad smile.

She rested her head on his shoulder as he put his arm around the back of the swing and nudged her closer. For a moment he thought she might stay nestled in his grasp until she suddenly pulled away and told him she needed to check on Jack. "I just need to be sure he's sleeping. I don't want him to wake up and not know where he is or not be able to find me. I'll be right back."

When she returned she appeared more relaxed and sat back down close to Clay who took her hand in his and gently moved the swing back and forth in a lulling manner. "He was sound asleep, his arms wrapped around the stuffed horse you gave him."

Clay leaned to kiss her, and she responded. He kissed her over and over, and it was obvious to them both that this could lead to more. His hand grazed her breasts as he reached to draw her closer, and he heard a slight whimper that he interpreted as acceptance. As he cupped first one breast and then the other, she didn't stop him, and he began to feel aroused, which he knew he wasn't hiding well. As he kissed her again, he positioned himself to stand and drew her up in his arms. "Can we go inside?"

She hesitated, as if unable to let herself, but yet not strong enough to keep from succumbing to his desires and her wants. He took her hand and she followed, noticing the need that was building in his tight jeans, but once inside the house, a pall came over her, and she took control of her emotions. "I can't, Clay. Not tonight. I thought I was ready, but I'm not. I'm sorry." She turned and left him standing uncomfortably in the great room.

She woke before dawn feeling incredibly guilty for leaving him in the condition he was obviously in as a result of their actions. Furthermore, she felt like a silly, shy school girl who was afraid of losing her virginity to the captain of the football team if she rode in the back seat with him on a double date. It didn't make sense.

What was so wrong with sleeping with him? She didn't have to make a commitment. Making love didn't have to mean that she loved him or expected a long, lasting relationship. She was acting crazy. It was just sex. Women slept with men all the time with far less feelings than she felt for him. Besides, she had wanted him as badly as he wanted her, so what was the big deal? The big deal was that it was more than sex. It was a feeling similar to one she thought she could never resurrect again. She realized she was afraid of loving again.

She found him outside writing, and blushed with embarrassment as she saw him, his head down, lost in thought as his fingers flew across the keyboard. When he noticed her, he looked up briefly, and then down again, as if to say I don't want to talk right now. But Faith walked over and put her arms around his shoulders, and whispered. "I'm sorry, Clay. I am truly sorry. I promise I won't do that to you again."

He stood and said, "I have coffee and sweet rolls made—the gooey kind with cinnamon and white icing. I thought Jack would like them." He rattled on, pretending nothing had happened the night before.

When Jack woke he ran straight to the kitchen in his pajamas, calling out for Clay. "Can we ride?" Laughing, Clay asked, "In your P.J.s?"

Faith smiled. "How about some breakfast for a little cowboy? Then we will dress and have Clay show us the horses. He's made you yummy sweet rolls." She poured him a glass of milk, and sat out two rolls, which he gobbled quickly.

"Yum, these are good," wiping his mouth on his pajamas.

"Jack England, where are your manners? Not only did you eat like a pig, you didn't use your napkin. You know better, now don't you? I'm embarrassed," she scolded.

He hung his head, and whispered "I'm sorry."

Clay winked at Faith behind Jack, and took a long sip of coffee, before responding. "Forgiven, you're just excited, right?"

"Yes sir."

"Thank you for using your manners, Little Man. You want to make a good impression don't you? Maybe Clay would invite us back."

"Would you, Clay? I mean, if I use my best manners."

"Sure, fellow," tousling the little boy's hair that was sticking up all over his head from a night of heavy sleep.

Faith helped Jack dress in his new boots and the new jeans and western shirt she had bought him in Dallas. "We'll have to get Clay to help us with the chaps. That's beyond my pay grade."

"What's pay grade?"

"Oh, it's just a saying, Little Man. What it means is that I don't know exactly how to put them on you, so we'll let him." She noticed how straight he stood when she had him ready. As she reached to hug him, he wiggled from her grasp, and ran down the hall yelling for Clay. Smiling, she combed her hair and finished dressing, still feeling slightly uncomfortable about the night before, although it was evident that Clay wasn't going to let it ruin the trip.

Within fifteen minutes, Clay and Jack were riding Lee and Faith was on Madonna touring the ranch. "Faster," Jack squealed, as the three cantered at a steady, but slow pace.

"Y'all go ahead. I'll catch up or you can circle back for me," Faith suggested. When they returned Jack's helmet was slightly ajar and his face plastered with a smile as big as the ranch, and he talked so fast Faith couldn't understand exactly what he said.

"He's trying to tell you we jumped a gulch," Clay explained, with a crooked grin. "I held on to him," he said, reassuring her.

"It was neat. We went high."

"So, you're having fun?"

"A lot."

"Me too." And then turning to address Clay, she continued, "The sky is amazing. I'm not sure when I have ever seen the clouds move so fast only to be replaced by another group of blue and white bands," she said, readjusting her sun glasses while holding the reigns loosely so that the horse would trot toward Clay. "It's really peaceful out here; one can't help but sense the freedom and openness. This is nice."

"That's why it's sad what is happening to the land. I mean, this is as far south on the property that I feel comfortable riding with you and Jack. Beyond here, I never know what I'll find—broken fences, trash, and people trudging through the grass. When they do that, the cattle move again and again. Makes them thinner—harder to fatten and sell. Cows don't like people in their space, so that alone keeps Shane busy just herding them."

"I know it's hard because this land belonged to your father."

"And his father before him, but I'm just not cut out for this in the long haul. My heart's not here. Theirs was." He paused and whispered in the boy's ear. "Hey, I've got one more thing to show you," as he turned the horse and applied a gentle pressure to the horse with his strong legs. The stallion took the command and in a full gallop they headed for the barn. Clay yelled back to Faith. "See you when you get there."

"Whoa," Faith said as the mare reached the barn. Clay ran over and helped her, bragging on how well she rode and handled the horse. "I think anyone could ride her—she's so well trained. I haven't ridden a lot," she explained, blushing, but not elaborating.

Although she had ridden a few times with Tyler, she didn't feel totally adept so she had taken a couple of quick riding lessons at an arena in Frisco within the last two weeks in preparation for the trip.

Looking over at Jack who was now feeding both horses pieces of apple and sugar cubes as if he had done it many times, she was amazed that he wasn't the least afraid, and happy that he appeared so relaxed in the ranch setting. Walking over to him, she asked. "Can I feed Madonna?"

"Sure, Mom, but just one piece of apple. She can't have too much."

"Okay, I see."

Handing her a slice of apple, Jack said. "This is how you do it," as he gave the last sugar cube to Lee. Clay took the reins and lifted the saddles from the horses. Next he showed Jack how he brushed them, and together they finished the tasks of readying them to go back in the barn. Just then did Jack remember that Clay had said he had something else to show him so he began asking what it was? Clay smiled, and pointed to a bright apple red four-wheeler in the corner of the barn. Jack shrieked. "Can we go in it?"

"That we can. What do you say?" He asked turning to Faith.

Rolling her eyes, she answered, "I say, I'm going in and take another shower. I've had enough dust for one day. Have fun. Shall I make sandwiches when I'm dressed?"

Clay nodded as Jack crawled up in the driver's seat of the four-wheeler, and began turning the steering wheel. "That comes later. Maybe I should drive first," as he signaled for the boy to scoot over, which Jack did in a flash. "Here you have to wear this," Clay said, adjusting the same helmet he had worn earlier. "Fasten your seat belt, I'm starting the engine!"

⌘   ⌘   ⌘

When the two came in the ranch house, Faith was putting the finishing touches on the sandwiches, but she stopped to hear Jack tell all about how the two of them had driven all over the ranch, and how they had seen cattle and even a snake. Describing every detail, he giggled and explained how Clay had revved the motor and driven really fast twice, so fast that the dust swirled behind them.

"He popped a wheelie!"

"Oh, he did," raising an eyebrow. "Do you think you could stop talking long enough to wash your hands, Little Man?" Grinning, he raced off to the bathroom.

When he was clearly out of sight, Clay came around from the other side of the room smiling and catching Faith off guard planted a kiss solidly on her cheek. "Thanks for letting me get to know him, Faith; he's a great little boy."

Looking up at him she felt flush and for a moment wished he would take her in his arms and hold her close. "No, thank you, for being so good with him."

Jack ate quickly and then Clay showed him where he could build a fort in the courtyard using wood he had gathered for that purpose. "This is cowboy and Indian territory, so you need a fort. "I'll check on you in a bit, okay?" But Jack didn't answer because he was already picking up wood.

Lingering over lunch, Clay and Faith made small talk about the morning, and Clay explained that he wanted to take them into Douglas for dinner, and to look for a belt and buckle for Jack. "There's not much there, but it's the closest place, and it has some old western charm."

"I almost forgot to ask you. Are you really a Madonna fan? I don't know if she would be pleased to have a horse as a namesake."

Grinning, he explained that his dad had always wanted to go to South America, especially Argentina to see the gauchos and visit a real ranch there. "I wanted to visit the wineries so that was my college graduation gift—a trip to Argentina, Chile and Bolivia. Now that I've been to those countries someday I'd like to go back to South America—maybe to Machu Picchu and the Galapagos Islands. I see tours all the time advertising the two. Have you been?"

"No, I haven't really traveled very much. That's on my bucket list—travel in general. I'd love to go back to Italy, especially to see all the work my dad has done on his place. I've planned it several times, but something always comes up."

"I've never been anywhere in Europe; and I would love to see the Italian vineyards, plus all the other highlights, especially Rome. But the top spot on my list is France. I could get used to a week in Paris and Versailles, and at least a week of touring the wine country."

"So, keep going. I'm not seeing the Madonna connection."

"In Bolivia we went to the southern shores of Lake Titicaca to a little town called Copacabana—Río it's not, but it houses the shrine of the Indian Virgin, the Black Madonna, who is a beloved symbol of Bolivia. When I returned, my dad had bought me the black filly, hoping it would bring me home to stay I think, so I named her the Black Madonna."

"Was that your favorite place?"

"No, I really liked Argentina. The beef there is the best ever—it's raised on grain and a hormone-free diet. We ate at La Cabaña Las Lilas, one of the most famous steakhouses in the world. Of course, the Malbec from Mendoza wasn't bad either. Buenos Aires is a great city. Have you been?"

"No, but I think I would like it—the tango and shopping—that's my kind of trip."

"It has a mixture of Latin and European culture that is vibrant and inviting. The cobblestone alleys and waterfront give it a European flair, but then the music, history, and art let you know you are in South America, which I found very interesting."

"So what was the best part?"

"It was fun watching my dad interact with the gauchos. I think it took him back to when the cowboys were the folk heroes of the west just like they are there in the pampas. I think there is a certain amount of romance connected to life of the cattle and grain barons as well as the lowly nomadic gauchos who have inspired poets, writers and artists for several hundred years."

"Did your mom go with you and your dad?"

"She did, but she shopped and visited the Recoleta Cemetery. Sounds grim at first—both the shopping and the graveyard," he said with a chuckle. "But I have to admit I wished I had visited the cemetery after she described the century old magnolias and the seven thousand tombs of the rich and famous. She saw Eva Perón's black marble grave. Mom said the people there all refer to her as Evita as a term of endearment. "Don't cry for me, Argentina' is etched on her headstone. Bet you didn't know that!"

"You should go on Jeopardy," she teased.

Ignoring her while trying to look hurt, he continued, "In Chile my mom and dad stuck to the museums and took a tour of Santiago while I spent two days visiting the vineyards and wineries. We all went to Valparaíso to see where the cruise ships come in, and lost a few coins at the casino, which is even easier than in Las Vegas. It was a great trip—the last one we ever did together...," his voice trailing off.

Faith reached across the table and took his hands in hers. "I guess we better check on Jack, although I could sit here all afternoon and listen to your stories."

They need not have worried, because he was busy in play, finding a way to fashion the wood and an old bed sheet into a pretty good fort from which he was busy shooting make believe Indians he saw lurking in the courtyard. They watched in silence before going back inside for more conversation and a couple of quick stolen kisses.

After a brief stop at the Douglas Western Store where Jack became the proud owner of a hand crafted leather belt and buckle that carried his name, they ate at the restaurant of the historical Gadsden Hotel, known in southern Arizona for its vaulted stain glass skylights that run the length of the long ceilings and Italian marble staircase with a genuine Tiffany window at the top.

Jack ate his burger like he hadn't had food in months while Faith and Clay each savored a T-bone and salad. The two hundred cattle brands painted on the walls, including the one Clay pointed out as his, kept the tired little boy busy while they visited with the Cochise County Sheriff who had stopped in for a cup of coffee and slice of pie.

Although Sheriff Harris Noble was several years older than Clay, they had known each other since they were boys and Clay had even worked on the campaign when the sheriff was elected four years before. His dad had been sheriff for more than twenty-five years before he retired, and that was the only job Harris had ever wanted. Both he and his dad had worked tirelessly to find the men who killed Clay's dad, and Clay knew that it haunted them that they could never solve the crime.

The two men exchanged notes about the most recent happenings in the areas, and reminisced about the time when living in southern Arizona was more carefree and peaceful, explaining incident after incident to Faith, who apparently from the conversation, had already been mentioned to Harris in earlier discussions. He had smiled when they were introduced and commented that he felt as though he already knew her. She didn't broach the subject, but his smile told her that her name had come up before.

Clay explained that Harris often stopped by for coffee in the mornings as he drove the lonely county roads, checking out complaints or surveying the damage done by a busy week of migrant crossings. Their early morning talks revealed a lot about each man, and what he hoped to make of his life. Clay knew that Harris was doing what he loved and that he would never leave the county, but he worried that harm might come to him because law enforcement was his passion, and he was fearless. One of his deputies had been killed in the line of duty a year earlier, and there had been threats made on Harris's life on more than one occasion.

His wife had left him a couple of years back for one of her professors at the University of Arizona where she had taken a series of classes in geosciences over a five year span, and it had broken his heart, especially when she took their eleven year old son to live with her in Tucson. Harris tried to keep him every other weekend, but that was becoming more and more difficult because of his schedule and demands on his time. On occasion, he had even had to drop the boy off at Clay's house when he got a call to a crime scene during his off-time.

When Jack got restless and sleepy, Harris said his good-byes and Clay picked up Jack and carried him to the truck where he promptly fell asleep in the back seat with his head on a pillow Clay had thrown in just in case.

⌘　⌘　⌘

Clay was beginning to uncork a bottle of his best Bordeaux when Faith stopped him. "I don't think we have time right now for that." He looked at her with a surprised expression just as she took his hand. "Because I'm going to seduce you!"

A smile touched his lips as he dropped the corkscrew from the other hand and turned around to draw her near to him. He studied her for a minute to be certain he had heard her correctly. He couldn't think about another night without her, without making love to her. He kissed her and looked into her eyes, with a questioning look. "Are you sure about this? I don't want you to do something you'll regret later."

"I'm sure, Clay," as she began unbuttoning his shirt, and rubbing her hand gently over his chest.

"What about Jack?"

"You wore him out today; he'll sleep through the night." By now she was releasing his belt, and he knew she was serious. Taking her hand, he led her into his bedroom, and locked the door behind them. Slowly, he began undressing her as she did him, and within minutes they were both naked in each other's arms. He kissed her lips, and then her neck, and breasts, stopping long enough to look at her well proportioned, yet slender body. His fingers moved over her body, finding her most intimate part, and he teased her until she trembled with excitement.

She reached for him and felt his hardness as he slid on top of her. "Please Clay, I need you. Love me with everything you have." Their urgency increased and when he entered her, she clung to him and breathlessly moaned, wanting him, moving together in his rhythm as the force of his muscular body pushed him deeper inside to the moment of ecstasy.

For the longest time, he held her, touching her damp face, not wanting to release her. When he finally did, he eased off and rested on his side, sliding his hand between her legs, feeling her soft moistness until she grew more and more excited. "Please Clay, once more, please."

She reached for him as he pulled himself on top of her, kissing first her breasts and then moving lower and lower until she shuddered with anticipation and exhilaration. And then when he knew she could wait no longer he entered her with a powerful thrust, and they came together as one.

The heightened passion left them drained of energy, and for almost an hour, they lay next to one another, listening to the steady breathing, searching each other's eyes for answers to unasked questions.

Finally, Faith pulled the covers to her breasts, and sat up in the bed against the headboard, which creaked slightly. "I think I have time for a glass of wine," she said softly. He slipped out from under the sheet, pulled on his underwear and jeans, and turned on the lamp by the bed.

Returning with two glasses and the bottle, he handed her a small tray of cheeses and crackers. "You can eat crackers in my bed anytime," he said with his crooked grin that she had come to expect and like. "I don't know about you, but I'm hungry," as he popped a piece of cheese atop a cracker in his mouth, and washed it down with the red Bordeaux.

She blushed, "That was quite a workout. Do you have any idea what time it is?"

He turned and glanced at the clock on the side of the bed where he was sitting, his back propped up on two pillows against the head board. "It's almost one-thirty. Are you planning on going somewhere?" He asked, laughing and taking another sip of wine.

"I thought I might should check on Jack."

Smiling, he said, "I looked in on him when I went to the kitchen. He's out like a rock. You're good for at least five more hours," he winked as he leaned over and kissed her.

"Don't start tempting me."

He sat his glass of wine on the night stand and reached for her again, this time brushing his hand against her breasts. "You're beautiful, and you have a beautiful body. I could look at it all night."

"You aren't so bad yourself." She admired his muscular arms and legs that were obviously that way as a result of working on the ranch, and his thin torso that flattened against her when he pressed his manliness into her waiting body. Just thinking about it made her want him again, and within minutes of finishing their first glass of wine, they were once again clamoring for more of what each had to offer, determined to satisfy all the pent up desires begging to emerge.

After the last drop of wine, and a long good-night kiss, Faith gathered her clothes and went to the bedroom where she had slept the night before.

⌘　⌘　⌘

It was after nine when Faith forced herself out of a bubble bath, and found Clay sitting in the kitchen talking to Jack while they both ate cereal. "Hi Mom. Me and Clay are having breakfast. I thought you were never going to get up."

Smiling she said, "I didn't sleep well. I seemed to have rolled and tumbled the first part of the night. But now that I have had a few good hours of rest and a nice bath, I'm good as new."

Clay stood and poured her a cup of coffee. He wanted badly to kiss her good-morning, but refrained, although it was not easy. She looked so fresh, and smelled heavenly of lavender and rich herbal essences.

"Jack and I have been discussing our day, and he wants to ride the ponies again. If you want to stay inside, I have some excellent reading materials." He winked, and handed her his first book. "This one's probably my worst, but you probably should read them in order; that is if you are interested."

"This is a gift, being able to just relax and read. It's not something I get to do often." When she finished her second cup of coffee, she helped Jack pick out his riding clothes, and saw the two off before settling in on the porch swing with an overstuffed pillow and the book, which she quickly became engrossed in, not hearing Jack and Clay come back in a couple of hours.

Jack rushed toward her almost in tears. "I don't feel good. I upchucked all over the four-wheeler, but Clay didn't get mad at me." He was several feet behind the boy when he explained that Jack had seemed to feel fine when they left, and then he started complaining about his stomach hurting. At first, he thought the ride might have made him nauseous, but even after they stopped for awhile, he got sick again.

Faith reached and touched her son's forehead and it was unusually warm. "I have some medicine in my suitcase that I never leave home without so let me give him that and maybe if he can sleep awhile he'll feel better." Clay rushed forward and scooped the boy up in his arms and carried him to the bedroom where he gently placed him on the bed. Pulling off his boots, Faith helped him out of his jeans and told him he could sleep in his shirt and underwear. She patted his head and gave him a kiss. "I'll be right out here if you need me."

After a light lunch of salad and fruit, Faith and Clay talked about his writing for awhile, and then he left her to her reading while he answered emails and took care of paperwork for the ranch. Jack slept most of the afternoon, but woke up around six, cranky, clingy, and restless. Clay opened a can of soup for him, but he only wanted his mother to do anything for him. Faith turned on the television for him, and made him a bed on the couch where he slept off and on as he watched cartoons.

This was their last night at the ranch, and Faith had hoped that she and Clay could spend it the same way they had the night before, but it wasn't looking like that would happen. Jack couldn't help that he was sick, and they couldn't help that they wanted each other. Around eight Clay grilled chicken and vegetables outside, and Faith joined him while Jack was sleeping.

Over a bottle of Chardonnay, she explained that Jack would be restless and fidgety tonight having slept so much during the day, which would restrict her from stealing away for their time together. Telling her he understood, she saw the disappointment in his face, and felt the tug in her own heart, but this was the way life was with a child, another obstacle in their relationship that was already complicated by her being in Dallas and him on the ranch. The afternoon had given her time to think, to sort things out, to be reasonable and not emotional in her decision-making.

"I'll move to Dallas and get a place there. I'll do whatever it takes to keep this relationship going."

"You can't just leave this ranch and all it meant to your family."

"Someday it will sell. I'll put it on the market this week."

"Then what? You love the wine country so if there is any other place for you, it should be there."

"I can write in Dallas and drink wine there," he said, trying to bring a smile to his lips and lighten up the conversation that was going the opposite of what he wanted. "My books are doing well. I have enough money from the royalties. This can work, Faith. You'll see."

"I can't see. I'm sorry, Clay."

"Didn't last night mean anything to you? I mean, didn't that tell you that we're good together, that this is deeper and stronger than we are?"

Looking down into her glass she noticed it was empty, and she felt the same as a shadow came over her and tears welled in her eyes. In silence, she sat the glass on a nearby table and walked over to Clay whose mouth turned down and shoulders sagged. He no longer looked like a tall, fit rancher with a lopsided grin; instead a lost little boy whose world was crumbling. Reaching up, Faith touched his ruggedly handsome face. "Last night proved to me that I am capable of loving again. I'm just afraid, Clay, afraid of hurting you and scared about the possibility of losing again. It just seems easier to let it go now, before something happens."

With a wrenching, hollow feeling in the pit of his stomach, he said, "But you are stronger than that. I've seen how you are. People can't live their lives in fear of the what ifs."

"My whole life I have been stalwart and resilient when others around me were not, but now I feel so vulnerable because I know that life can be cruel and merciless, that you can think that you are on top of the world, and the next minute that world has imploded," she said softly.

The chicken sizzled on the grill as Clay halfheartedly flipped each piece over and turned the propane lower. With tongs he moved the foil holding the vegetables where the heat wouldn't reach them, and poured Faith another glass of the white wine. The moon was full and it illuminated the western sky as he looked up at it as if to ask for help or guidance. He was stalling, hoping he could think of the right words, anything to convince her to let things take their course, to give it the chance it deserved.

Taking Faith in his arms he looked directly in her eyes and he finally responded, "Sometimes, the story has a happy ending;

sometimes the characters live happily ever after, but in the first chapter it's hard to know. Unfortunately, life doesn't have a table of contents, but I'm willing to take a chance on the epilogue. Look, I can never be your first love; all I'm asking is to be your last. That's all I'm asking, Faith. That's all."

"I should have never allowed myself to feel this way."

"Why do you keep punishing yourself for the past that you can't change? You're not being fair to yourself or me, or for that matter Jack. He needs a father." He stopped, fearful that he had said too much, stepped out too far, pushed her to the brink. Drawing his eyebrows together with his hands on the bridge of his nose, he revealed his worry, his concern.

"We said we would take this slow. I need time, Clay."

Feeling defeated, he took the chicken off the grill and gathered everything onto one tray. Jack was still sleeping when they went inside, and they ate in silence, picking at the food, moving it around on their plates as though it were pieces of a puzzle that didn't fit anywhere. When it was obvious that dinner was over, Clay stood. "I'll get this," as he started to clear the table alongside Faith.

He stopped, and looked at her longingly. "Whatever happens now, I just want you to know, I will never forget last night or for that matter any of the time we've had. And I won't let you get away without a fight."

The next morning both Clay and Faith tried to be upbeat for Jack who was apparently recovered because he chattered all the way to the airport. As hard as they tried, their conversation was stilted, their emotions raw from a weekend of peaks and valleys, highs and lows. Clay couldn't remember when saying good-bye to someone was so difficult, and Faith felt a twinge of regret for having second thoughts.

⌘ ⌘ ⌘

chapter
twenty-four

Clay called the morning after she and Jack arrived home as if nothing had happened, as if he hadn't heard that she had told him they needed to put distance between them. *Hell, wasn't there plenty of that—about a thousand miles.*

"Hi Clay," she responded warmly, trying to hide the surprise in her voice.

"Thought I'd just say hello and tell you about my day so far."

"Your day?" Looking at her watch, she said, it's only eight in the morning."

"Well, I started at five this morning. The migrants really trashed the ranch this weekend. Shane and I picked up so much garbage it would make you sick. There must have been two hundred plastic water jugs, not to mention discarded clothes," he said, with disgust in his voice.

Without so much as a pause, he continued. "The drug-cartel was involved for sure because some of the stuff had been painted black. That's a dead giveaway. But we also found eight phone cards and several western union receipts. Maxwell may be dead, but it hasn't slowed down."

"Yes, like you have said many times, as long as the border is not sealed off they will continue to come," Faith offered.

"Don't you think Maxwell is the one who hooked up with the cartel to begin with, and they worked together?"

"That's what José led me to believe."

"Well, now that he's gone, the kidnapping of migrants has started again. A lot of them are being held for ransom. Not long ago, they found a shallow grave of bodies about fifty miles from here inside Mexico. Did you hear about it?" Clay asked.

"No, but I'm not surprised. Of course, Maxwell did his share of holding guys for ransom. José told me stories of the way he had guys who didn't pay killed or they cut off their fingers and toes until a relative sent money. Remember, he had the woman killed," she said, disgustingly.

"I think Maxwell was so ruthless, he may have done some of the dirty work for the cartel. They may have even split the money and the routes."

"You're right. I don't think José even knew just how connected Maxwell was to the cartel. I think that association had grown over the years as the cartel got more powerful. Guess we will never know."

"October is always the worst month because that's drug harvest time in Mexico and we aren't even close to fall. My dad was killed in October. It may be a long summer."

"I worry about you Clay."

"As long as we keep allowing this, these poor people will continue to come and to die. The only ones who win in this are the corrupt coyotes and the drug lords. We have to seal the border, and it's as if nobody listens."

"I hear it every day because I deal with the other side of it—the ones who want to do it right, to become legal citizens through a process that is in place. Only trouble is that process is broken too. It is frustratingly slow, expensive and typically bureaucratic. Of course, everyone thinks an immigration attorney only helps the illegals. Nothing could be further from the truth."

"I can see where you would be as discouraged as me. We don't make it simple."

A few minutes of small talk and their conversation ended, but Faith had trouble concentrating after she heard his voice. Though sounding upbeat; there was a hint of tension, which she attributed to their last discussion before she left Arizona.

Later in the day she checked her email, but there was nothing from him, and the next day he didn't call. *Maybe she had made the right decision; maybe he finally agreed with her.* Two more days passed, and she decided he wasn't going to fight after all. In some ways it made it easier, but she had to admit she missed him.

She looked at the picture of him she had taken on the ranch. His Stetson shielded his eyes, and she wished now she had taken one without the hat, but she saw his twisted, funny grin, his broad, muscular shoulders, and his pronounced Adam's apple. The photo with Jack showed a gentleness that would be easy to hide by others his size, but she hadn't missed it in the way he would scoop him up in his arms or his measured caution in saying just the right words to garner the little boy's attention.

A generic email couldn't hurt so she wrote a short one and pushed send, but at the end of the day there was still no answer. After dinner, she was restless, edgy, and without further thought she picked up the phone, and called Clay's number. When he didn't answer, she wondered if he had looked at his caller ID and decided to let it ring. She deserved this; after all she had said she needed time, and he was apparently giving it to her.

When the phone rang several minutes later, Faith suddenly experienced a sense of relief. No one in her family usually called this late so it could only be Clay. She raced to the phone and answered with a cheerful hello.

"Faith, this is Sheriff Noble. Have you heard from Clay in the last few days?"

"No, I haven't. I've tried emailing and calling, but he hasn't responded."

"We have a problem."

What's wrong? Tell me he's okay?"

"I don't know. It appears he's been kidnapped by the Mexican Mafia or a fringe group. We really don't know much at this point. Shane didn't see him for a couple of days, but just figured he had stayed in Tucson when he took you to the airport or had maybe even flown with you. Then this morning he found Clay's horse, still saddled, just roaming up and down the fence line.

"Shane called me and we went in the house, which had been busted into and ransacked. They stole his guns and broke into the safe, but I can't tell what else is missing. Fortunately, the inside cameras have given a description of the intruders, not that it helps us much right now because they're all obviously in Mexico and so is Clay probably."

"So he wasn't in the house when they took him?"

"No, not according to the cameras, and we don't have concrete evidence that they did, but that's the way it seems right now. Either that or they've killed him. We don't know anything more."

Shock and fear gripped Faith as she sat down to take in the news. Holding back tears, she tried to act composed, but her nerves were making it difficult. "Has this happened before? Has anyone else in the county been kidnapped?"

"Not here, but there have been several along the border, and as you know countless inside Mexico."

"But why Clay? Why would they want him?"

"All I can figure is money, and the fact that he joined the Minute Men after his dad was killed and did a little work with them along the border. Other than that we just don't know. I'd feel better if we got a ransom note or some kind of communication, but we have nothing to go on."

"Can you see faces on the tape the cameras got?"

"Yes, they're actually pretty clear. There's three of them, and plenty of tattoos to identify somebody by if we had anyone who could help us, but we don't."

"This is a long shot, Sheriff, but as you know I have a client in prison for being Maxwell's deputy. He's been in that area a lot and knows the bad guys. Could you send me a copy of the tape and I'll pay him a visit. Maybe he can ID some of them—that might at least tell us what element we are dealing with."

"I can overnight it in the morning, but Faith, you know we may be too late. These guys are ruthless. They kill for the hell of it, because they enjoy it. And if they don't kill them right away they torture them. I've heard of them peeling their fingernails off with pliers or burning them with torches from automotive body shops. It's not uncommon for them to cut off a guy's testicles or behead him and send the head back to his loved ones."

"Stop! I don't want to hear anymore. I don't want to think about it. We have to find him. As soon as I get the tape I'll go see my client. Then I'm flying there."

"I'm not sure what good that would do, Faith. I called you because I wanted to see if you had by any small chance heard from him, that maybe he had been able to get a call out or something. That's why I called. I didn't want to upset you, and don't really know what the relationship is between you two, except Clay talks about you a lot."

"Send me the tape, Sheriff. I want to help. Will you please call me the minute you hear anything, please?"

"Yes, I'll be in touch if I know anything. Good-night."

Faith was shaking when she hung up the phone. Pacing, she didn't know what to do, where to turn. If only she could talk to him and know he was alive. If only she had told him she loved him, a fact that had become abundantly clear to her over the course of the conversation with the sheriff. She might never get the chance to tell him. What a fool she had been.

⌘   ⌘   ⌘

The note came to the sheriff's office the next day, followed by a grainy black and white picture of Clay blindfolded with his hands tied behind his back. It was impossible to tell where they were keeping him, but the message was loud and clear. The kidnappers were demanding money and lots of it.

Sheriff Noble read the scribbling carefully several times. This was no flash kidnapping. They weren't going to release him quickly, and they were serious; he had no doubt. If he didn't get a million dollars and the deed to the ranch to them within the week, they would start cutting off his fingers, and he knew they meant what they said. He called Faith and gave her the news.

"I'll get the money. Did you send me the tape? Oh sheriff, at least he's alive."

"Maybe, you can never be sure with these guys. More often than not, families pay the money and they kill the victim anyway; sometimes they're already dead when the money is delivered."

"I have to be hopeful. If all they want is money then we can handle that."

"Who knows what they really want? But one thing I know is I hate like hell to give them anything, but this time I'm too close to the victim to take chances. I'll call you later."

Later was sooner than she thought. A second letter had come mid-morning, and this time it gave the terrible, gut-wrenching insight that nobody wanted to know. Faith was involved more than she realized, maybe even the reason for the abduction. The note read: *We saw the bitch lawyer with our man here. We've been watching. Just missed the boy, but we'll take the cowboy instead. She shouldn't have messed with Maxwell. We'll get his revenge.*

When the sheriff had finished reading the letter to Faith, she was hysterical. "This is my fault. They have to be connected to Maxwell's group—that's clear. Oh, my gosh. I'll get the money today. I'm not sure how because I can't put that much together if I empty every savings account I have, plus Jack's portion of the life insurance he got from his father. But, I'll think of something. Maybe my father can help or my boss."

"Wait, Faith. Let's talk when you get here tomorrow night. I don't trust the phones. What time is your flight?"

"Provided I get the tape early, it's more than a four hour drive to the prison so the earliest flight I can take doesn't get me into Tucson until nine fifteen."

"I'll have my deputy pick you up, and you'll stay at my house where you'll have round the clock security. Let's hope your guy can help."

⌘　⌘　⌘

It wasn't a visiting day, but Faith was able to convince the warden of the urgency of her visit with the information she shared.

At first, José was less than forthcoming and preoccupied with his upcoming marriage to Tami, who he described as a beautiful beauty operator from Houston who sent him long, loving letters.

After seeing her photo Faith understood why she didn't call herself a stylist. She must have worked at the Curl Up & Dye, she surmised. Nonetheless, José was totally enamored by her, and babbled on and on about what she had selected to wear to her wedding, and how he would be connected by telephone, and on and on. She tried to listen patiently, knowing the importance of building rapport with this kind of person. She had done it during the trial, but memories are short in prison. *Her wedding* were the optimal words as he explained that her children and a minister would be at the church, and help her celebrate afterwards.

"What if I try to convince the warden to let you get married in a room here?"

His face lit up, and his bad eye moved erratically, and he got so excited that he began to stutter. "Y…Y…You cou…could do that?"

"Well, I can try. Some prisons allow it, some don't. But I won't even think about it if you don't cooperate with me. You should also remember that I can write a letter or two when it comes time for your first parole hearing. Right now, that letter certainly wouldn't be positive."

"J…Just tell me what you want from me."

"I want you to look at these pictures that I had made from a tape and tell me if you know these guys. Don't even think about lying," she warned, pulling the photos from a brown envelope. She laid them out on the table and waited, watching José's expression change from forced stoicism to a visible frown. "Well?"

"Yeah, I know all of them. They're out and I'm in this shithole."

"So, tell me everything you know, including names."

Pointing to the guy on the left with the scar over his right eye, his arms riddled with tattoos, he said, "This is Rafael Torres—he was one of Maxwell's lieutenants, who had a cushy job in the Naco area because he paid off a Border Patrol agent early on who helped him. Actually, the BP was on our payroll. Anyway, I'm sure when Maxwell went to the pen, the gravy train ran out so he's probably ganged up with the Mexican Mafia or started a syndicate of his own. Not the brightest star in the sky as Maxwell would say. I'm sure he needs money because he's not smart enough to run a big operation on his own.

"Now, this second guy is a different story. Maxwell called him "the wizard," because he was always coming up with ways to screw people around. He's also the most unscrupulous, which is why Maxwell liked him. I've seen him rip the skin off a guy's back for smarting off to him. He's strong as an ox and sly as a fox. See that scar all the way down his face? Guy took a knife to him, and the wizard came right back, took it away from him and stuck it square in his heart. Blood was running down his face on to the other guys. I remember it like it was yesterday."

What seemed like a bolt of lightning went up Faith's spine, and she could almost visualize the torture that this guy could impose on Clay. "Keep going; what's his name?"

"Emilio Cortez. He's called M, pronounced 'eme' for short. The last guy is a clown. Hector Flores. He's just M's flunky. Meaner than shit but can't carry through on anything without fucking it up. Oh, sorry."

"So did you ever see any of these guys after you were arrested? Think hard, this is important."

A grin came to his face that had become almost pasty after his months in prison, quite a contrast to the tan on top of his natural coloring that he carried when Faith first met him. "I never said anything, but M and Hector were at the trial the day I testified. You should have seen the look they gave me. Of course, they always wear those dark glasses, which they think makes them look suave. M can dress up really good, and he likes to strut his stuff. He probably thought Maxwell was going to beat the rap and he would look good for being there for support—probably get a promotion, like my job since it was plain I was coming here no matter what."

"So in other words, he would know what everyone at the trial looked like and who they were." Suddenly, she remembered seeing the two guys. It made sense now; they were the ones at the back of the courtroom.

"Exactly, and he has a photographic memory, which is why he remembers everybody who has ever crossed the border while he's working. Hell, all those guys look alike to me when they cross, carrying the same shit, wearing the same shabby clothes, but to M they were like faces on a billboard. If one ever tried to stiff him without paying, he'd just as soon shoot him in the back as eat a tamale, and the guy loves his tamales and beer," he said with a chuckle. "I never liked him because I didn't trust him. Always figured he would stab me in the back to get further up Maxwell's list. So why are you asking me all this?"

"Because they've taken a friend of mine hostage—kidnapped him and want a large ransom. The guy they kidnapped was at the trial, and they saw us together." She didn't elaborate on the fact that she had spent the weekend with him and that they had made passionate and unabashed love for an entire night or that she missed him terribly and was scared beyond belief for his life. Instead, she asked him what the reason could be that they chose him. Could it be for money, revenge or both? Or was it something else entirely.

"Where does this guy live?"

She explained that he had a twenty-five thousand acre ranch at the Arizona-Mexico border that he had inherited when his father was killed more than likely by the drug-cartel.

"Then I'd say it's a combination of money and revenge—both against you and him. They probably think he knows too much. Did you know there are a couple of tunnels on some of those ranches?"

Shocked, Faith encouraged, "No, tell me more."

"Hey, what's in this for me? If anyone ever finds out I told you this shit, they'll come looking for me."

"Well, they'll have a hard time getting in here just to visit, and I doubt they'll want to join you."

"Yeah, but if any one of them ever gets in here accidently—you know, like I did, then they'll kill me."

"Look, we'll cross that bridge when we come to it. I can always get you moved."

"I don't want to be moved. Tami moved from Alabama just to be close to me."

"You're here because of me. You could have been in a Supermax, but I convinced the court to put you here. Come on, tell me about the tunnels." She looked at her watch. This was taking longer than she anticipated and she had a plane to catch, but she needed to find out as much as she could. She had caught José at a weak time, almost vulnerable, because of the upcoming wedding. The next time, he might not be so agreeable or helpful.

"The cartels and Maxwell's group worked together to carve out several tunnels from inside Mexico through to some of the ranches. They've been there three or four years. One of the ranchers found out about it—discovered it one day. Never got to share the news though—Tito blew him away, right there on his own ranch."

Faith gasped, and then tried to cover her astonishment. That had to be Clay's dad, although Clay had never talked about the extent of his wounds, of how exactly he was shot or how bad the scene must have been. This also meant there was a tunnel on the property, and by all indications neither he nor Shane had any idea. "Who's Tito?"

"Oh, he's dead. Apparently, he was messing around with one of the women married to a cartel leader. Didn't go over so well, when the lead dog caught them in bed in some sleazy hotel, all wrapped up in each other's arms, naked. Next day, the owner found both of them lying in a pool of their own blood. The gunman had cut off Tito's balls and stuffed them in his mouth. Must have been a little guy or the story is exaggerated." He laughed heartier than Faith could ever remember.

"So where do these guys—M, and the other two stay most of the time? Where could we find them?"

"They pass freely along the border, plus they have fancy homes in Mexico, but they spend time in both places. But let me warn you. The Mexican police are on their side. They've been paid off so don't go expecting to try to get their help. They'll take your money and double-cross you in a second, plus they'll give the word to M in a flash, and they'll take your friend deeper and deeper or kill him, if they haven't already."

"Could they hide someone in the tunnel?"

"Sure, you can't believe the little tentacles in those tunnels. You could hide a guy for years."

"How do they breathe?"

"They don't for long. I didn't say you could hide him **alive** for that long."

She thought she had heard enough as she stood to leave. Gathering up the photos, she carefully slid them back into the envelope. "Thanks, José. You've been helpful."

"You won't forget about the wedding, will you?" He had a hopeful, almost boyish look on his face. "I want to tell Tami on Friday when she comes to visit."

"I'd hold off on that until we find out the warden's decision. I don't want her disappointed, but I'll do everything I can. She must be a heck of a woman."

"Oh, she is. The best. Just wish I could show her how much I love her—you know what I mean, don't you?"

"I believe I understand what you're saying, but I can't help you with that," thinking it might take a lot of Viagra for poor old José when that day finally came.

⌘　⌘　⌘

On the plane to Tucson, Faith had a lot to sort through in her mind and in her notes. *Geez, it seemed that Maxwell was working from the grave.* She had wanted to talk with the sheriff before she took off, but he had warned her about the phones. She was a little nervous about the officer picking her up at the airport. If these guys were as brazen and ruthless as José had described, they might know she was arriving and have a foil there waiting to kidnap her as well. Most of all she was worried about Jack and grateful that her mom had agreed to come on short notice and take him home with her to East Texas until this ordeal was over. Suddenly, she was in a cold sweat. This had gotten crazy.

When she stepped off the plane and found the baggage claim, she looked up to see the sheriff himself. She didn't know when she had been so glad to see a man in uniform. As he came forward, she could see the concern in his face, the tiny lines on his tanned and weathered face that she figured had developed over the last four years as a result of a demanding job, a dissolved marriage, and too much sun. He was too young to look this tired.

Taking her luggage he smiled forlornly, "I thought I'd just pick you up myself. Figured this would be a good time to talk on the drive back."

"Thanks Sheriff, but is that the only reason or were you worried I might go with the wrong person in a stolen uniform?"

"Clay told me you were the strongest, smartest lady he had ever met. Now, I believe him. Here's my car. I get to park in a special place." He winked. "One of the few perks of the job, except a free cup of coffee now and then. Don't believe those doughnut jokes," he said, laughing. Faith was glad to see him loosen up to some extent because the news she had for him would set that lightheartedness back a few hundred years.

When they were safely in the car she began telling him what José had related to her, relying on her notes rather than sheer memory. She didn't want to miss anything. When she reached the part about the tunnels, the sheriff banged his right hand on the car dash. "Shit, how did we miss that all these years? We should have known Dwight—Clay's father had stumbled on something. We just kept telling ourselves that he approached the wrong person coming across his land, but now it all makes sense. He discovered what they couldn't afford for him to know, so they killed him and we were all too stupid to figure it out."

"Don't be so hard on yourself. You couldn't have known. Maybe he didn't. Maybe your original theory is right. Clay obviously didn't know about it either."

"Nope, we've been outsmarted. That's the whole damn deal. They think differently than us. They're just too freaking cunning for us stupid Anglos. Now, they have Clay, and their tunnel, and that's not enough. They want our money and your first born if they could get him."

A shudder went through Faith remembering that the note had mentioned Jack in so many words. Thank God that hadn't happened. She didn't know what she would do. It was bad enough that they had Clay, but her Jack, her little boy; nothing could ever be that bad. At least Clay was strong. He could defend himself as much as was possible. But not Jack. If they ever got him, she knew she would never see him again. She was worried to the point of nausea that the same might be true of Clay.

"There is some good news. I didn't want to tell you on the phone. Homeland Security is involved and they have agreed to provide the money, albeit it, slightly bogus. Anyway, it's the best bogus you'll ever find so before they realize it's worthless, hopefully, we'll have Clay back on this side. Trouble is, they sent the note demanding money, but they didn't give us details about how, when and where. Now, it's just a waiting game—who knows how long?"

Two days passed and no one had heard from the abductors. Faith was numb with fear, and the longer she waited the more she believed the worst was happening to Clay. She could only imagine what he was going through, if he were even alive. All she could do was pace, and call to check on Jack. From their conversations he appeared to be totally content with his grandparents, who she knew were doting over him. Nevertheless, she couldn't help but feel guilty being away. This, however, was something she had to do, for Clay, for herself.

Finally at the three o'clock shift change of the third day, a call came in to the sheriff. The kidnappers wanted their demands met and they wanted them that night, but they had added one major kicker and that was they wanted the *bitch lawyer* as they called her to make the drop-off.

Sheriff Noble didn't know if they were aware that Faith was there, but assumed they did. With that stipulation, however, he needed time for ICE to bring in a female agent to act in her place. No way was he going to let Faith actually do the drop, but the agent needed to act like her, walk like her and have an incredibly close resemblance. Any diversion from a perfect plan could cost lives, and not just Clay's. He stalled, telling the caller the lawyer hadn't completed drawing up the deed although the fake document was sitting on his desk.

This was a risk as well, and double-crossing whoever the kidnappers were was going to cause problems down the line, but he would deal with that as it came. Right now, the only thing he could handle was the present predicament. Every day brought new ones at the border so he had learned early to deal with the most pressing, the most imminent.

"I want the captive handed over to us simultaneously as the money and deed are exchanged. And it has to be on U.S. soil," the sheriff demanded.

Silence gripped the other end of the line, and for a minute he thought he had killed the deal, but it had to be that way or the captors would run with the money and Clay and continue upping their orders. "Deal?"

After another lengthy pause, he could hear conversation in the background, and then finally the answer he had been waiting for as well as instructions where the exchange would be made, which ironically was probably the very place they took Clay from his horse days earlier. Now, he and ICE had until sunset the next day to get it all together, but first they had to find the perfect match for Faith, and they had to do it fast.

Within an hour, investigators had entered in Faith's weight, height, color of hair, eyes and other pertinent data, and the databank came back with a female agent working out of southern California near Tijuana, which was good news because she could be there early the next morning and spend time with Faith, learning every important nuance. The only drawback was that the agent had greenish blue eyes and needed blue contacts before she arrived in Arizona, which would take a few extra hours.

The following day was one of the longest days Faith could remember. If things had been different she would have enjoyed Petra Morales, the Border Patrol agent who would be her decoy. Lively and perky, Petra was a few years younger and about ten pounds thinner than Faith, which she explained was necessary because the bullet proof vest would add the difference, and her hair was not so wispy. All in all Faith thought they shared enough likeness that at night no one's suspicions would be raised. Their coloring was almost identical, and Petra explained her mother was from Denmark and her father Mexican American, so she was a nice blend of the two.

She had what Faith laughed and said was a wicked sense of humor, and acted as though the assignment was just another day at the office. The agent wasn't nervous, or if she was she didn't show it. Only once before had she been called on to do a similar task, but even then it wasn't as dangerous as the one she was facing.

As the hours clicked off, Faith called and asked the sheriff to allow her to accompany the group making the exchange in one of the other ICE vehicles, but his answer had been an emphatic no. Actually, she heard the ICE agent in charge in the background scream, "HELL NO!"

She understood their caution, but desperately wanted to be there for Clay. The only concession was Sheriff Noble promising he would have a deputy bring her to headquarters as soon as possible.

As day ushered in the first illusion of nightfall, ICE agents and the sheriff and two deputies were in the field posed for the exchange. Harris Noble found an overpowering sense of relief as he saw the truck pull up at sunset with Clay sitting blindfolded in the back seat. He had no way of knowing what condition he was in, but he thought he saw a slight movement, which would indicate he was definitely alive and not just propped up to give the disguise. No one moved as the vehicles faced each other from fifty feet away, and time seemed to stand still until darkness fell.

Four men of various sizes and shapes exited the kidnapper truck, two holding Clay by either arm as he struggled to walk with his feet tied together. It had been a long, bumpy two hour drive from the cave located in a canyon somewhere in northern Mexico where they had kept him blindfolded and tied up for almost two weeks. He had actually seen nothing during that time, and eaten very little, but what concerned him the most was that he had heard his captors laughing and talking about the *bitch lawyer* being the drop-off person. He would rather die than put her in harm's way. The apparent leader of the group shouted for her to come alone, but the lead ICE agent hollered that one agent would accompany her to receive Clay while she handed over the money.

"No deal!"

The ICE agent in charge turned and searched Agent Morales' eyes for an answer. He didn't like the idea, but he didn't want to lose this now. "Let me go. I'm okay with it," she assured him.

"Okay, we've got your back," he said, begrudgingly as she opened her door and eased out. Simultaneously, the agents and sheriffs' deputies opened their doors and crouched behind them, looking straight ahead at the armed gunmen holding Clay.

When she stepped up to the kidnappers, she took the dirty scarf away from Clay's eyes and looked squarely at him, waiting for his eyes to adjust. Slowly she reached for his hands and cut the ties from them and then his feet. As soon as he could focus, he knew the agent wasn't Faith, and he felt relief. He was free to walk, and she motioned for him to do so, wondering why the gunmen were being so cooperative. For the first time, she was sweating, and she didn't know if it was out of fear or the vest.

She was armed, but because the gun was hidden, she felt defenseless. Suddenly, when Clay had taken no more than five or six steps, one of the gunmen lunged forward and grabbed her. Another jumped to help, but when he did, he fell, knocking her to the ground, a mistake that probably saved her life and cost him his.

Gunfire broke out as agents hailed bullets at all four men, while deputies covered Clay and continued shooting, dragging him to the truck. Then the night grew abruptly quiet and all four kidnappers lay bleeding and still. Agent Morales pushed one of the dead men off of her, and stood, miraculously unscathed, given the flying bullets. And in the mayhem she had managed to retrieve her gun, and was able to shoot the first gunman who attacked her.

Seeing a trail of blood to his truck, Sheriff Noble raced over to find both his deputy and Clay bleeding. He couldn't tell exactly where the blood was coming from, but radioed for two ambulances. By the time the paramedics had arrived, he determined that neither appeared to be in life threatening situations, but Clay had been shot at least once in the arm and the deputy had wounds to both arms and legs.

A quick assessment of the gunmen indicated that they were the same men on the camera in Clay's house plus one other who had no identification. "I'll clean up here, boss, and call the coroner, if you want to go to the hospital in Douglas with these guys," one of the deputies volunteered.

"First, I have a young lady waiting to see Clay that I promised to retrieve. I'm sure it's been a long night for her. Agent Morales did great, but I don't think she takes the place of the lawyer when it comes to Clay," he said winking at the female agent and his deputy.

⌘   ⌘   ⌘

Relief was too small a word to describe Faith's emotions when she saw the smile on Sheriff Nobles' face. "He's okay, Faith, but he took a hit to his arm so he's at the hospital in Douglas. Grab what you'll need for the night because I'm sure he's not letting you get away this time."

On the drive to the hospital, the sheriff detailed the shoot-out, obviously proud of his men, and satisfied that the two agencies had worked in perfect unison. "Your decoy was remarkable. She's one tough gal. Sort of reminds me of you. Oh, I forgot; she was supposed to," he said, smiling, but suddenly looking extremely tired and haggard; the stress had taken its toll, and the release of tension had left him drained. "Do you know what your plans are now? I mean will you be staying a few days?"

"I'm hoping to take Clay home with me, if I can convince him."

"I think that is a great idea. I've already sent one of my men over to clean up the mess these guys made at the house. I'm sure Clay will want to determine what they took besides his guns. They cleaned those out, but what he had in the safe, only he knows. I do know most of the important stuff was in the lockbox at the bank, because a long time ago he gave me the other key in case he was gone and needed something. I checked on it and it's untouched."

"Any idea how long he'll have to be in the hospital?"

"Wouldn't even guess. Tell you the truth, I couldn't tell how bad the wound was because he's a guy who handles pain well or tries to anyway."

Faith looked away momentarily, knowing that unfortunately she had seen another side of him when she had been the one causing the hurt, a tender side that ached when he was wronged. She never wanted to do that to him again, and hoped he would give her the chance to make it right.

Seeing him at the hospital for the first time took her back. She hadn't expected him to be so pale and wan, thin and gaunt, but all the tubes and machines were what really scared her. The nurse must have noticed her stunned expression because he quickly introduced himself and explained that Clay had just returned from surgery. The bullet was lodged deep in his upper arm, and in order to do no further damage, it had to come out without delay.

"He's a lucky man, another four or so inches, and he would be a dead man. That's how close it was to the heart. He'll be okay; just needs some rest. Tomorrow morning, the sight of a pretty woman, and he'll be on the mend."

"Thank you. Can I stay right here?"

"Sure, I'll get you a pillow and blanket. I can bring in a more comfortable chair if you like."

"I'm fine. I want to be right here when he wakes up." Her thoughts took her to other times when she had sat in similar settings, holding Tyler's hand, wiping his brow, and praying that the cancer would retreat. It hadn't, of course, but now she had the chance to support another man that she had grown to love and who she knew loved her.

She had almost lost him, first from her foolish decisions, and then by heinous acts by evil men, but this time she had heard the words, *he'll be okay*. Those precious words were like soft music from an old violin. She reached and took his hand. It felt smaller than it had two weeks before when he had traced the lines of her body with his fingers, and brushed her moist hair from her face after he had brought her to the pinnacle of fulfillment and passion. Watching him sleep, his breath uneven, reminded her of how different he looked now than when he had curled up next to her, satisfied and spent from their love making. She smiled, anxious for him to wake and get well, to take her to those heights again.

⌘ ⌘ ⌘

She was sleeping in the chair when he awoke, and despite his discomfort, he smiled broadly and gazed at her face. He could have stayed that way, just looking at her, much longer, but the shift change brought still another nurse, this time a loud, disagreeable one who obviously had rather have been anywhere but on duty at seven in the morning. Startled, Faith woke and saw Clay trying to smile, as the portly nurse rearranged his pillow that didn't need it, and changed out the IV.

"Good Morning, Faith," he said, his voice raspy and scratchy.

Jumping up, she put her hand to his forehead and brushed back his hair, which was dirty and unkempt from his long ordeal. "I was so worried, Clay." She paused, her hands trembling. "I thought I would never say these words to another man. "I love you." She kissed him gently on the cheek. "Whatever, we need to do, we'll make this work."

Smiling he reached for her hand, noticing immediately that she was no longer wearing her wedding ring. "I love you, too. Even if I had to nearly get killed for you to realize it, I'll take it."

"Oh Clay, I realized it earlier, but I was just being stubborn."

"I don't want to disturb you two, but I need to check on the patient," the doctor said, walking into the small private room. He looked more like a professional wrestler than a doctor, but much too old for the ring. What little hair he had made a circle around his head, but for some strange reason that Faith couldn't quite understand, he had dyed it a motley brown, or at least it had come out that way when someone had applied the coloring. With hands the size of salad plates, he pulled back the cover over Clay's arm, undid the bandage and checked the wound. "I saw a lot worse in Viet Nam; you're just damn lucky those guys didn't have machine guns. Must have been amateurs. The cartel would have blown you off the face of the earth."

"When can I go home?"

"Couple of days probably, unless some kind of infection sets in. But it looks okay right now. The emergency room doctor did a good job. Just out of med school, but he's okay. Everybody needs to start somewhere, and end somewhere. Guess this is where I'll call it quits. The nurse will dress this shortly. See you tomorrow."

When the door eased closed, Faith smiled. "Great bedside manner. You aren't jealous at the way I looked at him, are you?"

"Stop. It hurts to laugh. I think I have a few bruised ribs. The first night for some reason, my captors felt the need to beat the shit out of me. Excuse my French, but I really don't know any better way to describe it. But, I'm extremely lucky to have my fingers because that was what they kept saying they would do to me. Cut one off each day. I really don't know why they didn't. Maybe because after the first threat, I sat on my hands. Not really, but I sure thought about it."

"What did you eat?"

"I'm not certain. Remember, I couldn't see so the best I could tell from the taste it was mostly beans and rice, but one day some awful meat that made me sick as a horse. Come to think of it, it might have been horsemeat. A terrified look came over his face, just as he said the word horse. "Did they kill Lee?"

"No, he's fine. Everything is fine, except they stole your guns and whatever was in your safe."

His face clouded over. "The only thing in the safe was my dad's coin collection. I hate to lose that for sentimental reasons. Same way with the guns, but I won't be needing them anyway. I'm selling the ranch, Faith, even if I have to take a lot less than it's worth. I can't stay here. Not now. I would never ask you or Jack to ever visit me here."

"I told you we would make this work, but I'm glad you want to sell the ranch. They wanted Jack; did you know that?"

"Yes. I heard them talking. Most of it was in Spanish, and I guess they figured I didn't understand, but of course I did. It appears they had been shadowing me for several months, staking out the place. One of the guys saw me at the trial; then when you came, that was the icing on the cake. They saw the chance to hurt both of us, and they got me while I was out riding by myself. It's a miracle they didn't try to get us all while you and Jack were there. They were a little disorganized or they probably would have."

"Sheriff Noble certainly lived up to his name. He is, indeed, a noble man," Faith explained, praising him not only for good work but for his friendship to Clay. For the next two hours they talked about the chain of events and Faith's visit to see José, and all that his conversation had revealed. The biggest shock to Clay was the story about the tunnels, and how the discovery of one had brought his dad's fate.

To change the mood, Faith laughingly told him about the pending prison wedding, and reminded herself that she must call or email the warden that very day. She knew José was eagerly awaiting the news. When Clay appeared tired after visiting with her and then the sheriff, she kissed him and encouraged him to sleep, promising she would return with the biggest hamburger she could find and a chocolate shake.

"Now, that I'm not worried about your safety, here are the keys to my truck. This way you can come and go at your own will. You're still welcome to stay at my place until you fly out or whatever plans you two make," the sheriff offered.

"Did you get any sleep last night?" She asked with sincere concern.

"Like a baby. Good as new. How about you?"

"Not much, but that's okay. The nurses kept coming in and out. You know if you want to rest, a hospital is not the place. Clay was restless, and they must have woken him five or six times. Maybe tonight both of us can rest better."

⌘　⌘　⌘

chapter
twenty-five

Clay agreed to fly to Dallas with Faith, and they left as soon as he was dismissed from the hospital and could pack enough clothes for a couple of weeks. While recovering he had made careful notes and instructions for Shane who had visited him every day, and called his neighbor with the news he was selling the ranch. Though he made no commitment, the rancher neighbor showed interest in the land, provided he could get it below market value. Clay didn't tell the neighbor that right now the way he was feeling he might pay him to take it.

At the airport, the couple was met by Patrick and Sue, who quickly took to Clay. "As soon as you are up to it, Clay, we'll have to share a few bottles of wine. I understand you can teach me a lot," Patrick said.

Clay blushed, "I doubt that, but we can certainly exchange views. Faith tells me you're quite knowledgeable. This arm won't keep me from lifting a glass with my good hand. Matter of fact, I could use one now."

"Well, let's go home and uncork a few," Faith said, smiling at Clay. Turning, she asked hopefully, "Are Mom and Jack there yet? Mom said on the phone this morning that they would be. I missed Jack so much. Although he was in good hands, I couldn't help but worry."

"She and Jack are waiting at your house," Sue said, reassuringly. "They arrived right before we left to pick you up. He wanted to know if Clay brought a pony," Sue explained, laughing. "I took the liberty of telling him probably not. Thought it best to get that part out of the way before your arrival."

Clay gave Faith a worried look. "I should have brought him something."

"That isn't necessary. He needs to understand that he doesn't get presents every time he sees you."

"Yeah, but until I win him over, it might be a good idea."

"I think you've already done that. Maybe tomorrow you two can continue to bond while I'm at work."

"I'm just a little worried about staying there. This time it's on his turf. I don't want him to resent my time with you."

Patrick spoke up. "He's already been talking about you non-stop. Besides we've all said a few things to prepare him for the changes that may be heading his way," he said with a wink in Faith's direction.

Clay took Faith's hand. "We are still going to take things slowly, and not rush anyone's feelings or raise any concerns. As soon as I am mended I need to get back to Arizona, and take care of unfinished business. That will give everyone here a little breathing room."

"Who says we need room to breathe?" Faith asked, smiling and leaning into him as they reached Patrick's Land Rover. She knew Clay was playing it carefully, and she appreciated his guarded attitude about Jack, but now for the first time she wondered if he was having cold feet about the direction their relationship had taken.

In the car Patrick offered to pick up Jack and Clay for lunch the following day, and Clay jumped at the chance to have time with Faith's father. This would give him a chance to determine how her family was feeling about another man coming into her life.

When they arrived at Faith's, Jack and Alice met them at the door, both sporting huge grins and offering equally full-size hugs. Jack spoke first. "Can I see where the mean men shot you?"

"Later, Jack. It's still pretty sore," Faith chimed in, hugging her son.

But his attention was on Clay. "Wow, you're like a real cowboy!"

Clay grinned. "Without the Indians. So how've you been, sport?"

"Good, are you going to be my daddy?"

The room became instantly quiet and nobody seemed to be able to penetrate the silence except Clay who knelt down on one knee and looked Jack squarely in the eye. "How would you feel about that if it happened someday?"

"Okay, Grammy says I need a daddy and that Mommy needs you." Clay smiled at Alice, who at that moment had a horrified look on her face. He gave her an understanding and reassuring look that said out of the mouths of babes and grandmothers all is forgiven.

Turning back to Jack he continued, "Well, only you can decide the daddy part. Nobody can ever take your daddy's place. You were his long before me, but given the opportunity, I might just make a really good stand in."

"Okay," and then Jack became bored with the whole subject and raced off to get a toy.

"Well, that was a real eye-opening homecoming," Faith offered, hugging Alice, who she knew was worried that she had been outed by her grandson. "It okay, Mom; you've never been one to keep your opinions to yourself, even with a five year old." Her response broke the tension, as Patrick came back into the room with a bottle of wine, obviously not out of hearing range of the entire happening. "I propose a toast to Clay's recovery and for Alice's as well." Everyone laughed easily. "Dad, will you put Clay's luggage in the back guest room while I put mine away, and then let's go out on the patio, and enjoy this vino."

⌘   ⌘   ⌘

The next morning Faith rose earlier than normal, trying not to disturb anyone but Alice who joined her for coffee. She knew her Mom had plans to leave early to drive home, so she wanted to spend a few uninterrupted minutes visiting with her. While they talked they shared the task of making blueberry muffins, which they had done so many treasured times when Faith was growing up. They both loved the smell of the warm muffins as they came out of the oven, and the memories they evoked. How many times had they talked about boys or grades or other issues that plagued Faith like any typical teenager as they cooked them or some decadent dessert and then shared it guiltily, both feeling better after spending time together? "I like Clay. All kidding aside. He's good with Jack."

Faith smiled, "Yeah, he's good with me too. You know, Mom, I never thought I could love anyone like I loved Tyler."

"Loving Clay doesn't lessen your love for Tyler. That will never change. But there's room in your heart for both; Tyler understood that long before you did."

"I know. I was scared to face the whole love thing, and in some ways I still am. But it seems so natural loving him, just like it did with Tyler."

"You'll do just fine. You always have. Okay, Hon, this old woman has miles to go before she rests, and I have a pretty good man waiting for me too." She stood and gave Faith a kiss on the cheek. "Call me."

"Be careful, Mom. Where's your bag?"

"Everything's already in the car. See you soon."

"Thanks for everything. Drive safe—and the speed limit," knowing that the last part of her request would go unheeded. Alice was on her third speeding ticket for the year. The only time she drove the speed limit was when Jack was in the car, and even then, she fudged a few miles an hour. She had acquired so many tickets in the last few years that Faith refused to help her although as a lawyer it would have been easy. She figured that would encourage her to continue, and Alice needed very little encouragement for anything she felt strongly about—and getting from point A to point B fast was something she believed in.

She waved to her mom from the front door, and then scribbled a note to Clay and Jack to accompany the muffins she covered and left on the counter. *You boys enjoy and behave. Don't eat so much you make yourselves sick. I needed to get to work and catch up. See you this afternoon. Love ya.*

Faith couldn't believe the pile of mail and papers on her desk, but before she even had a chance to look at any of it, Mr. Jackson stuck his head in the door. He was always at the office before any of his partners or employees and Faith often enjoyed a conversation with him before beginning her day. Of course, he wanted to know every detail and even quizzed her some about Clay.

If anyone would be tentative about the relationship she was afraid it might be Mr. Jackson. She really wasn't even worried about her in-laws. Her mother-in-law had reassured her countless times that they understood that the day would come when she would remarry, but her boss had loved Tyler like a son as well, and she knew he was nervous about her falling for someone else. He had never gotten over losing Tyler, and he showed it perhaps more than anyone else Faith knew. Carefully, she relayed the last week's events as she broached the subject of Clay.

"So what's your feeling for this guy? I mean, you haven't known him very long."

Faith smiled, "I didn't know Tyler anywhere close to this long before I knew he was the one for me."

He slipped wearily into the chair in front of her desk, and sat his coffee cup on a coaster that he found after rummaging under the mound of paperwork. "Don't mind me, Faith. You know I want the best for you, but I worry, plus I don't want to lose you from the firm. You're the best damn lawyer I have."

"You know you and Mrs. Jackson will always be special to me, no matter who else is in my life. To tell you the truth, I don't know where this will all lead, but to be fair to you, I'm quite fond of him, so only time will tell."

"That's all I can ask from you. Glad you're back." He rose, his shoulders sagging, and Faith knew it pained him to think about any changes to her life or his firm for that matter.

"Hopefully, I won't have any more exciting adventures for awhile. And thanks for understanding."

Giving her a backhanded wave, he took his leave and sauntered down to his office where his secretary, who had just arrived, was trying to straighten it enough to make it presentable for visiting clients. Faith laughed. The man didn't have many flaws, but office tidiness certainly wasn't high on his list of virtues. Law books were strewn everywhere as were stacks of papers and journals.

The problem was he knew where everything was, which drove his secretary crazy. About all he would allow her to touch was the out box and his yesterday's dirty cups of coffee, which he left not just in his office but everyone else's he entered with a cup in his hand. She had worked for him for more than twenty years so she was used to his ways, but that never stopped her from trying to change them or to refrain from giving him grief about them. It was an office joke about the way she huffed and puffed each morning while she looked for ways to make his office more desirable, and Faith and some of the other senior attorneys were convinced he did it to aggravate her.

Once years before, just to play a prank, Tyler had scattered ten cups around the room and post-it notes on tables and chairs just to hear her rant. Everyone got a laugh out of it, except her of course. But she was a terrific secretary or administrative assistant, which she insisted on being called. Every employee knew if something needed proofed or checked to take it to Doris. She could find a missing comma like a knitter could find a dropped stitch.

Before Faith could read all her mail, the phone started ringing. The first was from an old friend from college who wanted to invite her to a baby shower, and the second was from the warden where José was incarcerated. He had received her email and just wanted to confirm that he had agreed to allow José and Tami to tie the knot in the employee break room.

"Hey, do you know the difference between a love bird and a jail bird?" He asked, laughing loudly into the phone. Not giving Faith a chance to venture a guess, he said, "Love birds can fly away!"

Then he told her that although the wedding would have vending machines and an old refrigerator as a backdrop the couple was elated with his decision. "I don't think you should miss this. You may not get another chance for an opportunity like this. Heck, they might even ask you to be matron of honor."

Amused, she thanked him, but gave her regrets. "Sorry, I'm afraid these nuptials will have to go forward without my presence, but I promise to send a small gift for the bride when I get her address. What do you suggest?"

"Maybe a vibrator!" His voice boomed with laughter.

"Where's your compassion," she teased.

"That was never in my job description."

She and the warden had actually become friends over the course of José's short stay, and they shared a common sense of humor relating to some of the occurrences at the prison. He assured her he would email her about the ceremony and freeze her a leftover Twinkie from the reception.

The next call was the biggest surprise. She recognized the voice immediately although it had been years since she had talked to Jeff, her reporter friend in Boston. The last time he called was right after her wedding when he had begrudgingly offered his congratulations to her and Tyler, with a warning to Tyler that he best be good or he would be ready to step in and take her away. Although he had said it teasingly, Faith knew he meant it. She liked Jeff and admired his journalistic abilities, but from the very beginning he simply wasn't her type, and she knew it, although he didn't want to accept it.

The time they had spent as friends during her father's trial had been fun, and in a roundabout way, each had contributed to the other's success although that wasn't what the friendship was about. The trial itself had given Jeff the story he needed to show his bosses he wasn't just another fledgling reporter from the Midwest, and it was almost as if Jeff had found the very witness Faith needed to change the course of the trial.

"What on earth brings this call out of nowhere?" Faith asked, astonished to hear his hello.

"Hey, I've been meaning to call for several months. I saw your name associated with that big smuggler trial. You keep me amazed. How have you been?"

It was as if no time had lapsed since their last conversation. His voice was even, yet Faith noticed he had acquired some New England accent. "I'm great. Apparently you are still in Boston," referring to his inflections.

"Yes, still at the newspaper, except I'm managing editor. No more ambulance chasing or hanging out at city hall digging for stories for me. Now, I get to send out the rookies," he laughed. "Seems as though I write the news and you make it. That was quite a trial."

"Yes, but my part was small; actually it happened before the trial."

"I doubt that anything you do is ever small. It sounds like your part was the deal breaker. I always knew you were good. Glad I was on the ground floor and saw your very first trial."

"You're the same ol' Jeff. You gave me confidence you know."

"We gave each other confidence, but you had poise and composure—I'm still working on those."

"What else is going on in your life?" Faith asked, interested in catching up with her old friend.

"Well, when I finally decided you would never let go of Tyler, I married a scientist. Actually a rocket scientist—for real. She's from New York. Can you believe I married a woman from the city? No, can you believe she married me?" He laughed, not stopping for her to answer. "We have a three year old daughter and another girl on the way."

"That's great, Jeff. I hope one of these days I can meet this lucky woman."

"Yes, same here. Speaking of lucky, how's Tyler? When you two left here I thought he was the luckiest guy in the world. He had it all, looks, brains and a beautiful woman lawyer at his side. I was jealous and felt a little sorry for myself."

"There was a lengthy pause, and Faith struggled to find the right words. "I guess you could say his luck ran out, Jeff. He died five years ago from cancer. It's been hard."

Stammering, "Faith, I'm so sorry. I didn't have any idea. I would have never been so flippant or light about it. I'm truly sorry for you—for both of you."

"It's okay. I understand. It's certainly not something you expect. The only thing good to come out of it except some beautiful times before he got so sick, is our wonderful son, Jack. Tyler never saw him, but I try to keep his memory alive."

"I hardly know what else to say," Jeff said, noticeably taken back. "Let's try to stay in touch. Do you ever come to Boston? I really would like to introduce you to my family."

"It's been a long time since I was that direction. Immigration law doesn't take me that way much," she said with a chuckle.

"One last thing, and then I'll let you go. How's your dad?"

"Gosh, a lot has happened since we last talked. He and my mother married, and they live here in Dallas part of the year and in Italy the other time. He teaches a couple of classes at SMU one semester, but I think this may be his last year. If it weren't for Jack, they would be in Italy all year. They love it there, and of course their friends Carmella and Stefano are getting up in years, but they still manage to make and drink a lot of wine," she explained, her voice now more lighthearted.

"That's pretty cool that they got together after all they had been through. You should write a book about them. It would be a bestseller."

"I doubt that. They don't talk much about any of it anymore— seems it's one of those topics best not discussed except maybe by them. At first their relationship was a bit rocky I think, but they never said much to me once they married. Plus, I know it took awhile for them to heal, yet their love was stronger than the pain. They seem truly happy now, and intent on making up for lost time. Alice married too, so I'm the only single one around."

"Are you seeing anyone? I mean, it's none of my business."

"Well until just recently I could say no, but I met a rancher from Arizona at the trial. He's also an author—writes westerns. And I think he's quite special. We'll see."

"Well, let me know, will you? I'll be happy for you this time. Can't say I was too excited the last time." He said with a slight laugh. "Life gives us rotten lemons sometimes, and I never quite figured out how to make lemonade out of them. But then I guess that's why we have wine. You taught me how to drink it, and I have a couple of glasses each night. Here's to you, Faith. It's been great talking again."

"Thanks, Jeff. I'm so glad you called. Let's not wait so long. I promise to stay in touch."

When she hung up the phone, her thoughts took her back to the first time she saw Jeff, how young and fresh he looked, and how naïve they both were—just starting out in their careers. A lot had happened in those eight years.

Returning to her mail, her mind wandered again, this time to Clay. It was after ten, and she figured that since he hadn't called, he didn't want to bother her. She was anxious to know how his morning was going so she called him. He and Jack had finished breakfast and were watching cartoons, just what the doctor ordered, he explained, although he claimed he didn't recognize any of the new characters. "What happened to Scooby-Doo?"

"Sponge Bob shot him—happens all the time. But you need to know; Scooby-Doo has risen from the ashes or retirement and is back in new form. You may not recognize him, but he'll jump on you too."

"Ouch!"

"Are you talking to me?"

Clay laughed, "No, Jack. He just hit me with a pillow. I was going to stop taking my pain pills, but maybe I should reconsider. I think he forgot about my arm. His energy level in the morning is pretty remarkable."

Faith laughed. "Are you telling me? I left out clothes for him to wear with you and dad to lunch. Just be sure that he finds them, okay?"

"Did you lay mine out too?" He teased, "You know I'm hurt."

"You can only use that excuse so long. I'm ready for you to be mended. I miss your strong arms," she spoke softly into the receiver.

"I can't talk right now. I'm being smothered by a friend of Sponge Bob's. I'll call you when we get back."

"I'll try to be home early, but I haven't really accomplished much so far—not even finished going through the mail. The phone keeps ringing. Later, bye."

Faith worked through lunch, nibbling on an apple she had brought from home and a bag of crunchy Cheetos she had purchased from the vending machine. *I would scold Jack for eating this* she told herself, but she continued to chew the cheesy chips until the only thing left was the orangey film on her fingers, which she quickly noticed had extended to an important document on her desk.

She reached for a bottle of water hoping to remove the smudge and congratulated herself for drinking it instead of a Coke, trying to feel better about the mess she had made as well as her indulgence. The remainder of the afternoon went quickly without further interruption, and she made notes for some research she was having one of the clerks do for her, before leaving instructions for her secretary about another pending case. Since she had been out of the office more than usual, she promised to return tomorrow, a fact that she knew thrilled neither her secretary nor the clerk.

She had been planning to relieve her secretary of her duties for a couple of months but each time she decided she couldn't wait any longer, it turned out to be the wrong time. First, Bliss told her that her ex-husband was three months behind in child support, and then there was a sickness in the family, and before long the secretary was pregnant by her latest boyfriend who had moved in with her and didn't have a job. Now, the timing was really wrong so Faith was biding her time again, but hating it because Bliss's mind was definitely not on work.

Although the secretary had come highly recommended, she had never proved to be as skilled as Faith wanted, plus she missed a lot of work, and Faith blamed herself for not checking out her references better. In hindsight, Faith realized she had probably been fired from the last place, but when Faith hired her, she needed someone fast. Even if she had to use a temp, she would never rush into such an important decision again.

Part of it was because her last assistant was so terrific, fast, thorough, dependable, and always on time, an employer's answer to prayers. Actually Faith had plenty of lead time but was uncharacteristically slow in hiring a replacement after finding the pool of applicants not to be the best. Her old secretary had given her several months warning and had even stayed behind with the children until the end of the first school semester although her husband's promotion and transfer to Oklahoma with the oil company had come several months earlier. Finally, Faith hired an older woman who came with outstanding credentials, but she had only worked at very small law firms. She lasted three days, complaining that there was just too much work. So Bliss it was.

It was hard not to compare the new one with the old, although Faith admitted there was no comparison causing her to depend on her clerk for way more work than she should. Recently she gave her a hefty raise to compensate for the heavy load, but still it wasn't the best of situations.

She was anxious to get home, and when she drove up she noticed Patrick's vehicle parked out front. The two must be hitting it off she decided, although she was faintly disappointed she wouldn't have Clay to herself. Both men were laughing, reclining in the two chairs flanking the fireplace when she walked into the den, and Jack was sleeping on the couch, apparently tired out from wrestling with Clay.

"Well, you two look relaxed."

"We are, indeed," Patrick exclaimed. "I thought I'd stay here to give Clay reinforcement."

"Reinforcement for what?"

Meekly Clay gave her an appealing glance. "Well, your dad and I were talking over lunch, and we thought it might be fun to go camping up in Oklahoma this weekend."

"Just the two of you?" She knew she sounded selfish, and wished it hadn't come out that way.

"No, No, all of us. You, Jack, and me, plus Patrick and Sue."

"Do you mean real camping, like in a tent?"

"Well, when we first talked about it that's what we were thinking, but we checked on some cabins up on Broken Bow Lake, and figured that might go over better with you and Sue."

"Definitely," she murmured, still unconvinced. "Tell me more."

Patrick responded. "There are two cabins, each with two bedrooms and a great room and kitchen, right on the lake, close to the state park."

"And they have paddleboats, canoeing, trout fishing, all sorts of stuff that Jack will like."

Faith smiled. They knew exactly which buttons to push. She watched them as they acted like smug co-conspirators in a crime. "So how far is it?"

"Three hours," they said in unison.

"Well, I must say you guys have done your homework. Does Jack know?"

"No, we wanted to talk to you first, but we did look at fishing gear while we were at Academy," he said, looking sheepish.

"Do you think your arm's okay, I mean to be that active?"

"It's better every day. I won't be able to canoe, but I can fish and paddle boat.

"Then I guess it's a done deal; after all it's two against one, and when Jack finds out that will be three, although I'm sure I could get Mother's vote."

"Nope, already convinced her," Patrick countered, slyly.

"So, when is this all taking place?"

"Thought we would leave middle of the afternoon Thursday, around two or three, if you can arrange your schedule."

"I'll make it work. I'll just work through lunch again," she taunted. "The sacrifices we women make." Secretly, she was excited, but she wanted them to think they had pulled off a coup that only they could do together. She would let them think whatever for Clay to build a good relationship with Patrick and engender a bond with Jack. Going camping or whatever the real name for the adventure was certainly a good next step, especially after the weekend at the ranch.

When Patrick left, Jack was still asleep, and Clay and Faith had time for a few kisses, but nothing more. "I missed you today, Clay."

"I would tell you that I missed you, but frankly, I didn't have time. It was a busy morning, and then lunch, Wal-Mart and Academy"

"What did you do at Wal-Mart?"

"Well, you see, they had these toys..."

"Never mind."

"Hey, I haven't told you the good news. I got a call from my neighbor. He wants to buy the ranch. It's not a great deal, but it's okay. I've checked around, and it's fair enough, although he wants me to finance half of it."

"Do you mind?"

"No, if we were to find something in California, some land for a vineyard some day, then I could use half the money for the down payment and then have enough coming from that each month to make the payments."

She sat in the chair Patrick had left, and there were a few moments of strained silence. "Clay, we are going to have to figure this all out sooner than later."

"I told you we would take this slow. Look, I'm going back to the ranch on Tuesday and take care of all the business. I have to find a place for the ponies and horses, at least until I figure out what to do with them. I'll put a few things in storage. The neighbor is going to offer Shane a job to stay on so that's good."

Looking worried, Faith said. "Then what?"

"I need to finish the book I'm working on. My deadline is fast approaching, and I'm way behind. I'd like to get an apartment here, not far from here if there's such a thing. Then, we will let this play out like we both know it will."

"No, tell me. I'm not sure anymore. You seem to be backing away."

Inside Clay felt a tinge of something between guilt and satisfaction. He knew he had rushed her in the beginning, and that had pushed her away. When he finally understood her hesitation and fears, he decided to play it on her terms, only now, he realized that maybe she was more ready than he expected, but he wasn't willing to take any chances. His heart warned him to remain cautiously optimistic that he was right, but it also told him to tread gently, especially on her turf. He would marry her tonight if it were up to him, but so far this emotional roller coaster he had been riding hadn't been under his control. Searching her eyes, he said tenderly. "I could never back away from you."

His heart was in his throat. He couldn't hide his feelings; they were way too strong. He stared at her for a minute and then spoke softly. "A lot has happened in a short time. I knew the minute I saw you in the courtroom that I wanted to get to know you, and then I found out you weren't married, yet it was apparent that you were resistant to a relationship. I thought I would go crazy trying to convince you. I know that sounds foolishly romantic, but it's true."

Slowly and carefully, he continued. "From the first day, I watched you move among the others in the room. I smelled your fragrant softness as you walked by me, not even noticing my existence, and I saw another side of you as well—a strength and buoyancy that showed in every move you made." He smiled warmly, remembering.

"I rushed you in the beginning, and I almost realized that too late. And then I decided that anyone as wonderful as you was worth whatever time it took. And if that takes a year or ten, I'm willing to wait. As the saying goes, you had me at hello."

"Oh, Clay, I love you, even if you are a foolishly romantic guy. That's what makes you special." She went over to him and reached for his hand. "It won't even be a year—not if it's up to me."

⌘　⌘　⌘

Though it was almost summer, it was not yet unbearably hot in southeastern Oklahoma because of the rivers, crystal clear lakes, and protection of the sloping Ouachita Mountain range, overlooking the green, pristine forests and Beavers Bend State Park. Faith laughed and said they looked like the Beverly Hillbillies in Patrick's Land Rover, filled with ice chests, fishing gear, suitcases, and an assortment of swim toys.

Jack was hyper and giddy with excitement when they arrived at the cabins. As Clay tried to help Patrick unload, he nudged him aside. "Wait until that arm heals. You can do the dirty work next time. Here Jack, take some of these toys," but Jack had squirmed his way out of his mother's reach and was running to the lake.

"I'll get him," Clay called, already half the distance from the boy. They walked along the shore, and Clay threw a rock, skimming it across the top of the water. His eyes large with amazement, Jack picked one up and tried, but it fell short of the water, disappointing him, but not discouraging him from trying again. Taking his hand, Clay walked him closer to the water and picked up another stone, teaching him the logistics of throwing it just right. The next attempt hit the water and that seemed enough to satisfy Jack for the moment before he took off running after a squirrel that quickly found a tree and an easy escape.

"We better go help. Then we can come back," Clay bargained, returning to find the women putting up groceries in Patrick and Sue's cabin, and Patrick sorting out the fishing equipment.

"Hey Jack, I put your things in our cabin. SuSu and I want you to stay with us tonight. We've missed you."

"But I want to stay with Mommy and Clay."

"You can tomorrow night. Tonight we get you."

"Okay, but where's the TV?"

"There's not one, but we both promise to read you a story."

Faith was stunned, but she tried not to show it, and dared not look at Clay, who she knew was thinking Patrick was the greatest man on the planet.

The fire took forever to catch, and Faith wondered what they would have done without the day's newspaper that she had tossed in at the last minute and had planned to read at some time. After much cajoling and blowing, it lit, but took its own time burning until the coals were glowing red, then an ashy gray and finally ready for the burgers. "Let the flames begin," Clay shouted. The men blamed their fire starting problem on old charcoal and bad fuel while the women laughed at them, drank red wine and cut potatoes into wedges.

After the hamburgers and s'mores were gone, the bottles of wine drained to the last drop, and the final installment of the ghost story told, Jack fell asleep in Patrick's lap, and the adults said their good-nights. Warm from the fire and wine, their hair and clothes smelling faintly smoky, Faith and Clay quickly undressed, kissing and touching, while the water pipes clanked in an attempt to heat the water in the old cabin shower.

When Faith had wrapped his arm carefully in a black plastic trash bag, giggling like school kids, they stepped gingerly into the small tiled space, reminiscent of the 60s when baths were built for function, not pleasure. The shower head was anything but modern perched on the wall just over Clay's shoulders. A new white shower curtain, hung too high, allowed water to lap over the raised tile onto the bathroom floor, but it too was tile. None of this seemed to matter to the couple, and they hardly noticed the water running hot and then cold and hot again, just the steam off their bodies. Their body temperature was their only thermometer and it rose with every tantalizing stroke.

With sore ribs and a wounded arm, love making was more restrained than it had been at the ranch, but no less passionate or prolonged. As the sun filtered through the thin organza curtains, Faith lay curled under Clay's good arm, unaware that he had been awake for more than an hour watching her sleep.

⌘   ⌘   ⌘

Jack caught his first fish and it was a keeper, although the game warden might have disagreed. Clay helped him take it off the hook and weaved it onto the stringer as everyone gathered round to take pictures and congratulate Jack on his catch. His grin was almost as big as the small mouth bass and his eyes danced as he posed for photographs. After that he was relentless until he caught three more. By noon, he and Clay had enough for lunch, and although Jack had proclaimed he didn't like that kind of fish, as soon as the first fried piece came out of the cast iron skillet and cooled, he ate it and asked for more.

Patrick hated that he had not brought his golf clubs after seeing the eighteen-hole course, but was soon content to lie in the hammock and read Clay's first novel while Faith, Clay and Jack rode paddle boats and Sue visited the gift shop. It was a lazy afternoon that included a brief drive around the area and more fishing before a late afternoon picnic.

The remainder of the weekend was more of the same, relaxing and slow. Jack caught more fish and fell asleep early allowing Faith and Clay to enjoy the last night together. They took a blanket and a bottle of wine and went down to the lake where lying side by side, holding hands, they counted the stars.

⌘   ⌘   ⌘

Life returned to some form of normalcy when Clay left for the ranch, but Faith missed him, and Jack acted forlorn. He had become accustomed to his constant attention and asked often when Clay would return, begging to talk each time he called. Faith hadn't realized just how much her son needed a father, and Clay seemed poised and perfect for the challenge.

The sale and closure of the ranch proved to be even easier than Clay expected, but it was harder to pack away many of the mementoes and treasures that his parents had collected and passed down to him. Trying to be sensible rather than sentimental, he went through everything, choosing keepsakes wisely. What little furniture he wanted to keep, which included the domed trunk, he put in storage along with boxes of saved relics.

The neighbor took the horses temporarily with the understanding Clay would find an alternate place within the year and bought the remaining cattle that Clay didn't sell at auction. By the end of two weeks, a lifetime of memories were either packed, sold or given away, leaving Clay to ride the ranch one last time and say bittersweet good-byes to those important to him.

⌘　⌘　⌘

Clay was met with kisses and hugs at the airport, making the first time Jack saw any outward display of sentiment by Faith, which appeared not to faze him one way or another. He talked incessantly about the ponies, wanting reassurance that Clay had not sold them and that he could ride again soon.

After stopping for dinner, they drove home and opened packages that Clay had brought, a beautiful western blanket for Jack's room, which went unnoticed by him and set of cowboy and Indian action figures that got major attention. Faith's gift box held the most gorgeous turquoise and silver squash blossom necklace that she had ever seen, along with a matching bracelet and ring in the second.

They talked until long after Jack had been put to bed with a bedtime story from Faith, and then begrudgingly kissed goodnight, each going to their respective rooms, but wanting to spend the night together.

The next two days Clay searched for an apartment with two bedrooms and a swimming pool, knowing that would entice Jack to visit. Finding one about six miles from Faith's house, he signed a six months lease on a downstairs unit that looked out at the pool that was lined by crepe myrtle trees in full cherry pink bloom. Actually, the grounds were beautifully landscaped and the manager had convinced him that most of the renters were young professionals. At the price of the monthly lease, he figured there couldn't be many deadbeats, which was good because he remembered what it was like living in an apartment in college, and he never wanted that arrangement again.

Although he realized the one he chose wouldn't be the quietest unit, the terrace and its proximity to the pool was important. Buying new furniture would have guaranteed a more comfortable and nicer collection, but it wasn't his plan to be there long enough for comfort so he rented enough furniture to make it presentable, splurging on a desk for writing. Together he and Faith shopped for a minimal amount of dishes and glasses, along with towels and sheets and other incidentals. He encouraged Jack to bring over all the toys he wanted and sat up one corner just for him.

As soon as Jack saw the pool he asked Faith why they couldn't live there. Within a week Clay was settled in, and before long, Faith and Jack were spending more time there than he was at her house, primarily because of the pool, which had indeed been an easy lure for Jack who played for hours on each visit, giving the couple time to unwind and visit.

Jack quickly made friends with another little boy named Blake who was his age and had only a few other friends at the complex. He and his mother, who was recently divorced and worked in online marketing at home, had moved to their apartment a couple of months before. Although Blake visited his dad every other weekend he was lonely and Faith was glad that he and Jack had each other. Except for the occasional, "watch us," the boys played without interrupting the adults, save a few breaks for chips and juice, which Clay kept in a cooler near the pool.

Almost every night's dinner was something cooked on the grill, and occasionally Jack asked to stay over, which gave Faith the excuse she needed to spend the night, although they were still cautious about their sleeping arrangements. Quickly, a pattern developed and on days that Faith worked, he planned the menu and cooked; on other nights she brought salads or casseroles. During the day, Clay wrote, taking short breaks to Google real estate offerings in the California wine country. Each night he and Faith would talk about what he had found or who he had talked to about a vineyard that was available. He approached it practically, and though he hoped to find something in the near future, he was realistic and patient, giving Faith time to sort out her feelings.

One night after Jack and Blake had played for more than two hours in the pool, Jack asked Clay if they could have a burping contest, explaining that Blake and his dad had the weekend before and that he thought that was pretty cool. Clay laughed as Faith looked astonished. "What kind of contest, sport?"

"You know, where you burp and then I burp and we see who is the loudest."

"Oh, I get it. Sure, but from the look on your mom's face, I think we will do it when she's not around."

Jack's mouth turned into a toothy grin, the kind that goes from ear to ear. "I tried in the pool, but it didn't work."

"I think I know the trick."

The next day Clay called Faith and said he would pick up Jack from day care because they had plans. "Plus, I think he needs me to start teaching him how to really swim."

"That's a great idea. I've been thinking I needed to get him enrolled for lessons, but just keep forgetting."

"No need; I'll have him swimming in no time. I'd just feel better knowing he can, plus he's plenty ready."

"I need to run some errands so that's perfect. It will give you extra time, and I can be a little late without feeling rushed. If I bring everything, will you grill burgers?"

"Consider it done, but I'll pick up everything at the store. I need to stop anyway. Seems I'm out of bottled Coke."

"You never drink bottled Coke."

"I don't normally participate in a burping contest either, or at least I haven't in about twenty five years."

Laughing, Faith replied, "I forgot. Have fun. And please be finished before I get there."

Jack was waiting on the front bench of the day care, back pack in hand, when Clay walked through the door. Although Clay was now on the official list to pick him up, Faith had called ahead. Jack was delighted to see Clay and gave him a hug.

"Let's go, sport. I'm ready for the contest," Clay announced as the two got into the car. Handing him a large bottled Coke, he instructed, "Take a big gulp, all in one breath."

Jack did as he was told and then burped a loud, long rumble. A huge smile came to his face, and he took another guzzle of the carbonated soda.

"I think I'm beat already," Clay said as he took a swig, downing it quickly. He expelled a long burp, and both giggled. "Now you understand this is not very polite and we can't do it in public, right?"

"Yep, I mean yes, sir. But can we do it again until all our Coke is gone?"

"Sure, but this is just between us guys, okay? I don't think mommy would be very happy with our behavior," Clay said, winking.

"Okay, our secret."

When Faith arrived at the apartment, Clay was sitting by the pool in his swimsuit reading and Jack was splashing in the pool.

"Hi," she called. Clay and Jack looked at each other and then at her, their faces beaming. "You two look like you just swallowed a couple of flies. What's up?"

After a silly giggle Jack ducked and went under water.

"Call it male bonding. I really can't talk. I've run out of air!"

⌘　⌘　⌘

chapter twenty-six

At the office Faith had a bounty of unfinished business, and first on her list was contacting Harry Herrera to confirm the details of Maxwell's final hours as determined by the investigation as well as the substantial amount of money that would eventually go to Consuela. According to Harry, the prison report was short, but not exactly sweet. Maxwell had become increasingly belligerent over the course of several weeks before his suicide, with bouts of severe depression accompanied by screaming rage and verbal abuse, lashing out at the guards without provocation.

On several occasions, he had refused to eat, which didn't appear to bother anyone and only increased his hunger. Prison personnel had seen these actions personified in more than a few inmates; that's what Supermax was known to do. It's meant to be punitive; after all these guys are not in the slammer for stealing cars or smoking dope, although many may have committed those crimes in the beginning. So, they simply adjust, and come to grips with their circumstances, but not Maxwell. He had always called the shots, and the inability to do that caused him great consternation. Eventually the only solution was to end it, another bit of reality that brought no remorse from a single human being as far as anyone could tell.

The distribution of assets had proven a bit more difficult, which aggravated Harry who had not intended to spend a great deal of time on a seemingly easy task. He had figured he would be counting his money in retirement by this time, but Consuela was slow in signing the paperwork and so far hadn't submitted to DNA requirements.

Faith agreed to call and help him speed up the process, strictly on Enrique and Consuela's behalf and not his. Although he had been nice enough to her, she had absolutely no respect for him, knowing his lengthy connection to both Ridgeway's.

When she called Consuela, she first had a lengthy conversation with Enrique. He was such a sweet man, who held no disfavor for anyone, save Maxwell and José. Instead, he talked about his many blessings in spite of a less than easy life. Faith found her talks with him to always be uplifting for that reason, for no matter what life had handed him he saw the glass half full.

He braced her for the fact that he and Connie were having difficulty making a decision on the inheritance because it was tied to corruption, greed and unlawful conduct, not to mention the hurt it had brought to so many innocent people.

They were not certain they could in good faith accept any part of it. Consuela picked up the other receiver and confirmed her feelings to Faith, who listened intently. Although she understood, she wanted them to consider a way to make it more palatable. Patiently she talked them through many of their concerns, and suggested they sit down with Yoli and Cody. Promising to call them in a week, she encouraged them to consider all their options.

In the meantime she stayed busy tying up loose ends on several green card requests and working to help an eighty year old couple who were trying to secure a visa for a friend in Cordova, Argentina. The woman had been an exchange student in their home more than forty years earlier, and because they were getting up in years and wanted to see her one last time, they had sent her a roundtrip ticket to visit them. But, she had been denied a visa, and Faith couldn't figure it out except that since her husband had recently died, the government might consider her a risk of wanting to stay unlawfully in the States. After numerous phone calls and some persuasion, she was successful, which reminded her of why she had chosen this specialty.

Being an immigration attorney often left her frustrated because she worked with people who were trying to get into or stay in the country legally, but the process was so slow and cumbersome that it wasn't any wonder why folks took the illegal route. Just recently she had been working with a hospital who had recruited foreign doctors, but once the hospital reached an agreement with one, the administrator ran into obstacles, and from the looks of the back-log with the U.S. Citizenship and Immigration Service, the doctor could be retirement age before anything might be solved.

There were countless stories told to her from people who had been waiting for years for a green card, many who had married someone from a Caribbean island or even a European country, which is usually easier, only to be separated now, waiting because there was a glitch in the paperwork. Because of costs or fear, many had tried to go it alone, only to wind up in deeper trouble because of an innocent mistake. What troubled her most was when the rules changed in the middle of the stream, and she had seen that happen many times. Or the young man who came with his mother when he was a minor and when immigration services finally got around to his application he was twenty-one, too old for a minor's visa. Everyone played the blame game, and he came out the loser.

Faith had been working with one young woman for three years, and still there had been no closure despite her attempts. The client had met a young man from the Philippines on a cruise and they had later married. Because of the language problem, they had decided they would compromise and live in Mexico City, but when they watched a man get beheaded by a drug gang, they quickly changed their minds. Unaware of the problems they faced, they moved here, but shortly afterwards he was denied his application, and deportation procedures started. His application was so far down the stack of others that short of a miracle, Faith knew they wouldn't be living in the U.S. together anytime soon, though from recent developments thought she could now see a glimmer of hope.

The most depressingly sad case she had taken dealt indirectly with immigration law, but the impact of illegals in the country bore heavily on the actions that led to the case. She was contacted by a man facing years in prison who asked her to represent him. After several days of consideration she took the case although she had doubts from the beginning that she or anyone else could win—the odds were too overwhelmingly stacked against him.

The man, who lived along the Texas border with his wife and their one son, appeared to be a middle-class, hardworking, law abiding citizen until a terrible accident occurred. Evidence showed that a young illegal alien from Mexico was driving under the influence at a high speed when he ran a stop sign, plowing into the car driven by the man's eighteen year old son, who was to leave within days to play baseball on a full scholarship to the University of Texas. The illegal was unhurt, but the teen died at the site of the crash.

Within hours after the collision, the illegal alien fled across the bridge to Mexico. Distraught and heartbroken, the man pushed

U.S. authorities to find the driver, but their efforts failed although the father never really thought they tried. Losing his son he told Faith was the worst, but watching the Mexican national "get away with murder," as he described it was more than he could bear. After a year of failed justice, he took it into his own hands. He had heard stories that the illegal was coming and going across the bridge, and several friends of his son's who had seen pictures indicated that they had noticed him at local bars on both sides of the Rio Grande River.

So, undeterred the man took a large part of his life savings and hired a hit man to find and kill the illegal. The only trouble was the person he paid was an undercover agent who promptly arrested him. Faith lost the case, and the man got fifteen years in prison. The outcome was no surprise, but it didn't lessen her anguish for her client as she watched the guards take him away. But even her compassion didn't outweigh her knowledge as a lawyer, understanding that empathy and sympathy do not equate to mercy in a court of law nor are what's fair and what's right synonymous. The facts, however, brought her no solace.

Yet her job had heartwarming, positive stories and one was a young man whom she helped to get a green card, and though it took more than a year, he was never discouraged. On the day he received it, he asked Faith to accompany him to the U.S. Army Recruiting Office where he promptly joined. Six months later she received a letter from him, serving in Iraq, thanking her for not giving up on him. Those were the stories she cherished as she pushed clients to tackle the process legally, but she well understood their irritation at the process so out of kilter, so terribly lengthy and arcane.

Before a week had passed, Enrique called, and along with Consuela, shared the news of their decision regarding the ranch. Excitedly they told Faith that after sitting down with Yoli and Cody they had figured it out. The ranch could never be a home in the traditional sense—they knew that early on because of Maxwell and all his terrible associations, not to mention the awful memories that Consuela held. But with the right idea it was a perfect answer to redeeming a place, to giving back to those less fortunate or facing similar heartaches that they had once faced.

"Remember, I told you that my granddaughter died of leukemia?" Enrique asked.

"Why yes, Enrique. I very well remember."

"Well, we've decided to give the land and money to Yoli and Cody so they can open a working dude ranch for kids sick from cancer. Any kid with any kind of cancer from age seven to eighteen would qualify to come, regardless of their background or family situation. They'll just have to apply and have the stamina to play and work. Of course, we don't expect them to really work, but to understand responsibility and other lessons, while growing in their own confidence. We want them to be like any other kids while they're here, and we won't talk about their sickness."

"Oh, Enrique, that is a wonderful idea."

"We watched Trina fight a terrible battle, and we know what we want for all kids. We are all so energized. As you know, Cody has been working at a dude ranch near San Antonio, so he has some experience now. The ranch where he works is not for sick kids, but he's already started research and making plans for this one. It's going to be a lot of work, but it'll be worth it. He grew up on a ranch, so he understands a little of what it's like."

"So tell me everything."

"They want it to be a working ranch where the kids perform chores and take care of the animals. We know too well that when children get sick they often lose their self-esteem and think because they're ill they can't do anything. This won't make them well, but it will give them a week of fun, mixed with a little responsibility, and a sense of belonging."

"You said you are giving the ranch to Yoli, what does that mean for you two?"

He chuckled. "It means we won't have to work as hard as they will. I know what it's like to work from before dawn until after dusk, but these kids—you know Yoli and Cody, don't quite understand that as well as I do. Connie and I are satisfied right here in our own little world, that we carved out together, but we've promised to help out in the summer when most of the kids are there. The rest of the year, it will be up to them to keep it running. It won't be an easy life. That's a bigger piece of property than they can imagine. I'm not sure they really know where the land begins and ends, but they say they are up to it, and I really believe they are. This means a lot to them because of Trina."

Faith wondered too if they knew how many hours a day a working ranch required. After listening to Clay describe life on a ranch, she hoped they knew what they were getting into. But she also understood having passion for a cause, and she empathized for their pain in losing a child. She shared their awareness of the cruelty of cancer and what it does to a child, what it does to the family as well. She was careful to keep any discouraging thoughts to herself.

"The important thing will be to find good help. I doubt if they want to keep Maxwell's employees."

Enrique answered, "You know, I may be naïve, but I don't think some of them had any idea what kind of truly dreadful things Maxwell was into. The ranch was so apart from most of the other parts of his life, except of course, the constant flow of illegals. But when they got this far, they were so happy they apparently didn't tell others the horror stories that we know to be true. Several of the key people have asked to stay on, so we'll just have to see how it goes."

Faith agreed, "I can believe that. Those folks were just probably hard working, good West Texas people, who did their job, and kept their noses clean."

"Of course, we'll hire doctors and nurses who will live at the ranch during the summer, which means there will be lots of construction going on for awhile. Yoli wants to take the main house that is there and turn it into the bunkhouse for kids, but add more bedrooms so that each child only has to share with one other. Then we'll build some apartments for the medical staff and other personnel, a family house and a guest house for us when we're visiting. The original bunkhouse can also be used as an infirmary. As you can see we're still in the planning stages, but are wondering if you can help us with the logistics of the non-profit part and some other legal issues?"

"That's not my area of expertise, but I'll help every way I can. This is so amazing—better than I ever dreamed."

"Yes, and because there is so much money, this can be free for every kid, plus Cody suggested corporate donors, hoping to get people involved to help these kids and their families. We're going to name the ranch the Double D for the "d" in de la Peña, which is Yoli's idea, not mine." Enrique offered, seemingly embarrassed. "But we're calling the main house, Trina's Place," his voice cracked, but he continued. "It's nice we can do that in her honor and memory."

"For once, something good will come from this land," Faith offered.

"Yes, finally. Will you visit, Faith?"

"I'd love to. I'd like to bring Jack and Clay sometime. Would that be okay?"

"That would be great. Clay could give us some good advice since he lived on a big ranch for most of his life. And maybe when Jack's old enough, he will spend a week or two with the children here in the summer," Enrique suggested.

"Jack would like that. I'm sure he would learn a great deal about himself and other children."

"That's what this place is all about—understanding the goodness of life as seen through others," Enrique said, a smile coming to his face.

⌘ ⌘ ⌘

chapter
twenty-seven

In mid June Clay received a call from his real estate agent in California who explained he had found the perfect vineyard in the Russian River area of Sonoma County. Anxious to see it, he flew out, but within minutes of seeing the ninety-eight acre plot wished that Faith had accompanied him. Although he had at first imagined a vineyard in Napa, he fell in love with the idyllic setting and all that the area had to offer. Having lived in Arizona for so many years, the cooler climate of the valley, the longer growing season and the closeness to the Pacific Ocean hooked him.

Here he knew the rolling hills were often enveloped in evening fog that escapes to the ocean each morning, giving way to warm, even occasionally hot days and cool nights. The vines had seen better times. What the early frost the year before hadn't damaged, the smoke from the forest fires had tainted. Much of the land had been planted in Chardonnay, but because the owner had also been involved in a bitter and protracted divorce, those vines had been further neglected. Clay wasn't sure he could salvage any of them, and didn't know if he even wanted to try. Although replanting would be an expensive task, the prospects were not all negative because he could decide what grapes and where he wanted them on the land. He knew he wanted to grow grapes for Pinot Noir as well as Chardonnay and Pinot Grigio.

He had studied the growing patterns of this entire area and knew that the soil and climate were ideal for these varietals. Though difficult to grow, Pinot Noir was his favorite to drink, its distinctive texture a challenge that he was willing to accept.

Surprisingly, there was no house, but a barn and stable, and the realtor explained that the couple had lived in Guerneville and had planned to build before their marriage fell apart along with their dreams. Clay noticed a garden that held an overgrown tangled mess of dead vines that appeared to at one time have been a bumper crop of raspberries. As they walked and surveyed, an eagle perched on one of the stable posts, eyeing the intruders before he lifted his wings and flew away as if to say this is my land, I'll leave for now, but I'll be back.

Clay's brain was on overdrive as he sculptured out a Mediterranean chateau and found the perfect place for a hot tub or maybe a small pool for Jack. He was actually glad there was no house; it was a plus rather than a stumbling block allowing them the chance to design and create their own home, exactly what they wanted together.

But before he could even think about the property, he needed Faith to walk it with him, to envision a future in these rolling hills, close to redwoods, Christmas tree farms, and even a dairy down the road. Suddenly, he was fearful that she wouldn't be as in love with it as he was, that it would be too far from family and friends. She was a Texas girl, and he knew it was difficult to take a Texas girl out of her environment, the only place she had ever lived. Sure they had discussed it more than once, but talking about it and really doing it were two different things.

When he called her, she could hear the excitement in his voice, but also the unease that she might not share his affection for the setting. Trying to allay his concerns she promised to make arrangements for Jack, and fly out in two days, which was the soonest she could arrange. The Jackson's had volunteered in advance in case this should happen, and since Patrick and Sue had left for Italy the week before she was thrilled to have their offer and more pleased that she had just settled her most pressing case. She hated putting Judge at the kennel, but there wasn't much choice. Luckily Dusty could fend for herself a few days if the neighbor would check on her water and food. Cats were easier than dogs. Besides those arrangements, everything else could wait.

At the airport news stand she bought a newspaper and the only book that she could find that included anything about Sonoma. When she and Clay had visited before, they hadn't had time for anything but Napa, which she thought was wonderful, but she was curious and anxious about the parts of the wine country she wasn't familiar with. She thought it strange that she was even considering the idea of moving there. If someone had told her that a year ago she would have thought them crazy. What she knew about California could fill one page of a tabloid magazine and be about as accurate.

But she did know that lately, half of the people in her neighborhood had moved out of California and were getting twice or three times the house in Texas. They were tired of the taxes, earthquakes, mud slides and wildfires, but she reminded herself that none had lived in Sonoma. "Besides Texas has tornadoes and hurricanes," she said under her breath as if in a personal attempt of persuasion. Where was her adventurous spirit? Life was about choices and new beginnings she repeatedly told herself as she stepped off the plane.

On the ride from San Francisco to Sonoma County, Clay talked nonstop, hoping he could convince her of the land's beauty and potential even before she arrived. Although he was anxious and tempted to go directly to the property, he stopped for lunch at the quaint little roadhouse grill and lodge where he was staying, nestled along the Russian River near Guerneville. From there they drove the two lane roads through an area that reminded her of Tuscany until they came to the land for sale. He had a good idea this route might sway her. Listening to her chatter about the similarities delighted him since he knew how she felt about Italy.

Like a kid seeing a new bike, Clay jumped out of the rented car and before Faith was completely out of the car, took her hand and began showing her the vineyard. Pulling her forward, he pointed out how he would change the trellising and plant more along the hills where there was a noticeable absence of vines. "And here's where I thought we might think about a house, waving his hand to bring attention to a large knoll that gave way to a valley. You can see the mountains and the vineyards. Isn't it beautiful?"

She answered him with a smile. "It needs a lot of work. Are you sure that's what you want?"

"The price is right, and I can do most of the work myself, except of course, build the house, but I can oversee it, and start new grapes, and plant a garden, maybe some apple and olive trees. The barn is here and just needs a little customizing for the horses and ponies," his excitement and enthusiasm growing with each word of explanation.

"And how long do you think that would take?"

"A lifetime," he said taking her in his arms, and then quickly adding. "I think it could be ready for you and Jack by the time school is out next year. I've been hoping that maybe I could convince Shane to move here and help. I know he really wasn't too thrilled about working for the neighbor, so he might want a change. Besides, his choice of women is certainly better here, and he's been hinting that he's ready to settle down."

"Where would you live? And how often would I see you?"

"I haven't worked all that out in my mind because I didn't want to allow myself to think that far ahead without you seeing it." Pausing, he looked at her squarely, "What do you really think?"

"I think it is beautiful. I really do, but I know that I love you."

"So, does that mean you would agree to move here?"

"Not unless you ask me to marry you and steal me away."

"And what about your career? How would we work that?"

"I don't know; I haven't let myself think that far ahead," she said, mocking him sweetly. "Maybe if the offer were good enough and the proposal just right, I would stay home and have babies."

Shocked, he dropped to one knee and took her hand. "I had visions of how I would do this, all romantic and everything, but you give me no choice. I've been challenged. So, Faith, will you marry me?"

Smiling, she said, "I thought you'd never ask. I will, I will."

He stood and they embraced. Then reaching in his pocket, he took out a small box. "I have to admit that I have been carrying this with me for several weeks. I wanted it to be a surprise, but if you would rather have something new, I'll understand." He handed her the package and she opened it to find a ring with five large diamonds set in a single gold band.

"Clay, it's beautiful. And you picked it out yourself!"

Blushing he said, "It was my mother's. Do you really like it? I mean, you can select something else if you'd rather."

Wiping a tear, she answered, "No, Clay, No, this is much more special than anything new. It has history etched into it and memories worn throughout. Now, we can add ours too it. Maybe someday, I can pass this down to a girl of ours. How did you know what size?

"I guessed. Is it right?"

"It's perfect, and so are you!"

"So when do you want to do this?" He asked in earnest.

"You mean purchase the property or the wedding?"

"Both. And the sooner the better. I would do it today!" he exclaimed.

"Well, we can make an offer on the property any time you're ready, but the ceremony will have to wait—at least until I go shopping," she laughed.

Grinning, he said. "I know, but it was a nice try, don't you think?"

⌘   ⌘   ⌘

The next day they mulled over their decisions and crafted an offer on the land, hoping to get it for less than the asking price since the owners really needed to sell. Within hours, the owners countered, and they countered theirs. Their agent promised to call as soon as he had any news, but he encouraged them to find other things to do besides wait.

Just listening to him lightened their moods as they secretly snickered about him. Such a proper Englishman he was, seemingly misplaced although he had lived in the States since the early nineties when he came from London with a new American wife he had met at Oxford. Still he claimed he had never entirely acclimated to the Pacific West and certainly not northern California where the sun shined more than three hundred days a year. In a heavy British accent that had not been tempered by years of living in the States, he had told them he much preferred the fog and the overcast, cloudy days that reminded him of home to the sunshine. Also, in the middle of wine country, his preference was a pint of ale, and while most locals were casual almost to a fault, Clay had not seen him without his dark suit and bowler hat.

From his conversation with Faith, she quickly determined both he and his wife, a local artist/sculptor, were true intellects who loved to read the classics and visit museums all over the world. In the photos he shared of his wife and their two Scottie dogs, Faith decided it was a match made in heaven, or at least in Great Britain.

But he certainly appeared to understand the real estate market, so they heeded his advice and found ways to fill their time while they waited. Driving out to where the Russian River interfaces with the Pacific Ocean near Jenner, they walked the beach that was a temporary home to a handful of seals that rested lazily, unmindful of human visitors or the osprey that watched from a nest he had built in a broken tree limb. The rock formations and spectacular cliffs provided the perfect background as the couple strolled aimlessly, making plans for the land they hoped would soon be theirs.

"What do you think about a wedding on the knoll where we want the house?" Faith asked wistfully.

"Are you serious?" He asked, not believing what he was hearing.

"Yes, I think it would be gorgeous at sunset, as the fog is rolling in. Just something small, family and a few friends. Having it there would be a symbol of our starting out together—our land, our new lives together. Then maybe we could rent a restaurant where everyone could have dinner and wine, and that would pretty much be it. Of course, the next day we could fly to Paris and see the south of France. You said you wanted to do that someday, right?"

Surprised by her revelation, he replied hastily, "Yes, a honeymoon in France sounds magnificent and the wedding here would be a dream come true. Do you really think we could get away on a honeymoon? What about Jack?"

"He has so many people wanting to keep him, he'll be fine. As long as we promise to bring him presents, he'll rush us out the door."

"Guess we need the land first. I wish they would call." He said, nervously. Pausing, he continued in an anticipatory mood. "So when do you want the wedding? I need to do a lot of work clearing and cleaning to get the land in good enough shape for a wedding."

"Would August rush you?"

A smile overtook his face. "I'll work from first light until the sun goes down behind the mountains. Somehow, I'll be ready."

"I just thought we should do it before Jack started kindergarten. It's going to be so hard to be apart—you out here and us in Dallas," she said in a melancholy tone. "I've been thinking about it a lot, and it's still the best plan. That will give you a year of uninterrupted building and planting. Jack can go to school where he's looked so forward to going and I can finish up my cases—close out everything at the firm. Mr. Jackson is going to be upset, but he'll understand. Hopefully, we can meet here or in Dallas at least once a month. Do you think that's possible?"

"We'll make it possible. Do you want to start a law practice when you get here?"

"I told you what I want. I want a baby!"

"Well, I know just the man for the job."

"Yeah, me too," she said, leaning into him.

"You can't imagine how happy I am right now!" He said, putting his arms around her.

"I'm glad you were persistent," she said, smiling.

"Yes, me too. I knew a good thing the minute I saw you in that courtroom."

"You know, I'm slowly learning that everything that happens has a purpose though sometimes it's not clear at first. I never thought anything good could ever come from knowing Maxwell Collin Ridgeway III, but now I do. I would have never met you otherwise. In the end he got what he deserved, and I'd like to think we are too. I refuse, however, to give him credit for being coyote smart," Faith said, her voiced mixed with emotion, remembering his evil ways.

"Thankfully, that's all in the past; we have tomorrow; he doesn't," he said, kissing her tenderly.

They spent the remainder of the day at the Sonoma fairgrounds, mingling with hundreds of other people at the lavender and jazz festival, which they thought was a weird combination. Strange or not, it drew a crowd, an eclectic group of older folks competing in a swing dance contest and young people milling around, their babies asleep in backpacks.

Clay and Faith strolled along the booths manned by local artisans and growers selling every kind of lavender product imaginable. Faith stopped at a small stall where a tiny woman, with graying hair, pulled up haphazardly into a twisted knot, was making her own sachets. In her long lilac skirt and gypsy-styled blouse, she looked exactly as Faith had visualized an organic gardener from this area. After listening to the vendor talk lovingly about her garden, and how she tended it daily, harvesting the tall aromatic stalks when the blooms burst forth, Faith was unable to resist. She bought a bundle of fresh lavender in a petite grapevine basket and a couple of packets of sachet, their fragrance evoking relaxation and soothing comfort.

An array of musicians, some on sax, and others on trumpets and pianos, performed on various stages, each group reflecting a distinct quality or subgenre, ranging from bebop to Latin fusion. Listening, but not really hearing, the couple walked directionless, preoccupied with their thoughts, restless and antsy for an answer from their real estate agent.

Later, long after dinner, they received the call they had been waiting for and the news that they had just bought ninety-eight acres of wine country. Appropriately, they opened a bottle of Pinot Noir, savoring its velvety, lush richness, and toasted to their future together.

⌘　⌘　⌘

OTHER WORKS BY CINDY BRADFORD

Keeping Faith, 2009
Promises Kept, 2010

www.KeepingFaithTheNovel.com
www.PromisesKeptTheNovel.com

Made in the USA
Lexington, KY
21 February 2011